IF TOMORROW COMES

TOR BOOKS BY NANCY KRESS

IF TOMORROW COMES

BOOK 2

OF THE

YESTERDAY'S KIN

TRILOGY

NANCY KRESS

TOR

A TOM DOHERTY ASSOCIATES BOOK

NEW YORK

This is a work of fiction. All of the characters, organizations, and events portrayed in this novel are either products of the author's imagination or are used fictitiously.

IF TOMORROW COMES

A Tor Book
Published by Tom Doherty Associates
175 Fifth Avenue
New York, NY 10010

www.tor-forge.com

Tor® is a registered trademark of Macmillan Publishing Group, LLC.

The Library of Congress Cataloging-in-Publication Data is available upon request.

ISBN 978-0-7653-9032-5 (hardcover)
ISBN 978-0-7653-9034-9 (ebook)

Our books may be purchased in bulk for promotional, educational, or business use. Please contact your local bookseller or the Macmillan Corporate and Premium Sales Department at 1-800-221-7945, extension 5442, or by email at MacmillanSpecialMarkets@macmillan.com.

First Edition: March 2018

Printed in the United States of America

0 9 8 7 6 5 4 3 2 1

Readily will I display the intestinal fortitude required to fight on to the Ranger objective and complete the mission, though I be the lone survivor.

—from the Ranger Creed

Evolution is an indispensable component of any satisfying explanation of our psychology.

—Steven Pinker

IF TOMORROW COMES

PROLOGUE

Judith Ryan shoved her way to the front of the crowd, moving people with her elbows, her cane, and her age. It took her twenty minutes to get from the car to the cordon; the crowd was vast and Judith, eighty-five, was slow. When she reached the cordon, she was still five hundred yards from the spaceship, gleaming and silent on its little hill in the autumn Pennsylvania countryside.

"Step back, ma'am," the soldier said. He wore riot gear and a gun. "You can't go any far— I said to step back!"

"Please," Judith quavered, "my grandson—"

The soldier glanced quickly around, looking for a child that might have slipped under the cordon. Nothing. "Step back, ma'am."

"You don't understand! He's on the ship! I have to talk to someone and warn them!"

The soldier scowled. Nothing like this had been covered in his briefing. He fell back on clear orders and native skepticism. "Uh-huh. Makes no difference. You can't— Ma'am!"

Judith ducked under the cordon, even though the motion made her left knee buckle. She jabbed her cane into the grass to right herself. The soldier grabbed her. People nearby raised cell phones and cameras.

"My grandson! I have to warn somebody!"

More phones were raised. An officer strode across the area inside the cordon. "What's the problem here?"

Desperation wrinkled deeper the lines on Judith's face. "I have to tell someone! He's aboard the ship—I only just learned! I found something, a . . . but he isn't—"

"Her grandson," the first soldier said.

The officer glanced back over his shoulder and then at his watch. Then Judith knew. The ship was doing what the car radio said it might: lifting hours earlier than announced, perhaps to foil any last-minute attacks.

"Ahhhhhh," went the crowd, while news cams and crews scrambled to catch up.

The silver egg, dazzling in the sunlight, rose silently and without fire into the blue sky. The alien technology that had built her, only beginning to be understood on Earth, was of no interest to Judith. No one had listened to her. And even if they had listened, all she could offer was her unsubstantiated word, her heart-deep knowledge, the emblem she had found buried in the garden while mulching her roses. Nobody would heed any of that.

The officer, his face kind, said, "Ma'am, everybody aboard the *Friendship* got the most thorough physical and mental checkups possible. Your grandson will be fine."

Judith stared at him. He didn't understand. It was not her grandson she feared for.

Too late. Way too late.

CHAPTER 1

"I'm here," Leo Brodie said, slinging his regulation duffel onto the bunk and following it with his rifle, ammo, and dope log. "Christ on a cracker, I'm really here!"

He didn't expect an answer; the five-by-seven sleeping cubicle on the USS *Friendship* was empty. Flawless gray walls made of God-knows-what, human-designed wall screen, storage drawers underneath the two-foot-wide bunk—it all left Leo a strip of deck two feet wide to stand in. He'd been in more cramped spaces, but not for a while.

The knock on the door was expected. Leo flung it open. Owen Lamont stood in the narrow passageway. Leo flung his arms around him. "Owen! You're the one who got me here!"

Owen detached himself; too late, Leo remembered Owen's dislike of being touched. "Yeah, and now that you are here, we have rules you need to follow."

"Always," Leo said. "How did you—"

Owen shoved Leo aside, crowded into the room, and closed the door.

"—pull it off, Owen? My orders only came through yesterday; I was on transport all night. I'm not—"

"Not Seventy-Fifth, no. But you're still the best damn marksman in the entire Army. Could come in handy on Kindred."

"That's what they call World now? Fuck, every planet is a world!"

"That's why they call it Kindred. Don't you ever access the news?"

"No," Leo said. "Too depressing. Christ, it's good to see you! But why do you need the best damn marksman in the entire Army? You expecting trouble on Kindred?"

"Nobody knows." Owen's thin, deeply sunburned face lost its grin. "It's terra incognita, bro."

"Tara Inca Nina—Mayan girl. I knew her in Peru."

"The Incas weren't Mayan and the Mayans weren't in Peru."

"Whatever. God, it's good to see your overly educated ass again, Owen!"

"Lieutenant Lamont. Try to remember."

Leo mocked a salute and hugged Owen again. This was his best friend in the world, and fuck all those people who said they made a weird pair: exuberant upcountry Leo and serious, prep-school Owen with the most deadly skills in the elite Seventy-Fifth Regiment of the US Army Rangers.

They'd met in the Ranger Assessment and Selection Program at Fort Bening. Leo had been sent on recommendation of his CO in Brazil, as a result of Leo's hitting a target with the M107A1 sniper rifle at 2,100 meters. It had been a Holy Grail shot, straight-up luck, although it was true that he had the ability to nudge a little more out of his weapon than normal. Kentucky windage and Tennessee eleva- tion. He had finished RASP and gone on to Ranger School, the most physically and mentally demanding leadership school in the Army. There he had washed out during the mountain phase of training— well, not washed out, exactly, but the details were too embarrassing to think about. Leo was good at not thinking about things.

Owen, in contrast, had finished Ranger School, winning the William O. Darby Award for Distinguished Honor Graduate, and had joined the Seventy-Fifth. The Ranger tab gleamed on the upper left shoulder of his uniform. Since then he'd served in the Mideast and in the Panama Canal Food Wars, earning a Silver Star for valor under fire. Leo had been sent on a second tour in Brazil, but for the last two months he'd basically sat on his butt at Joint Base Lewis–McChord in Seattle, watching deployment after deployment kank as various political situations changed.

Leo said, "So how many troops aboard?"

"Six."

"*Six?* That's all? And you're expecting enough trouble for the Army to send a Ranger squad and request a sniper?"

"Nobody's expecting anything," Owen said with exaggerated patience. "That's the point, Leo. We have no idea what will happen on Kindred. But Colonel Matthews had to fight to get even six. It's a tiny ship, only twenty-one berths. Not our choice."

The ship's size, Leo knew, had been the aliens' choice, along with everything else about the *Friendship*. She had been built from plans left by the Denebs (who weren't from Deneb—Leo remembered that much) in exchange for—well, Leo didn't exactly understand what, but it had to do with biology and the spore cloud and the vaccines and other scientific shit. Apparently the Deneb ship, which had gone back to World—no, to Kindred—had been just as small, although he didn't know why.

He returned to what was comprehensible and immediate. "This Colonel Matthews—a good guy?"

"Yes. Did RASP five times."

"Impressive." Officers of the Seventy-Fifth didn't coast on old training; each time they were promoted, they had to do the assessment program all over again. The Seventy-Fifth had no overweight, out-of-shape leaders. "Who else do we have?"

"Three Rangers and you. Enlisted are Private First Class Mason Kandiss, Specialist Miguel Flores, and Specialist Zoe Berman."

"A girl Ranger?"

"One of only three and the only one with combat experience. Bomb expert. Don't look like that. She's off-limits, Leo."

Leo smiled. "Just fucking with you."

"Don't."

Leo nodded; he'd expected this. Everything in Owen's manner had just changed, from facial expression to body posture; the informal reunion was over. Owen was an officer and from now on that would be the relationship. Leo didn't mind. He'd rather serve under Owen—and this unknown colonel, since Owen vouched for him—than anyone else in the entire United States Army. He nodded again, to show Owen he'd gotten the message, and said, "Sir, can I ask who else is aboard?"

"Five ship's crew, all Navy under Captain Lewis, six scientists, and four diplomats led by the US ambassador to Kindred, Maria Gonzalez. Colonel Matthews has ordered fall-in at thirteen hours."

"Where?"

Owen smiled, reluctantly. "Well, that's a problem. Besides personal quarters, the ship's got the bridge, the common area you came through when you boarded, a storage bay full of supplies, and behind that an area that is wardroom and gym now—we share it with the Navy—and will be a laboratory on Kindred. It's crammed with lab benches and exercise equipment and a big foldable table. But it's all we have. Be there at thirteen hours."

"Yes, sir."

Owen—from now on and at all times, Lieutenant Lamont—left. Leo stowed his gear.

He didn't even feel it when the *Friendship* lifted, smooth as a dancer. If the wall screen hadn't suddenly blossomed into a view of Earth rapidly falling away, Leo wouldn't have known that liftoff had occurred. No strapping in, nothing—damn, that alien tech was something! And thanks to Owen, Leo was here. Really, really here.

Going to the stars.

What the hell was she doing here?

Marianne Jenner already knew the answer to that. All the answers, actually. She was, officially, Ambassador Gonzalez's assistant, the only one aboard who had actually met any Worlders. (No, Kindreders? The name change was beyond stupid, even for a government PR move.) She was, officially, the geneticist who had helped create the vaccine against *R. sporii* (only she hadn't, not really—other team members had done that). She was, officially, the person who had saved the *Friendship* (when it had been the privately built *Venture*) from destruction by the Russian ship bent on revenge, and so averted a war. She was, officially, the only one on ship with a family member on World. On Kindred. Whatever.

All that made her practically a national icon, at least for many people. Others hated her passionately. Marianne distrusted both groups.

Unofficially, much as she wanted to see Noah again (had it really been ten years since her son left Earth?), she was ambivalent about this expedition. The Kindred expedition to Terra had resulted in much good, yes, but also in the destruction of entire economies. Was Ambassador Gonzalez charged by the US government with anything other than establishing diplomatic and trade relations with Kindred? Over half the passengers were armed military personnel, both Army and Navy, with, she suspected, much more serious weapons in storage. Not to mention ways the spaceship itself might have been weaponized; the basic alien plans that Earth had been given covered only the hull and mysterious drives. Marianne distrusted the military. She especially distrusted military going to a peaceful planet that had not seen war in thousands of years. Why were Colonel Matthews and his men along?

There was a general meeting scheduled for the common area at 1:00 p.m. Meetings, in Marianne's experience, usually ended up 90 percent chaff to 10 percent wheat. Still, 10 percent wasn't nothing. She would go to the meeting. As soon as she had a nap. Liftoff wasn't for another hour, and she had not slept well last night.

———

Dr. Salah Bourgiba, biologist and ship's physician, watched the lift-off on the big screen in the common area, along with the other scientists and the diplomatic corps. Ambassador Maria Gonzalez sat beside him, her gaze intent on the screen, her face unreadable. Salah had no idea what was going on in her mind, although he knew everything there was to know about her body, medical history, and genome. He knew everything there was to know about all their bodies. Salah had long ago gotten used to the double vision demanded of doctors in social situations: *"Oh, what did you think of that movie?"* and *I hope she's had that mole on her neck checked out.*

Unlike the twenty-one bodies aboard, the ship itself was a mystery to Salah—and to everyone else, even the engineers who had built her. They might all just as well be flying on a magic carpet. Physicists and materials experts were still fighting about why the dark-matter drive worked, and the fights were vicious and public. Salah knew this because he read and spoke five languages, which was one reason he and not another physician sat here now, watching the Earth dwindle to a blue-and-white marble in a black sky. He picked up languages as easily as a dark suit picked up lint, and after studying recordings of Kindese (awkward name) for months, he was pretty sure he could translate for the other scientists and those diplomats who did not speak the language. Tend their bodies, aid their jobs— he was a full-service provider.

Except maybe for himself.

Studying his fellow adventurers, Salah thought that the least understandable thing about the *Friendship* might be the way that all twenty-one aboard her had just accepted liftoff. No gees pressing anyone down, no rocket boosters, no course corrections, no weightlessness. After five short test flights, everyone just accepted this miracle, this living room with fake-leather easy chairs and giant-screen TV moving through space, this alien technology out of *The Arabian Nights* by way of Apollo's chariot, as the new *normal*. The adaptability of humans dazzled Salah.

Ostensibly, the rest of the trip should be equally painless. The humans on Kindred had, after all, practically invited Terrans to visit, by giving them the spaceship plans. In fact, they probably expected Terrans earlier than ten years after the Kindred ship departed Earth. And by now the Kindred, having technology so much more advanced than anything on Terra, would have not only perfected the vaccine it took Earth years to create, but also vaccinated everyone against *R. sporii*. The planet had only one continent, one culture, a carefully controlled population, peace and plenty. Kindred would not suffer the devastation that had ravaged Earth when the spore cloud had hit, and they would be welcoming hosts to this small, unthreatening Terran delegation.

So why did Salah feel such unease?

Let this go well, insha'Allah.

Leo stood at attention until Colonel Matthews said, "Stand down." Leo relaxed his stance, at least as much as possible in a "wardroom" so crowded with stuff that the six representatives of the United States Army barely had room to stand between the table and the wall.

"Sit," Matthews said, and Leo blinked. Enlisted men didn't usually sit with officers. But, as Owen had already told him, this mission wasn't usual. Leo sat.

Matthews was old, maybe in his forties, but he looked like the kind of CO you could trust. Gray hair cut very short, pale blue eyes. That the other five soldiers were Rangers put Leo at a disadvantage, but he didn't detect any condescension from Matthews. Only—why was the CO wearing glasses? Eyesight had to be lens-free to qualify for the Seventy-Fifth.

Owen didn't look at Leo, and Leo didn't try to catch his eye. Lieutenant Lamont was second in command here. Leo didn't look at Specialist Zoe Berman, either, having been told not to, but he'd had a glimpse anyway—wow. Flores and Kandiss, like everybody else, were expressionless.

Where were the Navy guys? At the other meeting, probably, which raised some questions. Who was in charge of this mission, Army or Navy?

Matthews said, "This is an informal briefing to supplement what you've already been told, so feel free to ask questions. Our mission here is to guard and defend this ship and everyone on it. Because this is a diplomatic mission, ultimate authority rests with Ambassador Gonzalez, whose orders you will obey without question."

That answers that.

"The captain of this vessel, Captain Lewis, has final say over everything connected with the ship while we are in space. Once we are on the ground, command reverts to me unless and until we return to space. If Captain Lewis is incapacitated in space, his executive officer, Ms. Fielding, is in charge. If both are incapacitated, then command reverts to me, not to the other Navy personnel aboard. Is everyone clear on the chain of command?"

"Yes, sir!" from five throats.

"If I am incapacitated—"

Leo listened, but he wasn't perturbed. Such talk was just the sort of thing the Army, especially Rangers, did: anticipate trouble. This was a trade mission to a friendly planet. Their main job was to guard the diplomats and scientists against any stray crazy, defuse any situation like that without killing anybody if they could help it, and look impressive in dress uniform.

Although—why Rangers, then, instead of the usual Marine honor guard for diplomats? Rangers were a direct-action special operations raid force. And why a crack marksman taking up one valuable berth that could have been used for another scientist or Washington bigwig?

Leo didn't think he was going to get answers to any of that, but he couldn't help mulling over the questions. What the hell sort of trouble was expected on Kindred?

"We do not, of course, anticipate any trouble," Maria Gonzalez said. She stood at the front of the common room, the most spacious area on the *Friendship*, addressing the twelve people in easy chairs or seated around the small tables. Two Navy personnel, Executive Officer Anna Fielding and crewman Robert Ritter, were on the bridge, although Marianne couldn't imagine what they were doing there, since the ship pretty much flew itself and no one, including Engineer Volker, understood how. Maybe the Navy personnel were talking to Earth while they still could. The Army people were holding their own briefing.

Ambassador Gonzalez was forty-nine, a tall and elegant woman with black hair worn in a chignon. As the first-ever ambassadorial appointee to another planet, she carried enormous responsibility to make the mission go well, which she bore without apparent anxiety or doubt. The woman radiated a confidence that Marianne envied.

"If I repeat information you already know, please forgive me," Gonzalez said. Her smile was charming, if a little practiced. "We don't know much about how this ship functions, but our Kindred cousins"—a carefully chosen term, Marianne guessed, to remind everyone that the Kindred were human—"have shared their own experience with their ship. The star drive bequeathed to them—and now to us!—is best pictured with space as a piece of cloth. A handkerchief, perhaps. We are at one corner. The drive 'folds up' space until we touch the opposite corner, unfolds, and there we are. The Kindred said that about a week passed aboard ship while this metaphorical folding occurred, although when they sent their first ship—because as you all know, they had built two—and went to their ill-fated colony planet, the folding took only a few hours. So it does seem dependent on distance."

Marianne was not used to people who spoke in such long, grammatically correct sentences with so many dependent clauses, varied with punchier short sentences. Admirable, if slightly theatrical. Gonzalez was a pro.

"We thus expect to be in space for two weeks, although supplies have been brought for three months. We cannot, of course, eat the food on Kindred; our microbes are not adapted for it. The plan is two weeks of travel, a month on Kindred, two weeks back. During the journey out, you will have a last chance to learn or improve your knowledge of the language. The screens in your quarters, and we do apologize for the small size of the accommodations, can access voice lessons in Kindese, accompanied by English transliterations as best as we can produce. Just as a reminder: A caret in the middle of a word indicates a rising inflection, and an upside-down exclamation point a tongue click, like this."

The ambassador clicked. Marianne, who had no aptitude for languages, had pretty much failed at learning Kindese. Her tongue click sounded like she needed the Heimlich maneuver.

"On Kindred," the ambassador continued, "the scientists will have opportunities to interact with their counterparts, and the diplomatic corps will establish what I'm sure will be a long, mutually beneficial interstellar relationship with the government on Kindred. Which, of course, is made much simpler by the fact that there is only one!"

Obliging laughter. Gonzalez smiled engagingly. She was known for her abrupt switches from formal speech to the unexpected joke, the slang phrase in the right place. The media loved her.

Gonzalez waved her hand and said, "Piece of cake."

"We don't know what to expect on Kindred," Colonel Matthews said. "The plan is two weeks of transport, a month of occupation, two weeks' transport back. The natives could be friendly, but they don't know we're coming, and there is always the possibility they won't like it. At destination, the shuttle will convey rotating parties of five to the surface; one will remain on watch aboard unless otherwise informed. At the end of the meeting, Lieutenant Lamont will go over the various possible incident scenarios we've anticipated, with our responses. Contingencies include crowd riots, kidnapping, extraction scenarios, terrorist operations, outright military attack, infiltration of the ship or our Ranger base, and/or emergency evacuation of all personnel.

"Basically, all of us need to be ready for anything at all times."

Captain Alan Lewis now spoke. Marianne recognized him, of course—he was the famous astronaut who had saved the lives of two Chinese and one French astronauts at the ISS. Appointing him commander of the *Friendship* was a PR stroke of genius. Everyone but the Russians liked him; the Russians didn't like anybody. But the Russian spaceship, like the original American one, had been the target of domestic terrorism by the widespread, dangerous extremists who wanted no contact with Kindred because they held the Kindred responsible for the spore cloud. Which made no sense, but then, when did extremism ever make sense? Marianne was just glad that the Russian ship no longer existed. She had already tangled with it once.

Lewis had the same easy charm as Gonzalez—was that desirable in a ship's captain? Marianne didn't know. Certainly he looked the part, a handsome African-American in dress whites.

"I won't go over everything in your briefings," Lewis said. "You already know about shuttle deployment, planet conditions, and helmet requirements."

She knew. Kindred orbited an orange dwarf. Slightly larger than Earth but less dense, the planet's gravity was .92 gee and its oxygen content equaled Terra's at twelve thousand feet. They could have breathed the air, which was similar to Earth's, but would not because of microbes. Nobody on the mission had the same immunity to Kindred pathogens that the Kindred had developed over millennia, and so the air helmets were necessary to cover mouths, ears, eyes. Also, no Terran's gut microbes made eating anything grown there plausible. Ten Terrans had gone with the aliens when they left Earth, including Marianne's son Noah, and all of them would have had their microbiome completely changed. Examining these ten bodies was the major excitement for the two physician-biologists aboard, Claire Patel and Salah Bourgiba. Marianne saw them exchange small anticipatory smiles across the room.

"Drills will be held immediately following this meeting in the use of filter masks," Colonel Matthews said. "Remove your filter planetside and you won't die, maybe, but you risk infection from native diseases that you could then carry back to this unit. Removing filters inappropriately is grounds for court-martial. Does everyone understand that?"

"Yes, sir!"

Leo wondered if he could sight and shoot as well through the faceplate of some fucking filter helmet. He hadn't so much as *seen* the thing before, and he sure couldn't test it regarding marksmanship while aboard the ship. Had the CO thought of that?

"The shuttle, human built, is large enough," Captain Lewis said, "to hold everyone for transport but not as habitat, which it will become once we are on ground. Navy personnel will stay aboard the ship except for Lieutenant Yi, who will pilot the shuttle. Colonel Matthews plans to leave one of his soldiers aboard as well."

Why? That made no sense to Salah, but then, he had never been in the military. To prevent mutiny? Looting? Hijacking? Seriously?

"Although it will be a habitat, the shuttle will also make four scheduled trips to the ship to reload supplies, exchange personnel as needed, and allow our scientists access to the greater computing power of— Ladies and gentlemen, there goes the moon."

All heads swiveled to the wall screen. In a single eye blink, the moon loomed off to the left and then dwindled, no more than a firefly in the night. How fast was the *Friendship* moving? He would have to look it up.

Another miracle. Another adaptive normal. The meeting resumed.

"We have now passed the moon," Colonel Matthews announced. He must, Leo realized, be receiving information from the bridge. Well, cool—that's what the CO's data glasses were for, but they were so sleek and normal-looking that Leo hadn't even realized. Great tech!

The filter masks weren't too bad, either. The thing wasn't a helmet or a big-ass gas mask, after all. Made of some clear, flexible plastic, it fit snugly—really snugly—over his mouth and nose and sealed itself to his face. A bulge under one ear held some sort of tiny motor. The mask kept Terrans from breathing in microbes their bodies couldn't handle, but microbes in the air still could get on their skin and in "other orifices," so protocol would be to wear wet suits when they were out of base. At least, they looked like wet suits to Leo, covering pretty much everything. The gloves were thinskin and really flexible, but they were still gloves and he didn't like shooting with gloves. Another problem.

"Brodie," Colonel Matthews said, "everybody else has drilled with this equipment for weeks. Your duty roster includes sessions with Kandiss to thoroughly familiarize yourself with the equipment."

Leo nodded. He was the FNG—Fucking New Guy—and way behind the curve. But he was a fast learner.

Matthews said, "Duty rosters, including exercise periods, are as follows—"

The meeting droned on. Marianne fought drowsiness. She knew all of this information—everybody here knew all of this information. They'd had classes on it. Now the astrophysicist and geologist were reciting the known facts about Kindred's physical properties, along with speculations on its geologic history. When they finished—and please God, let it be soon—probably Maria Gonzalez was going to repeat what was known about Kindred social structure. What if Marianne pleaded a headache and—

The wall screen, which had shown black space studded with stars, suddenly went completely dark. The PA system said, "Captain Lewis and Ambassador Gonzalez to the bridge. Repeat, Captain Lewis and Ambassador Gonzalez to the bridge."

David Sherman, geologist, stopped in midsentence. He and the astrophysicist looked at each other. A moment later the PA said, "Dr. McKenzie to the bridge. Repeat, Dr. McKenzie to the bridge."

The astrophysicist disappeared through the door. Before anyone could stop her, Marianne followed him.

David Sherman struggled on a moment more: "As I was saying, the molten core of Kindred is . . . isn't . . ." He stopped again.

Stars reappeared on the wall screen.

In the middle of helmet drill—not hard, but Leo still had no answer about its effect on sighting targets—Colonel Matthews suddenly went intent, listening to something no one else could hear. Then he said to Owen, "Lieutenant, take over," and strode from the room.

The Rangers glanced covertly at each other.

Captain Lewis, affability gone, said tightly, "Dr. Jenner, you were not summoned. Please leave the bridge."

"No," the ambassador said, "let her stay. She's the only one with any experience with Kindred; maybe she can shed some light on this."

The door flung open and Colonel Matthews strode into the room. He addressed Lewis sharply. "Captain, I expect to be included in discussions when something of this nature occurs."

It seemed to Marianne that Lewis wanted to say something in the same tone as Matthews—Christ, not a turf war just six hours out! But Lewis was too good for that. He caught himself and said, "You're right, Colonel. My apologies. What has happened is that all communication with Earth has ceased. It happened at the moment the stars . . . blinked."

Blinked. That must have meant the *Friendship* had jumped from one side of the ambassador's piece of cloth to the other. But that wasn't supposed to happen yet! Or, rather, it hadn't happened that way when the Kindred ship approached Earth eleven years ago. There had been two weeks of sightings by NASA, SETI, the European and Chinese and Russian space agencies, and every amateur astronomer who knew where to point a telescope. The *Friendship* was supposed to have two weeks in the solar system before she jumped.

Greg McKenzie had been working at the computer. He said, "Ambassador, we've arrived. This is the Kindred system."

Marianne swiveled to face the wall screen. All she saw was a fuzzy orange disk in the black sky. Around it were other, brighter stars.

Gonzalez recovered fast. "Very well," she said. "We all knew that the ship's drive was preset to arrive back at Kindred, but I guess we didn't realize how quickly we would arrive. Captain Lewis, are we now traveling at normal ship speed?"

Marianne had to suppress an insane giggle. What was "normal" under these circumstances?

Evidently Captain Lewis agreed. "I have no idea, Madam Ambassador. Mr. Volker?"

The Navy engineer said, "We are traveling at the same speed as before we, ah, jumped. At this speed, assuming it remains constant, we are three weeks away from arriving at the planet."

"Thank you," Gonzalez said. "Captain, can we speak to the planet now?"

"I'll try."

Owen must have been equipped with some way to hear Colonel Matthews, or something, because he broke off in the middle of a sentence and said, "As of now, this unit is on red alert. Battle stations, *now*."

Four soldiers sprang up faster. Faster than Leo, standing bewildered and alone by the table, imagined possible, Owen had opened a bulkhead locker and he, Kandiss, Flores, and Berman were grabbing arms and donning armor. Owen felt like a fool. He didn't have a battle station, had no idea what he was supposed to be doing. A sniper was useless on a tiny ship. Owen said calmly, "Brodie, come with me. Cover me if necessary." He handed Leo his gear.

Cover him? Against what? Were they going to be boarded, or land, or . . . Leo did as he was ordered, automatically checking his weapon, copying Owen's movements, hoping for the best.

Marianne stood inconspicuously in a corner of the bridge while Ambassador Gonzalez addressed the tiny blue marble on the wall screen. "Kindred, this is the Terran ship *Friendship*, from the United States, built with the plans you left us when you came to Earth. We come now in peace and friendship." She then repeated the message in English.

No answer.

Gonzalez tried again, and again. Nothing. She turned to the engineer and the physicist, both of whom had been involved in building the ship. "Are we too far out?"

Volker said, "It seems so, ma'am."

"I want the recorded version of the message played every hour, and I want to be summoned immediately, awake or asleep, when there is a response. We don't know where their receiving equipment is, in orbit or on the ground, or in how many places."

No, they didn't know that. Although, Marianne thought, it was reasonable to suppose that a civilization so much further advanced than Earth had ultra-sophisticated detection equipment for anything out of the ordinary in their star system. Still—

Judy Taunton, physicist on Earth and Marianne's friend, had made some very disturbing speculations about Kindred.

Gonzalez said, "Open the all-ship frequency, please. I would like to tell everyone what the—"

"Oh my God!" McKenzie blurted.

Colonel Matthews said sharply, "What is it? Incoming?"

"No, no, I . . . my God, no, but I checked . . . let me run the program again!"

Gonzalez said, "What program? Inform us, Dr. McKenzie!"

The astrophysicist turned away from the computer and toward the ambassador. Marianne was shocked at how pale he looked, how shaky. If he fainted . . . But he didn't. McKenzie got hold of himself, although his voice quavered.

"The astronomical program checks the stars' locations against charts. We know what positions every celestial body should hold relative to each other, given observers' positions. None of them right now are as projected, they—"

Gonzalez said sharply, "You mean we aren't at Kindred?"

"Oh, we're there," McKenzie said. "But the aliens didn't tell us there would be a temporal dislocation. But . . . but from star positions, *there is*. Time dilation has carried us forward fourteen years from when we left Earth. And I'm assuming that returning will add another fourteen years. And they didn't tell us."

CHAPTER 2

It began almost immediately.

Salah Bourgiba had anticipated it, from the moment that the ambassador made her announcement. The other doctor aboard, Claire Patel, was a virologist, more of a researcher than a physician, although she was licensed to practice medicine. It was Salah who had extensive clinical experience, who did so well with medical patients needing psychological support. The background checkers knew that, of course, along with everything about everybody.

So they came to him, these young men and women who had just learned that when they returned home, everybody else would be twenty-eight years older, and they would not be. Who were expected to remain adaptable and tight-lipped and professional everywhere else on the ship. Crewman Robert Ritter, who had a wife and a three-year-old child. A month from now, little Susan would be older than her father. Dr. David Sherman, who was embarrassed to be asking help at age forty-one but who had parents who would be dead when he returned. Ambassador Gonzalez did not come to see Salah, although he knew that she was uneasy about establishing diplomatic relations now, when the spore cloud was imminent. She'd expected to arrive on Kindred fifteen years before that happened.

Branch Carter, the brilliant young lab tech and personal-hardware whiz, did come to see Salah. And, unlike many others, Branch was willing to express openly his rage.

Salah heard that rage even before Branch entered, in the passageway outside sick bay. Branch's voice rippled with anger. "Did you know?"

"What? No!" Marianne Jenner, who must have been passing by. "I didn't know any more than the rest of you."

"Uh-huh. You sure your son didn't tell you before he left with the aliens and you just didn't bother to tell the rest of us because you were so hell-bent on getting Terrans to World?"

"Branch, no." Her voice held compassion under its firmness. "This time dilation is as much a surprise to me as to the rest of you."

Silence. Salah waited. Whatever Branch said next would be critical.

"I'm . . . I'm sorry, Dr. Jenner. It's just . . ."

"I know," she said. "Don't worry about it." Then she did the best thing she could have done: her footsteps receded quickly along the passageway, allowing Branch to enter the infirmary unseen.

The small room had all the personality of a meat locker: two walls of bulkhead storage cabinets plus a blank wall screen, two walls of stacked metal bunks that could fold down if needed. If more than four beds were required, the ship was in trouble. In the middle sat two chairs and a collapsible table, now holding a box of tissues and the pot of coffee without which nobody on the ship seemed able to function. Salah, who drank tea, was prepared.

"Come in, Branch. Sit down. What can I do for you?"

Unlike Ritter, also twenty-eight, Branch Carter was direct. "I need a sleeping pill. I can't sleep since I heard what those bastards did to us."

Salah kept his tone neutral; the young man bristled with anger looking for a reason to explode. Branch's personnel file said he was extremely competent at his job, affable and tireless, and "of a disposition to work well with the scientists aboard." It did not say he was prepared to have his temporal place in the universe fucked with. Salah said, "You're assuming that the Kindred knew about the time dilation."

"Why wouldn't they? They brought their ship to Earth, and they sent a ship to a colony world, too—the ship that got infected with the spore cloud in the first place."

"Yes, that's true. But consider this—they may not have known they jumped fourteen years when they came to Earth, where they'd never before been. And if the colony planet is fairly close to Kindred—say, even in the same star system—their other ship might not have needed to jump, or the time dilation might have been so small they didn't notice it."

"Or they might have lied to lure us to Kindred, thinking that we wouldn't come any other way."

Was that the idea circulating among the younger people aboard? Maybe. Branch, the three youngest soldiers under Colonel Matthews, and two of the Navy crew were under thirty. Naturally they would talk away from their superiors. Salah leaned forward in his chair.

"If the Kindred lied, why do you think that might be? What would they gain from 'luring' us to Kindred?"

"A blood supply immune to the spore cloud. When they left Earth, remember, we didn't have the vaccine yet. Maybe they never developed it."

"Possibly. But of course, they are more advanced than we are, so they probably did develop the vaccine. After all, when the spore cloud hits Kindred a few months from now, the Kindred will have had years to prepare. In addition, they already have ten Terrans, the ones who went with them, to donate blood."

Branch ignored the second part of this argument, seizing on the first. "If they're so much farther advanced than we are, then why did they come to Earth for our help in the first place?"

A good question, and one that had been asked often: by scientists, by politicians, by media, by an endless number of conspiracy theorists. Never with a satisfactory answer.

"All I'm saying," Branch said, "is that I don't trust them now. They never told us that humans were immune, after all."

"If you haven't trusted them all along, why did you apply to come on this mission?"

The young man looked away, then back at Salah. Honesty wrinkled his fresh skin, and all at once he looked even younger than he was. "I wanted to go into space. I mean, who wouldn't? I jumped at the chance. But this is a dirty trick and I don't trust them now. That's all I'm saying."

"And all I'm saying is that you're a scientist. As a scientist, you owe it to objective truth to wait until you have all the facts before you make a judgment about the Kindred. When we get close enough for communication, we'll have more answers. Does that seem fair?"

"Yes. But . . . if they're so far ahead of us that they can build ships like this, why can't they pick up our communications from space? We could do that decades ago."

Another unanswerable question. Salah said, "I don't know. But let's gather all the facts before leaping to conclusions."

"Yes. Okay. That makes sense." Branch rose. He looked calmer now, the sleeping pill forgotten. "Thanks, Doctor."

"Anytime."

Salah made a note on Branch's chart. Then he sat for a while, thinking. The lab tech's underlying distrust of the Kindred should have been detected by the battery of psychological tests he took before being accepted for the *Friendship*. Not that Salah had ever really trusted psychological testing; except in extreme cases, it seldom revealed anything not obvious during an hour-long interview. Extroversion, novelty avoidance, reasoning ability, lying—a sensitive interviewer could ferret them all out with a few good questions and a lot of careful listening. People were just too complex for simple true-false tests.

Still, Branch's visit raised a question about the supposedly exhaustive background checks: What else had they missed? And in whom?

When Leo got to the wardroom, five minutes late for his scheduled exercise session, Miguel Flores sat at the table, reading on his tablet. Flores looked up briefly and scowled; he'd been scowling since everybody got the news about the time dilation. Well, it wasn't any worse for him than anybody else, and anyway there wasn't anything anybody could do about it. It just was.

Zoe Berman was already on the AllEx machine, doing pull-ups. Her arms bulged with muscle. She was long, lean but with definite breasts, and she had a face that belonged on an angel. Leo tried not to look. He climbed onto the bike, set the resistance for maximum, and began pumping. In his view, none of this equipment was any substitute for running or climbing, but this was what they had.

Twenty minutes later, Miguel cursed softly, closed his tablet, and left. There was no place to go except here, your bunk, or the common room, which was off-limits to the enlisted men unless you were on watch. At least they each had personal quarters, however small and cramped, instead of a barracks.

Leo said to Zoe, "And so another one crawls into his cave. We're all going to be hibernating bears before we reach the planet."

Zoe said, "Switch."

Leo climbed off the bike and onto the AllEx, and Zoe took the bike. She staggered a little getting on. Her eyes, huge and green, looked weird somehow. Cloudy. Leo said sympathetically, "Not sleeping well?"

"Shut up."

O-kaaay. Not a candidate for leadership awards. Leo did the required pull-ups, enjoying the play of his own muscles, the beating of his own heart, even the sweat that filmed his forehead. The time dilation, which was covering the ship with its own stink, didn't bother him all that much. His parents were dead; there was no love lost between him and the foster family that had raised him for the state money; he didn't have a girl. Earth twenty-eight years from now was sort of intriguing, and the Army would still be there.

The whirring from Zoe's bike slowed.

The Army was his real home, his bedrock, had been since he'd been eighteen. Basic, then sniper school, RASP (but don't think about that), then the 101st Airborne. Action in Brazil and that pissant skirmish in Turkey. The Army gave his life order and meaning. He knew guys who couldn't wait to get out, but not Leo. He was—

The bike stopped whirring.

Leo turned his head. Zoe slumped sideways, her eyes unfocused. Leo leaped up, just in time to catch her before she hit the deck. The bike seat and the back of her shorts were both covered with blood.

"Berman! Hey!" He eased her to the floor.

"Get away from me." A second later she clutched him. "Don't tell anybody!"

Tell anybody what? Leo didn't understand what was happening. Zoe gave him the most forced, horrible smile he'd ever seen. She said, "You never seen blood from a girl's period before? What are you, a virgin?"

"No." But this wasn't regular period blood like girls got, usually when you didn't want them to. Leo was sure of it. Zoe closed her eyes and bit her lip hard, and Leo saw that she was stopping a scream.

"You need the doctor."

"No! Just . . . just get me to my quarters . . ."

Leo eased her to her feet. More blood. Zoe staggered and he hoisted her into a fireman's carry. This was a miscarriage. But that wasn't possible, they'd all had a physical just two weeks before lift-off and the docs would have found a pregnancy. Appendix? Leo was hazy on where the appendix was—right side? left?—or whether it would produce blood.

"My quarters," Zoe said, and although there was no panic in her voice—Rangers didn't panic—and no audible fear, there was something scary.

Leo took her, dripping blood, straight to the infirmary.

The Muslim doctor—Leo wasn't good with names—flung open the door as soon as Leo kicked it. The doc was there alone. As soon as he saw them, he flipped down a bed from the left bulkhead and said, "What happened?"

Leo said, "I don't know. She was exercising on the bike and she slumped off. She said it's just her period but—"

Zoe tried to say something, then passed out.

The doctor's hands explored Zoe's body. He pressed and she revived and screamed. He said, "Comm on, private channel, Dr. Patel. Claire, to sick bay STAT, emergency."

The wall screen said, "On my way."

The doctor was undressing Zoe. To Leo he said, "Go now."

Leo was glad to go. In the passageway Dr. Patel pushed past him. In such a small ship, anybody could get anywhere really fast. Right now that was probably good.

He washed his hands; the washroom was empty. Christ—the passageway. Well, he could do that for Zoe, anyway. He got a towel, decided against it (Who did the laundry? He'd never thought to ask), and grabbed a lot of recyclable paper towels. Hoping no one saw him before he finished, he wiped the blood from the deck and bike.

Owen entered the wardroom just as he stuffed the towels into the recycle chute. "Brodie—aren't you on exercise rotation?"

"Yes, sir. Bathroom break."

Leo started doing pull-ups.

In his off-duty time, he knocked on the door of sick bay. The passageway lights had been dimmed to simulate night. The briefing in the common room, which even the Rangers had attended, had yielded a lot of math and astronomy that Leo didn't follow and two useful pieces of information: still no response from Kindred to the *Friendship*'s radio messages, and the spore cloud would hit the planet ten weeks from now. Why an hour-and-a-half meeting to tell everybody that? And why did the hour-and-a-half briefing have to fall in Leo's off-duty? But it was what it was.

"Come in."

Dr. Bourgiba switched off the wall screen, which showed the common room; he must have been watching the briefing. In the low light, Zoe lay asleep or knocked out on the bunk. Leo smelled disinfectant, a smell he'd never liked.

"I came to see how Berman is, sir."

"She'll be fine. Sit down, son."

Leo disliked being called "son," but he sat. The doctor said, "Did you know about Ranger Berman?"

"Know what?"

Bourgiba met his gaze squarely. The doctor's eyes were very dark, almost black. He looked in pretty good shape for a civilian in his forties, but he was no Colonel Matthews. Bourgiba said, "Ranger Berman was pregnant. Were you the father?"

"No!" Despite himself, Leo was shocked, which was ridiculous. "How could she be pregnant? They had physicals just two weeks ago! Anyway, she's a Ranger—too smart for that."

"Nonetheless, she was. An ectopic pregnancy—do you know what that is?"

Leo shook his head.

"The fetus implanted in a fallopian tube, not in the uterus. Tubes don't stretch. So when the pregnancy grows too big, the tube bursts and the patient bleeds internally. When Dr. Patel and I opened Berman, she had a liter of blood in her belly. But she'll recover fine."

Leo leaned forward in his chair. "Does anybody else have to know about this? I don't know how Berman got pregnant"—stupid statement, there was only one way—"but it would get her tossed out of the Rangers. Especially since she's the only female Ranger with combat experience and that's why she's on this mission. It'd be a huge stink and the Army would discharge her."

"Leo—discharge her to *where*? We're in an alien star system and in temporal dislocation."

Well, shit. All true. Still . . . "But they might discharge her when we go home. In twenty-eight years, I mean. And even now, aboard ship . . . she'll want to resume her duties, it's why she came. Why we all came. Can't you just say her appendix burst or something?"

Bourgiba didn't smile. Leo gave him credit for that. He said, "Any physician could tell the difference instantly. But I see what you mean—her unit and commanding officer might view her differently, as a female liability, and you don't think she deserves that, right?"

"Right."

"I won't falsify her records, but I will tell Colonel Matthews that her surgery was to address an abdominal problem that has been fully repaired. If he doesn't actually read her chart, that may be enough, and he probably won't read her chart because everyone has so much else to deal with. Ranger Berman should be able to return to duty in a few weeks. Will that do?"

"Yes. Thank you, sir." Leo stood. No way a Ranger was going to stay in bed for two weeks; by that time they'd have made planetfall. Zoe would be on her feet by the day after tomorrow.

Bourgiba said, "And you were not the father."

"No. I never met her till I came aboard."

"Are you two friends?"

"Not really. She keeps pretty much to herself."

Bourgiba looked at him more closely. "Then your concern for her is admirable."

"She's in my unit." Didn't civilians understand anything?

"I see," Bourgiba said, although Leo doubted that he did. "Get some sleep, Ranger Brodie."

"I'm not a Ranger. I'm just on temporary duty with—"

"Get some sleep anyway. You can visit Ranger Berman tomorrow."

When Leo returned to sick bay the next afternoon, Dr. Patel was there. She nodded at Leo and said in her pretty accent, "Ah, Ranger Brodie. Perhaps you would like to visit with Ranger Berman alone. If you need assistance, just activate the comm and call for me."

She smiled at him. Dr. Patel, who only came to Leo's shoulder, was as old as Dr. Bourgiba, but her smooth brown skin and dark curls looked good to Leo. All women were looking good to him lately—it had been too long—except for, now, Zoe Berman, which was weird because she was the most beautiful woman aboard. Something to do with her leaking blood all over him yesterday. Or maybe with her hard scowl.

The first thing she said was, "I suppose you ratted me out to Matthews."

"No. I didn't tell anybody."

Surprise, followed by suspicion. "Yeah? Why not? Against regs."

"Didn't think you'd want me to."

She looked at him a long time, until the expression in her cat-green eyes changed and she turned her head on the pillow so that her gaze rested on the ceiling. "I didn't know I was pregnant."

"Pretty stupid."

"Yeah." She wasn't offended, and Leo saw all at once that she wanted to talk. He pulled up a chair.

Zoe said, "It was a sort of farewell fuck. I got so little body fat that I was supposed to be immune. I always was before."

Leo nodded. His foster family, the one he'd stayed in longest, had had four older girls. Nasty, manipulative bitches that had bullied and hurt him, but Leo had learned to listen.

Zoe said, "I didn't even like him that much. But we were drinking and he was cute and he was *there* and . . . you know."

Leo knew. He'd had a lot of sex just because the girl was *there*. He could tell, too, from the way Zoe turned her head to look at him that she was done talking and that now he was supposed to say something personal. Girls did that. It was how they made friends. Figuring out this weird bit of girl-lore had helped Leo get a lot of them into bed, although that wasn't what was going on here. This might be better; he could use a friend aboard the *Friendship*. He was mulling over which piece of his personal life to offer when Zoe took that decision out of his hands.

"Why'd you wash out of Ranger School?"

"How do you know that?"

She rolled her eyes. "You think there wasn't a lot of talk about bringing you into the unit? A lot of poking around online?"

"Didn't think about it. But your poking didn't turn up the story?"

"It wasn't my poking. And Lieutenant Lamont didn't say anything, neither. Flores is pretty good on the computer."

Flores, scowling at his tablet, leaving the wardroom when Leo came in to exercise. "He didn't want me here."

"Nope. But he'll do what Lamont wants. Worships the guy. You still didn't say why you washed out."

"I didn't, exactly." Leo took a deep breath. Did he want to tell her this? Well, why the hell not. It was what it was. "I was there with Owen. Lieutenant Lamont, but he wasn't a looie then. We went to-gether through RASP and then Fort Bening, then we were in moun-tain phase and I got into some poison ivy."

"So? I did, too. Common."

"Yeah, but I'm allergic and didn't know it. I got blisters all over my body. That wouldn't have been too bad except that the blisters got infected. Sepsis, with a fever so high I hallucinated. Owen car-ried me back down the mountain. Saved my life."

"A natlee," Zoe said. "That's what my class called the natural lead-ers. But there's medical recycle. You could have gone through school again after you got well."

"Yeah." This was the hard part to tell somebody, especially a Ranger. "I decided I didn't want to."

"Yeah? And why is that?" Her tone was a challenge. Leo picked his words carefully.

"Nothing against Rangers. Christ, you guys are the best of the best. But lying there in the hospital, I just realized it wasn't for me. Not the service—hell, I'm a lifer. But what you just said—the emphasis on leadership. I'm just . . . not."

Long silence. Leo was thinking how to make his escape from sick bay when Zoe said, "Okay, I can see that. You're all right, Leo."

"Thanks."

"You, too. For not blabbing. Now get the fuck out of here so I can sleep."

"Yes, ma'am."

They grinned at each other, and Leo left whistling.

In the passageway the PA boomed. "This is Captain Lewis. Ambassador Gonzalez and Colonel Matthews to the bridge, please. Repeat, Ambassador Gonzalez and Colonel Matthews to the bridge. Ladies and gentlemen, we have contact with Kindred."

CHAPTER 3

Two weeks aboard ship. Marianne stood on the bridge; once again she was there only because Ambassador Gonzalez had requested her. She, in turn, had suggested that Dr. Patel be present. If Kindred was going to communicate information about the vaccines developed against the spore cloud, Marianne wanted the virologist to hear it immediately. Nobody had expected the *Friendship* to arrive so soon. This temporal glitch would add tension to the humans' expedition.

Not that there wasn't already tension. As the *Friendship*, now under the in-system drive, had flown toward Kindred, the ship had repeatedly hailed the planet. Kindred had never replied.

"We greet you from World," a voice said in Kindese. Marianne had learned a few useful phrases. *Tourist phrases,* her mind mocked.

Gonzalez said, "We greet you from Terra." Whatever the ambassador said next, Marianne couldn't translate, but she assumed it was more ritual greetings.

Captain Lewis said to his engineer, Joseph Volker, "Why isn't the wall screen showing images?"

"They're not sending any. The broadcast is on the same frequency as ours—I think it's coming from their ship on the ground, right . . . there." One of the bridge screens sprang to life with a stylized globe decorated with an asterisk, a dotted line running from that to a tiny icon of the *Friendship* in space.

The Kindred said something, and Gonzalez replied sharply. Marianne recognized the word "why," or at least one of the words for "why." Kindred, a complex language, employed different inflections for different states of being: absolute, tentative, in flux, and rotational.

The Kindred answered for a few seconds, and then silence.

Captain Lewis said, "Mr. Volker?"

"It isn't us. The channel went dead. I think . . . it might be because the Kindred ship just passed over the horizon as the planet rotated. Captain, they don't have any comm satellites in orbit that I can detect. None. And no space stations, either."

Marianne blinked. Terra had hundreds of communications satellites, most using laser-based communication systems in contact with Earth, with deep-space and Martian probes, with each other. Why wouldn't the Kindred, so much more advanced that they could build starships, also have them? It made no sense.

Gonzalez said, "The Kindred I was talking to—I didn't understand her title—said that the government would communicate again in an hour or so."

Volker said, "Then it can't be just that their ship is over the horizon. The rotation period is twenty-five hours three minutes."

Captain Lewis said, "Ambassador?"

Maria Gonzalez said, "We wait."

An hour later, communication resumed. Nearly everyone aboard had spent the time sitting in the wardroom with steaming cups of coffee. Ship's time was after midnight, but as far as Marianne knew, no one was asleep. One of Colonel Matthews's Rangers "stood watch" beside the open door to the bridge. (Why? What did the Army expect—a hijacking?)

Marianne eyed James Ramstetter, one of the ambassador's entourage. His official title was "Security" and ostensibly he was her personal bodyguard, but Marianne suspected he also worked for the CIA or NSA or FBI or maybe some Washington agency so secret she'd never heard of it. Maybe Gonzalez's chief of staff, sociologist Wayne Henry, and her economics adviser, Will Bentley, did, too. Or maybe these were merely the people needed to set up a United States embassy on an alien planet. *Don't be paranoid, Marianne.*

David Sherman said, apropos of nothing, "The spore cloud intersects Kindred in seventy-one days, Terran."

No one answered him; they all had this information already.

The wall screen brightened. The ambassador had made the decision to communicate openly, throughout the entire ship, whatever was said from Kindred. Even the infirmary, where Salah Bourgiba had one of the Rangers recuperating from some sort of minor intestinal operation, would hear and see the first transactions with Kindred.

The wall screen showed the planet, much larger now as the *Friendship* traveled toward it. No image had been transmitted from the planet. And the audio—

"That's *radio*," David Sherman, the geologist, said. "Listen to the static!"

There was so much of it that only a few words of Kindred were clear. Then, all at once, a female voice speaking unaccented English. "Terran ship? I greet you. This . . . garble garble . . . today . . . garble garble . . . land . . ."

"Who is this, please?" Ambassador Gonzalez said.

"Garble garble . . . more. . . . can't. . . . more tomorrow—"

David said, "Maybe they mean that when the planet brings the grounded Kindred ship in direct line on communication again—but why wait? And why radio? Their previous message was laser-based, like ours."

The staticky, unintelligible speech had continued to broadcast. Then, shockingly, a whole sentence came through static-free: "Do not attempt to land on World.

"Please."

———

"They don't want us," Mason Kandiss said to Leo and Zoe. For Kandiss, this was a long speech. The three of them crowded sick bay, Leo and Mason sitting on the two chairs and Zoe up in bed. Miguel Flores was on watch in the common area.

Kandiss was one of the biggest men that Leo had ever seen. His magnificent body bulged with the kind of muscle that came from daily climbing ropes, lifting weights, scaling walls, running for miles. He was spit-and-polish—you could be blinded by the shine on his boots. Zoe had told Leo that Kandiss was "the real shit." From her, this was high praise. "Plus," she'd said, "he wasn't one of the pricks who hassled me about women in combat, you know? He don't talk much, but he's okay."

Leo said, "If they don't want us—but wait, *who* doesn't want us? That was an American voice. Not an alien. So what's up with that?"

Zoe said, "Ten Americans went to Kindred with Noah Jenner. Well, nine and him. Maybe they run the place now? Naw, that's dumb. How could it even happen? They're supposed to be peaceful, this great culture with no war and shit like that."

Leo had heard that, too. He wasn't sure he believed it. Everybody had wars. "I'll tell you who *will* want us, any minute—Colonel Matthews. We're going to be—"

All three wristers vibrated. Kandiss said, "On. Kandiss here. Sir?"

"Battle stations immediately."

"Yes, sir," Leo and Kandiss said simultaneously. Zoe moved restlessly in her sick bunk. "Sir, Berman here. I can—"

"Negative, Berman. Stay where you are."

Kandiss was already out the door. Leo said over his shoulder, "Probably nothing will happen anyway."

"Yeah," Zoe said unhappily. "Probably not."

Nothing did, at least not until morning. Leo stood in full gear at his station in the corridor by the shuttle bay door, ready to defend it against nothing, and stared at the wall screen in the corridor. They were all over, those screens, so that nobody missed anything. Or maybe the screens were also security cameras watching the corridors—he didn't know.

The wall screen showed the planet getting bigger and bigger. The *Friendship* must be going really fast. Now you could see the one big continent coming over the horizon, scattered islands around it like water spiders on a pond. Probably now the planet would resume communications with the *Friendship*. Weird that they'd stopped during the night.

Kandiss had said "Maybe religion," which Leo thought meant some bizarre-o thing where everybody had to not bother the gods during the dark hours. Berman thought maybe they had iron discipline, with no talking after lights out. "For the whole *planet?*" Leo had said. "That doesn't seem realistic." Berman had said maybe it wasn't realistic, but how realistic was it that the Kindred never had wars and had only one culture? Dr. Bourgiba had once started to explain about how a small group of humans had been taken to Kindred 140,000 years ago and how they happened to be both genetically similar and basically passive types, until he'd noticed that none of the Rangers was listening to him. Bourgiba knew a lot, was really smart, but Leo thought the doctor was also somehow . . . hard to put a word to it . . . not all together. Inside. No, that wasn't right— Bourgiba wasn't nuts. It just sometimes felt like for all his smoothness, there was nobody really home.

Leo was getting sleepy. This battle watch came on top of a full day's duty and he hadn't slept in twenty-two hours. Well, shit, that wasn't so long. At Ranger School he'd done Camp Darby on three hours sleep a night, doing hard physical labor instead of just guarding a shuttle bay against nothing. Although . . .

Shit. He'd been asleep on his feet. Only for a few seconds, but if Owen or the colonel had seen it . . . Worse, he had a flash-dream of Berman, naked. Which was weird because he didn't really want her, despite those long legs and slim waist and firm breasts. Despite that face. He couldn't figure out why, either. Now, that Dr. Patel—

Clang! Clang! Clang!

"Prepare for possible attack," Captain Lewis said through the wall screen. "Repeat—" At the same moment Leo's wrister said, "Code one. Code one," in Owen's voice, and the wall screen in front of Leo glowed with another ship, shaped exactly like theirs, hurtling toward Kindred.

Salah stood on the bridge behind the ambassador's chair, the backup translator. The official English-Russian translator, Gonzalez's chief-of-staff William Bentley III, should have been doing this, but the ambassador had already made her decision. Bentley was on his way to his quarters.

Just in case, Gonzalez had said.

The Russian ship should not even exist. That was what the world had been told: the *Stremlenie* had been destroyed. But here it was, appearing from nowhere, erupting into space just as the *Friendship* must have done. Gonzalez spoke in Russian, hailing the *Stremlenie*, identifying herself and her mission. There was no answer.

The *Stremlenie* continued toward the planet.

Salah knew the history of this ship. Everyone knew the history of this ship. Russia had lost the genetic lottery no one had known would occur: a widespread allele in that already starving country had caused many more fatalities among Slavs than anyone else. The devastation from the spore cloud, plus climate change and totalitarian politics, had bred a virulent hatred of Kindred. Those Russian scientists who pointed out that the aliens had not actually caused the spore cloud were disbelieved, or shot. The aliens and the spore cloud arrived in tandem, therefore the cloud was a weapon aimed at Terra, and the Western countries were too deluded or soft or blinded to see that. The classified name for the *Stremlenie*, which had been made public only after the United States had barely averted Terra's first space battle, was *Mest'*: the *Revenge*.

"*Friendship* to *Stremlenie* . . ."

A burst of Russian. Salah translated for Captain Lewis, Engineer Volker, pilot Lieutenant Yi, and Colonel Matthews. "'*Friendship*, this is *Stremlenie*. Return to Earth now. We have no quarrel with you unless you interfere with us. Return to Earth now.'"

Gonzalez said in Russian, "What are your intentions?" Her voice was calm, but Salah saw the fingers of one hand curl so tightly into a fist that the ambassador's rings bulged away from her fingers.

On the second wall screen, the sunrise glowed across one-third of the Kindred continent.

Leo said, "Go, go!" He grabbed Dr. Patel from Kandiss, below him on the shuttle-bay deck, and hoisted her into the shuttle, along with a huge plastic case she would not let go of. Lieutenant Ritter was already at the shuttle controls; the engine hummed. Dr. Henry, Ramstetter, and Branch Carter were already strapped in. How many more? Leo ran through the memorized list in his mind—where the fuck was everybody? At least the ones that had shown up wore filter masks; you couldn't trust civilians to remember mission equipment. This was only a contingency plan, but everybody was supposed to act like they were really going to launch.

Zoe, in full gear, came to the shuttle door. Kandiss's face screwed into confusion.

Leo said, "No, Berman. Your orders were to stay in sick bay."

"Those were yesterday's orders. This is today. I'm on the first team list."

"*Were* on it."

"You got orders any different?"

Leo didn't. Kandiss shrugged. Zoe tried for the first step and staggered. Leo said, "Oh, fuck," grabbed her, and threw her in harder than he had thrown Claire Patel.

Where were the rest of them?

Owen appeared, carrying rifles and other weapons, both arms full and two slings on his back.

On the bridge, silence. The *Stremlenie* did not answer Gonzalez's question about their intentions. She had begun to repeat it when another voice spoke. "*Friendship*? I greet you. This is Noah Jenner speaking on Kindred. We are sorry not to communicate with you last night, but our equipment did not permit that."

Volker looked up briefly, frowning in puzzlement, before returning to his screens. Matthews scowled. Captain Matthews said into his wrister, "Get Dr. Jenner on the bridge. Now."

The ambassador said, "Mr. Jenner, we are a United States mission seeking to establish diplomatic relations with your planet. Do you speak for World?"

"No, but our . . . our rotational mother is on the way from . . . a distant city. Meanwhile, I'm here, much closer. There is a problem, Ambassador. It's not safe for you to land here just now. The spore cloud—"

A burst of Russian on the other frequency. Captain Lewis said, "Mr. Jenner, wait just a moment please. Thank you."

Salah translated the repeat of the *Stremlenie*'s previous speech: "'*Friendship*, this is *Stremlenie*. Return to Earth now. We have no quarrel with you unless you interfere with us. Return to Earth now.'"

Gonzalez spoke. Salah's stomach did an abrupt lunge. He translated. "'*Stremlenie*, this is the *Friendship*. Be advised that any attack on this ship or on the planet below will be considered by the United States as an act of war. I am authorized to say this by the president of the United States.'"

Noah Jenner's voice said, "What?"

Engineer Volker said, "The *Stremlenie* is changing direction, towards us. Calculating . . ."

Gonzalez said, "Doctor, go. Run. Captain Lewis, tell the shuttle to launch as soon as he's aboard."

Colonel Matthews said into his wrister, "Code one. Repeat, Code one."

Noah Jenner said, "An attack? By whom? What is going on up there?"

Volker, his normal stoic demeanor finally giving way, said, "Why don't they know? What the hell kind of equipment—"

Salah didn't hear the rest. He was running through the common room toward the shuttle bay, stomach flopping with every step, forcing his mind to stay clear of the hundreds of questions pounding it like bombs.

Dr. Sherman, the geologist, was aboard the shuttle; so was Dr. Bentley, the economics guy. Owen strode through the door, half dragging Marianne Jenner, who carried a laptop.

"Captain Lewis said I'm needed on the bridge! My son—"

"Please be quiet, ma'am, and sit down. These orders supersede Captain Lewis's. Brodie?"

"All but the other doctor." Leo blanked on his name, but it didn't matter. Owen said, "Kandiss, get him in one minute. If you can't, run back here."

"Yes, sir."

The doctor raced through the shuttle bay door. Kandiss pushed him aboard and jumped in. Leo slammed shut the door as the shuttle bay opened to the stars. He fell into his seat just as the shuttle lurched forward. The bulkhead, down near the floor, said BOEING; the shuttle had not been part of the very minimal alien plans but, rather, something added with current American technology. The lurch felt like the Greyhound that had brought Leo to the recruiting station when he'd run away from home—

Why think about that Greyhound bus *now*?

Don't think, either, of those behind on the *Friendship*: her crew, Captain Matthews, Miguel Flores, Ambassador Gonzalez. The Ranger unit's mission was to protect the ambassador, but she had overridden that when this contingency plan was created. Matthews, when he'd explained the plan to the unit, had clearly not been happy about it. But Gonzalez's authority came direct from the president, the commander-in-chief. Now this part of the unit's primary mission had become to protect her representative, Wayne Henry, until either the shuttle passengers returned to the *Friendship* or Ambassador Gonzalez was ferried to the ground.

Had the ambassador known a Russian ship was coming? Or suspected it? Did she stay aboard because she was the only one with direct authority the Russkies might listen to? Or—

It didn't matter. Leo's job was to follow orders, not question them.

Outside the shuttle window, a blinding flash of light.

Someone screamed. Another flash of light. Leo couldn't see what was happening. Did the shuttle have weapons? The *Friendship* must—

The shuttle abruptly turned, and Leo had a clear view. From one of the ships shot a beam of light, and the other one exploded in a sunburst. *Which one?*

The pilot, Ritter, said shakily, "Sir, the . . . the *Friendship* was fatally hit. No survivors possible."

Owen said, "Continue planetside with all possible speed."

"Yes, sir."

Sir. Owen—Lieutenant Lamont—was CO now, of Ritter as well

as the Army unit. They were all dead: Captain Lewis and his crew, Colonel Matthews and Miguel Flores, the ambassador, that physicist . . . all dead.

Don't think about that now. Leo awaited Owen's orders.

The pilot said, "Entering the atmosphere. We—"

The shuttle pitched and rocked—too much pitching. Ritter said, "We've taken a hit, sir." Smoke seeped from the back of the shuttle into the cabin.

Salah didn't know which of the women had screamed. Not Ranger Berman, surely, so it must have been Claire Patel or Marianne Jenner. Before he could see if either needed help, the shuttle was hit.

By what? Not the same beam—laser? alpha particles?—Salah was no physicist. But the shuttle didn't explode as the *Friendship* had. It lurched, and something somewhere began to smoke. Salah pulled his filter mask from his pocket and put it on; everyone else fumbled with theirs. If the young pilot could get it to the ground . . .

Lieutenant Lamont was saying over and over, "This is the *Friendship* shuttle. We are making an emergency landing. Come in, Kindred . . ."

Salah unstrapped himself and lurched to the front of the craft. "I can say that in Kindred, Lieutenant, if you wish."

Lamont said, "Go."

Salah found the strange and difficult words, short syllables interspersed with clicks and rising inflections that could totally change the meaning. But languages came easily to him, and he'd studied Kindred every spare moment for six months. "Kal^melᵢ hibdel . . ."

No response.

He kept on, as the ground hurled skyward to meet them. Trees, buildings, fields . . . then rougher terrain as steep hills rose toward distant mountains.

"Kal^melᵢ hibdel . . ."

Crash. They were going to crash.

Leo twisted in his seat and yelled to the civilians to assume the safest crash position, demonstrating what it was. The doctor sat in the copilot's seat, talking gibberish. Leo felt the engines turn off as Ritter took the shuttle into a long, controlled glide. Outside the window the ground rose. Where was Ritter going? *There*: a long, empty field at the base of a hill. Closer, closer . . .

The shuttle was hit again and black smoke filled the cabin.

They struck the ground hard enough to rattle Leo's teeth. Then he was on his feet, yanking people out of their seats as Owen pulled open the door. Kandiss jumped down. Leo threw the passengers at Owen, who tossed them to Kandiss, never mind who was injured, just get them out. . . . Marianne Jenner, still clutching her laptop. The lab kid, Dr. Sherman, the two doctors—Dr. Patel would not let go of her big suitcase—Christ on a cracker! Leo threw it down beside her. Zoe was unstrapping the two people farthest back, why weren't they unstrapping themselves, had the smoke overcome them . . .

Something from above hit the shuttle and it burst into flame. Leo jumped and rolled, instinct and training both taking over, a seamless whole. Owen landed to his right, and then Zoe on top of him. Her pants were on fire. He rolled her on the ground until it was out and then they were up, following Owen and Kandiss, who were dragging the civilians toward the hill.

No one else emerged from the burning shuttle. Not the pilot or Bentley or Henry.

Leo's legs wobbled under him. Not injury, something else . . . gravity wasn't right. He steadied himself.

Owen said, "Who is—" just as something happened that Leo had never seen, could not have imagined.

A beam of light swept across the sky, bright enough to show red against the pearly dawn. It swept from side to side before disappearing.

Then silence.

Someone quavered, "What was . . ."

"That was a weapon," Owen said flatly. "The same one that destroyed the *Friendship*. Kindred is under attack from the *Stremlenie*."

Dr. Sherman said, "But they must have counterweapons . . . an advanced civilization like this—"

No one answered him. Leo didn't see any counterweapons. He didn't even see any civilization. All he saw was a burning shuttle with nine survivors, marooned on an alien planet that either had not or could not come to their defense.

CHAPTER 4

Isabelle Rhinehart yawned, stretched, and rose from her sleeping mat. She folded it, put it away in the karthwood chest, and padded barefoot from her privacy room into the atrium of the house. No one was there; it was barely dawn. Isabelle made herself a cup of tea and, still in her night shift, opened the teardrop-shaped double door to the terrace beyond. Leaning on the railing, she sipped her tea and gazed at the valley brightening under the rising sun.

It was so beautiful: all of it, valley and terrace and house. Her lahk had built it two years ago, when Tony's job and Isabelle's art and Nathan's inventions had produced enough money. Well, mostly Nathan, and Isabelle was grateful to her lahk-mate, even though he was never home anymore and wasn't that nice a person to begin with.

Made entirely of karthwood, the house sat on the top of a low hill. Karthwood, which it had taken Isabelle a year on World to stop calling "bamboo," was the basic building material everywhere, and structures were designed for the natural curves of its hollow, tapering stalks, which were treated with natural salts against insects and weather. "Let the karthwood become what it chooses" was the construction motto, and what karthwood wanted to become was buildings with swooping curves, oval rooms, woven roofs lacquered against rain, sliding panels to open houses to World's semitropical air. Karthwood had the tensile strength of steel, the compressive strength of concrete, and the beauty of natural wood. In addition, as one of the few lighter colors in nature, its warm tan stalks were a welcome contrast to World's other vegetation.

But the fields and gardens were beautiful, too, in their more somber way. Vegetation used rhodopsin instead of chlorophyll; the darker coloration allowed less light reflection and more retention from World's orange sun. Skihlla rose above the horizon, suffusing the valley with its delicate light and glinting on the river that flowed to the east of the house until, beyond several other lahks, it fell in shining stages to the valley. From the garden below Isabelle's terrace rose the sweet, heady scent of pikaį leaves, perfuming the moist air. And now all of it, the whole lovely life her lahk had put together, might not last.

Isabelle drained her tea, raised the cup to the rising sun, and said in World, "Mother World, you are beautiful beyond compare."

"Bullshit," a voice behind her said in English.

Isabelle turned. "Good morning, Kayla."

"Yeah. Right."

So this was one of her sister's bad days. Kayla vacillated between staying in bed all day and complaining bitterly when out of it. Kayla had hated World for ten years, and it seemed to Isabelle that the hatred was growing. Isabelle recognized depression but had no idea what to do about it. Antidepressants did not exist on World. Medicine here, as on Earth, developed according to need. Isabelle, naturally robust, tried to be patient. But she had liked World from the beginning, even during the first difficult months of microbe-adjustment, financial dependency, and language ignorance, when the clicks and trills and inflected syllables of Worldese had swirled around her as incomprehensible as the insect sounds it resembled. Kayla still had learned no more than a few words.

She said, "I need help today, Kayla, in the studio, if you will."

Kayla snorted. "'Studio.'"

Isabelle hung on to her temper. "Please."

"You're just going to go on with this sham life as if nothing is going to happen? As if everything isn't going to come to an end in a few more months?"

Isabelle lost the battle with her temper. "I thought that's what you wanted! For World to come to an end!"

"Not us with it. Face it, Isabelle, when the spore cloud hits, everything ends."

Isabelle didn't answer. They'd been through this before.

Kayla gripped the railing and glared at the valley below. Figures moved, now, among the fields and gardens; bicycles sped along the roads. "Look at them, going to work like nothing is about to happen to them." Then Kayla's voice turned plaintive. "No, Izzy, I didn't want World to end. What I want is to go home. Have you forgotten home? Green trees and a yellow sun and cars and computers and steaks and—"

"Have *you* forgotten home—the home you and I knew? Welfare didn't exactly provide us with steaks or a car. Our cousin was shot outside the apartment building. Your child brought home a used needle he found on the sidewalk. The gangs—"

"So shoot me!" Kayla flared. "I remember the good stuff, and I don't want to die next month! When the spore cloud— Austin!"

Isabelle turned. Her nephew stood there in the Terran pajamas Kayla had sewn for him and insisted he wear, blinking against the brightening day. His thin face showed nothing. Sometimes he tried to make peace between his mother and aunt, which always filled Isabelle with shame; a thirteen-year-old should not have to take on that role. Today, however, he merely said in a flat voice, "We are all going to die?"

"No," Isabelle said, before Kayla could say anything. "You know we're not, Austin." She had explained it all to him more than once, even though once had been all that was necessary. The kid was smart. However, there was something of Kayla's negativity in him, too, which worried Isabelle.

Austin said, "We're immune, right. We're Terrans. But Mom is worried about all the people here who aren't. About everything falling apart and Worlders just losing it and going on rampages."

Isabelle turned on her sister. "What have you been telling him? God, Kayla!"

"The truth. I've been telling him the truth about what happens when a society falls apart! As in, you know, history!"

"World's history is not ours!"

"They're human, aren't they? That's what *you* always insist!"

Kayla's face shone with petty, pathetic triumph. Isabelle turned away in disgust, to find out exactly what Austin had been told and to correct it if she could. But Austin was no longer there. He'd gone into his privacy room, and when Isabelle whistled softly at the door to request entrance, he neither opened the door nor answered.

"Shit," Isabelle said softly.

The studio would have to wait. This was more important. Isabelle sat cross-legged on a pillow outside Austin's karthwood door and waited for the boy to come out.

He did, five minutes later, eyes wild. "Trajkal!" he cried in World. "On the radio . . . killed! A whole city—" He started to cry, tears flying off his face with the violent shaking of his head.

"Check weapons and then recon the area," Owen said, and Leo and Kandiss jumped to obey, even though Leo wasn't sure what "the area" actually was. The shuttle still burned, smelling horribly. They'd crashed beside a small, very irregular hill covered with boulders and purplish vegetation. Fallen rocks littered the ground, although away from the hill, the land was level. Owen had backed the civilians under an overhang of rock, almost a small cave. Zoe guarded them, weapon at the ready, even though Leo suspected she was having trouble staying upright. Dr. Bourgiba was bent over Dr. Sherman, treating his burns with something from Dr. Patel's suitcase. If that was all filled with doctor stuff, then it was a good thing that Dr. Patel had refused to let go of it. It was something they still had, anyway.

What else did they have? As they performed the weapons check, Leo cataloged their resources. His 107A1, the .50 caliber long-range sniper rifle zeroed to him. Four Mk 19 SCARs, Special Forces combat assault rifles; one of those was fitted with a modular shotgun system for ballistic breaches. Four Beretta sidearms. Ammo and hand grenades—Christ, no wonder Owen had staggered a little under the weight of the duffel. The gear they had all been wearing, even Zoe, who must have gone back to her quarters from sick bay to put it on right after Owen had told her to stay in sick bay. Filter masks for everybody. One person who spoke Kindese. No fucking idea where they were, or what kind of OPORD Owen could put together.

Leo conferred briefly with Kandiss. They went away from the burning shuttle, in opposite directions along the base of the hill. The sun rose orange, and it wasn't just the bright colors of dawn; it stayed orange. It looked larger than the sun on Earth. All the strange plants, broad-leaved and spicy smelling, were dark purplish. Leo felt himself adjusting to the lighter gravity.

Still no natives. Fields, with some sort of strange dark animal grazing in them. One raised its head, looked at Leo, and went back to chomping the purplish grass. Another trotted slowly toward a clump of brush and Leo saw a splash of pink paint on its rump.

A few of the dark, long-haired animals grazed on the hill, these with pale blue splotches on their necks. Choosing a spot with cover in case of ambush, Leo climbed partway up the east face of the hill. Light-colored, curved buildings in the far distance. A road, with something moving on it, too far to distinguish but the traffic was light and slow. In the very far distance, smoke rising from whatever the *Stremlenie* had destroyed.

And in the sky, two moons: one setting on the horizon and one fading in the growing sunlight.

He reported back to Owen. "No one in the area. Natives two

klicks off on a road paralleling here, not approaching us, moving at approximately ten klicks per hour. Animals which appear to be similar to sheep"—unless you counted the fact that they had three eyes—"that don't appear dangerous. Buildings two klicks away at eleven o'clock."

Kandiss returned from the other side of the hill. "Settlement about half a klick away. Two dozen houses, people in the streets talking, agitated but not armed. No military installations visible."

"Okay," Owen said. "Someone'll spot the shuttle fire soon, if they haven't already seen it. Just so we are all clear: This is now the Kindred squad, Second Platoon, Bravo Company, Seventy-Fifth Regiment. The mission now is to secure the area and let them come to us. If approached with hostile intent, defend as necessary. If they want to send in a negotiator, he—"

"There won't be hostile intent," Bourgiba said, and Owen spun around. Leo caught the brief flash of chagrin on Owen's face that he had not heard the doctor approach.

"Doctor, this is a military conference. Please return to—"

"There will be no hostile intent," Bourgiba said, just as if Owen had not spoken. "Kindred have no tradition of hostility, let alone war. Their society is peaceful, matrilineal, with its first principles those of—"

"I have read the briefing materials," Owen said stiffly. "Return to the others, please. Now."

Bourgiba did not move. He said softly, "I know your duty is to protect us. But with the deaths of both Ambassador Gonzalez and her second, Wayne Henry—"

"My charge is to protect you," Owen said. "And I am going to do that. Kandiss, escort Dr. Bourgiba back to safety."

Kandiss, looking startled, took a step forward. Bourgiba said quietly, "That won't be necessary. But, Lieutenant Lamont, bear in mind that this is a peaceful diplomatic mission to establish international and trade relations with the government on World. It is not about anything else, despite what happened here. It is especially not about what the *Stremlenie* desired, which was revenge. Against anybody, for any reason."

Bourgiba walked back under the overhang.

Zoe walked up, her face stiff with, Leo thought, determination to hide weakness. Owen said, "Secure the area. Report any movement at all to me. Brodie, you take the top of the hill. Berman—"

Under the overhang, Bourgiba was talking to Marianne Jenner. Dr. Jenner turned her head to stare at Owen.

Oh shit, Leo thought. The last thing they needed now was some kind of military-civilian turf war.

For two hours, nothing happened. Leo lay in his listening-observation post on top of the hill, rifle ready. He was glad for the Army's latest tech, a scope that could switch from a narrow field for accuracy at range to a wide angle like a spotting scope—especially good since he didn't have a spotter. He spent the time sweating in the growing heat under his gear and thinking over possible scenarios, knowing that Owen was doing the same. The Kindred might blame them for the attack on the city. After all, how would the planet know which ship had fired on them? They might send their own ship, or more than one if they had it and why wouldn't they, to sweep that red beam over this area, in which case all nine of them were toast. Or, Dr. Bourgiba might be right and they would send a negotiator to find out what happened. If they did, the negotiator might be a trick. Everybody in every city might be dead and the Rangers would have to defend the five civilians against looters or people bent on revenge or who-the-fuck-knew-what.

No, not five—four. The geologist, Dr. Sherman, was unconscious, and Dr. Patel said he would die of his burns.

Then what? The eight humans had no food or water, and couldn't eat or drink what they found without risking disease.

Bright spots: Dr. Jenner's son was some kind of high brass here. He wouldn't want his mother dead. And the Kindred had starships, or a ship. If this could be straightened out, maybe the Kindred would take the eight Americans home. The scientists and doctors agreed that with such advanced civilization, the Kindred would all be vaccinated already against the spore plague, so if they could be made to see that it was the *Stremlenie* and not the *Friendship* that had wasted that city . . .

Leo was a little surprised to realize how much he wanted to go back to Earth. Being away for a few months had been one thing. Even going back to an America twenty-four years later would be okay; the Army was still there and it was the Army he wanted. They were his family, his brothers, his purpose. But if this played out so that he never got to go home . . .

Don't think about it until it happens. And anyway—

Movement below.

"Group approaching north side of the hill," he said through his wrister. "Five people. No visible weapons."

"Transport?" Owen's voice said.

"Bicycles." That was a new one on Leo: enemy on bikes. After a moment he added, "Bicycles now abandoned. Group heading toward me."

Owen said swiftly, "Brodie, motion them to halt until I arrive, and cover me. Kandiss, with me until the natives are visible and then hold position at the base of the hill. Berman, stay with the civilians."

Brodie raised one arm and yelled, "Halt!" The people below him halted. Brodie sighted. Whenever Owen appeared, if any of the five Kindred raised anything like a weapon, Leo would take him out.

But—

Where would they carry weapons? The five people all wore dresses, even the men, pieces of pale cloth twisted around their bodies. Sandals on their feet, and carrying nothing. But again, this was an advanced civ and who knew what weird shit they had for weapons. Three men, two women. All tall, with coppery skin and black hair and huge dark eyes—too huge, like those sappy paintings of big-eyed kittens and dogs. Then one of them turned his head and through his scope Leo saw that the man's eyes were not dark but light gray flecked with gold.

The man called up the hill, "I am Noah Jenner. Please lower whatever weapon you have, we are no threat. I'm here to welcome you to World."

So this was Dr. Jenner's son. He looked just like the Kindred, except for the eye color. Owen came around the base of the hill with Kandiss. Kandiss took a position behind a boulder as Owen went forward. Both had drawn their Berettas.

The hill was small and Leo had exceptional hearing; he missed nothing. "I am Lieutenant Owen Lamont, United States Army, in charge of this expedition. Are you here in an official capacity, Mr. Jenner?"

"Yes. Well, as official as possible." He raised one hand, put it on his cheek, and pulled downward on the skin on his face—some sort of tension tic. Leo had seen his mother do the same thing.

Owen said, "If your delegation carries any weapons, place them on the ground now."

"We have no weapons," Jenner said. "Lieutenant, we want to talk to you. Did your . . . your military destroy our cities this morning?"

Pretty direct. Leo heard the strain and grief in Jenner's voice. Those were dangerous emotions. He kept his rifle trained on Jenner.

"No," Owen said. "A Russian ship fired on the planet, destroyed our ship, and then fired on our landing shuttle."

Jenner turned and spoke to the other four people, presumably translating. Their faces crumpled, looking suddenly much more human. Jenner turned back to Owen. "Why would a Russian ship do that?"

Jenner knew nothing—how could he? The Kindred ship, with him on it, had left Earth ten years ago. Before the spore plague hit, before whole economies collapsed across the globe, before Russians died in greater number than anybody else, before the vaccine was found.

Owen said, "Revenge."

"For *what*? All we did—"

We. Jenner considered himself Kindred, not Terran. Leo filed away this piece of intel.

"—was ask your help with finding a vaccine!"

"Some people didn't see it that way," Owen said. "Look, Mr. Jenner, I can fill you in on Terran history later. Right now, we have a problem, and so do you. Your planet is under attack, and our transport has been destroyed, both by the *Stremlenie*. We have the same enemy."

Jenner gazed at Owen, and Leo couldn't read the expression in those Terran-gray, alien-large eyes. Finally Jenner said, "Put away your weapons, Lieutenant. We won't harm you. But I don't think you realize that—"

"Noah!"

Leo turned his head the slightest fraction. Dr. Jenner was slipping and sliding over rubble on the rough terrain, Berman behind her. Ordinarily Zoe could have restrained Marianne Jenner with one hand, but Zoe had had surgery only two days ago. Behind both of them came Dr. Bourgiba, calling, "Ranger Berman! Don't—" Kandiss, behind his boulder, looked like he didn't know what the hell he was supposed to do. It was a zoo.

Owen said tightly, "Squad, stand down. Mr. Jenner, let's talk."

Salah sat quietly, listening as Noah Jenner deconstructed the universe.

Jenner sat cross-legged on the ground beneath the overhang. A short distance away, Zoe Berman "guarded" the other four Kindred, who sat in a huddle, not understanding the English being spoken but looking, Salah thought, more saddened than alarmed. One, an old woman, seemed to be the leader, but she hadn't asked Noah or Salah to translate for her. She merely waited, the coppery skin of her face set in the deep crevasses of age and grief. Her waiting, however, had not an air of resignation as much as of patience, with the trust that in good time she would be informed of everything she needed to make whatever decisions were necessary. Meanwhile, she grieved silently.

Mason Kandiss and Leo Brodie were "securing the area," whatever that meant under these circumstances. The rest of the Terrans listened to Lamont question Jenner.

"It wasn't just the city you saw destroyed," he said, and the grief of his expression echoed the old woman's. "It was three of our four cities." He named them, a litany of trills and clicks among syllables heavy with pain. "But we think the Russian ship has gone back to Terra."

"How do you know?" Lamont demanded. He, alone, remained standing, looming over the others, his weapons glaring to Salah even in the dim and orangey light. The day was heating up, even in the shade of the overhang.

"We don't, for sure. It could be on the other side of the planet. But—"

"Why can't you detect it with satellites or probes or your own ships? We could, with the *Friendship*." Lamont's voice was controlled but relentless, each word coming out like a small bullet.

"Ship. Singular. It was also destroyed in the attack. It sat in Kam^tel^ha."

This time Salah caught the name of the city: Beautiful-by-the-Sea.

"Your fleet consisted of only one ship?"

"There were two. The other, as at least some of you know"—he nodded at his mother, who sat beside him with her hand on his arm—"is contaminated with spores at the colony it was supplying."

"And you only built two?" Lamont was not even trying to hide his skepticism.

"Yes. Two. We had no need of more than two."

"A navy of—"

"It was not a navy," Lamont said. "Or an air force. Or space satellites. We have no military, Lieutenant."

"Uh-huh. So you're saying you have no starships left to get us home."

"That is what I'm saying."

Branch Carter suddenly shifted his weight on the ground, and Jenner gazed at him briefly before turning to his mother. Jenner's voice went reedy with strain. "I know you all thought that World must have an advanced technology. I thought so too, once. But I'm here to tell you that we do not. Our two star drives, plus plans to build the ships, were left for us, presumably by whatever race took humans from Earth to World 140,000 years ago. The plans were partly pictorial, partly mathematics, partly in symbols with a pictorial key or something like that—I don't pretend to understand it. But there were texts, all engraved on some metal that did not decay—the same plans that Mee^haoꭓ and his expedition left you on Terra ten years ago. And World understood them even less than you did. But we'd been left parts, too, in sealed containers that required a civilization far enough advanced to open. Including two star drives. It was sort of like. . . . like fitting together Legos. Or so I've been told. I wasn't here then."

Lamont said, "So you can't build another ship."

"We wouldn't even if we could," Jenner said. "We only assembled the last one because the spore cloud was—"

Claire Patel blurted out, "Why wouldn't you build another one? If you could?"

"Building one was a tremendous drain on our resources, and a tremendous violation to Mother World."

Claire looked confused, but Salah understood. They were now on religious grounds, or something close to religion.

"Violation?" Branch said.

"Mining substances, dangerous processing of them, radioactive waste—I'm not sure of the details. I'm not a scientist. But I know that the two ships were built only because of the spore cloud."

"And when you left us on Earth information about the ships, you just left out that tiny little piece about jumping ahead fourteen years during the trip here."

"We didn't know," Jenner said. "It was a shock to us to arrive here twenty-eight years after the *Embassy* left World. We thought we had twenty-four years before the spore cloud hit. We didn't."

Salah was doing rapid math in his head. But then, if the *Embassy* jumped fourteen years before it reached Earth and another fourteen returning here, and the cloud had been due in twenty-five years—

Jenner said, "Our calculations were wrong. We don't have your accuracy with astronomical measurements. But we know now that the cloud will come soon."

Salah said, "Our astrophysicist says—*said*—seventy-one days from now."

Jenner bowed his head.

Marianne Jenner spoke for the first time. "You couldn't accurately calculate the cloud's arrival. You don't have the physics to understand the ships you built. And you didn't have the biology, the genetics, to research and combat *R. sporii* yourself. So you came to Earth with hopes that we knew more."

"Yes," Jenner said.

Lamont said, "But you're—"

"No. We're not. Listen to me, Lieutenant. We have one culture and only one, because the land area of World is small and because the Terrans brought here were small in number and, maybe, because we don't have much genetic diversity. That's what I'm told, anyway. There were wars early on, but centuries ago one person gained control of huge swaths of land, presumably with an army, and she went on to establish the start of the civilization we have now. That was

Mother Lalo^. She was an extraordinary person, a . . . I don't know what you'd call it. Plant worshipper? Anyway, she established the principles for her kingdom, which eventually became all of World, that we still live by. That we must live by, to exist on this one continent without exhausting its resources. Respect for the land, first and always, which you can think of as ecological reality. No violence. Nothing that would lead to revolution, which means nobody starves, nobody is homeless, nobody is exploited. Family is all, not material goods, and a family is responsible for all its members. Government is made up of family heads, and decentralized whenever possible. Also, we practice strict population control. All of this is. . . . the word is untranslatable. 'Bu^ka^tel.'"

Marianne Jenner ducked her head, hiding some private expression. Salah tried to process everything he'd just heard. Jenner made Kindred sound like Eden. But these were humans, and Salah didn't believe in Eden. He said, "And all this works? These principles?"

"Most of the time, with most people," Jenner said.

"And when it doesn't?"

"We have laws, courts, punishments. But nothing like you have on Terra."

Lamont said, "Uh-huh. Mr. Jenner, about our immediate situation—"

Branch interrupted. "You must be mining ore. There are bicycles on your road!"

"Yes, we mine and manufacture and transport," Jenner said, "but as carefully as possible."

"Describe your level of tech, please. You have radios, don't you? That's why the *Friendship* couldn't raise your ship while it was on nightside and we weren't. Radios but no more advanced communication."

Jenner smiled sadly. "Yes. And you are . . ."

"Branch Carter."

Who now was, Salah realized, the closest thing the humans had left to an engineer or physicist.

Jenner said, "We have no space program except the ship that was destroyed in Kam^tel^ha. Radio and radio towers but not television. No phones—all communication over distances is done by radio. Electricity from wind, sun, water, and geothermal sources. Medicines but not laser surgery. Books, although we control how many are printed so as not to use too much paper. Think the 1940s, Dr. Sherman, and you'll be about right, with some exceptions. Big exceptions. No, better not think 1940s."

"Cars?" Salah said, despite himself.

"We could make them but don't, because we don't drill for oil. Most goods go by water; there are a lot of rivers. We have dirigibles—I came here by dirigible—but bicycles are the usual—"

"Wait," Marianne said. "You spoke to the *Friendship* from the Kindred ship, Noah. I heard you. But now you're here, and you said the ship was in the destroyed city."

"The . . . the best word is 'rotational mother'—sent me from Kam^tel^ha last night. Otherwise I would have been killed with the rest."

She said, "And your . . . your wife and child?"

There was a wife and child? Salah had not known that. Jenner must have told his mother before he left Earth. Was she Terran or Kindred? Interbreeding should be possible, there wouldn't be that much genetic drift in 140,000 years.

Jenner said, "That's why I was sent away. Everyone is returning to their lahks before the spore cloud comes."

"Lahk?"

"Their family groups. Large, as in extended families."

For a moment, Marianne looked as if she'd been slapped. Her son had just said that his family was not her. Before Salah could look away, the expression was gone. She said, "But by now you've developed a vaccine, you've had ten years, everyone in such a cohesive society must already be vaccinated . . . We vaccinated all of Earth against smallpox in less than ten years!"

Salah's stomach clenched. He knew what Jenner would say before he said it. So did Marianne and Claire, the other biologists.

Jenner said it. "We have no vaccine."

Branch drew a sharp breath.

Jenner continued, "We tried. But we don't know enough, not even with everything we learned from you on Terra, and we had to leave before you developed the vaccine."

Salah's stomach clenched. No vaccine, and the *Friendship* with all its supplies and databases destroyed. In another few months the spore cloud would cross paths with Kindred. The entire population, whose ancestors had been brought here before the spore cloud hit Earth the first time seventy thousand years ago, had no species immunity against *R. sporii*. There would be a few people with natural resistance, which was what had preserved the humanity of Earth even as it reduced the population to a few thousand in the famous "bottleneck event." But only a few.

Salah had worked in hospitals when the cloud made its second contact with Earth. He'd done twenty-hour shifts in Jordan, trying desperately to save those who, due to millennia of genetic drift, had lost their species immunity or who had weakened immunity. Many died. "Only" 5 percent in Jordan; 7 percent in the United States; 30 percent in Russia, whose genome had lost that particular genetic lottery. They died gasping for breath, their lungs filling with fluid, until they literally drowned.

Civilization on Kindred would disappear.

Marianne closed her hand around her son's arm. "You left Earth before we'd developed the vaccine. Ten of you. Many on Earth weren't immune to *R. sporii*, so some of you may be vulnerable when the spore clouds hit. Noah, *you* might not be immune."

Claire Patel said, "I have some vaccine. I brought it in that suitcase there. If you have any labs left standing, we might be able to synthesize more."

Jenner's already oversized eyes went wider. *"You brought vaccine?"*

Lieutenant Lamont said, "That's not our mission. Our mission is to establish relations and return to Terra."

Salah stood. He was aware that beside the young Ranger, he was short, a little bit flabby, old. Unarmed. He said, "We can't go home, Lieutenant. There is no means to go home. Vaccines are our mission now.

"We have to save as much of this planet as we can."

CHAPTER 5

Austin Rhinehart sat under a makfruit tree in the back garden and tried to imagine himself dead.

Everything would disappear, all of World. But then he would disappear, too, so how would he know he was dead? He wouldn't. Unless Old Mother Kee^la's tales of another world after death were true and Austin would join his ancestors in endless dancing and feasting. But Austin wasn't fond of dancing, and he didn't have any ancestors on World for his lahk, because everyone in it had come from Earth, a place Austin didn't remember. He'd been only three. Anyway, he didn't believe Old Mother Kee^la's tales. She wasn't even his old mother, only Graa^lok's; Austin's lahk was also missing old mothers.

And he wasn't going to be dead. He was Terran, and thus immune to spore disease. But everyone else was going to be dead: his best friend Graa^lok and Old Mother Kee^la and the teachers at school and Tiklal, whom Austin was supposed to apprentice to when he turned fourteen in two months. Only by that time, Tiklal would be dead, along with nearly everyone else on World.

Steven-kal came down the curving steps from the house, mounted a bicycle, and glimpsed Austin. He said in English, "I greet you, Austin. Aren't you supposed to be in school?"

"I greet you, Steven-kal. I was just going."

Steven-kal looked pointedly at his watch. "You are supposed to be there."

"I'm just going now."

"See that you do." He mounted his bicycle and pedaled off.

Fuck! Austin thought, borrowing a forbidden word from his mother's vocabulary. Steven-kal and his twin, Joshua-kal, were members of Austin's lahk. His mother didn't have any brothers, so Steven-kal and Joshua-kal had primary male responsibility for Austin, under the supervision of the lahk mother, who was Isabelle. Steven and Joshua McGuire—defiantly, he gave them their Earth names without the title of respect—weren't even here at the lahk very much, so why did they have to visit *now*? Austin hated all of them—not because they were unkind to him but because they had responsibility for him for another three years and nobody recognized that he, Austin, was already an adult and able to make his own decisions.

Well, they would learn that soon enough!

He smacked one fist into the opposite palm, which felt good so he did it again. Graa^lok ducked under the hanging leaves. "I greet you, Austin. What are you doing?"

"I greet you, Graa^lok. Nothing," Austin said. Graa^lok was learning English, which was one of the things Austin liked about him, even though Austin's Worldese was perfect. "You got here before the window for language closed," Isabelle-kal said, which Austin resented because that made it sound like the only reason he spoke so well was timing and not his own intelligence. The other thing he liked about Graa^lok was this: Graa^lok was the only kid on Kindred who had ever shown any curiosity about Earth.

Graa^lok said, "Are you ready?"

"I've been ready for a long time," Austin said. It was something he'd overheard Tony Schrupp say. Graa^lok looked puzzled for a moment but then grabbed Austin's hand. "Let us go!"

Austin pulled away; he didn't like being touched. It was another thing that set him apart from Worlders, who were all over each other all the time. But Austin wasn't a Worlder, as his mother kept telling him. He wasn't a Terran, either. He wasn't anything, and only Tony Schrupp seemed to understand that.

The boys darted from tree to tree, making a game of it, avoiding the road where people were bicycling around just as if they weren't going to die in a few months. But then Austin and Graa^lok doubled back because Graa^lok needed to use the bathroom, of all the stupid times, and Austin's mother caught them as they scampered down the stairs from the terrace to the garden.

"Austin!" she shrilled. "Come back here!"

"Going to school, Mom!" he called in English.

"No, come back, you and Graylock both, something horrible has happened!"

"Bye! School!" He ran as fast as he could with Graa^lok, who was shorter and fatter, puffing behind him. Whatever had happened would be his mother's usual exaggerated crisis. She would cry because she'd burned the vegetable stew or ruined the pillow she was sewing, and then Austin would feel like crying because he couldn't help her, and then he'd get mad because he didn't want to cry. Over and over. The real problem, Austin knew because he wasn't stupid even if he didn't belong anywhere, was that his mother hated World. Austin, who loved World, was thrilled that finally he and Graa^lok and Tony Schrupp and the others were going to do something about that.

The boys kept away from the roads, where people had stopped their bicycles and stood in little groups, talking and waving their arms. Austin and Graa^lok ran through the gardens till they reached fields. Through the fields where people weeded crops or sprinkled them with foul-smelling fertilizer from carts drawn by pel^aks, the patient and stupid beasts moving as slowly as if the warm air were thick as water. Through the grazing land beyond the village, where skaleth¡ grazed, their furry purple bodies splashed with different color dyes on different parts of their bodies to show who they belonged to. Shearing season hadn't come yet, and the skaleth; looked furry and content.

Well, *they* weren't going to die! Animals didn't get spore disease. Or . . . did they? Austin wasn't sure.

The boys slowed, Graa^lok flopping down on a patch of soft moss to pant. Austin offered him water from the canteen at his belt and Graa^lok drank greedily, water dribbling down the front of his wrap. "Don't waste it," Austin said, heard the echo of Isabelle's scolding words, and scowled. "We have a long way to go."

"Speak the English. I want to create practice. This is our third-last trip," Graa^lok said, unnecessarily. "Then, we did be away forever."

"Not forever. We'll come back to get my mother and your sisters. When everything's ready."

"Yes. Of course. But the other of Terrans in your lahk—"

"I told you, no." Austin deepened his scowl so that Graa^lok wouldn't ask any more questions about his lahk, which fascinated Graa^lok. Graa^lok's lahk was normal, living in a bunch of close houses with Great-Grandmother Kee^la as lahk mother, her son and daughter and their children and all the young cousins like Graa^lok, with everybody's father visiting instead of being thousands of light-years away on Terra. Austin would never be normal.

We'll make a new normal, Tony Schrupp said.

At the thought of Tony, waiting for them in the amazing new thing they were creating, Austin's scowl disappeared. "Get up," he said to Graa^lok in English. "We still have a long way to go."

Leo had rearguard in the transport, which was an open flatbed truck with benches and a sun canopy, like those things that tourists rode around on in Florida. "Electric," Noah Jenner said. "Slow, but we don't have far to go."

Leo hadn't heard where they were going. Owen had them all on alert, although the only thing they passed were an old man on a bicycle and some of the paint-splashed animals blocking the road. The other Kindred man got out and smacked them on their rumps until they moved. The big orange sun rose higher; the dark plants in the fields turned their broad leaves to follow it; Leo sweated in his armor and ignored the parched tingle of his throat.

At the front of the transport a radio spoke continuously in Kindese, the newscaster's voice sounding choked with tears. Noah, up front, seemed to be translating in a low voice for his mother and Owen, but Leo couldn't hear what they were saying. Dr. Bourgiba, near Leo, sat leaning forward, hands on his knees, straining to hear.

Dr. Patel said to him, "What's happening, Salah?"

He spoke quickly during a pause in the broadcast, clearly not wanting to miss anything, "Their three major cities destroyed, the major cultural and scientific centers and their starship. About twenty percent of the population dead."

Twenty percent? Leo had a hazy idea that in America, more than 20 percent of the people lived in cities. What he really wanted was evidence that the Russian ship had left the star system, but Dr. Bourgiba said nothing about that.

He added, "Decentralization of manufacturing and government, so. . . ." Leo didn't catch the rest.

More fields with either plants or paint-splashed animals, a big pond—and then they came to a settlement and Leo caught his breath.

He knew that he wasn't usually sensitive to beauty (except in women). Scenic views, important buildings, gardens—none of it stirred him. But he'd never seen anything like these houses. They were made of something like bamboo, all curving walls and swooping roofs, with decks and woven bits. Big ones, smaller ones, all surrounded by trees and connected by curving stone paths. It looked like he imagined the estate of some high muckety-muck in some

Asian country Leo would never see, but not exactly like that. He didn't know what it looked like.

They ascended a small hill and stopped in front of a structure surrounded by trees. Owen snapped orders and the platoon jumped off the transport and took shielded positions behind it or nearby trees. The old woman on the transport looked startled, and then *laughed*.

Dr. Bourgiba said, "Lieutenant, there is no need for defensive measures."

Owen didn't even bother to answer him. "Kandiss, Berman, secure the building."

A woman burst out of an upper floor onto a deck. Terran, though dressed in the same plain saronglike thing as Noah Jenner. She saw them and burst into tears. "You're here! You're really here—oh, thank God!"

She rushed down the stairs, saw Leo with his rifle raised, and stopped halfway down, hand to her mouth.

Noah Jenner snapped, "Put those guns down— Christ! This is my home, and you are guests! Kayla, I greet you—stop crying!"

Kandiss and Zoe ignored him, pushing past the woman on the stairs, disappearing into the house. A few moments later, Zoe reappeared on the deck. "Clear, Lieutenant. No other occupants."

"Inside," Owen said. Noah Jenner shot him a look of disgust and they all climbed the steps.

Inside was one large room, two sides open to the air but, Leo guessed, capable of being closed off with those woven wooden panels. Smaller cubicles on the side, all the doors open—probably by Kandiss or Zoe. A kitchen on one side, looking surprisingly like normal kitchens—a counter, stove, what might be a refrigerator. The rooms had no furniture except small, low tables of the same light wood as the house and a lot of big, heavily embroidered pillows, all in pale colors. The wood was pale, too, and the breeze blew through, warm and spicy. It was like being inside a basket at a flower show.

Jenner said, "You are welcome to my lahk," not sounding for a second like he actually meant it.

The woman, Kayla, said, "Have you come to take us home? When, oh when?"

Jenner said, "Weren't you listening to the radio?"

"No. Yes. For a while, but I couldn't . . . it isn't . . . Austin went to school like normal."

"These Terrans' ship was destroyed in the same attack that got the cities. I'm sorry, Kayla. Nobody is leaving World."

Kayla began to wail, a high-pitched shriek that pierced Leo's eardrums. The old Kindred woman, looking as disgusted as Jenner, grabbed her by the arm and dragged her onto the terrace and, it sounded like, down the steps into the garden.

Owen said to Jenner, "Who lives here and where are they?"

"The members of my lahk, which are the Terrans that came with me ten years ago. Some of them, anyway. Lieutenant, put down those ridiculous weapons. There is no danger here except what you and the Russian ship have caused."

Dr. Jenner stepped between the two men. "Noah, the big problem now is food and water. We can't handle your microbes. You had your entire microbiome changed, and we will need to do that. Meanwhile, we need a negative-pressure area with Terran atmosphere, the way it was arranged for us on the *Embassy*."

Jenner said nothing for a long moment. To Leo, it looked as if he was bracing himself for something he didn't want to say. Leo's hand tightened on his sidearm, which he had not received orders to holster.

Jenner said, "Mom—all of you—the setup that we had on Terra, the *Embassy* with its labs and the shuttle to orbit and the ship itself— all that was in Kam^tel^ha, the capital city, and was destroyed with it. I told you already that we didn't understand all that alien tech, and we never succeeded in duplicating it. The major hospitals and research labs were there, too. We have smaller clinics, one just down the hill, and maybe it can help. I'm no doctor. But in general, you will need to take off those masks and let your bodies adjust to World on their own."

Bourgiba said sharply, "Has anyone done that? Of the original Terrans?"

"Six of us allowed our microbes to be altered at Kam^tel^ha. Four refused. Of those, two died. The other two are fine."

Dr. Jenner said, "Which two?"

"Nicole Brink and Tasha McGruder."

The names meant nothing to Leo; he hadn't read much about the Kindred visit to Terra. He'd been fourteen years old, with his own problems.

Bourgiba said, "How long was the adjustment time?"

"About a week. A pretty rocky week."

Owen demanded, "You didn't answer my question, Mr. Jenner. Who lives here and where are they?"

Leo watched Jenner restraining his temper. "Myself, Kayla, her son Austin, Kayla's sister Isabelle, and Steven and Joshua McGuire."

Owen said, "Not Tony Schrupp or Nathan Beyon?"

"No. They chose to leave the lahk about a year ago."

From Noah's tone, this was some sort of breach, but Leo didn't know of what.

Owen said, "Where did they go?"

"To the mountains. I don't know where."

"You have a wife and child. Where are they?"

"With my wife's lahk, of course."

"Does anyone in this house possess any weapons?"

"*No*, and neither do you. You are guests here, Lieutenant, and Kindred does not permit guns of any sort. You will all relinquish yours and they will be locked safely away."

"That's not going to happen," Owen said.

Once again, Marianne Jenner stepped in. "Noah, not now. We

need water. Is there any sort of filtered water we can drink through straws or something?"

"No. Mom—"

She interrupted him. "I think it would be best if you took us to the clinic you mentioned, so we can see what supplies and facilities you have. We need to get acclimated as soon as possible because we're going to try to manufacture more vaccine from the amount we brought. Claire Patel here— No, Noah, don't look so hopeful, there aren't many doses. We thought the whole planet would be vaccinated. There's only enough for—Claire?"

Dr. Patel said, "A hundred doses. But we'll need at least fifty to synthesize from, if we can do that at all."

Fifty vaccines, and a whole continent of people facing the spore cloud, not counting the ones already dead in those cities. And Noah Jenner had a wife and child. Leo saw his face, the hunger and calculation, and knew that Jenner wanted two of those vaccines for the people he loved. So would everybody else, unless the doctors could make more. But even so, could they make enough for everybody in a few months, part of which was going to be spent sick from "adjusting" to the germs in this alien air? Didn't seem likely.

Now Leo knew how their mission would look on Kindred.

Shit.

Isabelle came home from the baker's, the basket of her bicycle laden with fresh-baked bread, her eyes red from weeping. Four cities. She had visited only Kam^tel^ha and knew none of the lahks in any of them, but they were Kindred and now they'd been murdered. The latest radio broadcast, which she'd heard in the teahouse, had said that the destroyer was a Russian ship. Isabelle wasn't sure how the Great Mother knew this. There was no way to communicate with the ship, if it was still around, because the Kindred ship had been destroyed in the Russian attack. The Great Mother had escaped death only because she'd been out of the capital, returning to her lahk like everybody else, to await the coming of the spore cloud. The cities had been half empty.

Half empty was still a huge number of deaths. And gone were the hospitals, the universities, the old Temple of Life.

Isabelle rounded the curve of road to her lahk and screeched her bicycle to a halt. The upper deck was full of people—*Terrans*. Terrans she did not know. Noah Jenner, whom she hadn't seen in a few months because he spent most of his time at Llaa^mohᵢ's lahk, stood among them. One, two . . . eight other Terrans, and four of them wore helmets and carried guns.

She dropped her bicycle, snatching up the bread, and rushed up the steps.

"I greet you, Noah. What—" She stopped dead. Two of the soldiers had raised guns. Isabelle had, a dozen years ago, dated a Special Forces guy. He'd been a dick, but she knew what she was looking at. These were Army Rangers.

Noah said, "I greet you, Isabelle. This is Isabelle Rhinehart, she lives here. Better be careful, Lieutenant, she's armed with loaves of bread."

A man stepped forward. Middle Eastern–looking, but no accent to his English, evidently the leader. "I'm Dr. Salah Bourgiba, Ms. Rhinehart. We're off the American starship *Friendship*, which was destroyed in the same attack as on your cities. Mr. Jenner brought us here."

Noah said, "I'm taking them to the clinic—best we can do. They need to drink, and the hospital at—"

"Yes, I know," Isabelle interrupted. "Where's Kayla? And Austin?"

"Austin's at school. Kayla's in the garden with Bahlk^a."

"Hysterical?"

"Yes."

Of course she was. Trust Kayla to make any complicated situation more complicated. Isabelle looked over the Terrans. So odd to see such pale skins on all but Bourgiba and the largest of the soldiers, who appeared to be African-American. And the hospital destroyed—

She said, "I'll come with you. I've been through what's ahead of you."

The older woman said, "You didn't have your microbes replaced before you reached Kindred?"

Kindred? Was that what they were calling World now? Dumb name. "No, I didn't. Are you Marianne Jenner? I recognize you from your pictures ten years ago. I was stupid then, I didn't trust Worlders to mess around with my insides and so I adapted the hard way. It's bad but it only lasts a week or so. Unless the doctor at the clinic— it's only a local clinic, don't expect anything fancy—can do something to help that's been developed since. We learned a lot from the trip to Terra, you know."

"But not, apparently, about the time dilation," Marianne said. She was not smiling.

"No. That was as big a shock to Mee^haoj and the others as it must have been to you. Lieutenant, you really don't need those weapons here. Although I have nothing but the greatest respect for the Seventy-Fifth Regiment."

Noah Jenner scowled. "Come on," he said. "We need to go."

Nothing but the greatest respect for the Seventy-Fifth Regiment. She was beautiful, smart—look how fast she grasped the whole situation— and kind. How old was she? Older than Leo, maybe, but Christ—her figure in that revealing sarong-thing, her strong firm arms. She wasn't dyed copper like Noah Jenner (or whatever they did to get his skin that color), but her face and body were tanned and her light brown hair streaked from that big orange sun. Or from something, anyway.

Was she married? He didn't understand this lahk thing, which had Noah Jenner living here and his wife someplace else. Maybe Leo could ask Bourgiba to explain it; the doctor seemed to know a lot about how Kindred worked.

He wasn't worried about surviving this "microbe adjustment." Hell, next to RASP and Ranger School and the whole poison ivy–sepsis incident, it would probably be a piece of cake.

Isabelle Rhinehart. Things were looking up.

CHAPTER 6

Austin and Graa^lok stopped at the mouth of the cave. Austin swiped the sweat off his face with the hem of his shirt. His mother sewed him Terran clothes, and although he usually wore a wrap, sometimes the Terran clothes felt better. And they kept his mother happy, or at least less miserable.

Graa^lok said, "Are you sure this is the right place?"

"Of course it's the right place," Austin said, hoping this was true. The mountains of World, old and worn down, were all full of caves. Some were stocked with supplies for hikers: some were gorgeous with gem-studded vugs that tourists visited; some had lakes or hot springs. However, those were mostly farther north than here, closer to the cities. This range was smaller and more isolated, amid farms and orchards. But it, too, held caves, some completely unexplored. A few small ones had crazy people living in them, those who didn't like the rules that Worlders lived by and so went off to live in small bands by themselves.

Well, come to think—that's what Tony Schrupp was doing. Only not really.

What Tony-kal was doing was saving civilization.

Austin tugged at the thick brush covering the mouth of the cave, mostly muktal^, which had unfortunate thorns. One pricked him and he sucked the blood off his wrist. "You could help, you know!"

Graa^lok didn't move. "These mountains are where they found the plans, you know. In a big cave. The plans for the starship, on titanium, and the sealed parts."

"Yes? How do you know?"

"Great-Grandmother told me. She was on the engineering team."

Austin, who'd never known Graa^lok's great-grandmother as anything more than a very old lady lying in bed, couldn't think of her as an engineer. She was even too old for the Council of Mothers, and engineers were young and energetic and inventive. Like Tony-kal and Dr. Beyon.

"Come on, we can squeeze through now. Don't break any sticks, we have to put all this brush back."

The two boys, Austin in the lead, crawled through the gap in the brush, which snapped closed behind them. They crawled along a tunnel barely large enough for their bodies; very quickly the tunnel grew dark. Twenty yards in, the tunnel turned sharply back on itself and the walls grew smoother; this part was human-made. A faint light appeared at the end. Then they were at the metal grill and Austin rang the bell.

A few minutes later, Tony's face appeared on the other side of the grill. "Austin?"

"And Graa^lok." It felt strange to talk to someone without first saying "I greet you." Sometimes Austin even addressed Tony and Dr. Beyon without the polite "kal" that identified them as members of his lahk. Austin relished these small acts of rebellion.

Tony said, "Did anybody follow you?"

"No."

"Did you bring it?"

"Yes."

Tony unlocked the grill and swung it open. A short drop led to another tunnel, taller and wider. The boys wiggled out headfirst and Tony lifted each to stand on the smooth stone floor. He locked the grill behind them.

Another door, solid metal, at the end of the tunnel. Tony unlocked that and they were in.

The cave was a large room giving out onto a deep lake fed by underground streams. They must have been warm, because the water was. Smaller tunnels led off in every direction. The uneven floor was littered with sleeping mats, bulging cloth sacks, tools, and a fantastic assortment of machinery. Some of it Austin recognized—a sort of heating coil, a small refrigerator—some he did not. He knew there was an air filtration system connected to the two chimneys that brought air to the cave, generators that used heat from the hot springs and World's magnetic field, equipment for a doctor. Everything had been brought in through the narrow tunnel, the larger machines in pieces. Austin didn't know how any of it worked; his mind couldn't seem to hang onto the concepts.

Graa^lok could. That's why he was here. He was unofficial apprentice to Nathan Beyon, who had been an important physicist back on Terra and who insisted that the next generation be well represented in this project. On World, Beyon-kal and Tony had made and sold transistors. Austin wasn't sure what those were, either, but he knew that everyone wanted them for radios and other devices. Beyon-kal had created the factory and oversaw manufacture of the transistors, somewhere near the central mountains where the mining and manufacturies all were, and Tony had sold them. They'd gotten really rich. Then they used the money to buy this mountain and create Haven.

When the spore cloud hit, some people would go in here, survive, and not come out until there was a vaccine or a cure.

Austin was incredibly lucky to be one of those people. He couldn't do science like Graa^lok, he wasn't a doctor or hydroponics farmer like some of the other Worlders that Tony hoped to persuade to come here, but he had his own jobs. Haven could save forty people. He, and his mother, would be two of them.

Of course, his mother was already immune to spores. So was Austin. But even though Terrans were immune, civilization was going to collapse—Tony said so—and it wouldn't be safe for even the Terrans to be above ground when there were desperate survivors. And to restart civilization, they would need girls who could have babies. That's where Graa^lok's sisters and cousins came in.

Austin didn't think about that part of it, except at night, alone on his sleeping mat.

Tony said, "Let me have it."

Austin pulled the bulky package from his pocket. He didn't exactly know what it was, but he'd memorized the Terran letters. His mother had taught him to read a little English, before she got too depressed about there being no English books to read. He handed Tony the package. Most of it was medicines, including one he recognized, a dry brown powder that his mother used to give him for earaches. Austin was hoping that no one at the clinic would take inventory of the stuff in the storage closets. With the spore loud coming so soon, why would they bother? That was his hope, anyway.

"Good man," Tony said, and Austin glowed inside.

He could steal anything. This lot hadn't even been that hard. The medicines came from the clinic right near their house. The other thing, the package with the Terran symbol on it and the English words, had been a little more complicated:

BIOHAZARD
VIRAL MATERIALS

To get that, Austin had gone with Noah to visit his wife's lahk and play with their little girl. Lil^da, whom Isabelle called Lily, was only nine and too young for Austin, but he used to play with her when he was a kid, and everybody seemed pleased that he wanted to see Lil^da again. Noah's wife, Llaa^moh¡, had gone to Terra on the World expedition there, which used to impress Austin. Llaa^moh¡ was a biologist. "Not the real thing," Beyon-kal always said, because there were no real scientists on World compared to Terra, but as Tony said, you had to make do with what you had. Austin had stolen Llaa^moh¡'s keys, gone to her lab, and stolen the "viral material." It had come from Terra. The cabinet had been triple locked, but Austin had been practicing on locks since he was eight.

Of course, stealing was wrong. Good people didn't steal, and nearly everybody on World was good, or at least they acted good and kept bu^ka^tel. That, Isabelle-kal said, was why the society could work "despite its many restrictions." But Noah's ethics class at school had also talked—briefly—about the rare times when it was necessary to break the law, such as if someone's life was in danger. Well, *everybody's* life was in danger from the spore cloud, and Llaa^moh¡'s lab hadn't found a vaccine even though they'd been looking for ten years, and Tony Schrupp was the only one saving people. Forty people, anyway. So it was okay for Noah to steal this viral material for Tony, and it would be okay for Austin and Tony, when the time came, to steal Llaa^moh¡, too, so she could keep looking for the vaccine. They would need a biologist and a doctor, Tony said, and he hoped that Llaa^moh¡ and a doctor could be persuaded to join them when the spore cloud got closer. If not, they would steal them. After all, it would save their lives! Llaa^moh¡ should be grateful.

"But . . ." Austin had said, man to man, "she won't help unless we bring Noah and Lily, too. And Noah won't be—"

"Leave it to me," Tony had said.

Beyon-kal walked out from the side tunnel leading to the lab. He was the oldest Terran on World, and on Terra he had been a really important scientist at someplace called MIT. Austin's mother didn't like Beyon-kal—not that she'd seen him very often. "He's creepy," she said, an English word that Austin didn't quite understand except that it had to do with not looking people in the eye and sometimes not answering when spoken to and being really smart at hard equations.

Beyon-kal—and why couldn't Austin even think of him without the respectful title? But he just couldn't—said, "Did he get it? Is that it?"

"Yes." Tony handed him the package.

"In *that* box? Christ, these people don't understand anything about safe handling."

Tony said, "Then stow it safer."

Graa^lok said in his rough English, "What be not right?"

For the first time, Austin realized that both men's jaws looked as hard as karthwood. If Austin hadn't been so pleased with himself, he would have realized it before. Tony said, "You didn't hear. Of course you didn't. You were hiking all day to get here."

"Hear what?" There was a radio in the cave, with a long antenna that went up one of the air chimneys. It would get an airtight seal around it once the spore cloud was closer.

Tony said, "The three big cities were destroyed from space. Some sort of laser beam—"

"Not laser," Beyon-kal said impatiently. "I *told* you."

"—and the World ship along with it. I'm sorry, kid. Did you have relatives or friends in—"

"The ship, too?" Austin's dream was to fly in the one World starship, to go out in space. "The *ship*? Who did it?"

"Terrans. Russians—that's another continent on Terra, not mine and Nate's. They also destroyed an American ship that was coming here, and so eight more Terrans are marooned on World. That's what Nate thinks, anyway."

Beyon-kal understood some World, but not very well. Tony had none. They needed Austin and Graa^lok to translate.

Graa^lok said doubtfully, "Will they be of your lahk?"

Tony said, "Speak English, Graylock."

"The new Terrans. In your lahk, Austin?"

"I don't know." He didn't care. That lovely ship . . . the Council of Mothers would never let it fly after the first time that brought him here. *Not necessary,* they'd said, which was pretty much their answer to anything different or fun. Tony said that was what happened when women got to run things, but even Austin knew that was stupid. Of course women ran the government; they had the babies and so could look out for people the best. Men ran plenty of things, including the expedition to Terra that had brought Austin to World.

And now there would never be another. Nobody knew how to build another ship. Also, neither of the two they'd built had accomplished what they were supposed to, and both had taken too much money and effort. Worse, their building had damaged the ecology of Mother World, which was only now getting back in balance. That's what Austin's teacher said at school.

Austin didn't know anybody in Kam^tel^ha or the other destroyed cities. It was sad that they were all dead, but not as sad as the loss of the starship, *both* starships, that—

He said abruptly, "Where is the Russian ship? Is it still here?"

Beyon-kal said, "Allegedly not. Come on, boys, I need some lifting done in the third lab."

That was another thing Austin did here. Translating, stealing, lifting. He was glad to be of use. The starship was destroyed, but civilization would not be, because of what Tony and Beyon-kal were creating here, now, with Austin's help. He was important. He was necessary.

Isabelle Rhinehart didn't go with them to the medical facility, which disappointed Leo. By now he had the relationships sorted out. Noah Jenner and the two other men who lived in the house, although they weren't there now, were married to native women, who all lived in other places (weird—why?) Kayla was Isabelle's sister; she had a kid that came with her on the first Terran mission to Kindred. The kid was supposed to be at school but school had been canceled because of the Russian attack and now the kid, Austin, was missing and Kayla was hysterical all over again and Isabelle had to go look for Austin.

"How old is Austin?" Dr. Patel said.

"Fifteen," Isabelle said. "Thirteen in Terran years."

Well, shit—the kid was just playing hooky. Leo had done that enough when he was thirteen (and done a lot worse, too). Austin would come home when he damn well felt like it. Leo suspected that Isabelle thought so, too, but she was humoring her wuss of a sister.

Owen called the unit together before they walked to the clinic. "This all looks legit so far, but nobody surrenders any weapons for any reason whatsoever. First priority is to assess situation, resources, terrain. If this medical procedure is judged necessary, we will undergo it in two shifts, first Berman and Brodie, and then Kandiss and me. Personnel not in clinic will take possession of the weapons of those who are. The immediate goal is to attain physical functionality to drink and eat on this planet, in order to carry out the larger goals of, first, defending civilian personnel and, second, discovering the means to return to Terra. Is this understood?"

"Yes, sir," Leo said, along with the others. But—return to Terra? Was that possible? How?

Zoe said, "Permission to ask a question, sir."

"Go ahead."

"How long does this medical procedure last and what do we do? Like, take a pill or an IV or what?"

Nothing so easy.

"Fecal transplant," Dr. Bourgiba said. "The quickest way to augment the gut biome."

"What's that?" Zoe said suspiciously.

The civilians, except for the two doctors, had already been taken into rooms someplace. The clinic turned out to be a short walk down the hill from Jenner's house. Leo and Owen had done a recon of the nearby town. The houses came in clumps, usually a big one surrounded by smaller structures, all made of that same light bamboo-like stuff in those same curves and weaves, with decks and open sides. Beautiful but hard to defend. The houses were set in a lush landscape of gardens, orchards, and fields connected by paths of smooth stone. He saw nothing that looked like factories or warehouses or office buildings, but the town center had what looked like stores and restaurants but could have been schools or temples or something really alien, for all he knew. The only large building was next to the clinic. Jenner said it was a combination school and community center.

Not too many natives around; probably they were inside, mourning their cities. The ones he saw were mostly tall, all coppery skinned, all with huge dark eyes like the ones in those sappy paintings his foster mother, the bitch, had hung around her living room. The natives walked or rode bicycles, although he saw one more electric transport and one heavily laden cart pulled slowly by a big stupid-looking animal.

The clinic was another bamboo-y building but more closed up and level with the ground. Leo saw Owen appraising it. He and Kandiss went into the small lobby, scoped it out, and came back outside. A native woman in loose white pants and tunic, more covered up than the usual wrap, led Leo into a small room with two scrubbed-looking raised platforms covered with what looked like plastic but probably wasn't. Leo had already observed that these people didn't use plastic. Canteens were metal; carrying was done in baskets; Isabelle's necklace was some sort of fake gold with wood carvings on it. Beside the platforms stood some metal buckets. An open door led to the head, which had—thank God for small favors—a toilet that looked pretty normal.

Dr. Bourgiba came in, translating for a native. "I'm sorry we have to put two in a room, but space is limited here. Accommodating all eight of us will be a stretch as it is. Dr. Patel and I have prepared everything. Lieutenant, which of your men goes first?"

"Negative," Owen said. "I want to see it first on civilians, including recovery."

Dr. Bourgiba blinked. "I don't think you understand, Lieutenant. This is the best way to make it possible for you to drink and eat, which you must do soon. We are all losing hydration in this heat. Recovery takes about a week. We must begin now."

Leo watched Owen, stony faced, come to a decision. It was true that they needed to hydrate; thirst made Leo's throat feel clogged with sawdust. Owen had no choice.

"Brodie and Berman, you first. Kandiss and I will observe."

Bourgiba didn't argue. "This is not going to be pleasant, I'm afraid. Please undress, everything off, including your face mask. Almost immediately the Kindred microbes will invade your lungs. The nurse here will give you some water to drink. And I'm going to insert a small capsule of native microbes into your rectum. Some of these should take hold and further your acclimation. In addition, they might serve to build immunity to—"

"Wait," Leo said. "Up my asshole? Some native's shit?"

"Yes. This is a well-established procedure on Earth, although there we would have the equipment to do it via colonoscopy. Undress and lie on your side, facing the wall."

Zoe said, "Wait a minute, I—"

Owen said, "An order, Berman. Go with Dr. Patel."

Leo handed his weapons and gear to Kandiss. The doctor drew on plastic gloves—they must have come from Dr. Patel's handy-dandy suitcase. Then Leo lay still for half an hour. Well, this wasn't so bad. He felt fine.

Soon after that nausea started, then vomiting, diarrhea, violent headaches, and the misery that made him sure he was going to die, and almost want to.

A nurse stayed with him, or somebody did. They were all a blur. He puked and shat and drank water and ate whatever they made him eat. Two days later—two lost, everlasting, fucked-to-hell-and-back days—he suddenly felt himself again. Weak as a puppy, but himself. His stomach stayed still, which was, he now knew fervently, what you wanted of a stomach. He was clean (who had done that?), lying on the raised platform in a clean room. Kandiss lay on the other platform, asleep, a huge dark lump. Through a window blew fresh, warm, scented breezes. Leo closed his eyes and slept.

When he opened them again, he was still clean, and Isabelle Rhinehart stood at the foot of his bed.

"Congratulations," she said. "You had it much easier than the others."

"They—"

"Will all live, all eight of you. Tough sons of bitches."

Her smile was glorious. Leo slept again.

Salah lay motionless, hoping that would still both the vomiting and the vertigo. Like most doctors, he was seldom ill; more delicate types didn't survive med school. Feeling this bad was new to him. But, he thought with the introspection natural to him, doing nothing was not.

Everyone he'd ever known would dispute that. Salah Bourgiba, polymath, Renaissance man. Respected physician, historian, speaker of five languages—six, now. But Salah knew, even if no one else did, that he had made only two independent decisions in his life: Aisha and applying for this expedition.

Otherwise, he had just drifted along the path marked out for him by others. The right schools and the right career choice, neither ever imperiled by the sorts of political activism—for the environment, the homeless, the economy, a dozen different idealistic causes—that had seized some of his classmates. The right hospitals for internship and residency, obtained partly by his own easy successes and partly by parental string-pulling that he had not asked about too closely. The right publications and board memberships and political stances, flowing from being born with the right connections. He had dotted every I, touched every base, filled out every required line on every form. Drifting, without decision, through all of it.

Ironically, it was this very lack of independent action that had gotten him selected for this mission. The government liked that he was a known and reliable entity. But others had urged him to apply. Then, having been chosen, the rest had also been well-marked and easy paths. Learn the language, study what little was known on Terra about Kindred culture, follow the leadership of Ambassador Gonzalez. It seemed to Salah that the last independent decision he had made, the last self-chosen action, had been Aisha, twenty-five years ago.

And look how that had turned out.

Bile rose in his gorge, and he turned to vomit into the metal bucket by his platform bed.

Austin woke in the middle of the night and bolted upright on his sleeping mat. He had the best idea of his life!

All around him, his lahk slept, each person in his own tiny private room: Isabelle-kal, Austin's mother, Steven-kal and Joshua-kal, who both were leaving tomorrow for their manufactures. Noah was not here; he'd gone to Llaa^mohį's lahk but would be back tomorrow.

The velvety darkness smelled of spicy pikaį in the garden below. A white moth—that's what his mother called them—beat its wings against the screen in Austin's window. The moth almost got through; the threads of the screen needed tightening again. Austin was supposed to do that tomorrow, as well as harvest culab. And turn the compost heap and bring a lot of stuff to Isabelle's studio for her sculptures. Well, he had more important things to do than lahk chores!

Tony needed a biologist. He had planned on Llaa^mohȷ because she knew the most about the spores. But now there were new Terran doctors on World! Tony didn't know that because the radio hadn't described what the Terrans did, but Austin knew. And all three doctors lay sick and helpless in the clinic. One would not be hard to kidnap.

Although there were soldiers here, too, with guns. Austin tasted both unfamiliar words on his tongue: *Soldiers. Guns.* Of course, Kindred had police, but they weren't really soldiers, and they didn't carry guns, only tanglefoam and water cannons and tasers. Still, the soldiers were sick and helpless, too, getting their insides changed so they could live on World.

Which doctor? Not Marianne Jenner. Too old, and she would probably be lahk mother when she got well again. (Would Isabelle mind not being mother anymore? Austin didn't know, but it was clear that the new Terrans belonged to this lahk and that Marianne-kal was the oldest woman.) So: Salah Bourgiba or the pretty little woman with the dark skin, Claire Patel. She might be easiest to kidnap, but Tony would decide that.

But it was Austin who'd had the idea! He lay back down on his mat, enormously pleased with himself.

Above him, the white moth squeezed through the sagging window screen and flapped around the room, trying to get out again.

CHAPTER 7

Isabelle stood with Llaa^mohį in the lobby of the clinic when a Ranger, Leo Somebody, walked shakily in. No, not a Ranger, his uniform had lacked the Ranger tab; this was the Army sniper somehow attached to Lieutenant Lamont's unit. He had recovered faster than everybody else. Barefoot, Leo wore only a clinic shift, in which his muscular body looked ridiculous. "I greet you," she said.

"Hi. Ms. Rhinehart—"

"Isabelle is fine."

"Isabelle, where are my unit's weapons? I checked on the lieutenant and the three others and they're still really sick and don't know much. Where are the weapons?"

"This is Noah's wife, Llaa^mohį. Private . . . uh, Leo."

"I greet you, Leo."

"Hi. The weapons?"

"Locked up," Isabelle said, and stood. This was going to be a confrontation.

"Unlock them." Leo's eyes were cold.

"I don't have the authority to do that."

"Who does?"

"The Mother of . . . of this governmental region ordered it. We don't have weapons, Leo. Not on Kindred."

"I do. Send for this mother person. Or whoever is in charge of your army."

"We don't have an army, either."

He stared at her. Isabelle wasn't frightened of him, but the steady gaze from those blue eyes was disconcerting. She said, "If you'll excuse us, we're busy. And you should probably be back in bed."

To her surprise, he left. Llaa^moh¡, who had some English but not much since Noah preferred to talk in World, said, "What did the soldier say?"

"He wants their weapons back."

"He may not have them."

"No."

They bent again over the table. On it stood Marianne Jenner's laptop. Before Marianne's fecal transplant, she'd told Isabelle that she had downloaded pertinent data onto it from dee-bees on the *Friendship*. Isabelle hadn't seen a computer for years. The previous expedition to Earth had brought back several, but had not succeeded in manufacturing them. Not only too complex, but also too far beyond the level of technology permitted on World. Isabelle understood how necessary that level was; World had only one continent, rich but limited in size. Worlders could not afford to exploit resources beyond sustainability. Everyone knew this, since it made a large section of schooling for the young, part of bu^ka^tel. Above all, respect and care for Mother World. Control population. Mine with care. Hand-make whatever did not require a manufactury. Even the transistors that Steve and Josh made, the transistors that earned the entire lahk its living, had taken two years to be approved.

The computers from the original expedition had been usable as stand-alones, once the voltages of World electricity had been adjusted. So had the gene sequencer and other equipment brought from Earth. But over time, the equipment had broken. Some had been repaired, but for the computers, no sophisticated parts were available, or could be made. As much vital data as possible had been printed, which mostly meant data on spores and on the progress made toward a vaccine before the original expedition had been forced to leave Terra hours ahead of the spore cloud. The data had not been enough. No vaccine.

But this was new data, on a new computer. Isabelle didn't know how to adapt it to World voltage; that might have been done in the destroyed capital. For now, the laptop was running on its limited battery. Isabelle translated the files Marianne had marked from English into World, and Llaa^mohǰ recorded the data. Most of the time, Isabelle didn't know what the medical words meant, or what their equivalent would be in World, but Llaa^mohǰ was a scientist capable of making accurate guesses, and they were doing the best they could until Marianne recovered. The spore cloud would be here in another ten weeks, and the biologist and two doctors all lay in bed with fever and vomiting and diarrhea.

"Turn on the radio," Llaa^mohǰ said.

Isabelle did, and for a few moments they both listened. No new attacks anywhere. Llaa^mohǰ was, of course, worried about her daughter.

Isabelle said, "I think the first reports were right. That Russian ship went back to Terra."

"They came all this way just to kill us!"

Isabelle looked away from the anguish in Llaa^mohǰ's dark eyes. Llaa^mohǰ didn't understand, of course she didn't. There were no wars on cooperative World, only the occasional murder over money or sex or just pure human craziness—and not very many of those. Nationality and patriotism, with its large-scale us–them duality, was unknown when there was only "us."

Llaa^mohǰ reached out and took Isabelle's face between her hands. "Listen to me, lahk-sister-of-my-husband. You must be careful of yourself. Noah has told me that there are Worlders who resent Terrans, all Terrans, because of the Russian attacks. These are not intelligent people. They think that all Terrans must be the same, because we Worlders are all so much the same. There is crazy talk in the villages closer to the destroyed cities. You must be careful of yourself, of Austin and Kayla, of everyone in your lahk."

Isabelle stared at Llaa^mohį. Was this true? In the face of the Terran attack on the cities, and the terrible spore-cloud attack still to come, were some Worlders no longer willing to keep what Noah had called "the Pax Worlda"? That was supposed to be a joke. But Llaa^mohį's urgency was no joke.

Us. Them. The Russians had created duality.

Isabelle said in World, "Let's bring this computer to town. Maybe someone there can recharge the battery."

Leo's legs still felt shaky; he ignored the sensation and left his room. The clinic was built in an irregular square around a sort of courtyard open to each room and the sky. In one room, Zoe and Marianne Jenner lay on two beds, Zoe asleep. Dr. Jenner looked back at Leo, then turned her head to vomit into a bucket. The room smelled terrible and Dr. Jenner looked worse. Leo's stomach roiled and he backed out hastily. A Kindred nurse pushed past him to go to her patients.

Kandiss still slept. In another room Owen lay open eyed but muttering. His wrists were strapped to the bed, which made Leo clench his jaw until he remembered, dimly, that his wrists had been, too. Hospitals did that, didn't they, to keep patients not in their right minds from hurting themselves or anybody else. *Well, all right, then. For now.* In the other bed, the lab assistant, Carter, was awake. He waved feebly at Leo. Dr. Patel slept on a floor mat in what looked like an office; Leo didn't go in.

He found what he wanted in the only room without windows. The only way to reach this room was through the courtyard, in full view of the staff. The door was locked, but it didn't look strong. Leo threw himself against it.

A man rushed across the courtyard, shouting in Kindese. Leo

threw himself against the door again. The motion made his head hammer and his knees buckle, but the door gave. Security here was shit.

Cabinets with wooden doors lined three sides of the windowless room, open shelves the fourth. Leo picked up something heavy from a shelf, a piece of metal equipment he didn't understand, and smashed the largest cabinet door, keeping at it until the lock gave. Cloth bags and glass vials. He began on a second cabinet.

"Corporal Brodie, stop." Dr. Bourgiba, shaky but upright, with a crowd of Kindred behind him. Leo scanned the group briefly. No one armed, no one moving toward him. He returned to smashing the cabinet door.

It was all inside: rifles, sidearms, armor, grenades, ammunition. Leo picked up a Beretta and checked it. Unloaded. Facing the group in the doorway, he calmly loaded it. "Doctor, don't try to interfere. These are our weapons."

"I see that," Bourgiba said. He spoke in Kindese to everybody else, who frowned and scowled and muttered and did nothing. Good thing for them.

"Tell them all not to try this again."

"Weapons are not permitted on Kindred, Leo."

"They are now."

Bourgiba let out a throaty sound, which might have been a sigh or a protest or a resignation. Not that it mattered which. Leo said, "I'm going to take these to my room. All of them. Nobody had better try to stop me."

"No one will. May I help?"

"No. You look like you should go back to bed."

"Try to understand, Leo, it's a different culture."

"I get that. But this is my culture."

Bourgiba spoke to the Kindred, who scowled and muttered some more and then drifted away.

To move the whole stock without leaving any out of sight, Leo had to carry the gear in stages. Some to the courtyard, more to the courtyard, then more, then the rest. Repeat to the door of his room, repeat until everything was inside. By the time he finished, he felt weaker than even Ranger school had ever left him. Bourgiba, who had watched the entire operation, said, "You need to hydrate. Then to eat."

"Is their water and food going to make me start vomiting again?"

"It didn't with me."

Leo considered his options. There weren't any. "Okay, then, food."

Bourgiba brought it himself, a polished wooden bowl of what looked like rice topped with what looked like fruit. Or vegetables. But it smelled good and Leo ate it, sitting on the edge of his bed, the unit's weapons piled around him. Bourgiba sagged against the wall. Kandiss slept.

Bourgiba said, "I need to examine you. Bodies vary in their transition to alien microbes."

Leo had already noticed that; he was deeply annoyed that Bourgiba seemed to have recovered faster than he had.

The doctor said, "The immune system goes wild with the intrusion of what it initially perceives as pathogens. Two of the original expedition died this way, and now we might also lose Marianne Jenner."

Leo stopped eating. Damn. He liked Dr. Jenner. After a moment he said, "Don't you need her to make vaccines?"

"Yes. Although Claire and I can do it alone if we have to."

Leo finished his bowl and waited to see what his stomach would do. It roiled a little, but not much. He felt less shaky now. "Lieutenant Lamont?"

"He'll be fine. So will the others. I expect them up by evening. Maybe longer for Zoe—her body just took a double insult, after all."

"She'll be up." Bourgiba didn't understand about Rangers. "What happens now?"

"The Kindred hospitals and research labs have been destroyed.

There are not quite ten weeks left to synthesize and administer vaccines, assuming we can make them. We'll work here—in fact, we already are. We have taken over two nearby buildings. More personnel and equipment are coming from other clinics, although the major sources were in the cities destroyed by the *Stremlenie*."

Leo thought hard. "You mean, everybody on Kindred knows this will be where to get a vaccine?"

"Probably not everybody. We've asked medical personnel to not share details with anyone."

Yeah, right, like that would happen if equipment and doctors were traveling across the continent and there was only enough vaccine for some people but not everybody. He said, "How close are the other two buildings?"

"One is about fifty yards away, a school. The other is across a field."

A security nightmare. "Which is bigger?"

"The school is much bigger. That's where we're setting up a lab now."

"Okay. Until Lieutenant Lamont takes over, I'm in charge of security here. Board up every window in the school and every window in this clinic that faces outward. Get workmen to build a covered walkway between the buildings, as strong as they can make it, not just those sliding woven panels. Get that done immediately."

"I don't have any authority to—"

"You have something everybody needs. Whoever owns these buildings will cooperate and so will the government. Promise them early vaccination if you have to."

"Leo, it doesn't work that way here."

Leo found his clothes in a cupboard. He stripped off the nightgown and pulled on underwear and pants. "Tell me, Doctor—are there rumors anywhere, on the radio or with the medical types arriving here now, of people hoarding food or fortifying their houses or generally getting ready to survive if they happen to be among the ones that the spore disease doesn't kill? Any rumors at all?"

Bourgiba was silent.

"I thought so. This place doesn't work that way, *now*. This is a peaceful place, *now*." He pulled on his boots. "But just in case it starts to work that way when things break down, we're going to be ready."

It was two weeks before Marianne was able to sit up in bed. She knew she'd nearly died. All her life she'd read accounts of people who'd survived plane crashes, cancer treatments, house fires. Every single one had said that, afterward, their appreciation of small things had deepened into gratitude for the glory of life.

She was really irritated that it was true.

The hard platform bed felt wonderful under her; the fruit she was brought to eat in small nibbles tasted better than any fruit she'd ever had; the karthwood of her clinic room gleamed like burnished gold. Sweet, faintly spicy air smelling of rain drifted through a small screened window. She was marooned on a planet about to undergo the death throes of its civilization, and she had never felt so alive.

Had Harrison Rice, her last romantic partner, felt this way in the brief time between his diagnosis and death? He hadn't said so. Stoic and detached, Harrison had kept his feelings to himself. But it had been his death that decided Marianne to come to Kindred and see Noah one last time. So complicated, the threads that mortality spun in human minds.

"Mom," Noah said—this strange Noah with deep coppery skin and huge eyes, surgically altered—"are you well enough to meet your granddaughter?"

Something clutched in Marianne's heart. "Yes!"

They came a few minutes later: Llaa^moh¡, whom Marianne had known as "Officer Jones" on Terra, with a thin child by the hand. "I greet you, mother-of-my-husband," Llaa^moh¡ said in heavily accented English. "This is Lil^da. Lily.'"

The child said, "I greet you, Grandmother," carefully shaping each of the English syllables, bravely lifting her eyes, as big and dark as her mother's, to Marianne's. A shy child, Marianne saw, unlike the two grandsons she had left on Terra. The grandsons she would never see again—no, don't think of that, this was Lily's moment.

Marianne held out her hand. Lily glanced at her mother, then came forward. Marianne was shocked at how thin her own hand was after weeks of illness, at how much effort it took to lift. The wrinkled pale fingers enfolded Lily's smoother ones. The child's skin was lighter than her mother's, darker than Noah's would have been without the artificial coloring. She had a small, heart-shaped face and a firm, generous mouth. "I greet you, Lily," she said in World. Marianne's eyes filled with tears.

"Mom," Noah said, "Llaa^mohị needs to get back to work, and you need to rest."

At the mention of work, tears vanished. Work had always been the great organizer of Marianne's life, the point of it. If her children had suffered from that, it was too late to make it right now, but not too late to go on contributing.

Llaa^mohị led Lily out. Marianne said, "The vaccines?"

"You need to talk to Salah or Claire about that. They're both recovered. What I know is that they're using the supply from Terra to . . . breed more? Make more somehow, but they haven't got it yet. There's a lab set up in the school. That kid you brought, Branch, is great with hardware—he got your laptop to function on our current. Now Isabelle is translating data from your laptop for our people, but we weren't as far along as you, and—"

"Why did you lie about that, Noah? I mean, why did Smith? And where is he, anyway?" "Smith" had been the leader of the first expedition to Terra.

"Mee^haoị is dead. Cancer. Would Earth have been as much in awe of Worlders if you'd known that all our tech was secondhand and that we understood it even less than you? Would Terra have been as willing to cooperate, or to voyage here now?"

Marianne didn't answer. She'd read history. The less advanced civilization was always either ignored or plowed under by the more advanced. Only the promise of advanced trade products had gotten the *Friendship* built; aggression and revenge had built the *Stremlenie*.

"Noah, help me up. I have to get to work."

"Out of the question, Mom. You're weak as a feather."

"You don't understand. I have to help. There's no way that Jones—your wife—uh—"

Noah smiled. "You never were any good with languages. Call her Lallie. Kayla Rhinehart does."

Marianne's flash of resentment at being compared to Kayla, even the brief glimpse she had of Kayla, dissipated in the need to be working. "Lallie and Isabelle won't know how I've organized the laptop files. Salah is a medical doctor, not a researcher, and Lallie doesn't even speak English, does she?"

"Not much. Claire Patel is in charge, and Isabelle is translating."

"No English at home, then? You really wanted to belong here, didn't you, Noah?"

"I never belonged anywhere else," he said, which was true, and not even his smile could soften the pain that his simple sentence caused Marianne.

Noah put his hand on hers. "I'm happy, Mom. Stop worrying about me. Tell you what, I'll see if Claire wants to bring your laptop in here so you can explain whatever needs to be explained. But you stay here and do whatever Salah tells you. Okay?"

Marianne nodded. "Noah, are you in charge here?"

"I am not. World is matrilineal, you know. The first expedition had Mee^haoȷ as a leader only because Terra is so patriarchal. Isabelle is the mother of my lahk. Of this . . . this scientific lab that suddenly got built here, one of the mothers on the Great Council is in charge. She's Lallie's great-grandmother, very old and not too well. She arrived yesterday and is at her daughter's lahk."

"Is she a scientist? Or was she?"

"No."

"There's a very old, non-scientist, great-grandmother in charge of the only effort on Kindred to produce a vaccine? That doesn't make sense!"

"In the United States you have—or had when I left—a president with no military service in charge of a huge army with nuclear weapons."

Marianne gazed at her son. When had he developed the ability, so lacking when he'd been on Terra, to riposte so effectively?

When he became happy, her mind said. Happy enough to replace despair with thought.

"All right, Noah. Bring the laptop and Lallie and Isabelle here, with Claire if she can be spared. And . . ."

"Yes?"

"The vaccine not being used for synthesis—you've vaccinated some people already, haven't you? Are Lily and Lallie among them?"

Noah looked away. All at once she glimpsed, perhaps for the last time, the child he had been: unwilling to tell her where he'd been and what he'd been doing, unwilling to risk her displeasure. Then the child vanished and he said, "Not yet. There isn't enough for everyone."

"And on Kindred everybody is treated equally. Bullshit. You're a capitalist society, aren't you?"

"More socialist. But with really constrained capitalism, yes. But it's not my decision. The Council of Mothers—"

"More bullshit. The spore cloud is what? Two months away? Vaccinate your family. Now, while you can."

Noah said nothing. But she could tell he would not do it.

Marianne said, "One more thing. When can I see Lily again? Soon?

"Please?"

————

Austin squeezed through the tunnel, which seemed to have grown smaller since his last visit. He had wanted to come here sooner, but that hadn't worked out. No one was expecting him, but when Tony heard Austin's great idea, he—and Beyon-kal, too—would be really glad he'd come. Twenty yards in, when the tunnel turned sharply back on itself and the walls grew smoother, the faint light appeared. At the metal grill, Austin rang the bell. The door farther down the tunnel clanged open and Tony's face appeared, scowling.

"What are you doing here?"

"I wanted to—"

"Christ, Austin, I told you not to come here unless I asked you to! We don't want you followed, we don't want anyone to— Did you see anybody on the way?"

"No," Austin said, which wasn't strictly true. He'd seen a rancher rounding up skalethi for milking and, farther on, a group of people hiking toward the mountains, who had called to him. But he didn't know them or they him, so it didn't really count. "Tony, I brought you something!"

"What?"

"Something you really, really need! Let me in!"

Tony unlocked the grill and Austin wriggled through and dropped to the lower tunnel. Tony said, "You're all muddy. Give me whatever you brought."

"It's raining out there. I'll give it to you inside."

Haven had changed in the two weeks since Austin had been here. More food had been delivered to the shepherd's cottage Tony had bought as a drop point, and then lugged here. That was usually Austin and Graa^lok's job, but Tony must have done it this time. Beyon-kal did not lug. Machinery had been rearranged, and the cave was filled with a low hum.

"What's that noise?"

"Nathan is testing the air filtration system. Negative pressure."

Austin didn't know what that meant, but it didn't matter. Tony's eyes raked Austin, looking for bulges in the pockets of his rain wrap. Tony said, "Well, where is it? The thing must not be very big."

"It's not a thing, it's an idea. You know how you said you had to kidnap Llaa^moh¡ so you'd have a biologist to continue to work on the vaccine? And kidnap Lily so that you could make Llaa^moh¡ work? Well, you don't have to! The new Terrans have biologists, and they know more than Llaa^moh¡, and one is still a little weak "—he was fudging that a little, Dr. Patel had mostly recovered from having her microbes changed—"and would be easy to take! Plus, she's small and can't fight. I bet even I could bring her here—tonight! Or tomorrow!"

Tony stared at him. Tony didn't look happy. The first swirl of anxiety roiled Austin. He waited for Tony to say something.

"You think we should kidnap a Terran biologist who is creating the vaccine at a compound guarded by Army Rangers, two months before the spore cloud hits, taking her away from the work she's doing there and inviting Rangers, who are experts in personnel extraction, to charge in here and rescue this woman?"

Austin hadn't thought of it that way. "Well, you could . . . you could . . . she would be useful!"

"She would indeed. And if and when the time comes, we might save her life by bringing her here. But do you really think we wouldn't know about her and her potential usefulness without you coming here to tell us?"

"Well, how would you know? You have a radio, sure, but you don't speak World!" Yes—how *did* Tony know all about the Terrans?

A movement to Austin's left. He whirled around. Beyon-kal and Graa^lok emerged from the biolab cave. Graa^lok said, "I greet you, Austin."

Graa^lok was bringing news. Graa^lok was here, invited when Austin hadn't been. All because Graa^lok was better at machinery, better at inventing, already apprenticed to an engineer. It wasn't fair!

Graa^lok, his face wrinkling, repeated, "I greet you, Austin."

"Go fuck yourself."

Tony, unexpectedly, put a hand on Austin's muddy shoulder. "Look, kid, I know you meant well. And you're part of this team, definitely. But we don't want to attract any unnecessary attention. The Mothers still think we're just some crazy business start-up or something—well, I don't know what they think. But they don't know what our plans are, and we want to keep it that way. Don't come again until Gray-lock brings you."

Until Graa^lok brings you—when it was Austin who brought Graa^lok here in the first place! Really, really unfair!

But he couldn't risk making Tony angry. Austin said grudgingly, "Okay."

"Good man. Look, you can get something to eat before you leave, okay? I know it's a long walk."

Austin ate, his back turned pointedly away from Graa^lok. But Graa^lok came and sat humbly beside him. "I have something for to show you."

"I don't care! Leave me alone!"

"It's really wondful."

"The English is 'wonderful,' idiot."

"It's really wonderful."

"I don't want to see anything you made."

"I didn't make it, I found it. And"—Graa^lok leaned close to whisper—"Tony-mak and Beyon-mak don't know yet. I saved it for you first."

"I said go away!" But when Austin had finished eating and Graa^lok was still there, Austin said grudgingly, "Okay, what is this wonderful thing? It better be fucking amazing!"

Graa^lok looked carefully around. Neither Tony nor Beyon-mak was visible. Graa^lok led the way to a side tunnel, and Austin followed. Three feet in, the first of Haven's chimneys rose, letting in air and light, although not as much light as before Nathan Beyon had installed the air filtration machinery at the top. When it and the other three chimney filters were turned on, Haven would be safe from spores. Below the chimney, Graa^lok picked up a bactotorch and handed another to Austin. Each one held enough microbe-powered fluorescence to let the boys see the tunnels they walked or crawled through.

They went deeper into the mountain. This tunnel, Austin knew from previous explorations, branched and branched again, going on farther than they had ventured. Some tunnels were small, some slick with dripping water, some partially blocked by falling rocks. It seemed to Austin that they went a long way. His clothes were wet and filthy and he shivered with cold.

"Gray, how much farther?"

"Not too far. If I can do it, you can. You're stronger and quicker than me."

Austin warmed under the flattery, even though a part of him wondered if that was why Graa^lok said it.

All at once the tunnel widened and grew higher, and Austin could stand upright. A fall of rock blocked the way forward, rising halfway to the ceiling. Graa^lok said, "We go over this and there it is."

"There *what* is?" The rock pile looked unstable.

Graa^lok didn't answer. He clambered up the rockfall, which slipped and shifted under him, sending rocks crashing to the tunnel floor. But he got himself over it, and so Austin had to follow because he was, after all, stronger and quicker.

Beyond the rockfall, the tunnel widened even more into an irregular room. Graa^lok raised his bacto-torch and waited.

"Wow!" Austin said.

"Wow!" Graa^lok echoed, clearly savoring both the new Terran word and the sight he presented to Austin as proudly as if it were an illathil share. Gold crystals sparkled on the ceiling, on the walls, in heaps on the floor. Nuggets glittered at Austin's feet. Piles of white quartz sand glowed.

"What is it?"

Graa^lok said in World, "We had it at school, didn't you? It's the inside of a geode. The gold precipitates out from circulating water that gets hot from magma. Some of these caves have diamonds, too. That's where manufacturing gets the diamonds and gold to make things. You know!"

Austin didn't. If he'd had this in school, he didn't remember it. Certainly nobody had ever shown him anything like this. "Does Tony know it's here?"

"No."

"Graa^lok, we could take some of this back and sell it and get rich!"

All at once Graa^lok looked scornful, and much older. "Sell it to who? Manufacturing is going to end in two months, along with everything else! How can you forget that?"

"I don't! That's why I want to bring my mother here!"

"Anyway, this all belongs to Beyon-mak, because he's head of this new lahk."

"A man can't be mother to a lahk, idiot." But Austin didn't want to fight with Graa^lok. He knelt before a pile of rockfall, gold mixed with sand, and let it run shining through his fingers. "Hey, there's something buried here."

"What?"

"Don't know."

Austin clawed aside the gold-flecked sand. The corner of something poked above a layer of hardened mud. Graa^lok handed him a hammer—why was Graa^lok always better prepared than him?—and Austin whacked at the mud.

"Be careful! You might break it!"

But when they got the thing out, it was clear that nothing could break it. A meter-high, four-sided pyramid with large bumps scattered randomly across each surface, it was not dented, not rusty, not as heavy as it should be to have survived the rocks that had fallen on it. Austin turned its surfaces over and over in his hands.

"Graa^lok, have you ever seen anything like this?"

"No. But I think it's been here a long time. We should give it to Beyon-mak—maybe he knows what it is."

Austin didn't want to give anything to Beyon-mak. Resentment rose again in his mind, a warty snake resurfacing. "No. It's ours."

"Tony-mak owns this mountain. He bought it from the mother of the lahk Caɪlee^ah. She sold it because the lahk needed money for—"

"I don't care. It's ours."

"It's not. Bu^ka^tel."

Austin weighed the Graa^lok's stubborn expression, the difficulty of smuggling the object past Tony in the exit tunnels, and the effort of carrying it all the way back to his lahk, and decided to bargain.

"Okay, we won't take it. But you can't tell Tony or Nathan"—he felt daring calling him that instead of Beyon-mak, which boosted his confidence—"until we agree to tell them together. After all, we found it together, and anyway it probably wouldn't fit into their plans for saving civilization. Agreed?"

"Agreed," Graa^lok said, even though he didn't look happy and even though they had not, in fact, found it together. To make up for his agreement, Graa^lok said, "You should sleep more, or drink more water, or something. You look like turds."

Probably he did. He'd walked through the rain to get here, and now he'd have to walk through rain to go back. And he was not sleeping well. But he said, scornfully, "I'm fine. Leo Brodie hardly sleeps at all. He told me."

"When?" Graa^lok challenged.

"Two days ago. I talk to Leo all the time." This was pushing it, although Austin did try to talk to Leo whenever he could. The Rangers fascinated him. "They're trained to go without sleep. None of the Rangers sleep much, even the woman."

"You're not a Ranger," Graa^lok said.

Austin stalked back along the tunnel, when he wasn't crawling or climbing. Beyon-mak let him out the door, the tunnel, the grill. At the end of the entrance tunnel, he clambered through the camouflage bushes.

There, sitting on a wet stone in an even wetter drizzle, was Noah Jenner, waiting for him. Austin's insides turned sick.

"I greet you, Austin."

"I greet you, Noah-kal."

"What the fuck do you think you're doing?"

Austin thought fast. He had to protect Haven. "I was just exploring."

"Uh-huh. Alone, in the rain, without telling anyone where you're going. Your mother is frantic."

Austin said sulkily, "My mother is always frantic." He started to trudge away, but Noah rose and caught him by the shoulder.

"What is Tony Schrupp doing in there?"

"I don't know what you're talking about."

Noah grimaced. He loomed above Austin—why couldn't Austin be that tall? He had the wrong genes. His mother's fault, or maybe the unknown father on Terra that his mother would never talk about.

Noah said, "Tony Schrupp and Nathan Beyon are in that cave system under the mountain. They've been bringing in supplies and equipment for months. Do you think the Council of Mothers doesn't know that? I asked you what they're doing in there."

"It's a start-up company."

"In a practically inaccessible cave? Without a license from the Council? Hiring no workers? Come on, Austin."

Austin repeated, because he couldn't think what else to say, "It's a start-up company."

"To make what?"

Austin, lips pressed together, looked down at his muddy shoes.

"It's a survivalist refuge," Noah said. "And Beyon is too smart not to know that spores can get in, so he's got some sort of air filter mechanism, doesn't he."

This wasn't a question, so Austin didn't try to answer it.

Noah sighed. "Maybe he can do it. Although how he thinks they can stay in there forever . . . Austin, you're forbidden to go here again."

"You can't—"

"Your mom says so, Isabelle as lahk mother says so, and as lahk-male-head-adviser"—there was no word in English for this—"*I* say so."

Austin almost said *Then forbid Graa^lok too because he's in there right now!* But that would be childish, and Austin was no longer a child, so he didn't say it. He was quite proud of this maturity.

Anyway, Graa^lok was not in their lahk.

Noah said, "Promise me."

"I promise," Austin said.

"Good. Now let's go home."

Austin hiked faster than Noah, just to show him he was not a follower. Because Austin was going back to Tony's. It was terrible to break a promise, but this was a situation outside normal ethics. There was too much at stake. Survival was at stake. All the Worlders would die except for those with natural immunity, whoever they were. In the last two weeks, Austin had learned a lot about spore disease. After the cloud came, everybody still alive from natural immunity would loot and fight for the food that was left—Tony had said so. He'd said it had happened over and over again, on Terra, whenever there was a plague. All the places Tony had told Austin about—the collapse of a huge city called Rome, and food riots in another place called Brazil, and also a mountain named Donner where people got so desperate they *ate* each other. Worlders were no different; they were human, too. Austin had an obligation—an ethical obligation!—to help preserve civilization in Haven. Also his own life. He didn't think he'd do well with fighting and looting and eating other people.

Someday Noah-kal would thank him. If Noah wasn't dead first.

Austin plodded on through the mud and rain.

CHAPTER 8

Leo, in full kit and with his rifle in hand, walked compound patrol. That's what they were calling it, the two buildings now connected by a covered walkway: "the compound." One building, the "Big Lab," had been a school and the "Little Lab" had been the clinic, but now they were collectively the compound and the squad was securing it. Owen had the whole thing built in less than a week. Kindred workmen from the little town did anything he said, they were that eager to have the scientists find a vaccine against spore disease. They'd then cleared a hundred-foot bare perimeter around the east, west, and south sides of the compound.

There were three doors, to the south, east, and north. The north door, which faced away from the town and toward open fields backed by distant mountains, had sparked intense arguments between Owen and Isabelle. That side of the clinic held a big vegetable and herb garden circled by a shoulder-high wall to keep animals from eating the vegetables. Owen had wanted the wall torn down. Isabelle had fought for wall and vegetables, and had won: "How do you suppose we'll feed you, Lieutenant? You're posting a soldier on the roof during each watch anyway—surely they can manage to see anything that approached over all that open grazing land to the north?"

Owen also had built a ready room on one side of the compound, made of triple-reinforced karthwood and stone, with doors opening both into Big Lab and out to the perimeter. The four of them slept there, one six-hour off-duty each day. Actually, it was six hours and eighteen minutes, since the day here was longer than on Terra. Leo would take any extra eighteen minutes of sleep that he could get. The ready room held four metal cabinets brought from the clinic, each with a lock. Owen, Kandiss, Zoe, and Leo kept their weapons there, separately—"The better to foil thieves," Owen said. "Four locks are harder to crack than one." Since the only people with any way of getting into the ready room were the scientists inside the compound, the lockers struck Leo as one more example of Owen's military caution. Or his general suspiciousness of Kindred. Depending on how you looked at it.

Owen had put together an OPORD with all the mission-essential elements: assessment, capabilities, civilian considerations, possible courses of action. Leo didn't know everything in Owen's mind, but at least he understood patrol. Like today, his often took place during the daily afternoon rain, which was also the daily siesta time, although not for the Rangers. Leo didn't mind rain; he'd been deployed to Brazil during the food riots.

Beyond the perimeter lay the refugee camp, which Leo also circled in his patrol. It wasn't properly a refugee camp; these people all had homes somewhere else. They were camped here to wait for vaccines. They had no guns, no IEDs, no grenades, no weapons of any kind. And in the past two weeks, the only Kindred who had ventured onto the bare perimeter was a child, whose mother pulled her back with smiles and what sounded like babbled apologies.

Leo didn't understand the camp. In Brazil, the refugee camps had been violent places, with fights over food, over places to put tents, over soccer balls, over name-calling. None of that here. Food and water came in on carts every day. Privies were cleaned. Sections of the river were set aside for bathing and washing clothes, apparently on some sort of schedule that everyone respected. Everybody was polite all the time, sharing and helping and keeping their kids in line.

Not that many kids, either—apparently every person only got one "tallied" to him or her, and then the mother's brother was responsible for raising the kids, who lived in their mothers' lahks. Crazy. Even crazier was that people didn't seem to mind that much government control over their personal affairs. Nobody in Tennessee would have stood for it, not for a minute.

"They're polite now," Owen had said. "There's no vaccine to fight over yet."

Well, that made sense, sort of. Maybe when the spore cloud got closer and if there wasn't enough vaccine to go around—

"There won't be enough," Owen had said. "It's six weeks off. When this place pops, we take out anybody rushing the compound. They will. There are males of fighting age there, plenty of them, and they'll get desperate."

The unit had all nodded, but something about the way Owen had said it bothered Leo. Under that Ranger calm was a kind of what— eagerness to start shooting? Well, nothing wrong with that—Rangers always found battle more exciting than waiting, they were trained for active missions. Still—

The rain started—you could set your watch by it—and the old people covered their cook fires and went into their tents. Leo spoke to Zoe, on watch duty on the compound roof, over the private radio frequency they had set up. "Zo—what are the refugee tents made of?"

"How the fuck should I know?"

"Well, they don't make plastics. Not good for the environment. So it must be something else, maybe cloth treated with some pine resin or something. See anything from up there?"

"If I did, don't you think I'd of already told you?"

This was inarguable. Leo said, "I'm going in now."

"Roger that."

His breath quickened; this was the only part of patrol that wasn't exquisitely boring. He nodded to Kandiss, on duty at the compound entrance. At any given time, three of the four of them were on duty and one was asleep. Owen always took night duty. Leo walked inside to begin his check on the interior rooms.

Rough walls had been erected in the Big Lab, which before must have been just one open room—how the hell did any kids learn anything? Well, they must have. The place swarmed with Kindred scientists. Branch Carter was explaining something to a bunch of them, but the translator was Noah Jenner, not Isabelle. There were machines and objects Leo didn't understand, but everything looked okay. Mostly he was ignored, but Dr. Patel gave him a quick smile. Dr. Bourgiba did not.

He took the covered walkway from the Big Lab to the clinic. No sick people in it now, unless you counted Marianne Jenner, who wasn't exactly sick but wasn't well, either. She spent a lot of time sitting up in bed, helping other scientists understand stuff on her computer. The rest of the time she was doing experiments with leelees.

As soon as Leo opened the door that connected the clinic part of the compound to the covered walkway, the leelee smell made his nose wrinkle. Inside the leelee lab, it was far worse. The small space was crowded with stacked cages, benches with equipment, and a big locked metal cabinet like the weapons lockers in the squad's ready room. The vaccines, Leo knew, were kept in there.

Two Kindred kids were supposed to keep the cages clean, Isabelle's nephew Austin and a fat kid called Graylock who spoke pretty good English, but either they weren't doing their jobs well or else leelees smelled like that even in clean cages. Not putrid or anything—nothing near as bad as the camps in Brazil—but sort of sour, like milk going bad. And the weird little animals chittered all the time, like insects. Dr. Jenner had told Leo that the leelees were a lot like mice, but Leo couldn't see it. Smaller than mice, the creatures were furless, short-tailed, with round purplish bodies. Part of their energy came from photosynthesis, part from eating.

"They look like skittery plums," Leo had said.

Dr. Jenner had smiled. "I meant their genomes. They're the closest mammals here to human genomic structure."

That was beyond Leo's pay grade, so he'd just nodded and filed the information away. Maybe it would give him something to talk to Isabelle about.

She stood on what was left of the floor space between Dr. Jenner and two Kindred scientists. Automatically Leo scanned the men for weapons (where? They just wore those brief pale-colored dresses) and the room for dangers, but everything looked clean. Dr. Jenner was showing the men how to do something to a leelee, and Isabelle was translating. Leo's heart skipped a beat.

She wasn't beautiful, exactly, not like Zoe and little Dr. Patel were beautiful, but everything about her appealed to him. Leo knew he was good-looking—enough girls had told him so—and usually he was good with women, talking easily to them and flirting and, if he wanted to, getting them into bed. Isabelle was different. He felt tongue-tied around her, maybe because she was older than he was, and she treated him like . . . what? A friend. Not a friend like Zoe, who understood Leo's world because it was her world as well, but like the friend-of-a-friend whom you might respect but thought you had zero in common with. Like that.

Dr. Jenner said to Leo, "Everything's good here, Ranger."

He didn't correct her. Her attention had moved back to the leelee, and anyway nobody on Kindred cared about the distinction between the Seventy-Fifth and the US Army. To the Kindred, the squad were all Rangers.

Leo checked the rest of the clinic, the locks on the two outer doors, one in the kitchen and one in what had been the lobby and was now filled with lab benches. He was halfway along the walkway to the Big Lab when a woman screamed.

Three seconds to reach the Big Lab. A Kindred stood there with his arm around the neck of Branch Carter. In the Kindred's hand was what Leo recognized instantly as a homemade pipe gun, pointed at Branch. The Kindred was shouting something in his own language, and people poured from the surrounding makeshift labs and sleeping cubicles to stand, hands pressed to their mouths and wide eyes wider, at the edges of the room.

All at once they looked alien to Leo: long spindly insect arms and legs, big dark reptilian eyes. All of them, not just the intruder holding the skinny human a foot shorter than he was.

The intruder could fire the weapon. The gun could—probably would—blow up, wounding or killing both him and Carter. Leo could drop him—his sidearm was already in his hand—but the impact might set off the homemade gun. . . . homemade? The thing looked pretty finished.

His thoughts were almost simultaneous. Adrenaline coursed through him. The Kindred was still shouting. Now Leo caught the one Terran word, hard to decipher in that accent: *vaccine*. The fucker wanted some of the precious vaccine. What did he think, that he could just waltz in here, be given a syringe, and stroll out?

Leo heard his own voice saying calmly, "Give him something he can think is vaccine."

No one moved. No one understood his English. Then Dr. Patel stepped forward, something in her hand. Behind him he heard another voice, speaking Kindred loudly: Isabelle.

Claire Patel walked up to the Kindred and held out her hand. A syringe lay on her palm. The intruder, holding the gun and Carter, had no hands left to take it. Dr. Patel smiled; only the throbbing of her temples gave away her fear—and approached the intruder. No one else, maybe, could have done it; Dr. Patel, weighing maybe ninety pounds, looked as threatening as a child. She put the syringe into a pocket of the intruder's wrap.

Isabelle continued to talk in Kindred. Leo would have given anything to know what she was saying. Leo would have to make a decision soon; the fucker was backing away, toward the door, his arm tightening around Carter's neck. No way Leo could let them get out of here.

The man shouted something back at Isabelle and kept moving.

Leo said, "Isabelle, tell everyone to get behind doors. *Now.*"

She did. A small part of Leo's mind was astonished at how quickly and completely lab personnel followed directions. He'd seen platoons less disciplined.

Then—*yes*. Leo caught the movement before anyone else did. Carter—because he was choking or because he was being taken away, flailed in the intruder's grasp. For a fraction of a second, the intruder's body was exposed. Leo fired.

His bullet hit exactly where he intended: the left knee. The intruder screamed, let go of Carter, and fell to the floor. The gun did not explode; it skittered across the floor and came to rest against a closed door. Leo was on the intruder, and it was all over.

"How the fuck did this happen?" Owen demanded.

The unit stood at attention in front of him. The homemade pipe gun, disassembled, lay on a piece of cloth at his feet. He glanced at it in disgust, although it was clear the thing didn't merit disgust. Made from two pieces of steel pipe, with a wooden dowel and nail making up the firing pin, the gun resembled the Philippine guerilla gun, utilizing blow forward action. Leo had seen such guns in Brazil. But this was a much sleeker version; the pipes had been sanded so that the barrel slid perfectly inside the receiver. The stock had a wooden block in front of the end cap so that if the receiver end threads failed, the end cap would not be blown into the user's face. The stock was smooth, with some sort of material acting as grip.

The problem with all these pipe guns was that you got only one shot—after firing, the barrel had to be removed and the spent shell pulled out by hand. That hadn't seemed to deter the attacker, who was now being treated by Dr. Bourgiba and questioned by Noah Jenner.

"Brodie," Owen said, "where were you?"

"On interior patrol, sir. In the walkway between buildings." Owen already knew this. "Permission to speak, sir."

"Go ahead."

"There aren't enough of us, sir. We can't cover everything. And if one Kindred could make this weapon, then a lot of them can."

"Do you think I don't know that, Brodie? Is that what you think?"

"No, sir."

"I'm glad you don't think that. Because I know this will happen again. I know there aren't enough of us to secure this facility adequately. I also know this should not have been allowed to happen. Berman, why didn't you observe the Kinnie from the roof?"

Kinnie. Leo hadn't heard the word before. They way Owen said it, it sounded ugly. Brassie. Towelhead. Gook. Jap. Chink.

Zoe said, "No answer, sir, except that he might coulda crossed the perimeter to the south, while I was watching what looked like suspicious movement in the east outer edge of the camp, sir. Kandiss went to check it out."

"What kind of suspicious movement?"

"Males of fighting age moving in, like . . . coulda been drills."

"Armed?"

"Not that I could see."

A diversion? If some group in the camp was that organized, the squad was in trouble. Three soldiers awake at one time . . . not enough.

"Kandiss, where were you? Did you see this 'drilling'?"

"No, sir."

Zoe said, "Sir, they'd stopped by the time Kandiss reached that section of the perimeter."

"And you—any of you—have never seen any more of these

weapons, or anything resembling them? Or anything else that can be construed as a weapon? Molotovs, IEDs, anything?"

Three no-sirs.

Brodie said, "Permission to speak, sir."

"Go ahead."

"We need more eyes, sir, as you said. We should start training Kindred to supplement patrols."

Something moved behind Owen's eyes. "Because that worked out so well in Brazil, right, Corporal Brodie? At, for instance, Brasília?"

Leo was silent. He hadn't been at Brasília, but he knew all about it, as did everyone in the entire world. Fourteen US-trained and armed insurgents had—all fourteen of them—been infiltrators. They had slaughtered fifteen Marines who had trained and trusted them, and then an entire village of women and children.

Owen said, "We aren't arming Kinnies any more than they're doing themselves. Christ, all that propaganda about how these are genetically and socially peaceful people . . ."

Leo blinked. "Genetically and socially peaceful"? Not the sort of language that found its way into any debriefing he'd ever been in. Well, Owen was smart and college-educated.

And the Kindred, whatever they were genetically and socially, were human. Humans got desperate.

Owen said, "From now on, standing orders are twenty-hour duty shifts. Roof watcher reports anything suspicious directly and immediately to me. No more fuck-ups. Another Kinnie gets inside, and the fuck-up is facing court-martial when we get back home. Got it?"

"Yes, sir!"

Back home? Did Owen still think that was happening? How?

"Dismissed," Owen said.

Leo bent to once again examine the parts of the pipe gun. There could be a whole factory making these somewhere—except, wouldn't the Mothers object? And what had the Kinnie been shouting before Leo dropped him? Maybe Leo better start learning the language.

He'd picked up a fair amount of Portuguese on duty in Brazil. He didn't have the kind of language ability that Dr. Bourgiba did, and opportunity to study was limited because they were going to stand twenty-hour duty shifts, but you could learn a lot just keeping your eyes and ears open. And—wait!

Maybe he could ask Isabelle to teach him. Half an hour, fifteen minutes carved from his sleep time . . . yes.

Two hours later, a dirigible floated toward the camp. Kandiss, on roof watch, used the squad frequency to detail its landing a mile away from the lab. Then he said, "Okay, a . . . a procession coming toward us."

Owen's voice, sharp on the radio frequency: "What kind of procession?"

"It looks like . . . four men carrying a platform on poles. Canopy, open sides . . . woman lying inside."

"A body? Dead?"

"No, sir. Really old. Not headed here, swerved toward Noah Jenner's house on the hill."

Where the Terran lahk lives, Leo thought, and then corrected himself: *lived.* Nobody was left in the beautiful karthwood house except Isabelle's sister and her kid, Austin. Jenner and Isabelle had moved into the compound; the McGuire brothers had returned to their "manufactures" in the central mountains; nobody seemed to know where the other two males, Schrupp and Beyon, lived now. Or, if they did know, they hadn't told Leo. Well, that had been typical of most of the foster families Leo had grown up in: people moved away, leaving no forwarding address. No biggie.

But the big house up the hill from the compound wasn't Noah Jenner's house, it was the lahk's, and Isabelle headed the Terran lahk. Hadn't Kandiss learned anything about how this place worked?

Leo also knew, even if Kandiss did not, who the very old lady was. The Mother of Mothers had arrived.

"What will you do with him?" Salah asked. He'd removed Leo Brodie's bullet from the attacker, and cleaned and dressed the wound.

"He'll get a trial," Isabelle said. "Or rather, he would have gotten a trial if there had been time. He might still get one. But with the cloud coming . . ."

"I'm surprised all the civic and business machinery has functioned this smoothly this long."

Isabelle took a sip of her wine. "Oh, I don't know, Salah—if, say, an asteroid were going to hit Earth and wipe out everybody in three weeks' time, do you think most people would riot and loot and go in for orgies, or would they just go on living their normal lives?"

"Some of each, I think. But you're right—here there is more of the latter and less of the former than on Terra."

They sat on karthwood chairs in the courtyard of the clinic, watching the stars come out. Inside, the rooms swarmed with scientific activity, but there was at the moment nothing for Isabelle to translate or Salah to doctor. The refugee camp, that amazingly orderly group of people not going on with their normal lives, preferred their own doctors. Salah and Isabelle held glasses of fruity wine. It was too sweet for Salah's taste, but that and a thin sour beer were the only alcoholic beverages permitted on Kindred.

"Permitted." Kindred had totalitarian control without totalitarian force, a combination that endlessly intrigued him. So did Isabelle Rhinehart, but he wasn't ready to admit that yet, not even to himself.

"You lost your three main cities. Yet government and business and everything else are carrying on."

"We lost so many." Grief in the drawn lines of her face, the droop of her body. "But World is pretty decentralized. Manufactures are all located away from cities. People are making do, around their mourning."

"I'm sure decentralization helps. Still, it's remarkable that Kindred society exists at all. In fact, it shouldn't. It's such a delicate balance between local rule and overarching beliefs."

"I guess so."

"I think a society's ideas about what it means to be human shape its institutions, and then those institutions shape individuals, because they must adapt to the system. But you can only stretch biology so far. Hierarchies—pecking orders—are built into human DNA. On Kindred, the possibility for fragmentation must be a constant threat."

"Not really," Isabelle said. "Bu^ka^tel."

She had tried to explain the word before, and hadn't really succeeded. Isabelle, though very intelligent, was not an intellectual. But as far as Salah could grasp, bu^ka^tel—the three syllables had rising inflections that he could never quite duplicate correctly—was the basic ethical and organizational principle on Kindred. It somehow combined law, rank, sharing, and maternal responsibility in a rich mixture impossible for the American mind to sort out. Rank neither trumped law nor was law; Kindred was not an oligarchy. The rule of Mothers carried both heavy expectations and the expectation of obedience from everyone else. Only, however, within the limits of sharing, which limits were somehow bound up with maternalism. Even women who didn't birth children were "mothers" because children belonged to the society as a whole, except when their allegiance belonged to their lahk, or something like that. Maybe. What was clear was that everyone, mothers and men and lahks, belonged first to World, as stewards of its ecology. All of that checked runaway consumption, even though the economic structure made room for capitalism as well as socialism. There was no government welfare, since a lahk was deeply responsible for everyone born into it.

But there were still elements of bu^ka^tel that Salah felt eluded him completely.

He returned to the more concrete subject of the intruder. "A trial of his peers?"

"No. Of mothers in the local jurisdiction. Only mothers can serve as judges, because mothers have the greatest investment in the future."

"On Earth," Salah said, "there are countries—small ones—that only permit men who have served in the military to vote because they have earned it by risking their lives."

"We don't have a military. Kindred chose to build institutions around life, not death."

"Not really fair, Isabelle. Too easy."

"I know." She frowned; her profile in the faint light looked classical. "When I first got here, I was so confused by everything. It just seemed wrong to deliberately choose not to make all the tech they could, to not let everyone have as many children as they wanted, to be so . . . *controlling*. Fascist. And then there was a period when I decided World was a utopia. It's not, you know—don't make the mistake of thinking that. We have crime, legal disputes, income inequality, all that shit. But no real poverty because working wages are controlled and families are obligated to take care of shiftless Uncle No^kal^te and idiot cousin Ko—and they do. No unhappy marriages because spouses stay with their own lahks as much as they choose, and marriage contracts are time-limited. No starvation because the continent grows food almost faster than it can be harvested. So now . . ."

"Now?" he prompted.

"I love it here." She said it so simply, and with such pain, that Salah fell silent. More stars appeared, strange stars in strange configurations. Lights shone from the rooms around the courtyard, their yellow electric circles not reaching Salah and Isabelle.

She said, "The prisons aren't terrible but they aren't luxurious, either. No basketball courts or college courses or any of that crap.

They're places of punishment for hurting the social group. But sentences are short and recidivism is fairly low."

"Is there capital punishment?"

"Yes. Take a life, lose yours."

He tested her. "What is the recidivism rate?"

"Three point eight percent."

He was sure then. Something in her voice had alerted him, and her precision about the number made him sure. "You've been in prison."

She turned to look at him. He could just make out her smile. "You're perceptive. Yes, on Terra. I was a scrappy kid. Juvenile offender, for grand theft auto. Plus a few other things, later. Then I wanted to get a job and go straight, and nobody would hire me. When Noah said anyone with the L-31 mitochondria could leave Earth, I volunteered. Kayla and Austin—he was three then—came with me because. . . . well, because."

Salah could guess at the reasons. Isabelle was the strong one, the "scrappy" one. Kayla, with no skills and mother of a toddler, depended on her sister. Kayla had gone uneasily to World, and now blamed Isabelle for it every minute of every day.

He said, "But you were bright. You did well in school. Your speech patterns, your breadth of knowledge—"

"That's enough about me," Isabelle said, with more than a touch of belligerence. "What's your story? Why did you volunteer for this mission?"

Salah drained his wine. How much of his face could she see in the dim light? But she had been honest, so he was, too. "I don't know."

"You don't know why you volunteered to leave your planet and go to God-knows-what? You don't know?"

"I'm not sure I know why I've done anything in my life." Except Aisha, but he was not going to tell her that stupid story.

A figure passed above them on the roof, a Ranger on patrol. From its bulk, Mason Kandiss.

Isabelle said, "I tried to volunteer for the Army. They wouldn't take me."

"Why not?"

"Heart murmur."

Instantly he was again a physician. "What are the details? Did you get a prognosis?"

She chuckled, a low sound that, to his surprise, went straight to his groin. "Easy, Doctor. It's nothing fatal. But the Army didn't want me."

But I do. Salah suddenly felt wary: of her, of himself. He stood. "I think I'll make one more tour of the labs. Check on Marianne, and make sure nobody has caught some weird Kindred disease."

"We call it 'World,' you know. Not 'Kindred.'"

"I know."

He made his way from the courtyard into Big Lab, which hummed with urgent, organized activity. Claire gave him a tired smile. Marianne Jenner was asleep, looking wan. Two more heroic women. This place abounded with them. Of course, there was also Kayla.

"World," not "Kindred." He would have to remember. In the walkway from the clinic to the Big Lab, he passed two World scientists, tall coppery men with big dark eyes, chattering to each other. Each said, "I greet you, Salah-mak."

"I greet you, Beelaɟ. I greet you, Kal^cho." He wished they would not address him by the honorific for a superior. He was a stranger here.

I love it here, Isabelle had said.

He was a stranger who probably would have to stay forever on World. Or what was left of it, after.

CHAPTER 9

There had been no time to build a biosafety level 4 lab. No time, no materials, no expertise at the level required. The imitation of Terran facilities, where Kindred had been carrying on its fruitless search for a vaccine, had been destroyed in the Russian attack, along with its researchers. Marianne, Claire, and Branch improvised.

"Put in the mice," she said to Branch Carter. The young tech acted as if he hadn't been seized by a homegrown terrorist and nearly killed. After the first shock of discovering the time jump, Branch had seemed to adopt a stance of energetic we-must-carry-on. Well, they were all carrying on. Branch's ability with hardware was turning out to be indispensable. As equipment, solicited and bargained for by Noah and Isabelle, arrived from clinics around southern Kindred, Branch modified it to create what they needed. He cannibalized some items to create something else. He jerry-rigged and connected and improvised, a human version of duct tape.

Branch said, "Dr. Jenner"—she'd given up on getting him to call her Marianne—"they're not mice."

Of course they weren't. They were leelees, rounder and smellier and purple. But Marianne had spent years working with mice; old tapes die hard.

Branch brought three of the animals to one of the two glass cages on the bench. Airtight, each cage had been rigged with a negative-pressure system and three redundant air filters, the best available on Kindred, with specs that should stop R. sporii. One advantage: R. sporii was large for a virus. But if the filters didn't stop the spores, if they got loose from the lab, Marianne might kill a lot of people before the cloud did. But there was no choice; to test the synthesized vaccine, you needed to first determine that something was susceptible to the disease, then vaccinate that something, and then expose it. Leelees were the something they had that was closest to the human genome.

Spores for the experiment had come from Claire's suitcase. She'd admitted freely to the vaccines, which used inactivated pathogens. She had not, however, admitted to the sealed packet of live spores also in the suitcase. Only a handful of people knew that the means to bring on a spore cloud early resided in the locked metal cabinet in a corner of the leelee lab: the compound researchers, Terran and Kindred; Isabelle; Noah; the Mother of Mothers. Marianne did not want to start a panic. Branch, who seemed immune to the leelee smell, slept in the lab, guarding the cabinet and the experiments.

What had Claire been thinking, to bring live spores down in the shuttle? Had she suspected that there was as yet no vaccine on Kindred? Marianne had asked her.

"Yes," Claire had said in her musical accent. "It always struck me as suspicious that the Kindred traveled all the way to Earth for help in developing a vaccine. I mean, when they were advanced enough to build a spaceship." She'd looked Marianne straight in the eye as she said it. Marianne had not replied; Claire was not the person she needed to have that conversation with.

Soon.

The leelees, one held in each of Branch's hands by their short tails, chittered. He dropped them into the negative-pressure cage. Claire Patel and the two senior Kindred scientists, Llaa^moh¡ and Ka^graa, watched, all of them taut as guitar strings. Ka^graa's mouth twisted in a grimace. Branch turned on the filtration systems and negative-pressure blower, and pressed the lever that released live spores into the cage.

The leelees scampered and chittered.

The spores took about twenty minutes to shed their dormancy and begin to propagate—or, at least, they had taken twenty minutes on Earth. Incubation period for the disease was three days in mice. Who knew what it was in leelees? Eventually, the leelees would be either dead or still scampering. If dead, Marianne had her test animals. If not, they would have to move on to another animal. If they ran out of either species or time, the synthetic vaccine would have to be administered to humans with no testing.

The problem with that protocol, of course, was that the vaccine would've been synthesized using available processes, grown on available cultures, guessed at with inadequate facilities. The synthesized vaccine would not be the exact duplicate of the Terran version, and the Kindred bodies were not the exact duplicates of Terran bodies, so who knew how well—or if at all—the synthesized version would protect?

She watched the purplish animals sniff the glass walls of the cage, climb over the pieces of karthwood that Branch had put in. At least behind glass, they could be neither smelled nor heard.

Branch said, pointlessly, "Now we wait." Ka^graa nodded. He and Llaa^moh¡ were picking up English quickly, but it scarcely mattered. Everybody knew they had to wait.

Marianne, weary, went to her own bed. Unlike everyone else, she had a room to herself, in what had been a closet. In both the clinic and Big Lab, bunks were jammed wherever possible. No one wanted to be away from the work, and Lieutenant Lamont had insisted on as much containment as possible. Only Isabelle, Noah, and Llaa^moh¡ went back and forth to the karthwood lahk house on the hill. Kayla and Lily were there, too, under the care of a sister of Llaa^moh¡.

On the wall of Marianne's closet were photos of her two children and two grandsons on Terra. She had tried to reconcile herself to never seeing them again. This had not worked. As she lay on her pallet, looking up the photos, she dashed away tears. *Stupid.* If she was here, she lost Elizabeth, Ryan, Jason, and Colin. If she was with them, she lost Noah and Lily. That was just the way it was. She stood up, carefully stripped the photos from the wall, and put them on a shelf under the supply of wraps that Isabelle had given her.

She was deeply asleep when loud knocking on the wall woke her. "Come in!"

Branch stood silhouetted in the light from the room beyond. "Dr. Jenner, you said you wanted to know when the leelees died."

Marianne looked at her watch. "The incubation period is *two hours?*"

"Yes. I witnessed the deaths and made notes. It was respiratory. I sealed the cages."

"Good." The notes were important; they could not remove the mice for autopsy without releasing spores into the air. But now they knew: the leelees were susceptible to *R. sporii.*

She said, "Just let me get dressed and I'll be right there. Claire?"

"She's there. The whole team is. And Dr. Jenner—"

"What?"

"Your son is here. Noah. He wants to see you right away."

Alarm coursed through her. "Why? What's wrong?"

"I don't know. But he says the Mother of Mothers is up at the big house and wants to see you right away."

"Fuck, no," Owen said. "I can't spare anyone to escort her. She ought to realize that."

Leo said carefully, "She didn't ask for an escort, sir."

He had stopped Dr. Jenner and Noah as they left the compound by the clinic door. Leo, on door duty, had told them to halt. All the while he was asking their intentions, he'd watched the refugee camp a hundred yards away, where cook fires burned and people moved around, green in his night-vision goggles. His orders were to not permit anyone in, anyone out after nightfall. The problem was that Owen didn't have the authority to give that order. Leo's choices: violate an order, force civilians against their will (it was clear that the Jenners had wills of their own), or ask the CO for clarification and look like a wuss. He'd called Owen, who was asleep.

"Brodie, hold them there. On my way."

Leo said to Dr. Jenner, "Ma'am, can you tell me the reason you want to leave the safety of the compound?"

Noah said, "Don't tell him anything, Mom. Ranger, you can't hold us here."

"I'm only asking your destination and intentions."

"Neither is your business."

"*Noah*," Dr. Jenner said. "Ranger, we're going up to the lahk to see the Mother of Mothers."

The old lady that Kandiss said had arrived this afternoon. "It's not a good time for a social visit, ma'am."

"It isn't social," Noah snapped. "Step aside, please."

Owen strode up to them. "Dr. Jenner, I'm sorry but you can't leave here."

Noah said, "The hell I can't!"

"*You* can, Mr. Jenner. You do, often. But Dr. Jenner is vital to creating vaccines, and my charge is to protect that mission. My unit cannot spare the troops to protect her away from the compound."

Before Noah could speak again, Dr. Jenner jumped in. "Why don't you get more soldiers by training some of the Kindred?"

Christ, for an old lady who looked exhausted, she was feisty! Her hand rested on Noah's arm, keeping him from saying anything else. Leo, face impassive, waited. Leo already knew the answer—Owen didn't trust the Kindred because any one of them could be an infiltrator—but he wanted to know what Owen would say.

"Because I choose not to, ma'am. Now will you return inside or will Corporal Brodie have to carry you in?"

Noah stepped forward. What the fuck—Jenner wore one of those girlish dresses like they all did; he was unarmed; he was tall but skinny and not very muscled. Owen was a *Ranger* in full kit: armor, helmet, rifle, sidearm. What did Jenner think he could do?

"Noah, no," his mother said. "I'm going back inside. We can resolve this in the morning."

"Mom—"

"No."

Leo almost felt sorry for the guy—ordered around like a ten-year-old by his mother. But Jenner didn't look humiliated, just angry, and not at Dr. Jenner. She had pointedly turned and headed back inside. Noah strode off into the night.

"Back on duty, Brodie."

"Yes, sir."

Five minutes later Leo toggled his radio to the private frequency he shared with Zoe, on roof duty and undoubtedly observing the whole thing. She said, "Jesus, Leo."

"Yeah. And you didn't even see Lamont. Something's eating him, Zo." Leo thought. "I mean, more than everything eating everybody."

"Yeah. I noticed."

"See anything strange from up there?"

"Nope."

"Good."

An hour later, her voice sounded on his wrister, this time on the squad frequency. "Alert. Code two. Near perimeter breached, seven o'clock."

He raced around the compound to the site. A litter was entering the perimeter from the direction of the house on the hill, carried by four strong fighting-age males. On it, sitting against a pile of pillows, was an old woman. Christ—the pillows could conceal more pipe guns, explosives, anything. Leo unslung his rifle and released the charging handle; it made an audible clack. "Go back. Now," he said, in Kindese. Behind him, he knew, Zoe crouched at the edge of the roof, weapons at the ready. Owen had gone back to the ready room to snatch a few hours' sleep; Kandiss was on patrol.

One of the litter bearers, scowling, jabbered at Leo in Kindred, too fast for him to catch any words.

"Go back," he said, not gesturing, not taking his hands off his rifle or his eyes off the group. At the edge of the camp, figures paused, grouped, started forward. More men, a few women. Nobody armed, as far as he could tell, but you never knew.

Movement behind him. At the same moment Zoe said, "Isabelle Rhinehart. Not armed."

She ran from the compound to Leo. "Don't shoot!"

"Tell them to go back to your lahk, or else inside the camp. Now."

Isabelle called to the litter bearers, saying Christ knew what. Leo felt his adrenaline pumping. If the men laid down the litter or the old lady reached under the pillows . . .

Isabelle said, "They're not leaving. But I told the men to not let go of the litter with even one hand."

God, she was quick! "Tell the old lady to keep her hands where I can see them. While they go back."

"They're not going back, Corporal. That's the Mother of Mothers."

And what kind of stupid name was that for a president or dictator or whatever the hell she was? It sounded like a nursery-school teacher. But Isabelle talked some more, and the old lady raised her hands. Then she squinched her behind along the litter to the edge, painful slow movements. The men lowered the litter to within a few inches of the ground, scowling at Leo.

Isabelle said, "I'm going to help her. I'll stay out of your line of fire. Okay?"

He hesitated. Orders were nobody in, nobody out. "She can't come in."

"I vouch for her. Leo, you can't shoot a hundred-and-two-year-old mother. Or me."

A hundred and two? But those weren't Earth years. Still, she looked a hundred and two. When she tried to slip off the edge of the litter, she staggered and fell. One of the bearers let go of his pole with one hand and reached it toward her. Then he glanced at Leo and put his hand back on the karthwood.

Isabelle ran forward and helped the ancient woman to her feet.

Leo said quickly, "Don't shoot, Zoe."

"Jesus, Leo!"

"On my responsibility."

She held her fire. Kandiss came toward them at a dead run, side-arm drawn.

Isabelle and the Mother of Mothers tottered across the perimeter. And Leo let them because Isabelle was right: He couldn't shoot her and a hundred-and-two tottering old bird, even if he was court-martialed for disobeying orders. If he shot, Terrans would never again be trusted on Kindred. Also, there were hundreds of people in that camp; even unarmed, their sheer numbers could overwhelm the squad and then what would they do to the other Terrans inside, to the whole vaccine program? The Ranger creed said *I will complete this mission, though I be the lone survivor.* Well, this was the way to complete it: by disobeying Owen's order.

And Leo wasn't a Ranger, anyway.

It took a long time for Isabelle to get the old lady across the hundred yards of cleared perimeter and into the lab door. By that time, people from inside the compound crowded the doorway, but nobody challenged Leo's order to stay inside. The door closed. Kandiss said, "Returning to outer perimeter, unless . . ."

"Stay here for now," Leo said. "I'll wake Lamont." What was he doing deciding this? Kandiss outranked him! One lousy alien planet and the command structure fell apart? Not if Owen had anything to say about it.

Kandiss said only, "Camp is quiet."

"Great," Leo said. He could feel the adrenaline still coursing. It had nowhere to go. The feeling was sour, like too much bad beer you couldn't vomit up. He knew that Zoe and Kandiss felt it, too. Rangers were trained for action. Inaction was hard.

He called Lieutenant Lamont.

Salah didn't know that anything was going on outside until it was all over.

He'd been reading on his bunk, one of three stacked in the ex-storage room he shared with biologist Ha^jakᵢ and Branch Carter, although Branch now slept in the leelee lab. Salah had about fifty books on his tablet, which was good because he wasn't ever going to get any more. Marianne might have some on her laptop, but file transfer was beyond Kindred. Still, as long as the tablet held out, Salah could reread *War and Peace* or medical journals now decades out of date, or the poetry of al-Mutanabbi.

Austin Rhinehart flung open the door without knocking. "Doctor! Isabelle wants you! Ranger Brodie almost shot the Mother of Mothers!"

Salah stared at Austin, flushed with excitement. What the boy said made no sense. When he didn't answer right away, Austin turned sulky, deflated at the lack of response.

"It's true. And Isabelle wants you." He vanished.

Salah caught up with him in the middle of the milling, gesturing crowd filling the central area of Big Lab. He caught phrases in Kindred:

". . . did not know the . . ."

". . . should not be permitted . . ."

"Mother of Mothers . . ."

". . . attack . . ."

"Austin," he said, grabbing him by the shoulder, "What happened? And where is Isabelle?"

"The Rangers almost shot the Mother of Mothers because she crossed the perimeter and Isabelle stopped them and she's with Dr. Jenner. Hey, Graa^lok!" He plunged across the room toward his friend.

Salah pushed his way through the crowd to the clinic and Marianne's room. The tiny space was jammed with people: Marianne, Claire, Isabelle, Ha^jakį, Ka^graa, Llaa^mohį. At least there were no Rangers present. Propped up on pillows on Marianne's bed, puffing with exertion, sat a wizened woman with fantastically lined copper skin. There were cloudy white circles at the edge of her filmy dark irises. Her bare feet extended straight in front of her, the toes dusky blue and the legs swollen.

Cyanosis, edema, arcus senilis, cataracts. Probable congestive heart failure. This lady was very sick.

Isabelle made a curious gesture that Salah hadn't seen before: a small circle with two fingers in front of her forehead. Some sort of salute, maybe. She said in English, "This is the Mother of Mothers. You address her as Ree^ka-mak. She wants to speak to you in World."

Salah said, "I greet you, Ree^ka-mak."

"I greet you, Salah-mak." Her voice was low but clear, without the quaver of her dying body. The filmy eyes had followed the sound of his voice. How much could she see through the cataracts?

She said, "You come from Terra, the long-ago place."

"Yes." Beside him, Isabelle translated in a low murmur for Marianne and Claire. Salah hoped his Kindese was up to this. Tenses in this difficult language were very complicated. In addition to past, present, and future, different inflections indicated different states of being for each: absolute, tentative, in flux, rotational. There were also degrees of rank carried by different wording. He could not afford miscommunication here.

Ree^ka said, "You bring vaccines to prevent deaths from the spore cloud." Tentative state of being. He matched it.

"We bring some vaccines and we try to make more."

"So Marianne-mak says. She says you have enough already for fifty of my people."

"Yes."

"How will you decide who will receive these fifty gifts of life?" Future tense, in flux.

There had been conferences about vaccine allotment among himself, Marianne, and Claire. There actually remained fifty-two vaccine syringes; two had been reserved for Noah's wife and child. Salah knew that in giving way to Marianne on this he had subverted what he was going to say next before he'd even said it, but it had not been possible to deny Marianne. Or Noah. Salah said, "That is for the people of World to decide."

Ree^ka-mak said, "You are not saying everything."

How did she know? For a nanosecond, bizarre thoughts swept through Salah's mind: telepathy, primitive magic. But of course it was not that. Either the Mother of Mothers had a highly developed ability to hear the nuances in voices, which sometimes happened with the blind, or else she was on a fishing expedition. Salah repeated, "That will be for the people of World to decide."

"There are many people outside this lahk who wish that vaccine."

"Yes."

"You have brought soldiers with weapons to keep them out."

How to explain the Ranger unit that had somehow morphed from an honor guard into a self-appointed and dangerous entity with its own ideas of what should happen here? Salah knew a refugee camp could be dangerous; he'd spent two years in the Mideast with Doctors Without Borders. The Rangers protected the compound, for which Salah was grateful, but he didn't trust Lamont and his three war machines. "The soldiers keep them out, yes."

"Until they do not."

"I cannot say what will happen, Ree^ka-mak. Perhaps it helps if the Mother of Mothers speaks to the camp."

"I have spoken."

When? Then Isabelle murmured to him in English, "Through the radio and through the lahk mothers."

He said to her, "There was a radio broadcast? Were we told about this?"

"I only learned it myself ten minutes ago. We've been busy in the lab, Salah. But maybe one of us should monitor the radio."

"Yes." As he and Isabelle spoke, the Mother of Mothers watched—no, *listened*—sharply. Salah said to her, "I ask what Ree^ka-mak said to the camp."

"I told them they must be patient," she said, and the tense was one Salah had not heard before.

"What . . . may I ask what the camp replied?"

"It is not a single thing, this camp."

That he could well believe. Humans, even in a united cause, were individuals. Salah waited.

"Some in the camp said yes to patience," Ree^ka-mak said. "Some did not reply. Do you understand what that means, Salah-mak?"

"Yes," he said, because he did. He'd been here before, in far different cultures, but with the same situation.

When the Mother of Mothers spoke again, the tense was clear to him: future absolute. "Some will attack to get the vaccine."

As soon as Isabelle had translated, Branch pushed forward. Salah had not heard him come from the leelee lab. The young man blurted out in English, "Won't the others in the camp try to stop anybody trying to steal vaccine? There must be cops there! Are there cops there?"

Isabelle said, "Yes."

"Won't the cops stop the others from rushing us?"

"Translate, please," Ree^ka-mak said sharply.

Isabelle did. The Mother of Mothers, an old and dying woman, leaned back against her pillows and closed her eyes. It was Isabelle who answered Branch.

"Nobody knows, Branch. Nobody knows."

CHAPTER 10

Salah took every opportunity to talk to Isabelle. There weren't many, but he watched for them. He noticed that Leo Brodie was doing the same thing, exchanging a few words with her as he went on and came off duty. Once Salah found them in the tiny clinic kitchen at one of the few times it was not occupied by Kindred cooks making huge pots of vegetable stew. Brodie and Isabelle laughed as they brewed coffee, or what passed for coffee here. Salah could not drink it; evidently Brodie could. He was trying to speak Kindese and she was correcting his pronunciation, which was terrible. Still, Salah was surprised at how much Kindese Leo had picked up.

But he could discuss things with Isabelle as far beyond the scope of someone like Brodie as a planet beyond an empty moon. He out-waited Brodie. When he finally left the kitchen, Salah said to Isabelle, "I know you're on radio duty now, but another quick question about World culture? I want to know as much as I can."

"That's good. Leo does, too, and I think he's the only one of the squad who's really considered that they may be here for the rest of their lives."

Salah didn't want to talk about what Brodie did or did not con-sider. He said, "Two questions. First—did the Kindred ever really ex-pect us to come here? Or did they leave us the ship plans fully expecting that since we didn't have the ready-made parts they did, we would never be able to build any ships?"

Isabelle hesitated. Finally she said, "I've asked myself that. I don't know the answer, and I couldn't get any answer from anyone here."

"The Council of Mothers must have known that trade with Terra, free emigration from Terra, could disrupt Kindred's entire delicate culture."

"I don't know. I'm only a junior member of the Council, you know."

"But it—"

"Salah, I don't know."

Or else she didn't want to know. He dropped back to an easier question. "I never see any religious practices on Kindred. What is religion like here?"

"Lukewarm." Isabelle smiled. "Well, not uniformly. There are different groups here and there, and a few are still fervent about ancestor worship and a mother goddess, but mostly it's just leftover songs and customs."

"Probably goddess worship was what led to your matrilineal culture."

"Probably." She didn't seem much interested in this idea. "But bu^ka^tel is what matters. Salah—why do you dislike Lieutenant Lamont's Rangers so much?"

The question caught him off guard. "I'm a doctor. I dislike organizations devoted to death and maiming."

"Not fair."

He didn't care if it was fair or not. Jealousy kindled in him, a small destructive flame. "Why do you like the soldiers so much?"

She spoke slowly, considering. "They're not pampered. They've all seen action, risked death, killed people if they had to. I think all that makes you come to terms with what the world is. They don't blow small stuff into major catastrophes because they know what big stuff actually looks like. They don't whine. They just carry on."

Salah recognized in this description the antithesis of Isabelle's sister. He did not say this. "I think you may be romanticizing the army."

"Maybe. Maybe not."

"Back to religion, if I may. What is one of these leftover customs?"

"Well, illathil, but you probably already know about that."

"I don't."

She seemed surprised, and then amused. "Really? Nobody told you? Well, you'll see for yourself. It's only two days off."

Marianne sat on a big pillow embroidered with flowers and watched the alien celebration unfolding in the open central area of the Big Lab. She had wanted to use this time to try the newest iteration of the synthetic vaccination on the leelees, but Isabelle had gently explained that was impossible until illathil was over. "It's supposed to go on for two days, but because of the circumstances, we'll compress it to a few hours. But no one will do anything else until then."

"But what is it?" Marianne had asked. All the Kindred scientists had disappeared into their bunk rooms and reappeared wearing red wraps, as startling a change from their usual vegetable-dyed duns and pastels as if a zebra had suddenly sported turquoise stripes.

Isabelle smiled, half-upturned lips on her weary face. All of their faces looked weary: with work, with worry, with uncertainty. "Salah asked the same thing. And Leo Brodie. It's not easy to explain. It's part religious ceremony, part party, part dance. Once illathil was more religious and probably very solemn, but now it's about family, mostly. Like Christmas on Terra for people who don't even believe in God. It's about family bonds and—really important—the redistribution of wealth to keep things more equal. It doesn't matter where you are on World, you go to your lahk for illathil." She paused. "Only not this group, this year."

"Like Christmas? They give gifts?"

"Oh, much more than that. We—the music is starting! I have to go. I'll explain more later. Now I'll just say that after the dancing, everybody gives away one-fifth of everything they earned or made since the last illathil. It's called a 'thumb.' Bank accounts, stock holdings, real estate—whatever."

"One-fifth?" Marianne said, incredulous, but Isabelle was already gone. She had rushed into a corner, stepped into a bucket, and joined one of the circles forming to the weird, atonal music. Her feet were covered with red dye of some sort.

Each circle held ten people. They weaved in and out, making precise figures on the floor with the red dye on their soles. To Marianne's surprise, the Mother of Mothers was part of one circle, sitting propped up on pillows while the other nine Kindred danced around her. She thrust out one red-dyed foot, left a mark on Ka^graa's ankle, and laughed. Austin and Graa^lok were there, too, Austin looking as bored as Marianne's sons had looked at family parties when they were thirteen. Bored, but there. "We teach our children very intensively to follow our ways," Noah had told her.

Noah danced in a different circle from Llaa^moh¡. Well, Marianne supposed, it wouldn't do to give away one-fifth of your holdings to your own wife. One-fifth! Even Mormons tithed only a tenth. No wonder no one was poor and homeless on World.

"Pretty amazing, isn't it?" Salah said. He dropped to the floor beside her. Across the room, Claire stood clapping to the music. They were the only three not dancing. *We haven't got anything to give away,* Marianne thought. Except, of course, a possible vaccine to save the lives of the dancers. Maybe. With luck.

"Salah, will you help me with the leelees? I want to administer the next trial now."

"Yes." He rose and held out a hand to help her up, but Marianne noted how his eyes never left Isabelle, whirling and stamping in the closest circle. Oh—so that's how it was. Marianne waved at Claire, who followed them.

In the deserted clinic, Branch slept in the locked room with the leelees and the live spores in their secure cabinet. An excellent guard, he woke the instant that Claire's key turned in the lock. Rising from his pallet, his hair falling into his eyes, he looked even younger than he was. "Marianne?"

"We're going to do the next vaccine trial. No reason not to—we four aren't illathil-ing."

"I'll take notes," Salah said.

"Okay," Marianne said. "Branch, is the next neg-pressure cage ready? Then get three more leelees."

On roof duty, Leo radioed Zoe on patrol. "What's all that going on in the camp? Here the whole damn building is shaking."

"The fuck if I know," Zoe said. "They've all gone crazy. But it don't look like dangerous crazy."

He spotted her, green in his night-vision goggles, at five o'clock and coming toward him from the east edge of the camp. She maintained an easy jog, weapon at the ready but, as far as he could tell, the Kindred paid her no attention at all. They had bonfires going high and they were dancing around in circles.

"Who's playing the music?" Leo asked. He couldn't see any musicians.

"It's not live. It's on, like, some weird old-time machines. Not even electronic."

"Like a gramophone?"

"How should I know? Leo—all their feet are *red*."

Adrenaline surged. "Blood?"

"No, some kind of dye. Do you think it's, like, a preattack thing? I heard that some enemy in Brazil did that."

"They did, yeah." He'd seen it, and afterward looked it up on the Internet. The article had explained about Japanese kamikaze preattack rituals, too—surprisingly interesting. Sharing sake, wearing their swords and elaborate belts embroidered by their mothers, composing death poems or songs. The rituals in Brazil had been starker but, like the Kindred now, had involved body paint.

But in Brazil, Leo's unit had received briefings whenever there was any kind of local festival, so they'd know what to expect. Had Owen received a briefing on this? Although—who would Owen receive a briefing from? It wasn't like they had a PR liaison attached to the squad. And given Owen's feelings about World, plus how busy all the native scientists were, maybe nobody had thought to tell Owen anything about this festival. If it was a festival.

Leo considered. Owen was inside the compound, doing the hourly check of every room. He'd be outside in a few minutes and would see the dancing for himself. But if the same thing was going on inside, it probably wasn't a preattack ritual, not unless all the scientists were in on an assault, which didn't seem likely. Let Owen make the call.

Evidently Owen decided that dancing didn't lead to attacking, because the squad's orders didn't change. Yet.

One of the World scientists should be in the leelee lab, Marianne thought, in case the synthesized vaccine actually worked this time. Or else she should wait until illathil was over. Isabelle had said it would only last a few hours and, contrary to custom, that nobody inside the compound would drink anything alcoholic. But Marianne didn't want to wait. They had only a little over a month until the spore cloud hit. Pretty soon Salah would need to administer the fifty-two doses of original vaccine to whoever was going to get them.

Branch carried three of the foul-smelling leelees by their three-inch tails. Two days ago they had been vaccinated with the latest attempt at synth-vac. The animals chittered and squirmed, looking like animated purple ping-pong balls. He dropped them into the cage. He released the spores. The negative-pressure machine hummed softly.

Ten minutes until the spores released. Then a few hours until the leelees died. She wasn't holding out much hope—they'd had so many trials already.

"Branch, do you want to go watch the dancing?" He'd been in this room day and night for a week.

"No, thanks." His eyes never left the cage. Well, if he'd preferred dances to science, he wouldn't be here in the first place. Not for the first time, Marianne wondered what would become of Branch after much of Kindred was dead. He was only twenty-four. Would he marry a Kindred woman (if any survived) as Noah had, help rebuild Kindred society, try to preserve as much Terran science as he could? What would the next generation on Kindred look like, born of sixteen Terrans and whoever among the Kindred either received those fifty-two vaccinations or else happened to have natural immunity?

One hundred twenty-six minutes to go.

At 2100 hours, Zoe went off patrol to sleep and Kandiss came on. "What is all that?" Kandiss said, and Leo explained the whole thing over again. If he listened hard, he could hear strains of the strange music coming through the roof. So it was going on inside, too.

Was Isabelle Rhinehart dancing? She was Terran, not Kindred, but she dressed like them, felt like them.

From the far side of the camp, Kandiss radioed the squad. "Sir, Kandiss reporting. The Kinnies are drinking. I think alcoholic. Some staggering, one young male vomiting in the bushes."

Leo hadn't seen that; for the first time, he wished he'd had a spotter with him, the way snipers always did on Earth. He swept his gaze over the camp. Owen said, "Brodie?"

"Confirmed, sir. Signs of drunkenness."

"Okay. I'm getting Berman back on duty, opposite side of building to me. Don't let anyone cross the open zone from the camp. One warning, and if it's not obeyed, fire. Roger?"

"Roger that."

"Roger that."

Leo knew just how dumb drunken men could be—occasionally, he'd been one of those drunken men, although never on duty. But these Kindred had no tradition of military discipline. That made the Rangers despise them, but Leo felt differently. They just hadn't had the training, was all. He still thought the squad should identify trustworthy Kindred—Isabelle and Noah would know who—and train them to help with surveillance and infiltration. Arm them lightly, maybe. Even unarmed, assets in the camp would help with intel.

The dancing got wilder. Then it stopped and people disappeared into tents. Leo crouched, ready for action, hoping there wouldn't be any—another way, he knew, that he differed from the three Rangers. *How many people have you killed?* Austin had asked Leo, half fascinated the way boys always were by snipers, half repelled. "Eleven," Leo had said. And if he had the choice, he would make each of those kills again; he'd been protecting Marines on the ground. But that didn't mean he enjoyed it.

Especially not here, against men armed with homemade pipe guns.

A group moved inside the perimeter on the south side of the compound, facing the hill leading to Jenner's lahk.

Zoe yelled something in bad Kindese: *Go back now!* All of them had learned that sentence, practicing until Owen was sure they had it right. On the roof, Leo tensed.

The group staggered back into the camp.

Okay, not that time.

He scanned ceaselessly, the tip of his rifle moving back and forth: a full slow 180-degree scan of the camp, quicker on the 180 to the north and west, then another slow scan. His SCAR was fitted with its telescopic sight, infrared laser, and tactical light. Mounted under the barrel was the grenade launcher, the 40mm grenades to act as force multipliers during a firefight. His ammo belt bore the maximum number of cartridges. He didn't want to use any of it.

Ten more minutes. Marianne, who'd dozed off while sitting in a chair and so nearly fallen off it, woke up. Spores, invisible and deadly, had permeated the recycling air of the cage for two hours.

The leelees scampered. Chittered. Sniffed the glass.

Breathed.

Eight minutes.

Kandiss said on the squad frequency, "Activity, east side of camp. Men, no women or kids, entering a single big tent. Not looking drunk."

"Hold position and observe," Owen said. "Do you have cover?"

"Affirmative. Large tree, but there are buildings behind me."

"Brodie, do you have him?"

"No, sir." The far eastern edge of camp was where somebody's lahk started: gardens, orchards, outbuildings, and a big house. Christ, anybody could be in those houses, with any accumulation of weapons. Owen had wanted to clear out all the buildings, but what good would it have done? The squad didn't have the troops to hold the objectives after clearance, and it just would have pissed everybody off.

Leo couldn't see Kandiss; he must be somewhere in one of those groves of trees. Leo would know exactly where when Kandiss fired. Meanwhile, all the tents he could see, even though his scope, looked alike. Which one did Owen mean?

He knew a few moments later. A group of men emerged. Leo focused on them, following their progress through the camp. Everybody else was drinking or talking or . . . the couple having sex in the shadows didn't realize Leo could see them. *Get a tent,* he thought, too tense/ready to be envious.

Leo said, "I got them, sir. Walking toward the compound, all carrying bags."

Owen said, *"Everybody's* carrying bags. They're giving gifts to each other. It's fucking Christmas."

"Roger that, sir."

"Kandiss, circle counterclockwise back to the compound and take the north doorway. Berman, keep the south. Brodie, anybody sets one step into the open zone and you fire. No more warnings."

"Yes, sir."

Below him, the north door opened. Leo called down in English, "Whoever opened that door, get the fuck back inside and lock the door!"

The door closed.

Two minutes past the time the leelees should have started writhing and gasping for breath. Instead, one of the animals tumbled another one to the ground and climbed on top of her.

"Yes!" Branch said.

"Give it more time," Marianne said, but she felt hope blow through her like fresh salt air. Sex, not death—maybe they had the vaccine this time. . . .

They were clear in his scope now, a dozen men, approaching the edge of the perimeter. They must be clear to everybody in the camp, too, because all the music and dancing and talking was stopping. Silence spread out in waves around the group of men, followed by frenzy. People pulled their children into tents. Some fled to the far edge of the camp and then out of it, prudently scattering. A few darted toward the group and jabbered, waving their arms. The advancing enemy unit—because that's what they were now—ignored their fellows, moving purposefully toward the perimeter, facing the Big Lab door where Owen waited. Zoe, in response to Owen's order, rounded the building to join him. Kandiss circled the camp toward the compound at a full run, but was still a quarter klick away.

In the enemy unit, hands reached into the bags they carried.

Leo tightened his grip on his rifle, sighted, and waited for the men to set foot onto the perimeter.

Below him, the east door opened behind Zoe and Kandiss, a faint click that registered on Leo's above-average hearing only because he was hyperalert.

Ten more minutes passed. Claire, who'd come in with Salah from the illathil, said in her calm, pretty voice, "I think we did it," and then let out an un-Claire-like whoop. Marianne felt her vision blur.

She had not teared up at any of the research advances on Terra that had led to this moment. So many steps to a vaccine, so much strife, so many deaths. But here, on a planet not her own, she was on the verge of crying: from release of tension, from relief, from momentary joy before she let herself remember that they still had to synthesize a planetful of vaccines, using outdated or jerry-rigged or completely missing machinery, on alien cultures in makeshift petri dishes, to protect immune systems that had evolved different defensive pathways.

Salah laughed, a deep masculine guffaw. He seized Claire and they danced a jogging step. Branch grinned like a Halloween jack-o'-lantern, wide enough to split his face. The leelees made high sexual squeaks as they mated.

Claire said, "I'm going to fetch Llaa^mohj and—"

The leelee lab door flung open and Austin Rhinehart stood there, his eyes almost as huge as a Kindred's, vegetable dye crusting the teenage feet that had grown faster than his body.

"There's an attack coming!" he cried. "And Isabelle went outside to try to stop it!"

Salah seized him by the shoulders. "Isabelle? What happened?"

"Lemme go!" Austin tore free and glared at Salah. "I opened the door to go outside because illathil is so boring! And Leo Brodie on the roof told me to go back inside so I did. But I told Isabelle because I thought somebody should know and she said to stay inside but she was going toward the door without telling anybody else so I came to tell you!" Austin looked triumphant, frightened, excited.

Thirteen, Marianne thought numbly. He was thirteen, so of course he looked excited. Was it really an attack? To get the vaccine they already had?

"Salah," she said, turning toward him, but he was already gone.

Zoe slipped behind the barricade Owen had had built there, primarily from an old refrigerator. If the natives had had any military sense, they would have taken her out before she got that far. They didn't have any military sense. Leo knelt, sighted, braced himself.

The men at the rear of the little group pulled from their bags pipe guns and—yes—an object the size of a cookie jar.

"Possible explosive device," Leo said. "Composition and strength unknown. Enemy has halted just short of perimeter."

Kandiss ran around the side of the building's north door. Again, no Kindred fired. But all four soldiers' attention was focused on the men with the weapons—were they a diversion for an attack from somewhere else?

When the east door again opened behind Zoe and Owen, Leo's first thought was, *We're fucked.* Someone inside could hurl an explosive and take out Zoe and Owen from behind, then let the enemy rush in without even having to breach . . . Then he heard the door click again, locking.

Owen yelled to whoever had come out, "Get the fuck back inside!"

Until the infiltrator moved away from the walls, Leo couldn't see who it was. Then she moved, heading diagonally across the perimeter toward the enemy. Isabelle.

She carried nothing and wore only a short red dress, her light brown hair greenish in his night scope. So many complicated emotions tsunamied through Leo that for a moment he couldn't breathe. Only a moment, though—he steadied himself.

Someone in the enemy group yelled something; a second later, Leo realized what the word was. "Vaccine!"

Owen said, "Brodie, warning shot."

He fired high above the camp. Women screamed. The group huddled closer together—the reverse of what they should do. Owen shouted to Isabelle, "Go back inside! Now!"

She ignored him, turning instead to look up at the roof. "Leo, don't shoot! All of you, don't shoot! Let me talk to them—please!"

Owen had two choices, Leo realized: Let her join the enemy group or shoot her, because she wasn't going back inside. Isabelle turned and ran toward the camp. Now if Owen, Zoe, or Leo fired, they risked hitting Isabelle. She could be taken hostage. She could be killed with a pipe gun or IED or even a fucking *machete*, right in front of Leo. If that happened . . .

Leo waited. None of the enemy had crossed onto the perimeter. Isabelle stood in front of them, waving her arms and talking. It seemed to Leo that the men were listening, but he couldn't be sure. He lined up a shot at the guy holding the cookie jar, a shot that wouldn't hit Isabelle. Stupid fucking civilian . . .

Christ, she was brave.

Whatever she was saying, it seemed to be working. The pipe guns were lowered. Eight of the dozen men seemed to be arguing with four others. They were all young, all jacked up. Leo felt the familiar strain: adrenaline with no place to go, a kind of mental blue balls. He didn't want to kill anybody unnecessarily, but—

Eight of the four turned back. Isabelle argued with the others. Leo couldn't tell who was winning. Then the south door opened, and Salah Bourgiba ran around the building toward Isabelle.

Fuck fuck fuck—

Before Owen could even get out his order to go back inside, the man with the cookie jar swung his head to see a Terran male running toward him. He hurled the cookie jar at the compound, screaming, "Vaccine! Vaccine!"

The cookie jar landed halfway across the perimeter and exploded. Leo fired.

The man went down. The other three ran, weapons lowered. Owen yelled, "Hold your fire!"

People screamed, running blindly in the dark. Leo could see them all, along with everything that was there and—more important— everything that wasn't. The IED had blown up without scattering shrapnel, without breaching the building, without touching Zoe, Owen, or Kandiss. It was the sorriest bomb he'd ever seen. Isabelle was all right. Even that stupid ass Bourgiba hadn't been injured. But the Kindred that Leo had shot lay dead just inside the open zone.

Fuck.

Salah blamed himself for the death.

If he hadn't stupidly, without thinking it through, run toward Isabelle . . . But he'd seen the pipe guns the men from the camp carried, he'd known how heavily armed the Rangers were, he'd seen Isabelle vulnerable and exposed to both sides and some atavistic masculine instinct had strangled all thought except to protect her. Protect! How? She was better equipped to deal with unrest in the camp than he could ever be, and the Rangers were trained to accomplish their objectives as efficiently as possible. Which that prick Lamont had done: only one man had died.

Salah's fault.

He stood in the bathroom of the compound, needing to calm himself before he returned to the meeting going on in Marianne's room. Illathil had abruptly ended. Ree^ka-mak had been told everything that happened. In the camp, the Kindred mourned their dead. The Rangers were on high alert, or code red, or whatever they called it, against further violence. Branch remained on duty in the locked lab with the leelees, living and dead, and the safe holding vaccines and spore packets. And here Salah was, stupidly standing in a bathroom, his back against the door, trying to gain control of himself.

Salah's father had been Muslim but his maternal grandmother had been French, a Catholic. Words from the Mass, which he had not thought about since his grandmother died thirty-five years ago, hammered at his mind in three languages:

Ma faute, ma faute, ma très grande faute.

Mea culpa, mea culpa, mea maxima culpa.

Through my fault, through my fault, through my most grievous fault.

A soft knock on the door. "Salah?"

"Coming, Claire." He ran the water briefly and came out.

She said, "It wasn't your fault."

He looked at her: tiny, sweet-natured, smart as hell; in some ways, Claire Patel was the heart of the Terran expedition. Younger than Marianne, more mature than Branch, more driven than Salah. But, this time: wrong.

Then she said the only thing that could help him: "Isabelle doesn't blame you."

He touched her shoulder briefly and they went back to the meeting. Ree^ka-mak sat upright in Marianne's bed, her face a fantastic topographic mask of sorrow. Her half-blind eyes, however, were steady. She said, "The people who attacked this place of healing must be named and"—Salah did not know the Kindese word—"and that will be done. Salah-Bourgiba-mak, I have decided that you will carry me to the camp to talk to the Mothers gathered there."

A shrewd move. She was the only one who could calm the camp, and if he carried her, no one would attack him. They would see that she did not hold him—or any of the Terrans—responsible.

But Isabelle, who had been translating the Mother of Mothers' words for Claire and Marianne, said in Kindese, "That may not be possible, Ree^ka-mak."

"Why not?"

"The Rangers have forbidden any Terrans to leave the compound—anyone, I mean, of the new expedition, who is involved in creating the vaccine."

"I will talk with Lamont-mak. Also with the Terran who killed Belįlak^ha."

"That will not be possible, either."

"Why not?"

"The soldier's superior is responsible for his . . . his group's actions, and Lieutenant Lamont will not explain them to you."

"They do not recognize my authority?"

"Over our people, yes. Over Terrans, no."

"Then do they recognize Marianne-mak's authority over the Terran lahk?"

"No," Isabelle said.

Salah realized that Ree^ka-mak knew all this already; she was making a point.

"Then," the Mother of Mothers said, "Lamont-mak recognizes no authority but his own?"

Yes. And history had shown, over and over, that military authority unrestrained by civilian control was the harbinger of disaster. However, Salah knew he was biased; he didn't like or understand the Rangers, not any of them. Isabelle did.

Isabelle said, "The ambassador that Lieutenant Lamont recognized as authority died in the Russian attack. I think the Rangers are trying to carry out her orders, which were to protect Terrans on World. Mother of Mothers, the man who killed Belįlak^ha was doing that. The Rangers could have killed many more of the men who attacked from the camp. They did not. Neither Lieutenant Lamont nor Corporal Brodie is at fault here."

"I do not blame them."

"Nor is Salah-kal to blame for rushing to me."

"I do not blame him. The people to blame are in the camp, those who made weapons and used them to try to obtain vaccines before others. Salah-mak will take me to the camp, and one soldier will go with me so that all can see that I know where fault lies. Now that Marianne-mak has created more vaccine, we must create a plan for giving it. This will not be easy. It is also not a Terran concern. This is my order: Give the fifty existing vaccines to everyone in the compound, immediately."

"There are fifty-two, Ree^ka-mak."

"There are fifty to decide. Two have been reserved for Noah Jenner's wife and child. No one knows if the child will inherit her father's immunity."

How had she known all that? Conversations must go on among the Kindred scientists from which Terrans were excluded.

Ree^ka-mak said, "The two vaccines for Llaa^moh; and her child are approved. She has worked here on the vaccine. After you vaccinate the rest of our people within these walls, you will have twenty-six vaccines left. How fast can more be prepared?"

Marianne said, "I don't know. We will start right now and work day and night."

"Noah Jenner will give the twenty-six vaccines to people he trusts, to take to the lahks of the scientists here, divided equally. The Mothers of those lahks will decide what to do with their doses. Whoever receives them must travel here because when the spore cloud comes, death will be everywhere but here. Marianne-mak, would bringing more scientists here help create more vaccines faster?"

Isabelle translated. "No," Marianne said. "Tell her it's not a question of personnel but of time to grow the cultures."

"I understand. Then you must work. As soon as Noah-mak arrives, send him to me. Now we will talk about who gets the new vaccines you will create."

"One thing more," Marianne said, in English. "Does she understand that the synthesized vaccine proved effective in leelees, but that it has not been tested in humans? That we don't actually know how or even if it will work? There are strains of flu that mutate so fast we can't—"

Isabelle put her hand on Marianne's arm. "She knows, Marianne. Believe me, she knows. She—"

Branch burst in without knocking. Salah's heart began a slow, painful thud in his chest. The young assistant trembled and his eyes practically rolled in his head. "I only left for a minute! When Claire—Dr. Patel"—he blushed a deep, mottled crimson—"wanted to go outside to see what happened, I didn't want her to go, after the bomb I mean because it seemed too dangerous even though a lot of people ran out and then Rangers came through the compound to check it out, so I thought it was all safe, and everything was so confused—I ran after Dr. Patel and I must have left the door unlocked—"

Marianne seized Branch's arm. "What happened? Are the cages with infected leelees—"

"No, no," Branch said. "The cages are intact. But the safe was open. No live spores were taken, but all the original vaccines are gone. *Stolen.*"

It took a moment for Salah to process this: stolen. By someone inside the compound. The Kindred scientists, who were the only ones who needed it; all the Terrans were—probably—already immune. Who could possibly—

Isabelle's face had gone rigid as stone. She said, "Find Austin. Branch, Salah, Claire—"

"We'll all look," Claire said.

But a thorough search of Little Lab, of Big Lab, of every bunk room and closet, and Austin could not be found.

CHAPTER 11

Traveling at night was thrilling. It would have been better, of course, if he had night-vision goggles like the Rangers and if he didn't have his mother with him, but it was still thrilling. Clouds obscured the moons but Austin carried a flashlight. Bringing his mother now was necessary because there might not be another chance to get away like this. Austin had actually slipped right out the unguarded north door, the one in the clinic kitchen, when everybody rushed outside to see the bomb and the Rangers had been too busy to keep people penned up. Austin was proud of his ability to elude them.

He was proud, too, of all the rest of his plans. He'd hidden in a dark orchard until everyone was asleep. Then he'd gone into his lahk, collected all the things for the journey, and left a note before waking his mother. "I'm going to take you to a safe place," he'd whispered to her, pleased with how mature that sounded. Kayla had been confused at first, but she was in one of her quiet periods, and didn't that piece of luck prove that he was doing the right thing? He was going to protect her. That's what men did on Terra. Ranger Kandiss had said so, where lahks were different than here. This appealed to Austin, who wanted things different because he was.

"You all right, Mom?" he said in English.

She nodded, eyes on the ground. They were trudging through a field of sleeping skaleth¡, shadows against a line of trees. Kayla had said little. Austin knew the signs; soon his mother would start crying for no reason. He would be patient with her this time. Mature. He wasn't a child anymore.

"Here, drink some water," he said, offering her the canteen. "We still have a long way to go to safety."

"Their next assault," Owen said, "will be better planned. Only we're not going to let them make another assault."

Dawn stained the sky. Leo had had two hours sleep in the last twenty-eight. All through the night, the squad had maintained stepped-up surveillance. The refugee camp seethed with activity but no one stepped into the perimeter, and as far as Leo could tell, the activity was more about mourning than fighting.

Still, Owen was right. The camp held enough angry males of fighting age to mount another assault, and added to the desperation and boredom of every refugee camp that had ever existed would now be anger over the bomber that Leo had shot.

Not that the fucker hadn't deserved it. If he'd been better at making bombs, Isabelle would be dead.

Still . . . these were people not used to fighting, pretty terrible at it, and told not to fight by their leader, the really old lady. Something didn't quite add up here, but now wasn't the time to figure it out.

Owen said, "We're going into the camp for a search and seizure. All weapons, anything that looks like an IED or the makings for an IED. Standard search-and-seizure procedures."

Leo blinked. There were four of them and at least five hundred people in the camp, whole lahks, with more arriving every day. He risked a sideways glance at Zoe. She shifted forward onto the balls of her feet, eager. This was what Rangers trained for; the Seventy-Fifth was basically a direct-action raid force.

He said, "Sir, permission to ask questions."

"Go ahead, Brodie."

"Are we also looking for the missing kid, Austin Rhinehart, or the vaccines he stole?"

"No. Rhinehart isn't part of our protectee group. If you find him, you can report his whereabouts to Dr. Bourgiba. But if Rhinehart is armed and he attacks, treat him like any other insurgent."

The kid was thirteen. But again, Owen was right. In Brazil, rebels had used thirteen-year-olds as suicide bombers.

They received the rest of Owen's OPORD, did the precombat inspection, and moved into the camp as the sun rose orange over the horizon.

Leo worked with Kandiss. They entered each tent, herded the males outside under Kandiss's guard and the women, kids, and old men into a corner. Leo tore apart the tents' interiors, which took about two minutes because there wasn't much in any of them: sleeping mats too thin to hide weapons, cooking pots and dishes, food supplies in tightly woven baskets, clothing. A few books, toys, musical instruments. A radio, always. These people traveled light.

The women glared at him or cowered, and some of the youngest kids cried. Leo knew how he must look to them in his armor and helmet and weapons. In Brazil, he'd sometimes given candy to kids in the villages. Not here.

One little girl, bolder than the adults in her tent, stepped forward and shyly touched his boot.

No weapons or IED makings in the first eight tents. The camp was in chaos but it was a pretty controlled chaos—no resistance, no attacks. People stood where they were told and returned inside tents when the ends of rifles were waved in that direction. But Leo knew it wouldn't last, and it didn't.

When he emerged from the ninth tent, having found nothing, a group of Kindred rushed toward him. Kandiss turned from the men he had herded together. One of the rushers raised a pipe gun. At this range one of those could kill him, depending on what the fuck they'd devised for ammo. Leo shot him. The others dropped their weapons and raised their hands. From the corner of his eye, Leo caught movement. From another direction, an insurgent raised a pipe gun aimed at Kandiss. Before Leo could drop him, the man flew backward in a spray of. . . . *piss?*

No. Water. A group of three Kindred wielded a hose that shot out yellow water. The hoses were used to bring drinking, cooking, and bathing water to the camp from a pond, but Leo hadn't realized they could deliver such force. The man on the ground writhed and screamed. . . . too much screaming. He clawed at his eyes. The water had some yellowish chemical in it.

The water-cannon-wielding men, Leo now realized, had some sort of badge sewn onto the front of their dresses. Cops?

Two of them rushed forward, yanked the blinded man to his feet, and cuffed him behind his back. The third turned off the hose and, incredibly, said to Leo in English, "I greet you, Ranger."

"I greet you. You police?"

But this was beyond the Kindred's English. He turned to the attackers, who had dropped their weapons, and began yelling at them. Zoe and Own jogged up. Owen said, "Report!"

Leo explained while Zoe and Kandiss covered them. Owen, expressionless, said, "Okay. Berman, take these insurgents into custody and tie them to those trees over there. Kandiss and Brodie, finish search and seizure."

They did. Owen walked to the compound, which again had civilians pouring out of it in response to the shooting, wearing nightclothes. To Leo these looked indistinguishable from daytime dresses. Owen began arguing with Dr. Jenner, Dr. Patel, and two of the Kindred scientists.

In the shooter's tent, they found sixteen more pipe guns and some bomb-making supplies. Weapons manufacturing on Kindred was stepping up fast. But no other tent held weapons and no one opposed their searches. Kindred glared at Leo resentfully.

As the squad left the camp, men took away the corpses of the two men, bearing them on their shoulders, their faces twisted with grief.

Leo took roof duty. He watched the camp. He swept his weapon three-sixty to make sure nothing crept up from behind. He sweated inside his heavy kit as the orange sun rose in the alien sky, above the sweet-smelling dark leaves of gardens and groves and fields. And he thought about what he had seen when the civilians flowed from the compound: Isabelle Rhinehart in the circle of Salah Bourgiba's arm, her pale hair loose across his shoulder, her lips open as she talked to him, his eyes gazing down at her with intensity and possession.

Salah wasn't sure how it happened. Isabelle was upset over Austin's theft of the vaccines, yes. She had stood mere feet away from the Kindred that Leo Brodie had shot, and it was entirely possible she could have been shot herself. The Mother of Mothers was dying. Bombers and shooters had appeared where none had been before. The world was ending, except for that portion of it that could be saved by synthvac. All that was true. It was a wonder that anyone remained sane.

True, too, that Salah had seen before the confused and sometimes startling reactions of people involved with so much death. Some froze. Some withdrew. Some numbed all feeling. Some became manic, some furious. Some turned to alcohol or drugs or, yes, sex.

He wanted to think it was more than that with him and Isabelle.

They'd come back from the camp, his arm around her, even though she didn't seem to need support. He wasn't sure what she needed until they walked down the covered passageway to the clinic and one of them—which? He wasn't sure—turned to the other. The kiss was brief, sweet, but not long; other voices rounded the corner from Big Lab.

Then they were in Salah's small room, on his sleeping mat, her brief wrap coming off more easily than his Terran pants, shoes, shirt. Even in the windowless room, she was lovely, a faint strip of illumination from alongside and under the hastily built door striping her body with light. She had a tattoo on her arm—a rose? He wasn't sure. It didn't matter.

He filled himself with the weight of her, the smell of her, the juiciness of her until nothing else mattered.

When they were finished, breathing quietly beside each other, she wanted to talk, but not about Kindred. About anything, it seemed, except Kindred.

"Where did you grow up?"

"Boston. You?"

"New Jersey. I wouldn't have gone to have my mitochondria tested in New York if it was any farther away. You know, when the Kindred were looking for those with the same haplogroup? All of us that came here are L-31. Their group."

Of course he knew that. All of Earth knew that. He said only, "But all of Kindred is not one lahk."

"No." She shifted on the pallet, pulling her leg slightly away from his. He regretted that. She said, "Are you L-31?"

"No. The US government wasn't as fussy as the Kindred."

"How old are you?"

For a moment he resented what felt like an interrogation, but only for a moment. This was Isabelle, more direct than anyone else in what had been his social circle. "Forty-five. You?"

"Thirty-three. I've heard you say 'Inch Allie'—are you Muslim?"

"'Insha'Allah.' There—I get to correct your pronunciation for a change."

She laughed but wasn't deterred from questioning. Salah had the impression that nothing deterred her. "Are you Muslim?"

"No, not now. I was raised in a lukewarm version of Islam, but my family's real gods were correct behavior and achievement."

"I see."

She didn't; the last thing Isabelle would ever worship was the kind of drifting along preset "right" paths that had characterized Salah's life.

"Are you—"

"My turn, Isabelle. Tell me about you. Your history."

She didn't hesitate. "It was bad. Kayla and I had an abusive stepfather. We left home as soon as we could and lived pretty rough. I did a term in prison, for grand theft auto and other things—nothing violent. Kayla tried to escape by getting married at seventeen—that didn't work out but at least she got Austin out of it. I was looking around for some way to change both our lives when the Kindred landed. This chance came and I took it."

I took it, not *we*. Isabelle decided for Kayla, and probably always had.

She said, as if she knew what he'd been thinking, "She's my sister. I'm responsible for her, before anyone else, because she's really just a child. You don't have children, do you, Salah?"

"No."

"Were you ever married?"

She had been so open, so honest. And they would never leave Kindred. Possibly he would die here, soon. All at once, for the first time, he wanted someone to know the truth about him. To know him. Or maybe he just wanted to make some definite decision for once.

He said, "Here is a fable. A very young couple marries. They don't know each other very well but that doesn't matter because they are so much in love. She's his only anchor, the only thing he wants. He admires that she is so sure of what she wants: to be a painter and create great beauty. He has to do something and so he drifts into becoming a doctor, a sort of default decision, and it turns out he is very good at it. She, however, does not become an artist. She lacks something—persistence, or talent, or resilience. Something. What she becomes is very unhappy. The world does not understand her, and does not give her what is due her. She begins to drink, which only makes her feel worse.

"She blames him because, after all, he does not feel this bad, and is that fair? It is not. So she does things that make him feel bad, too, like drink even more and sleep around. And that works—now he feels bad, too. But only for a while. After some time, he just works longer and longer hours to get away from her.

"Which, of course, is enraging. She blames him even more—he is neglecting her, which is in fact true. She does the one thing that can still make him feel horrible. She leaves him.

"And that works, too, for a while. He feels worse than he has ever felt in his life. But eventually he realizes that his life is actually better without her. He becomes slightly happier.

"But she does not. All her problems are still there—the failed work, the failed love affairs, the drinking, the empty days. In fact, her days are emptier still, without all the fighting. So she changes her mind and wants to come back to him.

"He says no.

"She pleads, cries, begs. He still refuses. She is stunned, panicked, and furious. Really furious. She wants to punish him for making her feel like this. She also wants to escape what her life has become. So she kills herself, leaving him a long letter explaining exactly why.

"And for the third time, this works. Completely. He feels incredibly bad, consumed with guilt. Because she is right—this is in part his fault. He, who helps others so effortlessly, has refused to help her, to recognize her despair, to do something, anything, for her. She, the only free choice he has ever made in his life, has won their catastrophic battle with each other.

"There is only one way he can cope with this. Well, two ways. He works more and more. And he turns off all feeling about his work, his patients, his life. The surprise is that this does indeed give him some peace. Years go by, and he is admired for his coolheadedness and competence and decision making, when in fact he has never made a real decision since he was twenty years old and married his wife. Who ended up dead, while he ended up happy."

Isabelle was quiet for a long time. Salah waited. Finally she said, "That's not happiness."

He didn't answer. A soft knock came on the door. "Dr. Bourgiba?" Branch's voice said. "Are you in there?"

"Yes. What do you need?"

"Somebody in Big Lab cut herself on some glass and said to go get you."

"Coming."

He fumbled in the gloom for his clothes. Isabelle sat up.

"Salah—after the spore cloud comes and almost nobody is left—"

"Yes?"

"This was sweet, although I certainly didn't plan to—I just want to say that I like you. But I'm not making any promises, for after."

"I know that," he said truthfully. Then, "Neither am I." A lie.

"Good. So we'll just see what happens. Is that all right?"

It seemed a staggering way to accept the end of civilization: *We'll just see what happens.* But, Salah realized wryly, pretty much his entire life could be summed up in the phrase.

He said, "Of course."

Insha'Allah.

Marianne woke from restless sleep. Everything creaked as she hoisted herself off her pallet. She was really too old to be sleeping on the floor. Too old, too pampered by American inner springs and memory foam. But on the plus side: *They had done it.* They had an effective synthetic vaccine, to replace the ones that young criminal Austin had stolen. (Why? Was he going to attempt to sell them?) The synth-vac was a triumph of will and luck over inadequate machinery and deficient knowledge.

On her way to the kitchen for a bowl of the vegetable soup kept perpetually simmering by the two Kindred cooks, she met Branch coming from Big Lab. The Kindred scientists, under Claire's direction, were hard at work manufacturing the new vaccines. Branch carried a mass of hardware in his arms; Marianne could barely see him around the machinery. When he did cock his head to one side, she was surprised to see him smiling. He'd been heartsick over his lapse in guarding the safe.

"Dr. Jenner! I found out something!"

"Is Austin back? Or Noah?" Noah had been away during last night's attack from the camp, but surely it would be on the radio and he would know about it by now.

"No, no, this is different. It's about the Kindred spaceship!"

Marianne blinked. Hadn't the ship, on which Noah and Isabelle and the others traveled to Kindred ten years ago, been completely destroyed in the Russian attack?

Branch saw her confusion. "The other ship, Dr. Jenner. The colony one."

Oh. The first ship the Kindred had built, which had become infected with *R. sporii* that killed everyone aboard. That was how Kindred had first discovered the spore cloud on its relentless path through the galaxy. Direct encounter on the colony planet.

"Isn't that ship still on a planet somewhere?"

"In orbit around it. The spore contamination came from an EVA. You saw the recording the Kindred brought to Terra, the last one the captain made."

She had. The recording had been horrific.

"But what I just found out from Llaa^mohį is that the ship is still sending signals!"

She was staggered. "You mean people are still alive inside?"

"No, no, everyone's dead. The *ship* is sending automatic signals. They were recorded all this time at Kam . . . Kat . . . the capital city that the *Stremlenie* destroyed. The equipment to receive the signals was on the other Kindred ship, and of course that's gone, too. But I think I might be able to rig up some sort of receiver to record them here!"

"Why? If it's just ship's signals, position, and planetary data and such, what good would it do us here?"

Branch seemed to not understand the question. "They're signals, Dr. Jenner. And I might be able to receive them. I'm only going to work on it when there's no need for me in Big Lab."

She saw, then, that he needed to do this, needed to do something to make up for letting the vaccines be stolen. That was how Branch saw it, anyway. For not the first time, Marianne ruminated on how very often brilliant young men invested themselves in pointless problems. But she was fond of Branch, and so she smiled and said, "Go to it. Good luck."

"The only place to set this all up is the leelee lab, but that's good because I can keep an eye on the leelees." He unlocked the door.

The animals, dead and alive, now stank like sewer rats and chittered like crickets. Moving away, Marianne heard Branch cry out. She turned back and ran into the room.

The cage of leelees treated with synth-vac was ominously quiet.

Marianne stared through the glass. Two of the three leelees were dead. The third moved sluggishly, coughing, obviously very sick.

The synth vaccine had provided only partial protection, and not for long. They had failed again.

Austin and Kayla arrived at the cave entrance at midmorning. Why was his mother so slow? She wasn't that old, maybe the same age as Dr. Patel. But at one point in the night she just lay down and slept on a patch of thick grass, not even telling Austin she was going to do it. Just lay down and closed her eyes. The rest of the time she trudged along, eyes down, like she didn't even care that Austin was rescuing her from the collapse of civilization. Didn't even care!

All his life, Austin had known there was something wrong with his mother. He never knew, one tenday to the next, whether she would be laughing and talking fast and thinking up adventures, or staying in bed and crying. He learned to take his requests and problems to Isabelle or Noah. But Kayla was still his mother, and she and Isabelle were the only members of his lahk—Graa^lok always pointed this out when they had a fight—who should *really* be in it, by blood. Isabelle said that Kayla couldn't help her strange behavior; the problem was genetic and there was no medicine for it on World because Worlders didn't get this disease.

Yet another reason to let civilization collapse without Austin and Kayla! World would be sorry when it lay in smoking ruins and they were safe in Haven.

If only she would walk faster.

Eventually, they reached the cave. "Mom, I'm going to go in first. Then when the doors inside are open, I'll come back out for you." He had to do it that way; if he went first, she would never get the bushes arranged right to hide the entrance. Noah knew where the cave was, but Tony didn't know that Noah knew, and Austin didn't want Graa^lok arriving from his lahk's illathil and tattling about badly placed bushes. Austin and Graa^lok weren't getting along so well these days. Graa^lok's fault—he always thought he was so damn smart.

Austin crawled along the tunnel and rang the bell. A few moments later Beyon-kal's face appeared at the grill, looking annoyed. "Austin? What are you doing here?"

"I got away," Austin said. "We did. In the confusion after the bomb."

He expected Beyon-kal to say breathlessly, "What bomb?" but was disappointed. Beyon-kal said, "It was on the radio."

"Me being gone was on the radio?"

"No, of course not. The attack on the compound was. Do they have a vaccine yet?"

"No. How did you understand . . . is Graa^lok here already?"

"Yes. What are *you* doing here?"

This wasn't the welcome Austin had hoped for. "Let me see Tony."

"I'll decide if you see Tony or not. For the third time, why did you come?"

"I'm here for good. I brought my mother. This was our only chance to escape while—"

"You brought *Kayla*? Now?"

"I just told you, Beyon-kal, we might not get another chance to escape! The Rangers aren't letting people in or out of the compound!" This was not strictly true; only the Terran scientists weren't allowed to leave, but Beyon-kal didn't know that.

Beyon-kal said flatly, "We can't have you here. Your absence—and Kayla's—will attract attention."

"Graa^lok is here!" Austin said, hating that he sounded like a little kid.

"Graylock's lahk is not researching a vaccine, surrounded by a refugee camp, or watched by radio reporters from around the entire continent. Yours is."

Reporters? Austin hadn't known that. It made him feel kind of important, which restored some of his confidence.

"Unlock the grill. I have to see Tony. I have important information."

"Tell it to me."

"No." When had he ever before defied Beyon-kal? Never. But now was different.

Beyon-kal scowled. Austin stared him right in the eyes, no blinking. Beyon-kal unlocked the grill.

"I'm going to get my mother," Austin said. And then, as Beyon-kal retreated along the tunnel, "Tony will really want to hear my information!"

Just as soon as he invented it.

He got Kayla through the crawl tunnel, going ahead of her to help her down to the big tunnel. She fell heavily but wasn't hurt. She still had not said a word. Austin went back to bring in his pack and rearrange the bushes. When he returned, Kayla was right where he'd left her, staring at the rock floor, tears falling from her eyes.

"It's okay, Mom." He hugged her briefly—he was too old to hug his mother but this was different—and led her through the open metal door to Haven. Tony waited, looking furious. Graa^lok stood behind him.

"Austin, what the fuck—"

"She left a note," Austin said. "I wrote it. Nobody will miss her or come looking for us. It's only two more weeks until the cloud. We're staying."

"You're not."

"She is," Austin said. It came out higher and squeakier than he intended, and he tried again. "My mother is staying. She won't be any trouble."

Kayla sobbed softly. Austin's heart swelled with pity, with irritation, with fear, with love. He had to save her!

His words came out in a desperate rush. "Listen! I have information you want! I'm friends with some of the kids in the refugee camp"—Graa^lok shifted his weight but said nothing, which was a good thing or Austin would have slugged him—"and they told me when the next assault on the compound will be!"

"So?" Tony said.

"So that's your only chance to get Claire—Dr. Patel—out of the compound and into Haven. You're going to need a doctor, you said so yourself, and she knows how to doctor Terrans, a lot better than any World doctor would. When an attack on the compound comes, everything is really confused. Shooting—Leo Brodie shot three Worlders so far, you probably know that from the radio. And a bomb! The confusion is how I got away. Dr. Patel and I can escape during the next attack. I can bring her here."

Tony said, "She won't want to come. What are you going to do—drag her here?"

"No, she does want to come! That's the information I was coming to bring you. I heard her say to . . . to Dr. Jenner that she's afraid of what will happen when everybody in the camp rushes the compound to get vaccines."

"You said they don't have vaccines yet."

"But they *will*. Or at least they might. She's afraid of the collapse of civilization." There—that should make Tony believe, because it was his own phrase. For good measure, he added, "She's really little, you know."

Tony said, "So say that I believe you. Dr. Patel wants to come to Haven. You can bring her here. How are you going to do that if you and your mother are 'here for good'?"

Austin hadn't thought that far. "Well, I misspoke. My mother is here for good but I'm going back. To bring Dr. Patel."

Tony looked at Beyon-kal, who rolled his eyes. Finally Tony said, "Okay. Here's the deal. Kayla can stay. You go, and when the refugee camp assaults the compound, you guide the doctor here. But if you're followed by Rangers, you don't get in—no, don't ask stupid questions, of course Rangers can track you. If you come too soon, like in the next eight days, you don't get in. I don't want a Ranger assault on Haven, but after about eight days they're going to be too busy with the collapse of civilization to chase you. If you come back without Dr. Patel, you don't get in, and your mother goes out. Got it?"

"*What?* But you said—"

"It doesn't matter what I said before. We started Haven before we knew we had Rangers to deal with, didn't we? Haven is both impregnable and defensible, but we only have so much food before we come out again after everybody's dead, and we need to keep the supplies for essential personnel."

Graa^lok blurted out, "But that's not fair!"

"Yes, it is," Tony said. "Harsh, but fair. When you're older—both of you—you'll understand that survival sometimes means tough choices. You bring me a doctor, you earn your place here."

Indignation choked Austin so much that he couldn't speak.

Tony softened. "I'm sorry, kid, but that's the way it is. Look, I'm sure you'll bring the doctor. We need her. When you do, you're in. And you can stay a little while now to get Kayla settled and to rest up. Start by getting her to stop crying, okay? Thank you."

Leo had perimeter patrol. Everything in the camp was quiet, and it seemed to him there were fewer people. Maybe some had gone back to their lahks, away from any more potential violence. Smart people.

The ones that remained ducked into their tents as soon as they saw Leo, or stood their ground and glared at him, or looked down at their sandals. In Brazil, an American sniper who had already shot three natives would have been screamed at, or had rocks thrown at him, or worse. He didn't understand these people.

A movement behind some bushes. Leo tensed, turned. But it was two tiny girls playing with a little pile of toys, probably farther from camp than their mothers knew. Both looked up from dark eyes huge in their coppery faces and smiled at him.

"I greet you, halhal^bem," Leo said in Kindese, hoping he had the word right for their age and status, hoping he hadn't called them a coffeepot or some damn thing.

They chorused back, without fear, "I greet you, Ranger-mak."

He couldn't linger. The little girls could even be bait, a trap, although he hadn't seen anything suspicious and Kandiss, on roof duty, was tracking him. But as he jogged on, the small incident warmed him, the only good thing that had happened in the last twenty-four hours. Maybe longer.

On the farthest edge of the camp, at the farthest distance from the tents, two men approached Leo from a grove of trees.

He halted, raised his rifle, said in Kindese, "Stop."

They did, and raised their hands above their heads. But that didn't rule out suicide bombs. Leo repeated, "Stop."

"Yes," the older of them said, in English. The word had a click on the end of it like so many of their words did, which Isabelle said changed the meaning but Leo didn't know how. "I greet you, Leo-mak."

"I greet you," Leo said, because what the fuck else was he supposed to say? This wasn't a tea party, but it wasn't an attack, either. Not yet. And how did they know his name?

The younger man turned his shoulder toward Leo, a sinuous twisting of his tall body, and pointed one finger downward to call attention to the patch sewn there. The same patch that the Kindred who'd turned on the water cannon last night had had sewn onto the front of his dress. The man said in careful, halting English, "I am police."

"Yes," Leo said.

"We help you. No more vee^al¡ss."

It took Leo a moment to get the word: *violence.*

Was this a trap? Or were these guys offering to be informants? And how did they learn English? He said nothing, waiting to see what they said next.

"Come."

No way. It smelled like an amateurish ambush. He said, more harshly than he intended, "No."

The older man smiled sadly.

The younger didn't seem all that surprised. He said, "We tell you." Slowly he raised one foot a few inches off the ground in the untrimmed weeds.

Leo tensed, but he let the guy shake his sandal until a piece of paper fell out. The two men nodded and, hands still raised, walked back into the camp. When they'd vanished, Leo picked up the paper, his mind busy. The men had probably been observed from the camp, but it might have looked like Leo stopped them, raised his gun, and spoke to them instead of the other way around—you could spin it that way.

The paper was a map. A big shaded block for the compound, the proportions exact for its two buildings and walkway; Leo had walked the roof enough times to know. The perimeter zone was shaded more lightly, and the tents drawn in curving rows. One tent fairly close to the south door was circled and inside it were drawn pipe guns.

Leo put the paper in his pocket, finished the perimeter patrol, and called Owen.

"An ambush," Owen said.

"Maybe, sir. But I could check it out."

"If there's a suicide bomb in there, then we lose you. Go, but take Berman to cover you and each of you take a Kinnie kid as hostage. Carry them in front of you. I'll give the fuckers that, they don't use kids as bait. Not so far, anyway."

He hated the idea. It was what insurgents had done in Brazil, and children had died. He wanted to say to Owen *We don't do that, it's not us.* But, then, this wasn't Brazil. The Kindred wouldn't kill their own kids in order to destroy an enemy holding them; Leo knew that about Kindred, knew it clear down to his bones. Kids shouldn't even be here in a war zone, but lahks stuck together no matter what. Blood here really was thicker than water. And Leo had just been given an order.

"Yes, sir," he said.

He radioed Zoe on their private frequency, destroying the last half hour of her allotted sleep, and she cursed him with several inventive combinations of filth he hadn't heard before. But in three minutes she was beside him in full kit. "This better be worthwhile, Brodie."

They strode into camp. Two little girls walked by, carefully balancing a bucket of water between them. Leo shook his head. He picked instead a pair of boys whose parents did not seem nearby, and

Zoe scowled at him; he'd hear about this bit of male chauvinism later. Leo and Zoe each held a child tightly against their chests with one arm, sidearm in the other. Leo could feel the child's fear radiating up his arm, like an electric shock.

"Stop! Don't move!" He said it in Kindese. The two men and one woman inside the tent froze, looking grimmer than stone. The tent held more guns—Leo noticed that each batch they confiscated was more sophisticated than the last—plus small devices and collections of chemicals that he didn't recognize. Leo and Zoe made them carry it all across the perimeter to the door of the clinic and dump it just inside. Then he let the children go. Zoe stood guard over the three adults, whom no other Kindred had tried to join, against the compound wall. Although what the fuck were they going to do with the insurgents? They couldn't take prisoners.

Just before Owen arrived, Salah came out of the leelee lab and stared at the pile just inside the south door. "What's this?"

"Confiscated weapons."

"And the metal cans?"

"You tell me. Could be bomb-making chemicals. Stay here, Doctor. Lieutenant Lamont might want you to translate."

Salah stiffened at the tone in Leo's voice. "I doubt those Kindred will tell you anything useful, not voluntarily."

The two stared at each other. Leo knew what Salah was thinking: *Would you torture a Kindred for information?* It was the wrong question. Before interrogation, you needed a place to actually hold prisoners, which they did not have. Nor did they have personnel for interrogation. They were four soldiers and they were getting no help from the civilians here. He turned away in contempt from Salah.

Whom he could not stop picturing holding Isabelle. Kissing Isabelle. Fucking Isabelle.

Irrelevant, Brodie.

He said to the doctor, "Put all this stuff somewhere safe. Now," and went back outside before Salah could answer.

Kindred informants had led them to this weapons cache. Leo would have to again raise the idea of recruiting and arming trust-worthy Kindred to supplement the unit. Christ, weapons could be pouring into every third tent in the camp, carried in with food sup-plies or any of the other things that kept this the most organized and cleanest refugee camp in the universe. The squad needed help. Leo found Owen.

"No," Owen said. His cheeks had hollowed and his eyes some-how retreated farther into his head. Or maybe just something in his eyes had retreated, gone so far inside that Leo couldn't see the Owen he'd known. Sure, Owen wasn't sleeping much, but none of them were, and anyway Owen had always been able to take more physical punishment and deprivation than any other three Rangers put together. This was different.

"Brodie, don't be so credulous. Those informants were softening you up. Once they gain access to our weapons and—"

"We wouldn't have to arm them with our weapons, only—"

"Did I ask for your opinion on ordnance?"

"No, sir."

"I didn't think so. Return to duty."

"Yes, sir."

Leo was off duty. This was his three hours to sleep. He tried, lying on a pallet in the ready room, but sleep eluded him.

Isabelle. Salah. Isabelle with Salah. . . .

Kindred making their clumsy guns to take by force vaccines that didn't exist. No, the guns existed for more than vaccines. *They think,* Isabelle had told him, *that all Terrans are the same, and it was Terrans who fired from space and destroyed their cities.* Well . . . but . . . didn't Owen think all Kindred were the same? Dangerous enemies. Didn't Kandiss think so, too, and maybe even Zoe?

Some Kindred were enemies, sure. But if Russia attacked the United States—

Which Leo was never going to see again. They were stuck on

Kindred forever. So didn't it make more sense to try to understand Kindred, to sort them out into dangerous and nondangerous, to think about after the spore cloud because Isabelle had said that some Kindred might have natural immunity and survive . . .

Leo wasn't used to this sort of thinking, and he didn't like it. He hadn't had these thoughts in Brazil. But, then, he'd known he was going home from Brazil. Thinking about the situation here felt almost as bad as thinking about Isabelle and Salah. But the only other thing he had at the moment to fill his sleep-deprived brain was almost as bad: two tiny girls playing with their toys, smiling up at him from huge dark eyes in their coppery faces, regarding him as an immensely interesting object that threatened them not at all.

CHAPTER 12

Kindred had plant-based drugs, including powerful opioids. The opioids had surprised Salah. Ree^ka refused all drugs, which did not surprise him.

She lay in Marianne's room, now hers (Marianne must have squeezed a pallet in someplace else; Salah had no idea where). Although she had refused medical examination, Salah judged that Ree^ka would not survive another night. He hoped that after this critical meeting, she would take the opioid. He understood that she wanted her mind clear now, but he knew of no aspect of the Kindred worldview that would preclude palliative care after the Mother of Mothers had handed down her last decrees. Surely some version of hospice must be included in bu^ka^tel. The Kindred considered themselves stewards of each other as well as of their precious, limited continent.

Ree^ka turned her head on her pillow, and did not succeed in suppressing a faint groan.

Wherever there were narcotics, there was an illegal market for them. That, too, was an aspect of life here that Salah needed to assimilate. If he was going to be here for the rest of his life—and since making love to Isabelle, that didn't seem such a terrible prospect—he needed more than the language. He needed the culture it served, because no one knew how many Kindred survivors might have natural immunity to *R. sporii*, as some Stone Age humans on Earth had. There was so much he didn't know.

Claire said, "Where's Branch? He left Big Lab to come here ten minutes ago."

Marianne said, "Probably in the leelee lab, working with the recordings from the ship. I'll get him. Don't start without us."

No one would. Marianne and Claire were in charge of what Salah now thought of as the failed vaccine program, although that wasn't really fair. In medicine, a partial success was not a failure, not even when the partial was very partial indeed.

The one leelee that had been sickened but not killed by *R. sporii* had begun to eat. Slowly, slowly the animal was recovering. There was no way to examine it closely, as there would have been in a biosafety level 4 lab; to break the seal on the improvised negative-pressure cage would have been to release spores into the lab. Kindred and Terran scientists had been reduced to watching it through the glass, to crouching on the floor to squint up at its turds from below, to rapping on the side of the cage to determine response, and other totally inadequate measures. But it was indubitable that the leelee now dragged itself around, ate and drank, sent forth a few faint chitters around its dead and decaying cousins, which also could not be removed from the cage.

Marianne and Branch returned, Branch looking as if he hadn't either slept or washed in too long. Everyone was working overtime, but Branch was also working at the hopeless task of decoding alien signals transmitted in alien code from an alien transmitter to a jerry-rigged device he did not fully understand. When she could be spared, Isabelle studied his notes to see if they corresponded to spoken Kindred. They did not.

Standing beside Ree^ka's bed, Isabelle slipped her hand into Salah's. Isabelle looked even more exhausted than Branch. Austin had not yet been found.

Noah Jenner came into the room, crowding it even more. With

Llaa^moh¡ and Ka^graa, eight people jammed themselves around Ree^ka's bed in a space the size of a large closet.

Claire said, "I think we have to go with the synth-vac we have. We can run one more leelee trial while simultaneously manufacturing as much vaccine as we can and starting to administer it. There's just no time to test more. We don't know how long it will take to become effective, and it offers only thirty-three percent protection . . ." She trailed off, clearly knowing how ridiculous that was.

Thirty-three percent on a sample size of three leelees. And the one leelee it had "protected" had sickened anyway. And that was in alien animals, not in humans. Who had, over 140,000 years, evolved immune-system differences from the Terrans the vaccine had originally been designed for. Not to mention that most vaccines needed at least a week, usually two, to protect anybody against anything.

To the low hum of Noah's translation, Claire finished with an unexpected note of defiance. "It's all we *have*."

Branch, with the audacity of the young, said, "So who gets it?"

Ka^graa said, "We scientists of World will not take the vaccine. It will sicken us and we must help with the manufacture. It is better so."

Salah's gaze dropped. Twenty-first century Americans did not bow; this was the closest he had to a silent gesture of respect. The Kindred scientists were giving their lives in the hope of saving even a few others.

But then the Mother of Mothers spoke, her voice abruptly stronger. "No. You will preserve some vaccine and take as late as possible before the spore cloud comes. Whoever survives of our people will need you. There is no disagreement possible."

Nor would there be any. Salah could see that.

Ree^ka continued. "The people in the camp are the worst of us. They have left their lahks. They have made weapons. They have tried to kill. Not all of them, that is understood. But they have defied bu^ka^tel to come here, and they must not be rewarded for this.

The vaccines will be given to the children in the camps. If they survive, Terrans will care for them."

Never had Salah heard such depth of sorrow in a voice, nor seen it as in the dark eyes of the Mother of Mothers. Ree^ka was facing not just the death of most of her people but of her civilization as well.

Marianne said, "Isabelle, tell her that we don't know how many Kindred might have natural immunity. Even the worst filoviruses on Earth have only a ninety percent kill rate, and *R. sporii* isn't a filovirus."

Isabelle said, "She knows."

They all knew. This wasn't Earth, and the Kindred were not nearly as genetically diverse as Terrans. There might indeed be some natural immunity, but on the first Kindred ship, everyone had died.

Ree^ka said, "Other lahks may come here now, those nearby. Llaa^moh¡ will know who to radio and in what order. Llaa^moh¡, you should bring your daughter and sister here now. They have my permission to leave their lahk."

Salah saw Marianne's face brighten.

The Mother of Mothers raised a feeble arm and pointed. Clearly, it took all her strength. "Marianne-mak, after the cloud, you must lead the Terran lahk to rebuild World. You must share this work with your soldiers. I so ¡mo¡mo^ you."

Another important word. But as Isabelle translated it as "sacred trust," her clutch on Salah's hand said that it was more than that.

Ree^ka faltered, and Claire eased her back onto her pillow. The Mother of Mothers closed her eyes, strength spent, and whispered, "Isabelle. Come . . . to me . . . soon."

The Kindred seemed to take this as dismissal and filed out. The Terrans followed, Branch half running back to the leelee lab and his machinery. Isabelle said to Salah in English, "There's nothing more you can do for her?"

"Only the opioids she won't take."

"Tonight?"

"I think so, yes."

"How will you set up the vaccination of the children?"

It would be difficult. As the Mother of Mothers had said, the people who had come to the camp, who had twice made assaults on the lab, were the roughest of Kindred society. Long ago on Terra, sociologists had made the observation that the worst enemies of any culture were its own young men between fourteen and twenty-four: not yet firmly anchored in life, testosterone raging, they were the ones that created both constructive revolutions and destructive gangs. Yet the camps held older men, women, children—had they followed their young rebels to keep lahks together, or because it was not possible, bu^ka^tel or no, to suppress the human bent to put self-preservation above survival of the group?

Isabelle answered her own question. "The Rangers will have to maintain order and bring the kids into the compound to be vaccinated inside."

Salah had trouble picturing that: Owen Lamont as kindergarten hall monitor. Before he could say anything, Leo Brodie came through the door from the walkway to the clinic. Salah caught the flicker in the soldier's eyes as he saw Isabelle's hand in Salah's. Another reason to distrust Brodie.

He said in passable Kindese, "I greet you, Isabelle."

"I greet you, Leo."

They each used the inflection for close friends? When had that happened?

Brodie would have continued on his pointless patrol, but Isabelle said, "Leo, I need to ask a favor."

"What?"

"Austin is still missing. I want to go up the hill to the lahk and see if he's there, plus bring Kayla here. Noah didn't go by the house like I thought he would when he arrived this morning, he just came straight here. Steve and Josh radioed that they can't leave their mining operation and aren't coming here. Ree^ka-mak says I may leave the compound only if I am escorted by one of the unit. Are you on duty? Will you walk me up there?"

Salah couldn't control his face. He felt it stiffen, felt his eyes narrow, and knew that Brodie saw it. Salah didn't want Isabelle to go outside, didn't want her to go with Brodie, didn't like that she had asked him. Probably she would have gone alone if the Mother of Mothers hadn't said otherwise. But Isabelle had asked Brodie.

Salah had a sudden picture of how they must look: a beautiful woman standing between a forty-five-year-old, slightly overweight doctor and a twenty-four-year-old, handsome soldier in superb physical condition. What a dreary cliché they were. Isabelle had slept with Salah, but was she regretting her choice? Did she believe in polyandry? He hardly knew her at all, only that she was the first woman in a long time that he'd wanted to know.

Brodie flashed a grin. "Sure, I'll take you, Isabelle. I'm just coming off duty. Let's go."

"Thank you." She smiled at him, and let go of Salah's hand.

The smile had been distracted; she was genuinely worried about Austin and Kayla. But it had still been a smile. Salah watched her walk by Brodie's side to the door.

He couldn't believe his luck. Isabelle had asked her favor just as Leo was coming off duty. Sleep-deprived weariness vanished in an instant. His mind raced, half on the safest way to protect her, half on the fact that he didn't actually have Owen's permission to leave the area. The CO hadn't said the unit couldn't leave while off duty, although the expectation was that all four of them would be immediately available for emergencies. Well, Isabelle's house was only half a klick away, and Leo was really fast, even in full kit. Also, it was up on the hill and Leo could surveil from there, see the whole area. Also, he would leave word with Zoe where he was going.

Owen wouldn't like it.

Owen didn't like anything these days. Sour as a croc with tooth-ache, Kandiss had said, which was the first time Leo learned that Kandiss came from Florida. Something was eating Owen, that was for sure—something more, that is, than the spore cloud and being marooned on Kindred and the constant tense state of jacked-up in-action. Something that Leo couldn't put his finger on. But what was Owen going to do—court-martial Leo? But, still . . .

Then Isabelle smiled at him.

The smile, sad and anxious, went straight to Leo's heart. She loved her whiny sister and that wild kid, Austin. Leo liked Austin, too, hav-ing been pretty wild himself at that age. So he said, "Sure." He visu-alized the route alongside the compound: skirt the camp, avoid the orchard and anyplace else easy to plant insurgents. Leo's action in Brazil had all been urban, but the principles were no different.

He radioed on the unit frequency, "Leaving the area for fifteen minutes, will report to you then."

"What the fuck?" Zoe said.

"Out, Zo!"

Isabelle said, "Who was that? Zoe Berman?"

"Yeah. She's all right."

"I appreciate you doing this, Leo."

"No problem." They were passing the edge of the camp now. No activity visible except a woman and an older man at a cook fire, some people sewing, a circle of older kids crouched over small stones . . . "What are those kids playing?"

"A gambling game. Sort of like Go."

He didn't know what Go was. "I didn't think Kindred gambled."

"Yeah, you guys either think we're all saints or else, like your lieu-tenant, all devils in disguise. Not true. We're human, just made nicer by a really good political and economic system."

We. Isabelle considered herself one of them. He said in Kindese, "I want know more by those things. Will you teach me?"

She stopped walking and turned to look at him. "Would you like to learn?"

"Yeah," in English. "Keep moving, Isabelle. No, not that way, over there. Longer but clearer."

She resumed walking. There was a little silence. Then she said, "Yes, I'd be glad to teach you. I'm amazed at how much Worldese you picked up already. Neither of us has much time, but we can fit in something. Now and . . . afterward. When we're not both busy for a while burying the dead."

Her honesty startled him. Leo had been trying not to think about after the spore cloud. That was how he'd gotten through Brazil: Think only about the day happening right now, the objective, the orders, the target. That had always worked for him before.

"Leo," she said as they approached the crest of the hill, "how many people have you killed?"

He hated that question, especially from civilians, who never understood. But Isabelle was different. "Eleven, mostly in Brazil. And every single kill was in defense of the Marine unit I was attached to."

"I get that," she said. "I'm not judging you."

"The others are," Leo said, again surprising himself. "Your friend Salah, for instance."

"He's a doctor. His job is saving lives, not taking them. But your unit is saving lives, too, by preventing even more violence."

"Yeah," he said, and they reached the lahk, which was a good thing because Leo's throat felt tight and he needed a moment before he spoke again. The bar girls and friends-of-friends he'd gone out with hadn't been like Isabelle. Nobody was like Isabelle.

"Stay here," he said, "while I check out the house. No, not there—stand behind that. I'll call you when it's clear."

"Okay."

The house was as beautiful as he remembered: swooping karth-wood—he knew the name now—curves, mellow gold in the orange

light, surrounded by the sweet-smelling dark foliage that would provide a fucking good cover for insurgents. And shouldn't the terrace
above him be open to the air at this time of day? The sliding panels
were all closed. Not good.

Leo circled the house. The north side stood flush to the ground,
with less cover. The door here was locked—if you could call that
lightweight contraption a lock. By now, he knew enough about
Kindred to guess that the lock wasn't supposed to keep anyone
out, just announce to visitors that nobody was here. If anybody did
break in, the lahks would cooperate to figure out who and go from
there. Or things stolen might just be given away in the next illathil.
Crazy system!

He easily smashed the lock with the butt of his rifle and cleared
the rooms, which was easy because there was nobody in them. On
one of the low tables, handmade like nearly everything here, was a
folded piece of paper addressed to Isabelle. Leo picked it up and
jogged back.

"Nobody there, just this note."

She read it and handed it back to Leo.

> Izzy—
> Austin and I going away to Steve and Josh. It's too dangerous
> here. Come get us after everything is over. At the mine.
>
> > Love,
> > Kayla

Leo said, "Who are Steve and Josh?"

"The other first-expedition Terrans in our lahk. They have a
copper mine in the central mountains and they're there a lot, but
of course they would have come back for illathil. Only—"

"Only what? Is something suspicious about that note?"

"No. Not really. Just that Kayla doesn't get along well with Steve and Josh. Nor does Austin. Still, if she's afraid, and she *would* be afraid here, with all the refugees and your unit . . . I wish she'd stayed here."

Leo didn't. If the mine was safer, then it was a better place for the kid to be. And he could do without Kayla, not that he'd seen that much of her. But she'd be around Isabelle all the time, after the spore cloud.

Don't think about that until the time comes.

"We have to go back, Isabelle."

"Yes, of course. The Mother of Mothers wants to see me. Alone."

"She does? What about?"

"I don't know. She's dying, Leo. Salah says probably tonight."

She let out a little gasp then, looking like she hadn't expected to. Tears filled her eyes. Leo, after a quick glance around for insurgents, shifted his rifle to one hand and put his arms around her. For one glorious moment, before she broke free and became herself again, he held her in his arms.

"Come on," she said, tears gone, "let's go."

All the short way to the camp, she talked to him about Kindred, a kind of crash course in how the place worked. Lahks, money, responsibility, Council of Mothers, mining, manufacturing restrictions, kids. Some of it Leo already knew and some of it he didn't but he listened hard to all of it, even as he kept a sharp lookout. He was a quick study when he wanted to be, and this time he wanted to be. The setup of her doomed society mattered to Isabelle.

At the camp, a teenage boy darted forward and threw a rock.

Instantly Leo had Isabelle behind him and his rifle pointed. The rock had bounced off his helmet; it had been aimed at him, not her. The boy, all thin coppery arms, brown knee-length dress too tight to conceal other weapons, arms out at his side, stared at Leo. The kid *wanted* Leo to shoot him. He wanted to be a martyr, a victim that insurgents could rally around. He was romanticizing his own death.

"Get lost," Leo said in Kindese. Then, in English, "Isabelle, move to the compound staying between me and the camp."

She did. Leo backed away, weapon at the ready, knowing without looking that Zoe was covering him from the roof. The boy shouted something and Isabelle started to shout back but Leo said, "No. Be quiet," and she was.

Inside the compound, he said, "What did the kid say?"

"He called me a filthy Terran turd."

Leo nodded, headed to the ready room, and waited to see if Zoe had reported Leo's unauthorized expedition to Owen, if Owen wanted to see him, what might happen next.

Isabelle crept quietly into Ree^ka-mak's room, prepared to leave if the Mother of Mothers was asleep. She was not.

"Come here, child."

Isabelle knelt by the bed and took Ree^ka's hand in hers. The bones and veins rose under the skin like karthwood twigs. Ree^ka's fingers felt icy.

"Tell . . . you two great things."

"Yes, Mother of Mothers."

"Afterward . . . heal the Kindred wound with the soldiers. Marry one."

It was the traditional way of forestalling conflict between lahks—and, once, monarchies on Earth. Married women remained with their own birth lahks; their brothers and male cousins were there to help raise children; marriage contracts were renewable or not every five years. In such a culture, closeness and fidelity between partners were mostly a matter of choice and good manners. Blood was what mattered, not pair-bonding. Marriage was easy, and easily changed. Children were not. Children bound lahks together for good.

"Mother of Mothers . . . I cannot do that."

"You can. One . . . contract."

"I'm sorry. Terrans do not—"

"You are no longer Terran."

It was the greatest compliment Isabelle could have been paid. She bowed her head. But she did not promise to marry anyone. Ree^ka had not spent much time around Terrans. Intelligent as she was, she apparently did not realize that marrying a Ranger would not create an alliance. Not even if Owen Lamont married sixteen Kindred women in rapid succession and fathered thirty-two children. The US Army did not work that way.

Ree^ka did not press her. Instead, she told her the second great thing. Isabelle's eyes widened. She half rose, dropping Ree^ka's hand. "What?"

But the Mother of Mothers had exhausted her strength. Her eyes closed.

CHAPTER 13

Marianne rubbed the small of her back with her left hand. She'd been standing at her improvised "lab bench" for hours. *I'm too old for this,* she thought for the hundredth time. Although weariness sagged the faces of even the younger people.

She had lost track of how many doses of vaccine they had made, or could make before they had to begin administering it. All the data was fuzzy because it was built on still fuzzier data. Would the vaccine protect humans at all? If it did, how long did it take to become effective? How would they give it to just children without a riot from the childless adults in the camp? How much would the Rangers cooperate in keeping the process orderly instead of protecting the Terrans by keeping them prisoner in the compound? What would everyone do after the spore cloud hit and they had hundreds of dead bodies to—

Don't think that far ahead.

Ka^graa said from his workstation, "You to go sleep, Marianne-mak."

She shook her head, forcing a smile. Ka^graa was learning English, even though chances were strong that he would be dead soon and all language with him.

It wasn't like her to dwell on tragedy. Always—well, almost always—work had been her distraction, her solace, her purpose. All at once, however, she wanted not to work but to see her family. She went to the closet where Noah, Llaa^moh¡, and Lily all slept on a single pallet. Llaa^moh¡ was working in the lab; Noah wasn't in the room; Lily lay asleep, dark curls tangled on her coppery cheek, clutching a stuffed toy of no species known to her grandmother.

As Marianne continued toward the leelee lab, which she could smell through the closed door, Isabelle came out of what had once been Marianne's room and grabbed Marianne's arm.

"I have to tell you something."

This wasn't like Isabelle. Marianne removed Isabelle's hand, which had clutched so hard it left dents in Marianne's skin, and said, "Ree^ka is gone?"

"No, not yet. But she told me something. Come here, into my room. Close the door."

Marianne did, her heart speeding up. *What fresh hell now?*

Isabelle said, "The Mother of Mothers says there is a way to call back the second Kindred ship."

"What?"

"The second ship. They built two, you know, from the alien plans. The first one was the colony ship that encountered the spore cloud first, after it jumped to wherever it was preset to go. It—"

"I know. Branch has been trying to decode that weird pinging still coming from the ship. But Ree^ka-mak says there's a way to call it back here?"

"Yes. They never did, because—"

"Because there was no point, with the ship infected with spores and everyone dead. And there still isn't, Isabelle. That ship is contaminated. If it came here, all it would do is bring the spore cloud earlier."

"Yes, I know that. But afterward—"

Then Marianne saw it. How had she been so stupid, so exhausted, so myopic? If they could call back the ship, then maybe they could go back to Earth. But—

"Did you say it was preset to go to this other planet? How could it go to Earth?"

"I don't know. But maybe there are scientists who have made progress on figuring out the drive—"

"Isabelle," Marianne said sternly, hearing too late that this was her tone for correcting graduate students who had just contaminated a lab sample with their own DNA, "if Terran scientists hadn't figured out the drive, why do you think Kindred scientists could? And where is this . . . this call-back device, anyway?"

"Well, that's part of the problem. It was on the ship that the *Stremlenie* destroyed. But apparently there exists somewhere another device that can call it back, only Ree^ka didn't know where it is."

"Ree^ka-mak didn't know? You told me there's no information on Kindred that the Mother of Mothers doesn't have access to."

"That's true. But this . . . device is only indicated on the titanium tablets with the plans for building both ships. It wasn't with the parts to build it. No one knows why."

"I see. Look, I don't think we should tell anyone about this. It's a ship we can't contact, can't recall, and so can't go travel to Earth in. But there are Terrans desperate to go back, and this will only just agitate them more."

"Lieutenant Lamont," Isabelle said. "Kayla. Branch. Maybe Steve. Yes, you're right. There's no point in agitating them more."

"Especially the Rangers."

It was the wrong thing to say; Isabelle had a far different view of the military than Marianne did. Marianne forced a smile and said, "Then we're agreed? We keep this quiet?"

"Yes. For now, anyway."

The two women stared at each other. Marianne had a sudden, surprising thought: *I wish this girl and not Elizabeth were my daughter.*

Disloyal, futile, disloyal. But it wasn't the first time that Marianne had realized how much more she had in common with—and how much closer she felt to—Isabelle and Branch and Claire than to her own three children. Parenthood did not guarantee affinity, and that was a sorrow that too easily turned to reproach. But she was tired of heaping abuse on herself. She unlocked the leelee lab. Branch looked up from the equipment on the floor, beside which he knelt like some sort of pagan worshipper.

Branch said, "Do they need me? I'm sorry, I just wanted to—"

"Why don't you find a bench for that thing so you don't have to kneel on the floor?"

Branch stared at her blankly; his knees and back were all young.

Marianne said, more gently, "How is it going? Actually, I don't even really know what you're doing here. Fill me in. The colony ship is sending pings . . ."

Branch jumped lightly to his feet. "I've made contact with the ship through this jerry-rigged receiver. The Kindred haven't even *tried* to listen to the pings since the real receiver was destroyed by the *Stremlenie!*"

"Well, they've been a little busy, Branch."

"Even so! There wouldn't be any human communication, obviously, but the ship was still transmitting some sort of data, probably positional and maybe also astronomical, and they just weren't interested. Can you believe that?"

Marianne could. The Kindred combined intense practicality with their almost spiritual belief in their stewardship of the planet. The colony ship was of no practical use—was in fact a practical danger—and it was contaminated. How many Terran words were there for "unclean"? Treif, marime, desecrated, haram . . .

She said, "So you're receiving signals. But—"

"But I can't decode them. I've tried every number system I can think of. Primes, Fibonacci sequences, Feigenbaum numbers, everything. I've tried turning them into electromagnetic radiation, at least within the limits of the equipment. Noah's been really good about bringing me whatever I ask for, if he can. I've tried to get text or visuals or sound or—"

"I meant, but what's the point?"

Branch blinked. "To know. To understand."

Pure science. Hadn't she been dedicated to it, once? Yes, but not for a long time, not since the Kindred had landed on Earth and announced that doom was on its way behind them. Since then, she had pretty much abandoned pure science for its bastard daughter, technology.

"I see," Marianne said, because she did, and her heart ached for him. There would be precious little pure science on World after the spore cloud. "Branch, I think you need to go back to the lab. There's probably more to do at your stage of the vac-prep by now."

"Yes. You're right."

They left, locking the door behind them, keeping safe a few chittering leelees, the negative-pressure cages of dead ones, and Branch's heartbreaking, Rube Goldberg attempt to reach out to the stars.

The president or whatever she was, that very old lady, died. The scientists inside the compound got it together enough to make some vaccine. Then they called a meeting with the Rangers to do a mission brief.

Leo could have told Marianne and Noah and the rest that this was a bad idea. Owen already had his mission and he wasn't budging from it. Protect the second-expedition scientists and then get the unit home. It really grieved Owen that he couldn't bring the bodies of Colonel Matthews and Miguel Flores back to Earth. A Ranger left none of his unit behind.

But Owen attended the meeting inside the compound—for the intel, most likely—and he brought Leo, who was supposed to be on patrol, with him. Kandiss and Zoe held the position outside—not that anything much had been happening. Right now the biggest enemies were boredom and sleep deprivation. In Brazil, Leo had seen those two cause soldiers to do stupid things. Well, from what Noah was saying now, boredom at least would be over soon.

"So we're going to begin the vaccinations tomorrow morning. The plan is for Isabelle, Dr. Bourgiba, and I to go into the camp and tell people that we are only vaccinating children. Then we'll escort the kids in twos and threes to the east wall, where doctors Bourgiba and Patel will administer the vaccines. Then we walk or carry that group back and bring the next ones."

"No," Owen said. It was the first word he'd spoken.

"What do you mean, no?" Noah said.

"I mean no. You haven't thought it through. You have vaccines outside the compound where people can see them, you're going to get a rush on the station. Huge. I don't want to have to shoot any more Kinnies than I have to."

Why did Owen use that word? It had become ugly, like gooks or towelheads, and Owen knew it. It was like he was trying to alienate the scientists. Or maybe he just hated the planet so much that the word slipped out.

Even Kandiss had acknowledged, grudgingly and in very few words, that Owen was being eaten up inside, although nobody was sure by what.

Owen continued, "Bring the kids inside if you have to do this. We'll cover you from both the roof and the ground and make sure the insurgents see that."

Noah, his face tight, said, "They are not insurgents. The children will be much more frightened, and the mothers much more anxious, if we separate them. I suppose we can bring the mothers inside, too—"

"No," Owen said.

Isabelle jumped in. "Noah, I think that Lieutenant Lamont is concerned about our safety. Even mothers have been used as suicide bombers on Earth, and—"

"We have no suicide bombers here!"

"—and the compound is more vulnerable if we keep opening and closing the gate. I'm not saying I agree with you, Lieutenant, but that is your concern, isn't it?"

"It is."

"Then what do you propose?"

Leo's heart swelled with pride in her, which was ridiculous because she wasn't his. But damn she was good! She was the real shit.

Owen said, "Don't administer any vaccine at all."

Leo blinked. What? The vaccine was what the scientists had been working on day and night! Why would Owen say—

"You told us that you don't know if the vaccine will work," Owen said, the words coming out like he was laying down automatic fire. "If it does, it only helps one in three, at best. That one will probably get really sick. You can't vaccinate more than maybe a few hundred kids anyway. Even if it's five hundred, then we get a hundred and seventy sick kids, many or most of who might die along with the native scientists, and you have twelve Terrans to theoretically nurse them, one of those a kid himself and five not even here: Schrupp, Beyon, the McGuires, Kayla Rhinehart. So six adults to nurse a hundred and seventy sick and dying kids."

He isn't counting the squad, Leo thought.

"And then when we go home, how are you going to take with us any of the kids that survive? There won't be room. And they would get sick all over again adjusting to Terra's microbes."

Go home? There was no way to go home. Looking at Own, seeing the set of his jaw like an erection, feeling the conviction rising off him like heat, Leo wondered for the first time if Owen was crazy. Battle fatigue, PTSD, whatever—guys got like that sometime. Except—

Everything Owen had just said was actually true.

Noah, his face as grim as Owen's, said, "Lieutenant, we *are* going to administer this vaccine. Your opinion is not being sought about that. It's being sought about the best way to do it without danger."

"You can't do it without danger."

The two men glared at each other, Owen in full gear and Noah in his silly pale dress, and Leo had a sharp image from Brazil: a fight between an imported mongoose and a viper.

Owen added, "Right now I'm getting reports from the compound roof of troop movements, heading here."

"Those aren't 'troop movements,' they're the arriving mourners for the Mother of Mothers' funeral!"

"Do you think I haven't seen insurgents use local customs to commit terrorism?"

Also true, Leo thought, and blocked his worst memories from Brazil.

Noah said evenly, "We are going to administer this vaccine. Period."

"Then let Kinnie scientists take it into the camp. All the second-expedition Terrans stay inside the compound, where we can do our job protecting you. The Kinnies can take care of their own."

Silence, except for the low hum of Salah's translation. Owen had used the offensive term deliberately, twice.

Noah took a step forward, fists clenched. Before he—or Owen—could do anything stupid, Isabelle again jumped in. "It's not a bad idea, Noah. We can take the vaccine into the camp. I've heard that there's anti-Terran feeling there, and that it's growing. If we Kindred are the ones to go in, not the Terrans, it might defuse any violence. Claire can teach you and me the procedure. Also Steve and Josh— they're on their way here, finally."

No. Not Isabelle.

Owen pushed it. "So I'm right that the Kinnies would attack humans?"

Appalled silence. Owen had to have said it deliberately, he was too smart to not know how that would be received, what was he playing at—

Noah said, "You are dismissed, Lieutenant."

Isabelle said hastily, "So we're agreed? Tomorrow morning the Kindred and I take the vaccine into the camp?"

Leo waited for Owen to say *Not you*. He didn't. He considered Isabelle and Noah to be Kindred, not Terran. And he didn't care if they were caught in any violence. They weren't part of his mission.

"I'm going, too," Salah said. "I'm a *doctor*. Let Claire stay inside, but you'll need all the translators you can get."

"No," Owen said, and strode out of the room before anyone could answer him.

The crowded, stuffy room smelled of contempt.

Leo returned to patrol, his head buzzing. As he jogged around the far perimeter, noon sunshine pouring sweat from under his helmet and down his arms, he saw the "troop movements" that Kandiss must have reported to Owen. He paused to raise his binoculars.

The land fell away just below where he stood, and he could see for kilometers. Fields, orchards, scattered lahks, the river tumbling in gentle stages from here to the bottom of the valley, shining amid the purplish vegetation. Dark birdlike things soared above the river. Up here, along the road about a klick away and two dozen strong, came a group of thirty Kindred. Some walked; some rode four-wheeled bicycles; a few were carried in open litters. Nearly all were women, and most were old.

Mothers. Come for the Mother of Mothers' funeral. Leo almost laughed, except that it wasn't funny. When Kandiss had reported, the procession was far enough away that he probably couldn't see it was an army of old ladies. Besides, insurgents often used as terrorists those people less likely to raise suspicion: kids, women, old men.

However, Leo would have bet his life that these weren't terrorists. They were the heads of lahks, like governors of states back home, come to bury a president.

"Procession coming up the road from the east," he reported. "Looks like a bunch of mourners. Mostly old women. I think they're heading to the camp."

"Copy that," Owen said. "Resume patrol." Leo watched a minute longer—they were *slow*—and then resumed patrol. The camp was quiet. Kindred took naps in the heat of the day, like Spanish or Italians. A sensible custom.

A lot of their customs were starting to seem sensible to him.

At the north side of the perimeter, a figure trudged toward him across a grazing field. Again Leo raised his binoculars. It was Austin Rhinehart.

Kandiss said from atop the roof, "Prodigal son returns."

Leo vaguely remembered something about a prodigal from the Bible, but he couldn't recall what. He waited for Austin to reach him. The kid looked filthy, exhausted, and miserable.

"Hey, Austin."

"Hey, Leo."

"Where you been?" And how did Leo get saddled with the role of truant officer? He didn't care where Austin had been. Except that maybe he did, and the boy looked so unhappy.

Austin said shortly, "I was gone."

"Well, I know that. You and your mother went with the Terrans who own the mine, right? The McGuire brothers?"

"Right."

"So where's your mom now?"

"Still with Steve and Josh."

"Uh-huh. And why are you back, and from the wrong direction?"

"Leave me alone! You aren't in my lahk!"

And give shit-thanks for that. But—

"Look, Austin," Leo said. "It's good you're back. But you're going to have some explaining to do. Everybody's furious about that vaccine you stole."

"What? I didn't steal vaccine! I didn't even know they made any yet!"

"Not vaccine they made. The original, from Earth."

"I didn't take it!"

Either the kid was telling the truth or he was a terrific liar. At Austin's age, Leo had been a terrific liar. He let the vaccine drop.

"Okay, you didn't take the vaccine. That still doesn't tell me where you were."

"With friends."

"Where?"

Austin tried to push past. Leo caught him by the arm. The squad needed whatever intel Austin possessed. "Listen, Austin. I like you. But you were somewhere mysterious and Lieutenant Lamont doesn't like mysterious. So you can tell me or you can tell him, and believe me, you'd rather tell me."

Austin's face changed. He didn't recognize good cop–bad cop— no TV on Kindred. And he was afraid of Owen. Which made sense— Owen was pretty scary these days.

Austin said desperately, "I told you. I was away, with friends. Someplace secret."

Leo loosened his grip a little and pretended a smile. "I had a se- cret castle at your age. Made of cardboard, in a tree."

"It's not a stupid castle in a tree! I'm not a kid!"

Leo realized his mistake. "No, you're not."

"I'm old enough to take care of my mother!"

"Where are you taking care of her?"

"Leave me alone, Leo! I'm tired!" He was blinking back tears.

"Where, Austin?" Leo tightened his grip again, just short of pain. "Who's there?"

"Ask Noah! He knows! He followed me there once!"

"Noah followed you there? Noah knows everything?"

"Not everything! I'm the only one who knows everything! Ow, let me go, you're hurting me!"

Leo didn't let go. Better this for Austin than what Owen might do. "What doesn't Noah know? Tell me that and I'll let you go, as long as you tell me the truth. What's at your friend's place that Noah doesn't know about?"

"Nothing important! Just a rusty old alien machine I found buried in sand in a cave! Well, it's not rusty, but—it's an alien pyramid! There! Are you satisfied? Noah knows everything else! Ask him!"

"I will." Leo released Austin, who rubbed his eyes and then glared through the dirt on his face. "How'd you get so dirty?"

"It's a fucking *cave*! Ask Noah!"

Leo believed him. Too bad he had to manhandle the kid to get the information. Although compared to what Leo had gone through at his foster homes on Terra . . . but this wasn't Terra. And Leo wasn't that kind of monster, and he didn't want this boy, Isabelle's nephew, to think he was. So he said quietly, "I'm sorry, Austin. I didn't mean to hurt you. It was just necessary. And can I ask you one more question? It's something you know and I don't, but I'd like to. Please."

Leo's tone—contrite, humble—clearly confused Austin. He said nothing, but after a moment he gave a grudging nod.

Leo said, "What's 'moe-moe'?"

"What?"

"I might not be pronouncing it right." Deliberately so; let Austin feel superior.

"You mean '¡mo¡mo^'?"

"Yeah."

"What do you want to know that for?"

"I'm curious. It's a word Isabelle used."

"And you like her. You want sex with her. Forget it," Austin said with the viciousness of the aggrieved young, "she's having sex with Dr. Bourgiba!"

Leo let go of Austin's arm. Immediately the kid looked scared. Leo said, "Go on inside the compound. Face the music there."

Austin looked puzzled; he didn't know what the phrase meant. Then he scurried away, looking back once over his shoulder, fearful, like Leo might shoot him in the back. But before Austin reached the compound, he called back to Leo, "I'm sorry!"

Leo nodded that it was okay, because it was. Austin had just needed to get back at him. Now they were even, and the next time they met, Austin would be okay with him again.

Leo radioed Owen to say there was a secret place somewhere that Noah Jenner knew about. If it was a weapons cache—and Leo doubted that, Noah was no insurgent—then it was Owen's job to decide what to do about it. If anything. It wasn't like they didn't have their hands full right here, come tomorrow and the vaccination program that might happen.

Or not.

CHAPTER 14

Branch knocked on the door of Marianne's new closet, where she had gone for a few precious moments alone with her granddaughter. Lily lay curled in Marianne's lap, asleep. Unable to talk to Lily except for a few broken phrases of Kindred, Marianne had played finger games with her and then with Lily's doll—small replicas of humans turned up in every known culture and so Marianne was not surprised by Lily's doll. Now the doll lay on the pallet beside them and Marianne cradled Lily, fingers against the child's skin, hoping that no fever would develop there.

An hour earlier, Lily and Llaa^moh¡ had received the synthesized vaccine.

So much agony had gone into that decision. Lily was half Terran—would Noah's immunity alone have protected her? Chances were strong that Noah had immunity, but what if he didn't? Also, might the vaccine itself harm Lily? The last thing Marianne had anticipated was using her granddaughter as a lab rat, but Noah and Llaa^moh¡ had made the decision. If Lily was going to sicken from the vaccine, her parents wanted time to care for her before they were inundated with sick children.

Later, Noah and Llaa^moh¡ would sit all night with their daughter, waiting. It had been both heroic and kind of them to first let Marianne have a precious hour alone with Lily.

"Dr. Jenner, can I come in?"

Annoyed at the interruption, Marianne called softly, "Is it important?"

"Yes!"

Which might or might not be true. "Come in."

Branch opened the door, obviously bursting to tell Marianne something. First, however, she put a finger to her lips and whispered, "What's all that noise in the walkway?"

"Austin is back. Marianne—"

"Austin? Does he have the original vaccine?" Bile rose in her throat. If the original, the *safe*, vaccine was here right after Lily had received the untested synth-vac—

"No. He says he didn't take it. But of course he did, and now he's lying so he doesn't get punished."

Marianne said nothing. She had raised difficult children—all three of hers, in different ways—and knew that difficult children could turn out all right in the end. Look at Noah, once an aimless addict, now a sort of leader to a sort of alien race. You never knew. Branch, at twenty-eight, was childless.

"But, Dr. Jenner, listen—"

"Keep your voice down, Branch, Lily's asleep."

"Oh. Sorry. But *listen*—I've got the transmissions from the colony ship decoded!"

"You have!" She had raised her voice, and Lily stirred on her lap. "You have?" she whispered.

"Well, partly, anyway. I figured out how to translate the signal to sound waves. Now I just have to clear the noise and—"

"You mean speech? But there's nobody left alive on the ship!"

"No, not speech. I tried that already. It's some other code, but not from a voice transmitter like the one we have—had—on the *Friendship*. From the ship itself, I think. It could be really useful astronomical data."

Useful to whom? The spore cloud was going to commit viral

genocide on the planet. Looking at Branch's excited face, the face of youth so easily able to compartmentalize that one thing at a time could fill his entire mental universe, Marianne did not say this.

"Good work, Branch. But aren't you supposed to be in the lab, preparing vaccine?"

"Aren't you?" A flash of anger, born of disappointment in her reaction. Almost immediately Branch said, "I'm sorry!"

"It's okay. Let's both go now." In the doorway behind Branch, Noah loomed. His dark gaze in the artificially coppery skin, those eyes surgically widened to look as much like a Kindred's as possible, had gone immediately to Lily.

"No fever," Marianne said, and let her son take Lily from her while Branch held out his hand to help her up so they could both go back to work.

Austin sat in the dark, in a former blanket closet, and scowled to keep back shameful tears. They would be sorry. In a day or two, they would all be sorry!

The blanket closet was empty of blankets, the entire stock depleted for people to sleep on wherever they could. Austin had yanked out the two bottom shelves so he could sit upright on the closet's floor. There wasn't room to lie down, but he was too mad to go to sleep anyway. Isabelle and Noah had yelled at him, threatened him, and accused him of what he hadn't done. He hadn't stolen the fucking vaccines! He wouldn't do that! Did they think he wanted Lily to die, or the scientists who were going to vaccinate all those kids tomorrow? Was that what they thought of him?

It served them right, what he was going to steal when he got the chance! If they thought he was a thief, then he would be one! That would show them!

Although that wasn't why he was going to kidnap Dr. Patel. It was to protect his mother, the only true member of Austin's lahk, the only blood member (forget Isabelle—she had betrayed him). "First, always, the lahk"—wasn't that what he'd been taught his whole life? It was! Bu^ka^tel! But now, when all he was doing was acting on that—

Noah had guessed where Kayla was. "You took her to Tony and Nathan, in the mountains, didn't you? Let her stay there for now. We have more important things to do here." And Noah had turned away from Austin, in disgust.

Isabelle hadn't been any kinder. "Just when we need you to act like a grown-up—you're thirteen, for God's sake!"

Austin *was* grown up! That's why he was doing this! And there were no gods on World, only lahks. Which he was acting to serve his lahk the best way possible, even if they couldn't see it. But they would be sorry when civilization collapsed all around them and they died in riots or starved like rats—Tony had been graphic about what those were—while he and his mother and, yes, Claire Patel, were safe in Haven. Dr. Patel would thank him one day for saving her life, just like Kayla would.

But first Austin had to get her there. He had a plan. Scrunched against the back wall of the closet, he went over and over the plan in his mind, until the thought popped into his mind to wonder what Leo would think of it.

No, Leo had nothing to do with this. Still, it would be nice if the Rangers survived the collapse of civilization, or at least if Leo did. They could help Tony rebuild. Then Leo, too, would be grateful that Austin had saved a doctor.

In the dark, he fingered the knife he'd stolen from the kitchen when Isabelle, still furious, had left him there to "at least eat something, for fuck's sake!"

Austin hoped no one would miss the knife before he needed it. He also hoped he wouldn't need it—but he was prepared to do whatever he had to. That's what courage was. Leo had once told him so.

Salah and Isabelle stood beside the doorway that connected Big Lab to the Rangers' ready room, that secretive hideaway. Lamont had just emerged, dressed in what looked to Salah like enough gear to take on the Russian army.

Watch your own prejudices, Doctor.

"They want a funeral?" Lamont said. "Here? Now?"

"*We* are going to have one," Isabelle said. "At my lahk house. I'm telling you so you know what to expect, Lieutenant."

"And what is that?"

Salah watched Isabelle choose her words carefully. Lamont looked like hell. He hadn't slept in days. The Rangers did sleep, of course, but not much, and apparently Lamont least of all. Salah noted the dark, puffy circles around Lamont's eyes, the jumpy irritability, the inhibition of the acoustic startle response. He couldn't see the mental signs, which was what Salah was afraid of. Nobody might notice those until Lamont showed impaired judgment, or hallucinated, or went bat-shit psychotic. Claire had tried to reason with Lamont about the need for the Rangers to sleep more, but she'd gotten nowhere.

And the worse Lamont looked, the worse the looks he leveled at Salah. No direct sneers or racist remarks; that was not his style. Just a lowering of inhibitions, gnawing away at the iron Ranger discipline, letting the underlying prejudices show. Salah, who knew everyone's medical history, knew what Lamont had been through when he'd been captured by people who looked like Salah.

Isabelle said, "The mourning ceremony doesn't last long. Ree^ka's body will be carried from the compound on the—"

"No," Owen said. "No one enters the compound."

"Noah will carry her body to the camp and it can be placed there onto the litter she came in on. Then all the mothers, including me, will accompany it up the hill to my lahk. What happens there need not concern you. The body will be returned to the soil that nurtured it."

"Buried? Burned?"

"Neither, and not your business."

Not buried or burned? What would they do with it, then? And it wasn't like Isabelle to be curt with the Rangers, whom she inexplicably admired. Involuntarily, Salah glanced up at the ceiling, where Leo Brodie wasn't even on duty; Kandiss was.

Lamont didn't react to Isabelle's rudeness; maybe he'd expected it. His gaze turned inward, maybe mentally measuring the distance between compound and lahk house, which was about half a kilometer. Not, Salah guessed, within firing distance of pipe guns or throwing distance of bombs or anything else the Kindred could devise, or Lamont probably would have burned the house down by now. Lamont regarded the Kindred with scorn for their military inexperience. Salah honored them for it.

Lamont said, "Permission granted, so long as none of my protectees leaves the compound," and Salah felt his gorge rise. Isabelle hadn't been asking permission. But she merely nodded, with neither subservience nor defiance.

When Lamont had left, Salah said to her, "Should Noah carry out the body now?"

"No, not yet. Tell all the second-expedition Terrans to go into the clinic. We Kindred need Big Lab for our farewell to her."

We. Our. There it was again, the line she drew between herself and him. At least Brodie, too, was on the other side of the line. Salah said, "Afterward, when the ceremony is over, will you come to my room?"

"Not tonight. I need to sleep before we start vaccinating tomorrow morning."

"I understand. But I meant to sleep."

"Not tonight. After the ceremony I want to stay and translate if the scientists need me, and then I promised Leo fifteen minutes of

Kindred instruction. He'll be awake and off duty, briefly, and since the Rangers are going to be here with us even after the cloud hits, it's important they learn what they're going to have to deal with. Leo is the only one so far who will listen to me. The soldiers don't sleep much, have you noticed?"

"Yes," Salah said. "I have."

From just inside the east door, which Zoe Berman had permitted to remain open so Salah could see this, Noah carried the Mother of Mothers across the open zone. Her body, wrapped in a light blanket but with her face uncovered, looked like it weighed nothing in Noah's arms. Salah, who had officially pronounced her dead, knew that ancient face had smoothed into lines of peace, almost of joy.

On the roof, Mason Kandiss covered Noah with an assault rifle.

The camp was quiet. Fires burned, sending spirals of smoke straight up in the still air. No rustle from the purple vegetation, no cries from children. At the edge of camp, four male litter bearers and nineteen Mothers, all that could travel here in time, waited in their pale wraps. Isabelle, almost as tall as the Kindred, was among them, distinguished only by her pale skin and light brown hair.

Noah moved slowly, although Salah doubted that Noah feared dropping Ree^ka. Rather, his pace matched the sense of solemn ceremony that overlay everything this evening. The Kindred in the camp were, by the Mother of Mothers' own admission, the least acculturated and most dangerous of Kindred's inhabitants. Yet the men and women, boys and girls, standing beside the Mothers all wore the same expression: respect, sorrow, profound acceptance. Some of them might have tried to kill Rangers; tomorrow some might rush the compound after vaccine; some might hate Terrans as an indivisible entity that had destroyed their cities, as so many groups on Earth had hated other groups as indivisible entities. But tonight they stood in respectful and apparently sincere mourning.

On Terra, Salah had seen people from the opposing political party jeer and taunt at the assassination of President Cranston.

He had seen cemeteries defaced, the gravestones scrawled with hate words.

He had been attacked by a patient to whom he had to give the news of an inoperable brain tumor.

A poem by Rainer Maria Rilke floated into his mind. The German original eluded him, although he did speak some German, but the English was there:

> Already my gaze is upon the hill, the sunny one
> At the end of the path which I've only just begun.
> So we are grasped, by that which we could not grasp
> At such great distance, so fully manifest—
> And it changes us, even when we do not reach it,
> Into something that, hardly sensing it, we already are—

What had grasped the Kindred, changing their Terran heredity into something else, something that all humans already were, or could be? Just culture, nurture, a kinder set of laws?

Yet tomorrow, there was a good chance some of these same Kindred would murder anyone who stood between them and a vaccine.

Noah reached the litter and laid Ree^ka's body onto it. The circle of Mothers gently but unmistakably closed around the litter, edging him out. Noah walked back across the open perimeter. A second German writer came to Salah, harsher than Rilke: "All things are subject to interpretation, and whichever interpretation prevails at a given time is a function of power and not truth."

"One down, a hundred thousand to go," Zoe said over their private frequency. Leo didn't think it was funny. For one thing, the old lady had maybe helped keep the insurgents in check. Sometimes Zoe didn't think far enough ahead. She was a terrific Ranger but not much of a strategist.

Leo had duty at the south door of the compound, facing the hill up to Isabelle's lahk. He had watched the funeral procession climb the hill, after which there hadn't been anything else to see. In a few minutes Owen would relieve Leo and Leo would get three hours' sleep, except that he was going to claim the fifteen minutes that Isabelle had promised him. No way he preferred sleep to that.

Zoe said, "Christ, I'm tired. Hey, Leo—all those waving flashlights at the funeral—what do you suppose they use for batteries if they don't have factories and shit?"

"They have factories. Just not near here. And the flashlights use biofluorescence."

"What the fuck is that?"

Leo knew the answer because he'd asked Austin, who'd asked Graa^lok and told Leo. "Bacteria in the flashlights that glows if you mix them with other bacteria."

"Really getting to know this place, aren't you?"

"Well, we're stuck here."

"Leo, you ever wonder if the Russian ship might return to finish the job?"

"Yeah, of course."

"No good—right? Can't reach it in orbit. We might rush their forces if it lands and they come out, especially if they think we're all dead. But their crew would just take off again and start shooting. We don't have anything that could take her down."

"We'd have to wait," Leo said; he'd given this a lot of thought. "Hide, wait until they're all outside the ship and feeling in control. Get the help of the local cops and train them. Force multiplication."

Zoe said forcefully, "Rangers don't do that kind of counterinsurgency shit. Lamont would never agree."

"Yeah, I know. You're not Green Berets. But—"

"We don't do that."

"We're doing a lot of things Rangers don't do. And Zo—if it helps us get home?"

"Well . . . fuck, it would be nice to go home. See my sister. Have a Big Mac. Get drunk at this great bar near the base."

Leo, moved by the unaccustomed wistfulness in her voice, didn't point out that if they got home, her sister would be twenty-eight years older than when Zoe left, her bar might no longer exist, and who knew if McDonald's would still be in business?

But then Zoe's voice changed. "Want to tell you something, Leo."

"Okay."

"I'm . . . shit, I'm a little nervous to go home. If we ever do. Twenty-eight years. Nothing'll be the same. I don't know about . . . you know. Adjusting and shit."

"I'm not sure we'll be going home, Zo." No matter what Owen said.

"Yeah. But what I'm thinking is—what if going is worse than staying here?"

"Well, the—"

"Twenty-eight fucking years! That's more years than I am already!"

Owen emerged from the compound. Leo said, "Gotta go, Zoe." Owen relieved him, and Leo hurried to the ready room, brushed his teeth, combed his hair, and went to wait for Isabelle in the tiny kitchen where their simple meals were either prepared by Kindred cooks or brought in by Noah Jenner. God, he was sick of vegetables. A Big Mac would be wonderful. Damn Zoe for putting it in his mind.

The kitchen had no chairs, so Leo leaned against the wall. He'd had only four hours of sleep in the last twenty-four, but he was too excited to feel drowsy, straightening when she came in.

"I greet you, Isabelle." She'd been crying; there were salt-tear trails on her cheeks. Leo wanted to lick them away.

"I greet you, Leo."

"How was the funeral?" Then, because that sounded stupid, he added, "Did everything go all right?"

"Yes. Ree^ka is ¡mundik¡."

"What does that mean?" He hadn't heard before a word that both began and ended with that tongue click.

"It means . . . it's complicated. Returned to the planet after an honorable life, with sort of overtones of joining the soil, almost like a wedding."

Weird—marrying a planet.

Isabelle said, "Say it. '¡Mundik¡.'"

He did, three times, until she was satisfied and smiled. "You really do want to learn. But let's start with something simpler, like basic conversation."

"In a minute. First I want to ask about tomorrow. I'll be on the roof with Berman, covering you when you take vaccines into the camp. But I want to know if there's anything the Kindred might do that would look suspicious to Zoe and me but isn't really because it's, you know, just customs we don't understand."

Isabelle's eyes sharpened. Leo felt that, maybe for the first time, she really *saw* him. She said, "Your lieutenant didn't ask that."

Leo was silent; he wasn't going to diss Owen, not even for her.

"It's a good question," Isabelle said. "I don't think there's anything weird, not for this."

"Lieutenant Lamont told you to not go into any tents, right? Make the kids be brought out to you, and stay within ten feet of the perimeter where we can cover you."

"He told us all that, yes."

Leo repeated it anyway. "If there's a rush on the compound, if people run past you toward the compound, hit the dirt and crawl *away* from the compound and the attackers. Try to reach a tree or other—"

"Lamont told us all that, Leo."

"Here's something he didn't tell you. Do you know a guy called Lu^kaj^ho?"

"No."

"He's a Kindred cop. He tipped me off to one weapons cache in the camp, and he and three of his buddies will be working the inside, on my signals. I can't describe him because they all sort of look alike to me—no, I know I'm not supposed to say that but it's true and I'll learn eventually—but if you get in real trouble, he or one of his guys will get you to safety if they can. You'll know it's him and not some kidnapper because he'll say a code word to you that I taught him. It's 'GI Joe.'"

Isabelle didn't smile. "Help just me, or help Salah and Noah, too?"

Leo met her gaze levelly. "Just you." And then, because he was learning to read her face, he said, "I wouldn't do that, Isabelle."

Slowly she nodded. "I know you wouldn't. I'm sorry, Leo. I know you wouldn't." She put her hand on his arm.

His anger, immediate and hot, dissipated. She was learning him, too. He was not—quite apart from his Army vows—not the kind of man who would shoot a rival. Or let him get shot, not if Leo could stop it. Which meant—didn't it?—that he and Salah *were* rivals, that maybe he had a chance with her.

Now it was her hand on his arm that burned.

She moved it to his face, briefly touching his cheek. Then the hand was gone and she said, "We only have ten minutes left. Let's learn some more Kindred conversation."

Marianne, almost too tired to walk, left Big Lab. They had stockpiled—how many doses of vaccine for tomorrow? She didn't know, but she did know it wasn't enough. But they were out of culture, out of syringes, out of time.

Passing the kitchen, she heard the low murmur of voices. Isabelle and—who? It didn't sound like Salah. Then the voice came again, a young and deep chuckle, and Marianne recognized Leo Brodie. What were he and Isabelle doing together?

Not her business. Still, it was good that someone could chuckle, could find something amusing right now. And Leo was the best of the Rangers, infinitely preferable to bristly and profane Zoe Berman or silent Mason Kandiss or Lieutenant Lamont, who more than the others filled Marianne with dislike.

She knocked softly on the door of the room where Noah and his family slept. No answer. Quietly she opened the door. Llaa^mohị was at work in Big Lab. Noah lay asleep, Lily in the curve of his arm. Marianne opened the door wider to let light spill into the tiny room. Lily breathed normally, her face with its skin lighter than both her mother's natural copper and her father's artificial tint, unflushed. The virus in the vaccine had not sickened her, at least not so far. Of course, it might not be protecting her, either. There was no way to know any of this until the spore cloud hit.

So much they didn't know. But hadn't the same thing been true on Terra, when she and Harrison and the others had worked so feverishly to create a vaccine that had not, after all, been necessary?

Harrison. Sometimes it bothered her how little she thought about him. She had lived with him for a handful of years, mourned his death from a heart attack, taken no lovers since. But she knew, in the deepest part of her only rarely admitted, that she had not loved him, not really. Nor her dead husband, Kyle, nor her most exciting lover, Tim. Her love had been reserved for her children and—further admission—even they had come in second to her work. She would never be mother of the year—any year. But one advantage of being in one's sixties was that you accepted who you were, for better or worse.

Marianne closed the door. It was good that Noah slept; he would need his strength for tomorrow. She needed to sleep, too. Now that Ree^ka was gone, Marianne's room was again her own. Unsuperstitious, she wasn't kept awake by Ree^ka's having died there. As soon as she lay on the pallet, Marianne slept.

Nonetheless, she dreamed—another rarity—of Ree^ka. The Mother of Mothers stood alone on a high hill. Below her swarmed leelees, hundreds of them, with human faces. Some tried to jump onto the hill to bite Ree^ka. Marianne could see their faces: Leo, Harrison, Branch, the dead ambassador Maria Gonzalez, Salah, and, most disturbingly, Lily. Throughout, the Mother of Mothers remained serene, raising her arms high and smiling, until the orange sun descended on her and she dissolved into mist and was no more.

CHAPTER 15

The sun stained a faint strip of sky near the horizon, the rest obscured by thick clouds. A stiff breeze bent the trees in the distance, and occasionally a puff of spicy scent rode the air through the open east door of the compound. Salah could have done without the wind, but at least it wasn't raining. Yet. Dawns were cool on Kindred and he shivered, but not from cold. He wore his Terran clothes, shoes and pants and jacket, and he needed to be quick out the door.

It was vaccine day. Lamont did not want Salah to be among those leaving the compound.

Steve and Josh McGuire had arrived during the night. The first-expedition brothers looked so much alike they could have been twins. Large, silent, shaggy, they looked exactly like what they had been on Terra and were now on Kindred: miners. Dirt seemed permanently embedded under their nails, in the seams of their faces. Isabelle had told Salah that they had always kept to themselves. The copper mine they had gone to work in fifteen years ago, they now owned due to a combination of superior expertise, insanely hard work, and isolation. They participated in no social activities near the mine. They had learned only as much of the language as necessary. Nominally they belonged to Isabelle's lahk, but they rarely visited, not even for illathil. They took no lovers; in the rich interconnecting gossip of the lahks, everyone would have known. They had come to the compound now, at the twelfth hour, only because of the spore cloud.

"I greet you," Salah had said, first in Kindred and then in English. They stared at him. Steve finally nodded; Josh turned away with a look Salah recognized. On Earth, he'd encountered it whenever he was the sole Arab-American in a conservative backwater town.

These were the Terrans that would accompany him into the camp.

"They're there only for protection," Noah said, "or at least the illusion of protection. Just to deal with any pushing and shoving. They look threatening, is all."

"They are threatening," Salah said. "They're armed."

"No, Doctor, that's not possible. We don't—"

"They're armed," Salah said flatly. "Ask them."

Noah, looking impatient, had asked. He'd returned slightly shaken. "They have guns. *Kindred-made* guns. I didn't know how the . . . they can't go into the camp like that."

"Isn't that Isabelle's decision?" Salah said, knowing it was. Isabelle was mother to the Terran lahk since Marianne, the oldest woman, had refused the position. Salah wanted as much protection as possible for Isabelle. If Steve and Josh had possessed guns for a while without killing anyone, they were probably not wild-eyed and trigger-happy.

Noah, defeated, held a long colloquy with the McGuires. The brothers kept their guns.

The vaccine team would go into the camp in three groups of three. Each group held someone who could speak Kindred to explain and soothe, a scientist to administer vaccine, and a Terran to handle any mild rebellion. For major rebellion, they had the Rangers.

But not accompanying them. Both Noah and Isabelle had argued with Lieutenant Lamont, who remained firm. More than firm; his air of sly triumph had driven Salah from antipathy to rage. He disliked the Rangers on principle, but for Lamont he felt contempt. Racists always deserved contempt.

"It isn't my mission to vaccinate Kinnies," he'd told Isabelle. "My mission is to protect members of the Second Terran Expedition and get them home safely, which is why none of them are going with you. Your so-called lahk can do what it likes, but my squad will provide you only with cover if you choose to retreat. That's all. I'm not risking good troops on a medical mission to insurgents, that has no chance of succeeding anyway."

Isabelle had asked mildly, "Do your soldiers agree with you, Lieutenant?"

"Irrelevant, Ms. Rhinehart. Subject closed."

Provide you only with cover. Which meant a chance to shoot Kindred if necessary, but not to make possible saving more lives.

That had been last night. Now nine people assembled in Big Lab: Isabelle, Noah, Ka^graa, the McGuires, three more Kindred, Salah. They walked through the east door toward the refugee camp, Salah in the center of them. It would take the entire US Marine Corps to stop him. He was a doctor; Isabelle was going; no punk lieutenant two-thirds his age was going to push him around. And what could Lamont, stationed by the east door with Zoe Berman, both in full kit, actually do to stop him? Shoot?

"Stop, Doctor!" Lamont said.

Salah kept walking, waiting for Lamont to seize him, or to order Berman to do so. Would she? Of course. Would the McGuires try to stop that? Probably not; their investment in this was minimal. They weren't the kind of men who avoided danger, but neither did they look possessed of humanitarian impulses. If Berman or Lamont fought with Salah, there was no doubt whatsoever that Salah would lose.

The order didn't come. It took a moment before Salah realized why. Lamont was protecting the second-expedition members, but only those he considered fully human. Despite his posturing, he really didn't care what happened to Salah as long as they had Claire as doctor.

Towel-head. Dune coon. Camel fucker. Salah had heard them all.

Just as they reached the edge of the camp, Salah looked back at Lamont. He couldn't see the lieutenant's face under his helmet and behind his goggles. But his stance was completely different from the man who'd bristled with irritable exhaustion last night. Lamont stood with alert confidence, every line of him controlled and full of power.

Why?

The camp had not been told that the vaccine was coming today, to avoid any organized rush. Nor did the refugees know that only children would be receiving the limited supplies of vaccine. But as the nine people approached from the compound, tents opened and men rushed out, stared, ducked back in. Women starting their morning cook fires stopped, eyes even wider than evolution had provided. Noah began in loud Kindred, "I greet you! We bring a gift for your children, who carry the hopes of all our futures—"

It had begun.

The sun disappeared behind the looming clouds, and the wind smelled of rain.

Owen was different this morning.

Leo knew it as soon as he saw the lieutenant, and immediately he knew why. *Shit.* Well, not Leo's call, and it wasn't like he hadn't done it himself. Only once, though. Once was enough.

His eyes met Zoe's as they went through weapons check, and then cut sideways to Owen. Leo raised his eyebrows. Zoe, grim, gave a small nod and put on her helmet.

They crouched on top of the roof, Zoe with her SCAR and Leo with the long-range sniper rifle. The nine people in the vaccinating groups crossed the perimeter. Salah Bourgiba was among them, which surprised Leo, but Owen hadn't stopped the doctor and that, too, was Owen's call. A sudden fragment from last night's conversation with Isabelle invaded his mind: *Damn, Leo, you're almost Kindred yourself in the way you accept authority!* She'd been teasing, but somehow the remark stung a little anyway.

She was there, too, walking beside Bourgiba. Now Isabelle, Josh McGuire, and a Kindred scientist split off from the rest and headed slightly north, toward a group of tents where three women stood outside, little kids in their arms or clinging to their legs. Leo moved his scope slightly in that direction.

The camp started to boil. That's how Leo pictured it—a big pot of water that usually simmered but now started to bubble faster, throwing off heat and steam. Some men and women went into tents; some came out of them. Groups formed, dissolved, reformed. Steve McGuire, bulky next to the slim Kindred, stood between Llaa^mohį and a woman who was screaming at her. Noah Jenner gestured as he talked with a group of men. Isabelle put her hand on a woman's arm, probably trying to persuade her to let them vaccinate her child. The woman first waggled her chin, which meant no, and then moved her head side to side, which—it had taken Leo a while to adjust to this—meant yes. She held out the kid, who immediately opened its mouth to scream.

"Christ," Zoe muttered, too low for the radio to pick up. "Chaos."

Owen said, "Brodie, report."

"No weapons visible, not yet. A group of men forming at eleven o'clock, they look angry. People rushing from tent to tent, probably spreading the news about vaccinating just kids."

"Copy. Berman, see anything different?"

"Seems there are more people total than yesterday. Maybe snuck in at night."

"Brodie?"

"Could be. Hard to be sure."

"Anything else?"

"No, sir."

But there was. Leo saw the Kindred cops he'd sort of recruited,

Lu^kaj^ho and three others, moving through the crowd. They had on the cloaklike things they wore for rain, although it wasn't raining. Did that mean they had weapons underneath? That wasn't part of what Leo had, laboriously, instructed them to do, and not part of Kindred life as Isabelle described it. Although Kindred life was obviously changing as it—maybe—came to an end.

"Something going on now at ten o'clock, four hundred yards," Leo said. "A group of men wearing cloaks, possible weapons underneath, moving toward Noah Jenner's group—no, they went into a tent."

Tension prickled Leo's skin like lice. For ten minutes, nothing happened. The three groups from the compound explained, argued, stuck syringes into kids. Women without kids in tow moved from tent to tent. Were they just spreading news, or were carrying messages about an attack? If Lu^kaj^ho detected the latter, he would signal Leo.

Jenner's and Bourgiba's groups moved farther into the camp; Isabelle's still worked the tents closer to the perimeter. The air filled with the cries of children, mingling with those of birds wheeling overhead.

No, not birds—these were closer to reptiles, Isabelle had told him, and were called . . . something that began with B or maybe P . . .

Then it all happened at once.

Lu^kaj^ho raised his arm in signal to Leo. Three different groups of men, boys, and a few women, all cloaked, emerged from three scattered tents and walked purposefully toward the perimeter. Two of them took a circuitous route, keeping groups of people or tents or vaccinators between themselves and the compound. The third, moving faster, came directly on.

"Here they come!" Zoe said.

Owen said, "The first motherfucker that sets one toe onto the perimeter, open fire."

Get down, Isabelle! But she didn't. She saw the men and began running toward them, leaving the Kindred scientist holding a child with Steve McGuire standing beside him. Did Isabelle think she could talk down this group? No chance. . . . Leo knew a full-out-fucking-serious attack when he saw it.

A man rushed into the open zone and Leo dropped him.

He hoped that would stop it. It didn't. The others hit the dirt but they didn't open fire. One of the men not in the group ran into the perimeter, pulled something from his cloak, and hurled it at the compound. Steve McGuire, closest, pulled a gun and fired, but someone else shot him in the back.

A bomb—the fucker had hurled a bomb. He would find out soon enough that a Molotov wasn't going to stop anything. These people had no idea what ordnance was, they couldn't make anything that could—

It wasn't a Molotov. A huge explosion at the east door blew out the wall of the compound, knocking Leo off the roof. He fell eight feet and landed hard, but a second later was on his feet, still clutching his rifle. Smoke thick as cotton filled the air. Leo coughed and stumbled, unable to see anything. Gunfire from above—Zoe was still firing. Kandiss and Owen, they'd been right in front of the east door. . . .

Figures rushed past him in the smoke and flying debris. The compound was breached and enemy flowed inside in search of more vaccine . . . was there any more? Incongruously, Leo realized he didn't know.

All this took only a nanosecond. Then some of the smoke cleared and Leo was firing at the enemy still running toward the compound. When they either were dead or had turned tail, he turned toward the east door. Kandiss lay there, his huge body still, and an insurgent was raising a pipe gun to fire. Leo swung his weapon around. But before he could shoot, a crack! came from his right and the enemy fell. Leo spun around. Isabelle stood there, blackened from smoke and dirt, holding Steve McGuire's gun.

"Get down!" Leo yelled, at the same moment that Zoe's voice crackled over the radio, "No more enemy approaching!"

"Fire if they do," Owen said. "Brodie, Kandiss, room clearing!"

"Kandiss is hit," Leo said. "I'm coming in."

Half the east wall was gone off the compound. Injured or dead lay on the floor of the Big Lab. Screams came from the clinic. Leo and Owen ran down the walkway.

In the first room, three Kindred scientists stood backed against the far wall. Two men stood in front of them, spinning around as Leo and Owen entered. The men both fired, but Leo and Owen were faster. The pipe guns sprayed the ceiling as the men fell.

Other rooms held more Kindred, one actually on his knees peering under a pallet for vaccine. All of them dropped their pathetic weapons and raised their hands. Leo kicked away the guns and Kindred scientists rushed in to tie them up.

In the last room, at the far end of the clinic, a Kindred held Noah Jenner's little girl, a knife at her throat. Marianne Jenner lay on the floor where he had flung her.

Leo didn't even hesitate. He had a clear shot, he had surprise on his side, he had the man's stupidity—the fucker didn't even hold the kid to cover his own face. Leo fired and the man's brains splattered on the wall behind him. He dropped Lily, who screamed and screamed.

Marianne Jenner moved, moaned, raised her head, and crawled toward her granddaughter.

Owen said, "Brodie, bring in Kandiss, then take the roof with Berman. I'll take the east door."

There was no east door anymore, but Leo got the point. He sprinted back down the covered walkway. The vaccinators rushed into Big Lab, including Isabelle and Bourgiba. But not enough vaccinators—who had been killed? Leo heard Salah say, "Isabelle, triage . . . where is Claire? Somebody find her—"

Kandiss was moving feebly on the ground. Alive, then. Leo dragged him through the nonexistent wall and over to Bourgiba. "Doctor!"

Bourgiba looked up from a Kindred that even Leo could see was too far gone to survive and ran to Kandiss. "Ranger, can you hear me?"

Kandiss moaned.

"Open your eyes and look at me."

Kandiss's eyelids twitched, then slowly opened.

"How many fingers am I holding up?"

"T-two."

"Excellent." Bourgiba asked a few more questions, peered into Kandiss's eyes with a tiny flashlight, removed his helmet and ran his hands over Kandiss's head. "You've probably got a concussion—there's a nasty bump on your head—but I think you'll be fine. Any other injuries?"

"No," Kandiss said, although Leo suspected there were. But he had seen Special Forces compensate for all kinds of serious wounds, just putting the pain and damage on hold until the mission was over. Airborne troops with injuries from a hard landing went on the assault anyway; soldiers bleeding enough to turn pant legs dripping red nonetheless took the objective.

Kandiss staggered to his feet. Leo said, "Join Lamont outside."

Bourgiba had moved on to the next body. People moaned and tried to move. Glassware, belatedly, fell along with its shattered shelf and smashed on the floor. Bourgiba yelled, "Somebody find Claire!"

Isabelle said, "I'll look."

Leo climbed back onto what was left of the roof beside Zoe. Nothing to the west or north. To the east and south, the camp was emptying as people ran, carrying kids and who-the-fuck-knew what else. It was chaos.

Thunder rumbled, and it started to rain.

Rain was good. Rain was wonderful. This planet *wanted* Austin to succeed. Proof: When the bomb exploded, Dr. Patel was standing in the Big Lab, and a piece of flying something hit her and knocked her down but didn't really hurt her! It couldn't have been better if Austin had planned it himself.

He had planned everything else. You had to be ready, be alert, so that when your chance came, you could grab it. Leo had told him that. Austin wore his Terran clothes, the jacket pocket bulging. In the smoke and confusion and gunfire, he'd grabbed Dr. Patel—Claire—under the armpits and dragged her away from the east wall, just like he was keeping her safe from any more explosions. Well, he *was*.

He dragged her into the kitchen of the clinic, tied her hands behind her back, and gagged her. Quick, quick, not much time, someone might come. . . . But everyone out there was shooting and screaming and nobody watched the kitchen. The door, which led to the vegetable garden, had finally been boarded up and locked because Lieutenant Lamont had insisted. Just before dawn, Austin had loosened the boards, leaving just enough nails to hold the karthwood in place, and stolen one of the multiple keys—easy job! Now he pried off the boards, unlocked the door, and peered out. Refugees might have circled around the building. . . .

But there was no one here. They were assaulting the east side, or maybe that and the south door, and the Rangers were busy stopping them. Everybody else was either hurt or tending to hurt people. Austin couldn't relock the doors or replace the karthwood, but he didn't have to. Noah would know where he was going, so no use trying to cover up his tracks. He just needed to get there with Claire before anybody came after them.

Her eyes opened. She looked around, tried to scream and couldn't, and began to kick him.

But he was prepared for that, too. He fished the bioplast box from his pocket, drew in a huge breath, and held the fluid-soaked cloth to her face. She struggled for a minute and then she was out again.

He dragged her away and gasped for breath.

This was the hardest part. He could be seen from the roof of the compound until he reached the karthwood grove fifty meters away. Ranger Berman was on the roof, firing—Austin could just see the top of her head from this angle—and might turn around. Austin dragged Claire as fast as he could across the stony field. Two grazing pel^aks, impervious to rain, raised their heads and stared, chewing. He was astonished that Claire was so light. Tiny, light, so pretty. . . . And it was a good thing he was so big and strong, not like that wimp Graa^lok. There were things Austin could do that Graa^lok, for all his brains, could not!

The clouds roared and a hard rain began.

Harder to drag her through the mud. One sandal came off and he put it in his pocket. Thirty meters to the trees . . . ten meters. . . . they were under the trees.

Austin put her down and bent over, gasping for breath. Only for a minute, though. He had to get her as far away as he could. Maybe they would think she disintegrated in the explosion and that's why they couldn't find her body. He didn't know much about explosions.

It would be easier when she came to. Then he could make her walk, even run. But what if she didn't come to? The knockout stuff was from school, they'd used it to knock out leelees to study. What if Austin had given her too much? What if she died?

Panicky, he stopped to put his ear to her mouth. She breathed.

She smelled of soap and flowers.

The rain tore through the leaves above them, pelting down.

"I shoulda known," Joshua McGuire said. "We use that explosive in the mines. Some of my miners went missing last week. I shoulda guessed, I shoulda checked the supply. . . ."

Salah moved his hand toward McGuire, stopped it, withdrew. McGuire was not the sort to welcome such a gesture. He sat next to his brother's body on the floor of the tiny room, formerly Marianne's bedroom and before that the Kindred equivalent of a clinic exam room, where the three dead had been taken. Two Kindred scientists had been standing close to the east wall of Big Lab when it exploded. Steve McGuire had been shot in the field with a pipe gun.

Another seven from the compound had been injured, two severely but not critically. Llaa^mohᵢ, Noah's wife, had a belly wound. A Kindred lab tech had his arm nearly torn off. They lay in what was now the ICU, after Salah's makeshift surgery. He longed for the sick bay equipment on the *Friendship*, or even the unknown hospitals destroyed in the *Stremlenie* attack, even though they had probably been decades behind Terran facilities. Llaa^mohᵢ would be lucky to escape peritonitis.

Noah had a concussion from having been hit in the head with a rock in the refugee camp. (A rock! In the age of star-faring!) Noah was dazed, with blurred vision and sensitivity to light. It was impossible to tell how badly off Kandiss was because the Ranger refused to leave his post long enough to be examined any further: "I'm fine, Doc." The best Salah could do was watch him. Symptoms of concussion could worsen over as much as three days as the brain swelled.

Three more Kindred inside the compound had been injured, none seriously; they'd been standing farther back from the east wall.

There were also dead and injured among the Kindred in the camp, shot by the Rangers. Salah didn't know how many. He would have treated them, but Lamont allowed no one to leave the compound.

And Claire Patel and Austin Rhinehart were missing.

"They're hostages?" Isabelle said, fear creasing her face into a caricature. Salah had left McGuire to his mourning and gone back to Big Lab. Shattered glass and broken equipment littered the floor. Beyond the huge hole in the wall, the camp looked quiet; a lot of people had fled. The rain had stopped. Salah bent over his last patient, a young lab tech, and began picking glass from his arm. The young man gazed at him from wide, dark eyes, refusing to cry.

"Hostages?" Isabelle repeated. "In the camp?"

"No," Lamont said. "Go back into the clinic with the others, ma'am. We can't protect you as well here. Doctor, can you move that man yet?"

"No," Salah said. He was finished with the young Kindred and the lab tech could easily walk, but he wanted to hear Isabelle, who was not leaving.

She said, "I don't want you to protect me, Lieutenant. I want my nephew back! And we need Dr. Patel. What are you doing about retrieving them?"

"We can attempt extraction once we know where they're being held. But my first priority is to secure this building. Now go back to the clinic."

Isabelle still didn't move. "I can go into the camp, talk to people, find out where they were taken."

"You're not among my protectees. If you want to go out there, I won't stop you. But I won't risk my soldiers guarding you, either."

"I'm going."

Salah stood. "Isabelle, no. It's too dangerous."

She rounded on him, and he understood that her fury wasn't really directed at him; it just had to go somewhere. "Don't try to stop me, Salah. You do your job here and I'll do mine."

"Isabelle . . ."

"You aren't going," another voice said, and Isabelle whirled around.

Leo Brodie stood on duty, his back to them, eyes and weapon on the camp. But his voice carried clearly over his shoulder.

"Brodie," Lamont said sharply, "this isn't your concern!"

"No, sir. Sorry, sir. But I have relevant information. Permission to speak?"

Lamont said nothing. Something in the quality of his silence, in his stance as he rolled forward on the balls of his feet, caught Salah's attention. Lamont wore his helmet but not his goggles, and Salah could see his eyes.

Oh.

Where had he gotten the popbite? He must have brought it with him; even if it was manufactured on Kindred, Salah couldn't see Lamont scoring a drug deal with a native. Popbite was a serious stimulant. It kept you awake and alert for days, but the price was steep: first, jitteriness. Then hallucinations. Then psychotic episodes.

Finally Lamont said to Brodie, "Permission to speak."

Brodie said, "There are tracks in the mud on the north side of the compound, leading toward the open fields and the mountains. The kitchen door is unlocked and the boards removed."

"Are you saying, Brodie, that Dr. Patel escaped? With that kid's help?"

"No," Isabelle said. Fury had replaced fear. "Claire wouldn't do that. Austin *took* her!"

Salah stood, nodding at the lab tech to go to the clinic. The lab tech stood but didn't go. How much English did he understand?

Lamont scowled. "You're saying a teenage boy kidnapped a grown woman?" But Salah could see Lamont's mind churning over this information, weighing the factors. Claire was tiny even for an Asian woman; Austin was strong for his age; the commotion and distraction of the assault on the compound and the aftermath of assessing the dead and injured . . .

Finally the lieutenant said, "Why would he do that? Sex?"

"*No,*" Isabelle said. "I don't know why!"

"And where would he take her?" Lamont now looked disbelieving; he had decided to blame the Kindred rather than Austin.

Brodie said over his shoulder, "He has a secret fort somewhere."

Isabelle said, "A *what*?"

"He told me once. He said he has a secret place—a cave, he said a cave, yeah—and that Noah Jenner knows about it. Also that he was going to take care of his mother there."

Isabelle stared at Brodie's back for a full twenty seconds. Then she tore off down the walkway, pushing past the exhausted people sitting on the floor along its walls, and slammed the door into the clinic. Lamont was grilling Brodie about the location of this cave, which Brodie said he didn't know, when Isabelle rushed back. "Josh says Kayla was never with the McGuires! Her note said she went on a supply dirigible but Josh said the dirigible arrived and Kayla wasn't on it. Austin—"

"Has both women trapped in a cave somewhere?" Lamont sneered. "A thirteen-year-old punk? I don't believe it."

"Leo, what else did Austin tell you?"

Brodie, without asking permission, said, "That's all, Isabelle. He was filthy and sandy, said he'd been digging around for old stuff in the cave and—"

"You're on report, Brodie," Lamont snapped. "Pay attention to duty before it becomes a court-martial."

"Yes, sir. Sorry, sir."

Isabelle ran back to the clinic, Salah right behind her. "Isabelle, wait. Noah is confused and dazed right now—"

"Not as confused as I am! Salah, Austin stole the vaccine, nobody else could have taken it, he stole Claire—is he psychotic? Is he like one of those mass murderers back on Terra? Those kids who shoot up their own schools?"

Ten years on Kindred and whatever she'd seen on Terra still lingered. Salah didn't know her past, didn't know Austin, thought lately that he didn't know much of anything. But he gave her his best opinion.

"I don't think he's a sociopath, no. I think he's a confused adolescent, and I also think he has help. He didn't take Claire and Kayla—if he did take them—to some kid-built secret fort in a shallow cave. Isabelle, where did those other two first-expedition members, Tony Schrupp and Dr. Beyon, go?"

"They have a company that manufactures transistors, way over in the coastal mountains. I told you, all manufacturing is confined to—"

"Are they there now? Are you sure?"

Isabelle was silent. "No." And then, "The Council of Mothers. They would know. I'm only a junior member but there's a senior group, Ree^ka was the lead, of course, but—I can radio."

"Are Schrupp and Beyon the kind to make survivalist plans for themselves somewhere? To believe that civilization is going to end and they better create a bunker?"

After a silence, Isabelle said, "Yes. They could be. I never liked either of them, but that doesn't . . . it could be. But why would they take in Kayla and Austin? Claire I can see, she's a doctor . . . I'm going to talk to Noah."

"I'll go with you."

The clinic was jammed with people in what was now post-op. Noah sat beside his wife's pallet, Lily on his lap and Marianne next to him, watching carefully for signs of nausea or confusion. Llaa^moh¡ slept. Noah looked a little more alert. Salah said, "How are you feeling?"

"Headache to shake mountains."

"To be expected. Still dizzy?"

"If I stand up."

"Any nausea, blurred vision, confusion?"

"I don't know."

"Count backwards from one hundred."

"One hundred, ninety-nine, ninety-six, no wait. . . ."

Isabelle burst out with, "Noah—what do you know about a secret cave that Austin goes to?"

"How do you know about that?" Noah said at the same moment that Marianne said "Cave?"

"It doesn't matter how I know!" Isabelle flared. "What matters is that you didn't tell me! I'm the mother of this lahk and—"

"Not so loud! Please!" Noah put his hand on his forehead.

"Sorry. But why didn't you tell me? Where is this cave? Are Tony and Nathan there? Is *Kayla*?"

"Kayla? No—isn't she? You told me . . . it's a little confused . . ."

"Isabelle," Marianne said in a tone that could have controlled an earthquake, "go easy."

Gradually the story emerged. Tony Schrupp and Nathan Beyon were constructing or had constructed a survivalist bunker in a mountain cave. Austin had been helping them with, Noah guessed, translation of radio broadcasts; neither man knew more than a few phrases of Kindred. (*Why?* Salah wondered. *If you emigrated, wouldn't you learn the language?*) Noah had followed Austin to the cave and then promised him that he would not tell the lahk if Austin agreed to not go there again and Austin had promised, an agreement he evidently broke. Yes, the Council of Mothers knew about the bunker; supplies and equipment had been going in for months. Noah knew nothing about Kayla's whereabouts, and this was the first time he'd heard that Claire was missing.

"That stupid kid! What does he think—"

"Easy," Salah said. "Don't get too agitated, Noah. We'll get them back."

"How? You don't understand, the entrance is small and probably impregnable, Beyon is an electronics expert and—"

"Easy, please."

"*Noah,*" Marianne said, and Noah subsided. The power of mothers, even if the son was nearly forty.

Isabelle stood. "Okay, I got it. You rest and don't worry, Noah. You either, Marianne. Leo will know how to get them out."

Leo. Salah surprised himself with a flash of jealousy so strong that his stomach jumped in his belly. She didn't trust Lamont, but Brodie. . . .

Salah thought he'd left this kind of sickening jealousy behind, long ago, with Aisha.

Lily whimpered and stirred. Salah laid a hand on her forehead. Still afebrile.

Marianne said, "Go now. Let them sleep. If the—"

The door flung open. Branch stood there. Like everyone else in the clinic half of the compound, he'd sustained no injury from the bomb, but now he looked so wild that he might be hallucinating. "Dr. Jenner!" he shouted.

"Branch! For God's sake—you woke Lily!"

The little girl started to cry. Llaa^mohį woke despite the sedative—the power of mothers!—and said, "Lily?" Noah put his hand to his forehead. Marianne grabbed Branch and dragged him into the corridor, Isabelle and Salah following. Against the corridor wall, two Kindred lay asleep, their usual sleeping areas destroyed in Big Lab.

"Marianne!" Branch said. "I did it! I got it!"

Marianne said, "Good. Great. But Branch, right now astronomical data—"

"It's not that! Come!"

They all followed him to the leelee room, which smelled worse than ever. Branch pointed dramatically to a complicated pile of equipment and said, "There! The code was convertible to sound and I did it!"

"Sound?" Isabelle said. "From the ship? Recordings?"

"No! Live! Real-time transmission!"

"Of what?" Marianne said.

"Listen! I'm going to turn it up—listen!"

Branch dropped to the floor and fiddled with analog dials. A light flashed briefly. Then Salah heard it. At first he thought it was coming from the cages behind him: chittering, very fast. But it wasn't.

Isabelle said, "Leelees? There are leelees alive aboard the ship? How?"

Branch said, so fast that he was almost chittering himself, "It was a colony ship, wasn't it? To a planet close enough for radio transmissions. Preset so that was the only place the ship could go. Big enough to hold animals and plants for a colony. When the people died, the animals didn't! The leelees didn't!"

Isabelle said, "Well, okay. They're up there, but the ship is still contaminated with spores because the colonists went outside and brought them in. Everyone's dead."

She didn't see it. Salah did, and Marianne had known the second the chittering began. She said now, sounding unlike herself, "The leelees aren't dead. There are spores there, but the leelees survived. Mutated immunity, or maybe a virophage since at least two survived to breed . . . let it be a virophage. Oh, God!"

Isabelle said, "What's a virophage?"

Salah said, "A satellite virus that infects larger viruses and can't reproduce any other way."

Marianne babbled at Salah, "*R. Sporii* is large enough to be a host, it could have coevolved with the spore cloud even though . . . but no paramyxovirus before now has hosted . . . no, that's not right, it's a new mutation . . . Isabelle! You said that Ree^ka told you there was a device to call the ship back to Kindred!"

There was? Salah looked at Branch; he hadn't known it, either.

"Yes," Isabelle said. She didn't look excited; maybe she didn't realize the implications. Salah did. If they could get their hands on a virophage that naturally killed *R. sporii* and it was airborne— insha'Allah, let it be a virophage and let it airborne!—they could release it on Kindred and it would fight the coming spores. Thousands of people might be saved. Maybe more.

Marianne seized Isabelle's arm. "Where is it? The device to call back the ship—does it still work? Where is it?"

"Nobody knows," Isabelle said. "It's gone. Buried somewhere in the mountains. Mining out the original tablets with starship plans. . . . they'd been there for 140,000 years! Getting them free took explosives. Caves collapsed, tunnels closed up, the ground shifted. Nothing but the coming spore cloud crisis could have led the Mothers to cause that much environmental disturbance. But Ree^ka told me that the call-back device is described in the tablets but wasn't with the drive or the plans.

"It's lost, and nobody knows where."

CHAPTER 16

At every slight rise in the ground, Austin expected to see someone coming after him: Noah or Isabelle or Leo or maybe one of the Mc-Guires, whom he'd only seen a few times in his life but remembered vividly. Big, silent, scary. Although why would the McGuires come after Austin? They didn't care about anything but their mines. No, it would be Noah or Isabelle or Leo. Maybe all three. All three would be a problem. Austin had a stolen pipe gun, but he didn't think he could shoot Noah or Isabelle, and Leo would probably shoot him first. Certainly Lieutenant Lamont would.

He'd dragged Claire into a sort of cover made of bushes, so he could rest. Rain pattered on the dark leaves above them as Austin sat cross-legged and ate a piece of makfruit from his pocket. It was dotted with lint. He ungagged Claire—they were far enough away that no one in the compound could hear her—and held out part of the fruit.

She ignored it. "What are you *doing*? Untie me!"

She didn't sound groggy at all. Maybe he didn't give her enough knockout drug. On the other hand, maybe it was good that she wasn't groggy—if she could walk, he wouldn't have to drag her. He launched into the speech he'd rehearsed.

"Dr. Patel—Claire—I'm taking you someplace safe. It's called Haven. There is food and water and safety from the collapse of civilization when the spore cloud comes. My mother is already there, and Graa^lok—do you remember my friend Graa^lok? Also two other Terrans and, soon, some Kindred. We're all going to rebuild civilization after the looters and other desperate people are dead, and you're going to be part of the rebuilding!"

Claire's mouth fell open. Raindrops dripped inside and she closed it again. Austin had always liked her pretty, lilting voice, but now she sounded almost like Isabelle. "Are you insane? *We're* trying to prevent the 'collapse of civilization'! Untie me immediately and take me back to the compound."

"I can't do that, Claire." There—that sounded definite and mature. Austin improved on it. "I'm sorry I can't do that, but I have the greater good to think of."

Claire tugged at the ropes around her wrists. They didn't give. She screamed. "Help! Help! Help me!"

What if someone was following them; could they hear her? But if anyone was following, they'd find Austin anyway; dragging Claire this far had left a clear muddy trail. Austin held his breath and waited.

No one came. When Claire finally stopped yelling, he stood up. How would Leo do this? Kind but steely. "Claire, we can do this two ways. You can walk with me holding that rope, or I can knock you out again and drag you, the way I did before. But your legs are all muddy and the back part of your wrap is nearly worn through and exposing your . . . uh . . . you."

He felt himself blushing.

Claire stared at him a long time. Then she crawled out from under the bushes, stretching the rope to its limit, and twisted her body with its bound feet in a complete circle. Austin, crawling out after her, knew what she saw: nothing. Empty, rocky fields in the rain, with the mountains rising abruptly ahead.

"We're going on now," Austin said. He wished that his voice was as deep as Leo's.

"Who was killed at the compound?"

"I don't know."

"Is the whole camp rioting?"

"I don't know. Yes. No. Not all of it."

"You are an idiot."

Austin didn't deign to answer that. He strode forward, tugging her to her feet and then pulling on her rope, and Claire was forced to follow. She stubbed her toe on a rock and cried out.

"Oh, sorry, here's your other shoe!" He fished it out of his pocket and handed it to her.

She couldn't put it on with her hands tied like that. Austin bent and tugged the sandal onto her foot, untied her ankles, and straightened. He hadn't known that small, pretty face could look so scornful.

Claire was a much better walker than Kayla. In another few hours, they reached the tunnel opening. Austin, who'd been a little deflated by her angry silence, felt better. They'd made it without being captured! Now she would see what her rescue was all about!

"I'm going to crawl in there and you're going to stay here until I tug on the rope. Don't be afraid, Claire, inside Haven is much different from the first tunnel."

"I'm not afraid. I'm furious."

Well, Austin could see that. He dropped to hands and knees, crawled to the grate, and rang the bell. When Tony appeared, he said, "I've got her. Dr. Patel. She's with me now."

Tony grinned. "Hey! Good man! Come on in, both of you!"

He unlocked the grate and helped Austin down the drop. Austin tugged on the rope until Claire appeared, her tiny body with space all around her in the tunnel, her rain-streaked face distorted by contempt.

Tony said, "Welcome, Doctor."

Claire said, "When the Rangers come after me, you are *finished*."

Austin said, "No, Claire, you don't understand. This place is impregnable."

"The boy is right," Tony said. "We made sure of that. Here, let me lift you down. Just beyond that farther door is Haven. Are you hungry?"

"Finished," Claire said. "All of you."

"If only we had a gene sequencer," Branch said.

"Stop saying that," Marianne said. She added, "Please."

They sat on pallets in the leelee room. It was the only room in the clinic not crowded with people, but it was filled nonetheless. With equipment, with the safe, with live and dead leelees, the dead and infected ones in their negative-pressure cages. That spared Marianne the smell of putrefaction; the live ones smelled bad enough. They chattered; the signals that Branch kept replaying from the colony ship chattered; Marianne felt her mind chattering and stuttering from going over the same limited data in her memory.

Much of the lab equipment had been destroyed by the bomb, but Marianne's laptop had been in the clinic, not in Big Lab. There wasn't anything on her laptop about virophages; she hadn't expected to deal with them on Kindred, and of course she'd expected to have access to the digital library on the *Friendship*. Virophages reproduced only inside their host viruses, like Russian nesting dolls, each smaller than the one that contained it. That required a host large enough, as viruses go. Also, the virophage had to be very small. The first one discovered was only fifty nanometers in size and had only twenty-one genes, thirteen of no known origin. It also contained a genetic segment of its host, which implied a genetic transfer between virus and virophage. To examine a virophage was to look at the earliest type of evolution, a trip back in time that made the fourteen-year jump from Earth to World insignificant. *R. sporii* might contain a similar segment of the virophage on the colony ship from some eons-ago encounter, so that when the two encountered each other again, the virophage moved in and set up housekeeping.

Viruses and their phages could have complicated multihost lives. The Argentine ant carried a virus, L. humile, that didn't much bother the ants but which attacked honeybees unfortunate enough to visit the same flowers or to get attacked by ants foraging for honey. Virophages seemed to be implicated in those encounters, although when Marianne had left Earth, the research was still controversial.

She could determine so much more if they had a sequencer to determine the genome of the virophage! They didn't have the virophage, either, but Branch, the hardware guy, seemed more obsessed with the lack of sequencer.

"If we had one," he said, "then after the ship is called back here, we could at least—"

"Branch," she said, with as much compassion as she could muster through her exhaustion, "the ship won't be called back here. The device is lost."

"But if we find it—"

"Branch—"

He said quietly, "I want to go home. The ship is our only chance to go home."

Marianne said nothing; there was nothing to say. She put her hand over his. A long minute later she said, "I'm going out for some fresh air. Back in a minute." Best to give him some time to control himself.

As she walked to Big Lab, a bit of eighteenth-century doggerel laughed at in graduate school came back to her:

> So, naturalists observe, a flea
> Hath smaller fleas that on him prey,
> And these have smaller fleas to bite 'em,
> And so proceed, ad infinitum.

"What are you smiling about?" Isabelle said, not entirely friendly. "I didn't think there was anything to smile about."

Isabelle stood in Big Lab, watching four Kindred rebuild the shattered east wall. Earlier in the day the three men and one woman had carted in karthwood, nails, tools, just as the bodies of the bomb victims were being carried out. Representatives of their lahks had come to take the remains of the two Kindred home, even though the spore cloud was so close that Marianne wondered if they would have time to reach their villages. She hadn't asked. The Kindred carpenters worked in silence. Zoe Berman stood beside them, her rifle trained on the workers; Mason Kandiss stood outside, scanning the camp. Undoubtedly Owen Lamont or Leo Brodie perched on the roof. Maybe both of them.

Marianne didn't answer Isabelle, who was in no mood to appreciate Jonathan Swift's doggerel. Instead she said, "The Rangers will go after Kayla and Austin once the compound is secure."

"Are you sure of that?" Isabelle said.

Marianne wasn't. She searched for something to ease the terrible twisted tension in Isabelle's face, to make Isabelle feel better. "Lily still isn't sick from the vaccine. So apparently it's not harmful."

"Which doesn't mean it will be effective."

"True enough," Marianne said. Isabelle didn't want to feel better.

Big Lab had been cleaned up, debris swept out and benches washed. It no longer looked like a war zone, and the rebuilding would be done by nightfall, although now they scarcely needed the space. It wasn't only corpses that were departing the compound; once it was secure again, the remaining Kindred would all leave for their lahks. They had nothing more to do here. The means to make more vaccine had been destroyed in the rush to steal it, and the remaining doses would be given to the Kindred scientists going back to their lahks, to do with as they wished. The only people left in the secured compound would be Marianne, Noah and his family, Branch, Isabelle, Salah, and the four Rangers. All of whom Lamont was prepared to defend until, apparently, the end of time.

And then, after the spore cloud, if any Kindred survived, it would be a whole new, and wholly unknown, situation.

Salah emerged from the walkway. He eyed the Rangers with dislike. "I wish it didn't look so much like slave labor, building their masters' dacha under armed guard."

"They volunteered," Isabelle said. "It's a form of atonement for what the others did."

"I know," Salah said. "But that's not what I came to say." He lowered his voice. "Come away from where they might hear."

Marianne and Isabelle followed him to the far corner. Salah kept his voice down. "There's two things I think you should both know, as lahk Mothers."

"I'm not—"

"Just listen, Marianne. I don't know how significant this is, but it seems it might be. First, I'm pretty sure that Owen Lamont is on popbite."

"What's that?" Isabelle said, which saved Marianne's asking.

"A street drug that acts on multiple brain centers to produce prolonged wakefulness and a sense of power. With prolonged use or in excessive doses, it promotes paranoia and then hallucinations."

Isabelle said sharply, "How do you know?"

"I'm a doctor, Isabelle."

Marianne said, "The other Rangers?"

"No. Not yet anyway. But of course, he might decide to share. Here's the other thing: Three times now I've seen Brodie in what looked like secretive conversations with Kindred at the edge of camp, when the other Rangers weren't around. The Kindred had pipe guns and Brodie didn't disarm them."

Marianne said, "I don't understand. What are you implying?"

Isabelle said, "He's *implying* that Leo Brodie is somehow cooperating with or encouraging violence in the camp. Why not say it outright, Salah? You think Leo is betraying us, betraying the Ranger creed, a thoroughly evil guy. Just spit it out!"

"I didn't say—"

"Yes, you did. The Rangers are dangerous to us, they're on paranoid drugs, they collude with killers, we shouldn't trust them at all. I didn't think you could be so paranoid yourself. Or so petty." She stalked back to the clinic.

Salah looked stunned. Marianne said, "She's just worried sick about her sister and nephew."

"Yes," Salah said, and then, "No. She . . . never mind. I'm sorry I spoke. I just thought the two of you ought to know what's going on with the Rangers." He left.

Going after Isabelle? Marianne didn't know, and didn't really want to. She pulled at the skin on her face. Too much was happening: to her family, to the Terrans, to the compound, to the planet. She stepped forward until she could see out of the rapidly diminishing hole in the wall.

The sun was just setting in a blaze of orange. One moon floated high over the eastern horizon. The brightest of the unfamiliar stars shone faintly; soon fainter stars would frame them, forming unfamiliar constellations that Marianne could not name. And somewhere out there, in orbit around another alien planet, was the Kindred colony ship, full of leelees infested with parasites that might save this planet. Leelees chittering, smelly, all alive-o, and unreachable.

Claire went all over Haven, inspecting shelves, studying equipment. At first Tony accompanied her, explaining, but she never spoke to him or acknowledged his presence. Nor did she acknowledge that her ass was partly exposed and very bruised from Austin's having dragged her. Austin tried not to look at that, and looked.

Finally Tony said, "Austin, *you* take her around. Just don't let her touch anything at all—nothing, you hear? And stay out of the room where Nathan and Graylock are working!"

They weren't rooms, they were just caves or parts of caves, sometimes with curtains hung from poles at their entrances. That was clearer than ever to Austin, seeing Haven through Claire's eyes. Caves with rough floors, or dripping water, or supplies stacked untidily on rough shelves of karthwood, or equipment brought inside in pieces and then reassembled, the tools and packing material scattered around, along with plates of half-eaten food. Behind a curtain, Kayla slept on a not-very-clean pallet.

When Tony had gone, Claire said, "Working on what?" She didn't look directly at Austin, hadn't looked directly at him since they'd arrived.

"What?"

"Tony said Nathan and Graa^lok are working. On what?"

"Equipment."

"What equipment?"

"I don't know."

"What does the equipment do?"

"I don't know." She was making him feel stupid. He hated her. He didn't hate her. He couldn't stop looking at her ass.

Claire said, "What medicines do you have?"

Glad to know the answer to something, Austin led her to the shelf stockpiled with glass jars and bioplast containers. Claire opened some, sniffed, squinted at the Kindred writing, series of squiggles and dots and lines. "Can you read this?"

"Of course."

"Tell me what they say."

He did, feeling important again, until Claire said, "I don't know what these are in English, or even if English analogs exist. I don't know what they're for. I don't know the conventional doses. You wanted a doctor, but as far as meds go, I will be useless to you without my own case of Terran drugs."

Importance crumbled. Austin clutched at her hand. "Please don't tell Tony that! Please!"

For the first time, she turned her head to gaze at him. "Why not?"

"He'll send me back to get your drugs! To steal them! And Noah and Isabelle will keep me there, they'll make sure I can't escape again, and the spore cloud is coming—"

"What do you think is going to happen when the spore cloud comes?"

"The collapse of civilization! Don't you *know*? Kindred will die, most but not all, and the survivors will be desperate, because some always survive a plague, and they'll steal and kill—just like they did in the camp, to get the vaccine! Only this time it will be to get food and wine and women . . . Tony told me! He told me how it was on Terra when Rome fell and the siege of Leningrad and the way the Indians massacred everybody at Cawnpore, even babies . . . and Leo told me about the Brazilian food riots! That's the way it always is with humans and no matter what Lieutenant Lamont thinks, Kindred are all human!"

Austin burst into tears. Immediately he hated himself for it, and then a moment later he didn't because Claire's face softened and she put her arms around him.

"Oh, Austin, it isn't always like that, and maybe especially not on Kindred where you have such different social systems from Leningrad or Cawnpore or . . . Rome! Why did Tony tell you all that? It wasn't fair, you're just a kid. Austin, listen to—"

"I'm not a kid!" And to prove it, he kissed her hard on the mouth and put a hand on her breast. She came up only to his shoulder and her bones felt light as a leelee's, so he was surprised at the strength with which she pushed him away. Comfort and sympathy were gone from her face as she stalked back to the main cave.

"Oh, for God's sake, Austin—*grow up!*"

———

Dawn brought more rain. Leo came off perimeter patrol around a quiet and nearly empty camp and reported to Owen, who was coming on duty. In the ready room, Leo took off his gear and stowed it in his lockbox, brushed his teeth, and glanced at the pallet he was not going to sleep on. At least, not yet, despite having had only four hours in the last twenty. Some things outranked sleep.

Isabelle waited in the kitchen. She'd made coffee, or what passed for coffee here. Leo searched for the word and found it: "Nakl."

"Very good."

"I didn't know if you'd come, what with . . . with everything."

"Teaching you is about the only good thing in my life right now."

Leo's heart threatened to burst right down its seam. Even if she only meant that the rest of her life was shitty—and that was what she meant, not that he was some shining star for her—it was still good. He sipped the nakl she handed him, even though he didn't like it.

Isabelle smiled. There was something wrong with the smile, something a little off, but she didn't give him time to figure out what it was. "Let's see how much you remember from last time. Tell me how to close the door."

He stumbled over the words but got them out.

"Good! Now tell me how to do it if I'm a mother."

Shit—she *was* a mother, and that meant different words. Leo found them, his eyes on her face.

"Good! Great!" Big smile—too big. Something was definitely off.

They went through several more phrases of conversation, and then Isabelle moved closer to him. Leo, no neophyte with women, thought: *Here it comes.* He was a little surprised that Isabelle would try to pull this, but then, the circumstances weren't the same as some college girl slumming in an on-base bar. He knew what she would ask.

She did.

"Leo," she said, taking his hand, "I need you to help me."

"Yeah?"

She kissed him. The press of her lips, soft and full on his, was so intoxicating that for a minute the kitchen, the compound, the planet were blotted out.

"I need you to go after Kayla and Austin for me, because no one else will."

Gently he pushed her away. "I can't, Isabelle. You shouldn't even ask me, and you know that. This isn't like you. Lamont will go after them when he can, maybe today."

"No, he won't." She was Isabelle again, straightforward and steely. He liked her better this way, although he understood why she'd tried to fuck him over. Family. Bu^ka^tel.

"Listen to me, Leo. Lamont isn't thinking straight. He's getting paranoid. Salah says he's on some drug—popbite."

"He is."

"You *knew*?"

"Fuck, Isabelle, we all use it when we have to. Maybe it didn't exist when you left Terra, but in the last decade . . . We all use it if we have to." He pushed away the memory of Brazil. "But listen, Austin and your sister are okay. Even Dr. Patel will be. So what if they ride out the spore cloud in some crazy survivalist bunker? Do you really think that those two Terrans will harm them? Tony and what's-his-name?"

"Who knows what they'll do!"

"The truth, Isabelle. Do you think they'll harm Austin or Kayla?"

Long silence. Then she said, "No."

"Then it can wait. After the cloud hits and we see what we're up against with survivors and vaccinated kids and all, then we can go convince Austin to come out. Or maybe they'll just leave the cave voluntarily. Why are they in there in the first place? They'll all be immune to spore disease."

"Probably, yes. But any Kindred they have with them won't be.

If they have some survivalist idea of restarting civilization, they'll have women with them. Claire Patel is too old."

"So how—"

Isabelle said, "Austin's friend Graa^lok has sisters. Young, pretty . . ."

"Well, there you go. And Austin's not a stupid kid. He makes himself useful, and he keeps an eye on what's around him. Sure, he's a little wet behind the ears, but he's sharp. He got his mother out there by fooling us all, didn't he? Dr. Patel, too. Those guys will want Austin around. He even finds them new stuff that might be useful, like that alien junk he told me about buried in the sand, and he can also translate anything that—"

Isabelle took a step backward. "What did you just say?"

Leo blinked. "I said Austin can translate any—"

"Before that!"

He had to make an effort to remember. "Austin told me he found some old piece of junk buried in the sand way back in a cave and . . . let me think . . . yeah, he said it was alien and wasn't rusty. At all. Isabelle—what is it?"

Her face had gone bone white. Was she going to faint? Leo reached out to grab her, but Isabelle was made of tougher stuff than that. She held onto a kitchen shelf and breathed deep. Then she said, "Go get Lieutenant Lamont."

"Whoa, you don't want to—"

"Do it. I'll get Marianne and the others. Tell Lamont it's urgent. Life-or-death urgent. No, tell him something else, something *he'll* want to hear.

"Tell him there might be a way to call a ship to take him home."

Salah Bourgiba wasn't convinced. Leo could see that. He thought the unrusty object that Austin had mentioned might be anything at all, a view that Leo shared, even though he didn't like sharing anything with Bourgiba. Dr. Jenner and Isabelle believed it was the call-back device but that, Leo thought, was because they wanted to believe it. Branch wanted mostly to get his hands on the hardware.

It was Owen who disturbed Leo.

He'd gone outside to look for Owen but found him instead in the ready room. Owen must have taken more popbite because he was hyperawake, counting his clips of ammo. They lay on the floor in lines straight as a parade drill, but Owen nudged one of them a fraction of an inch to the right. What was the point of that? Better not to ask.

"Sir, sorry to distur—"

"What?" Owen's calm, following so much irritability in the past week, was more unsettling than a shout or howl. The whites of his eyes looked yellowish, and the pupils were enormous. Not yet in armor, his weight loss was obvious. How much popbite was he doing? Every soldier knew the limits, as well as what could happen if you exceeded them.

Leo said, "Dr. Jenner and the others think they might have a way to call the colony ship back from wherever it is and use it to go back to Terra."

Owen went completely still. Seconds passed, during which Owen stared hard at something in the corner of the room. Leo turned his head, but the corner was empty.

Finally Owen said, "How?"

"Some device that Austin Rhinehart found in the mountains. He said to . . . they would like to discuss this with you, sir. In the clinic."

Owen put his ammo into his lockbox, locked it, and strode out. Since he had no orders to the contrary, Leo followed.

The Terrans had moved into the leelee lab, leaving the door open to let out some of the stink. Noah wasn't there. The leelees chittered—didn't the dumb things ever sleep? Well, if not, they looked better not sleeping than Owen, who reminded Leo of a twitchy jaguar he'd seen in Brazil.

"Lieutenant Lamont," Isabelle said. "We have two pieces of information for you. First, a few days ago Austin told Leo that he'd found an 'unrusty alien piece of machinery' in Tony Schrupp's cave, where Austin took Dr. Patel. Before she died, the Mother of Mothers told me there had originally been a device to call back the colony ship, World's other spaceship. It's been sending signals, as you know. Branch decoded them with that"—Isabelle pointed at a pile of machinery taking up a good chunk of floor space next to a rumpled pallet—"and there is a good chance that if we can get the device from the cave and use it through Branch's transmitter, we can call the colony ship back here."

Owen said nothing. His yellowish, huge-pupiled eyes did not blink.

Marianne said, "If we can get the ship here, there might be a chance that Branch could change its destination settings to Terra. After all, other settings aboard the *Friendship* were reprogrammable. Within limits, yes, but—"

"Why should I believe you?" Owen said in a calm, reasonable voice that nonetheless made Leo's skin prickle. "You want the hostages back. I said no. All of a sudden you come up with another reason for an extraction."

Bourgiba's eyes narrowed and he started to speak, but Isabelle put a hand on his arm. Smart Isabelle—she could do this better than anyone else.

Isabelle said, "I understand what you're saying, Lieutenant. But Austin spoke originally to Corporal Brodie, and I'm sure you trust your own unit's intel."

"Brodie?" Owen said, without turning.

"It's true, sir." Leo strained to remember Austin's exact words. "I caught him coming back to camp and he told me that Noah Jenner already knows where he goes, but that Jenner didn't know everything, that Austin was the only one who knew everything. The kid said that Jenner didn't know that Austin found 'a rusty old alien machine buried in sand.' He told me it's shaped like a pyramid. He didn't know what it was for."

Isabelle said, "Ree^ka told me the call-back device was pyramidal. Also, it's the only piece of alien machinery pictured in the tablets but never found. Geological activity over eons—"

Fuck geological activity. Leo saw that Owen had stopped listening. Owen stared at the floor, head down, an un-Owen-like pose. When he raised his head, his face looked somehow both twitchy and impassive.

"All right. We go after the call-back device."

Don't say thank you, Isabelle. This was a mission decision, not a favor or capitulation, don't let him think it is . . .

Dr. Jenner said, "Thank—"

"What do you want us to do?" Isabelle said, quick and loud. "Do you need a translator?"

Of course he didn't; the survivalists spoke English. But it was probably the first thing Isabelle had thought of.

"Wake Jenner," Owen said. "He can guide us to the cave. If he's too injured, then I need everything he knows about direction, distance, terrain, and the enemy forces inside the objective, including what weapons they might have. What is your second piece of information?"

This time, Isabelle let Dr. Jenner speak. "It's what's aboard the colony ship. Every time we've exposed leelees to spores here in the lab—"

"You have spores here? From Terra?"

Dr. Jenner looked surprised. "A limited number. What did you think we used to manufacture vaccines?"

Leo thought: *Did I know they had live spores?* No, he did not. The scientists had assumed everyone knew the science, and Owen had assumed their business was separate from his mission. Just as he'd tried to keep the squad separate and self-contained, using everything short of a nonfraternization order.

"Anyway," Dr. Jenner continued, "all the lab leelees that we exposed to spores died. But Branch has auditory evidence that on the colony ship, there are *live* leelees. That argues that they're somehow immune to the spores that killed the Kindred crew. It might be that just a few with natural genetic immunity survived and bred. But here on Kindred we haven't found *any* leelees with natural immunity. The other possibility is a virophage, a virus that destroys the spores, and if we can get the ship here and let the virophages loose before the spore cloud hits, and if the virophage proves to be airborne, it might save any of the population that can breathe it in. It's a long shot, but even so we— Lieutenant?"

Owen had turned away. No one saw his face except Leo, and he felt his own eyes widen. Owen's face jerked into a rage that Leo had seen only once before: in Brazil, on a suicide bomber rushing toward a group of Marines.

The rage vanished. Owen turned back to the others. "Bring me Noah Jenner. We start at first light. I'll take Specialist Berman with me. Private Kandiss and Corporal Brodie will remain here to secure the building."

Bourgiba said angrily, "We no longer need 'securing' because there's no more vaccine to—"

But Owen had already left the room.

Austin sat at a rough table with his mother and Claire, eating dinner. The cave was dim and cool. Claire had poked among the supplies and cooking pots and weird stove—Austin didn't understand what powered it—and produced a soup far tastier than the dry and cold stuff Austin had had before. Beyon-mak ate three bowls of it before disappearing back to his stupid old equipment. Tony, who'd also eaten three bowls of soup, kept looking toward the tunnel door.

Claire ignored them all, talking only to Kayla. "Can I ask how many hours of sleep you usually get in a night?"

Kayla shook her head, but then she answered. "Maybe ten. But it's not good sleep. I can't get up in the morning."

"What's the most pleasurable thing in your life, if you don't mind my asking? Your life at the lahk, I mean."

"Nothing is pleasurable."

There were more questions, gentle and kind—why didn't Claire talk to him that way!—until Kayla finally said, "Enough. Sorry. I can't." Her eyes filled and she went back to her pallet behind the curtain.

"Austin," Claire said, "your mother is seriously depressed. She has at least eight of the nine signs of clinical depression. Do you know if there are drugs for this on Kindred and what they're called?"

"Isabelle says there aren't." At least she was talking to him.

"What happens to people who are psychotic or schizophrenic or severely bipolar?"

"I don't know those words."

"I mean, people who can't function normally in society?"

"My mother's normal! She just wants to go home! She doesn't belong in a duịhn!"

"Is that an asylum? Perhaps not. But I'm worried that—" The tunnel bell rang three times and Claire startled. "What's that?"

Tony raced from a side tunnel to the door, unlocked it, and disappeared into the tunnel.

Austin said, "That's Graa^lok's signal. He's back."

Tony led seven women from the tunnel, followed by Graa^lok. Austin recognized Graa^lok's mother and two sisters; he'd known them since he was three. The other girls, all young, were strangers. All wore cloaks and carried large packs.

"Oh my God," Claire said. "You really think you can form a polygamous commune."

Austin didn't know what a "polygamous commune" was, but it didn't sound good. Or maybe it did. Graa^lok's mother smiled uncertainly and said in World, "I greet you, Tony-mak."

"Tony-kal," Graa^lok corrected. "We're a new kind of lahk now."

Another of the girls, the youngest, peered shyly at Austin. He stood up taller. She was even prettier than Claire.

Saving civilization might be great, after all.

CHAPTER 17

Leo stood on the roof, watching Owen and Zoe, both green in his night-vision goggles, as they set off north toward the mountains. The camp, its population a quarter of its former size, wasn't yet stirring. Were the Kindred left here the ones with no lahk to go back to? But everyone had a lahk. Maybe the vaccinated children and their parents were the hangers-on, the parents hoping to hand their kids over to the Terrans as the spore cloud hit and they themselves died.

But that horror would have to wait. Leo had another one to deal with.

Kandiss was on perimeter patrol. He would be back soon. Leo dropped from the roof and went inside the compound, where seven people slept. Plenty of room for them now.

In the ready room, he tried to smash the lock on Owen's lockbox with the butt of his rifle. It didn't give, and neither did the metal of the box itself. Okay, then—he'd have to blast it open, despite who might hear. Zoe was the explosives specialist, not him, but Zoe wasn't here. Leo fitted the silencer, even though silencers never really were, onto his rifle and blew the lock.

Congrats, Leo—you just qualified yourself for court-martial.

Owen had taken all the weapons, the full monte. His lockbox held only a photograph of a beautiful girl—who? Leo had no idea—a plastic bottle, and a Kindred box made of the stuff that Isabelle called "bioplast." Leo had almost forgotten what plastic felt like in his hand: smoother than bioplast, slipperier, somehow more slimy. The bottle held tabs of popbite. Leo knew what was in the bioplast before he opened it. But he'd had to look, had to be sure, had to prove himself wrong if he could.

God, he wished he'd been wrong.

He heard a sound behind him and turned. Isabelle stood there, dressed in some sort of flimsy nightie thing. She said, "I heard a noise and— Leo, what are you *doing?*"

"Nothing. Get out."

She stepped into the room. Leo snapped shut the box, but she'd already seen. "Those are . . . oh my God, the vaccines. Did you . . . no. *Lamont.*"

He stood. "I said get out, Isabelle. Go back to bed."

She ignored him. "He was the one who stole them. Lamont. When everything was so confused during that first assault—he was checking the compound before we all went back in even though it hadn't been breached . . . but why? Why?"

"I don't know," Leo said, but he did.

Owen, disliking Kindred since the moment they'd landed, more and more lumping all natives together as "the enemy," calling them "Kinnies" in that tone of utter contempt. Owen refusing to even consider training Kindred cops as force multiplication. Owen's paranoia about the camp made a hundred times worse by popbite. Owen clinging to the mission, which was to protect the Terrans and get them home no matter what, not letting anything or anyone deter him from that. Even if, in dawning psychosis, it meant making sure that as few Kindred as possible survived to interfere. The Ranger's creed said *I will complete the mission, though I be the lone survivor.*

It wasn't like he hadn't seen this before. In Brazil, a guy in his unit had gone crackers, started shooting up their camp one night, raving about voodoo and demons and Armageddon. He'd been doing popbite, too, but it hadn't needed that. Sullivan had been a little nuts even before he snapped. When he did, he'd managed to murder three Marines right in their own camp. There were always guys like that, couldn't take the strain, but . . .

Not Rangers.

Not Owen. Owen might strain but he didn't snap.

It still didn't make sense. There had to be more. Owen hadn't decided to go after Claire Patel until Dr. Jenner talked about that thing on the ship, the virophage thingy, that might save Kindred who breathed it in. Okay, so Owen was going for the call-back device so he could bring back the Kindred ship and help save the natives, long odds or no. But if that was true, then why steal the vaccines that had been the scientists' best shot at saving Kindred lives until Dr. Jenner came up with this new science? Why?

Unless Owen wanted not to recover the call-back device, but to destroy it. Unless he really wanted all the Kindred dead. Unless that had been his reason for coming on this mission in the first place.

No. Stupid idea, ridiculous, *disloyal*.

Why had Owen stolen the vaccines?

Leo scoured his brain for anything else he knew about Owen, any scrap of information. There wasn't much. Parents dead, raised by his grandmother Judith, liked the Pittsburgh Steelers, declined once to go to a bar with Leo and some guys because Owen had some sort of meeting to go to, a meeting he'd been secretive about . . .

The government would have vetted Owen for this mission. Looked into every nook and cranny of Owen's past. Only . . . look how many nooks and crannies they had missed about Leo's past. And Zoe's, too, from stuff she'd told him.

Not Owen. Leo wouldn't believe it. Couldn't believe it.

But if he were right . . .

The box of stolen vaccines was still in his hand.

Leo put it down, opened his own lockbox, and began adding everything in it to the gear he already wore. Isabelle was still talking to him, but he wasn't listening until she stood in the doorway, try-ing to bar him from leaving. "Are you going after them? Lamont and Berman? What is he going to do? It's the call-back device, isn't it? He wasn't interested in going after Claire and Austin until we told him Austin had that in the mountains and . . . No. He still wasn't in-terested, not until Marianne told him about the virophage. Leo—what is going on?"

"Get out of my way."

"Wait till I get dressed—I'm coming with you!"

Leo said, "You're not. You'd slow me down, give away my posi-tion, and distract me with keeping you safe. Isabelle, if you follow me, I'll disable you with a shot to the foot. Do you understand?"

Her eyes widened. She saw that he meant it. Leo lifted her by the waist and set her aside so he could pass through the doorway. Over his shoulder he said, "Don't tell Kandiss that I've gone, if he asks you. Go back to bed and pretend you never saw me."

She didn't answer. Leo let himself out the kitchen door, scaled the garden wall, and followed Zoe and Owen's tracks toward the moun-tains.

The sky turned orange and red.

Leo lay flat behind a slight rise. The Rangers weren't in any hurry, and catching up to them had been easy. Periodically Zoe scanned behind them but she wasn't expecting to be followed—certainly not by Leo—and keeping out of sight wasn't difficult even in this rela-tively open country.

How far was Owen willing to go? Leo had a pretty good idea of how Owen would breach the supposedly impregnable mountain for-tress, but depending on the setup inside, it might kill the Terrans as well, including Dr. Patel, who was one of Owen's protectees. And if Zoe objected—?

Zoe would not object. She was a Ranger: superbly trained, completely loyal to her unit, honed for just this kind of quick raid. *I will complete the mission, though I be the lone survivor.* A good creed—except when somebody's mission wasn't what everyone else's was.

Was that why Owen had pulled strings to get Leo on this mission? It had never really made sense to transfer Leo to the *Friendship* at the last minute; the Rangers had their own snipers. Had Owen thought that Leo wouldn't cross him, no more than Zoe or Kandiss would? If Leo was right and Owen was some kind of Army infiltrator from a xenophobic cult, if Owen had kept his hatred of the Kindred secret for years, then Owen was even smarter than Leo thought. Smarter than Leo, who'd spent years not thinking.

He would have to think now.

Owen had more knowledge, popbite, fanaticism, Zoe.

Leo had surprise.

They were moving again, hiking toward the mountains. As the terrain got rougher, it was easier for Leo to get closer to them and still stay hidden. If they talked, he couldn't hear it. Well, duh—they had left their wristers behind. One of the Terrans who'd designed this survivalist bunker was a physicist; who knew what he could detect with monitors inside.

Leo buried his wrister. He began to scan carefully for cameras, motion detectors, maybe drones.

At least nobody here had surveillance satellites in orbit.

In Brazil, Leo had shot Sullivan straight in the face.

Austin slept on a pallet in the middle of the central cave, along with Graa^lok, Tony, and Beyon-mak. The nine women had taken all the curtains and strung them together to make a new alcove, with all the best pallets. Austin had been pleased to see that Kayla had perked up a little with the arrival of Claire and the other women, even though she could talk only to Claire.

A noise woke him. At first he thought it was part of a dream, but then he came fully awake and the loud pinging continued. Graa^lok snored loudly. Beyon-mak was shaking Tony's shoulder.

"Get up, Tony. They're here."

Tony was on his feet so fast that his knees cracked. Austin sat up in the dim biotorch light. "Who's here?"

Neither man answered him. They went to the "monitor"; Beyon-mak did something; the pinging stopped. Austin moved quietly—maybe they wouldn't notice him—to stand behind them.

The screen, normally a flat blank rectangle set into a big wooden box, showed a *picture*. It was . . . it was the outside of the cave! Austin blurted out, "How did you *do* that?"

They ignored him. Beyon-mak was fiddling with knobs and muttering, "Fucking primitive system . . ."

Austin stared, fascinated. A word from his mother's laments for Terra jumped into his mind: *television*. But Kayla had described moving stories on television, not something real, right outside Haven. Austin looked at Beyon-mak with awe, which immediately changed to anger. Did Graa^lok understand this technology but not tell Austin that it even existed?

The picture went away in a flurry of white dots and another appeared: two Rangers walking toward Haven. The images were blurry, but Austin recognized both their walks: Lieutenant Lamont and Ranger Berman.

He said, "They want Claire!"

Tony half turned. To Austin's surprise, Tony grinned. "They won't get her."

"But . . . they're Rangers!"

"Who have no idea what we have here. Nada. Zilch. Haven is both impregnable and weaponized. Now be a good kid and go wake Graylock in case Nate needs him. And then keep the women away from here; they'll only get in the way."

"How do I—"

The grin vanished. "Any way you can!"

"Okay, yes," Austin said, although he didn't think he could keep Claire away from anywhere she wanted to go. And maybe not Graa^lok's oldest sister, either. He remembered her from when he'd played at their lahk as a child. Sher^llaa was sort of an Isabelle, and she had never seemed to like Austin much.

He went to wake Graa^lok.

Leo lay flat, camouflaged with brush he'd cut with his knife, studying the situation. He had circled around Owen and Zoe, moving faster, and was now between them and an abruptly rising, big, forty-five-degree hill. Or maybe it was a small mountain. It was where the tracks stopped, in front of dense brush fringing the base of the mountain. Through his scope, Leo could see the churned-up mud where people had gone into the brush and, he presumed, into a cave. Austin's "fort." Leo lay above the entrance and to the south.

Zoe and Owen had stopped to confer five hundred yards from the mountain base. No pipe gun could reach that far. But the two rogue Terrans had been inside for a long time, bringing in all kinds of equipment, and Beyon was some sort of fucking genius or something. They could have anything in there. Owen would know that. Also, the cave entrance would be fortified and maybe small. Zoe could maybe breach it, but not enter without being picked off like a rat in a barrel.

They were moving again. Zoe went south, Owen north, and they began to climb. Scoping out the terrain, or searching for a second entrance . . . No. Leo knew what they were doing.

Zoe climbed toward him. Silently, Leo slid in the other direction, careful not to dislodge any small stones. A few yards away was a shallow crevasse. Leo wriggled into it, pulling brush over him. He held his breath, rifle pointed upward between twigs, and waited.

He heard her boots on the rock.

She muttered, "Fuck."

Her shadow fell over him. If she looked down carefully enough, she'd see him. If she stepped wrong, her foot would go through the brush and she'd land on top of him. But she was testing each step carefully with her boot before shifting her weight, not taking her eyes off the terrain but not looking down, either . . .

Shit! Her boot felt the edge of the crevasse and her head swiveled . . .

Leo leaped up from his crouch and grabbed her. She wasn't ready, and he was. She yelled, "Enemy here!" which was right because now Leo was the enemy, but she had no radio and Owen was too far away to hear her. Zoe fought like the warrior she was, but Leo was stronger and he had the advantage of surprise. Still, no way he was going to win this quickly unless he either killed her or . . .

When he had the chance, he kicked her in the belly and she slumped to the ground, eyes rolled back in her head. He cuffed her hands behind her and barely had time to tie her ankles together before she was bucking and kicking with both legs together, her eyes furious and accusatory. She shouted loud enough to wake the dead.

He sat on her long enough to tape her mouth. Then, much more gently, he rolled her into the crevasse.

"Sorry, Zo. I have to stop Owen. He's going to destroy the planet."

Zoe shook her head, her mouth working under the tape. Leo could imagine what she was calling him. But there was no time to explain, and his nose ached and shed blood from where she'd gotten in a good blow. He dumped the brush on top of Zoe and stalked Owen, on the other side of the mountain.

Something exploded.

"Tony Schrupp. This is Lieutenant Lamont, US Army. Can you hear me?"

Austin stood ten feet from the flat TV window. He held out his arms on both sides to keep anyone else from going closer, but not only would this have been futile, it wasn't necessary. Austin's mother and the women of Graa^lok's lahk stood in a semicircle behind him, still as rocks, watching. Graa^lok stood beside Beyon-mak and Tony. Claire had circled to the side, and only Austin noticed that she had a kitchen knife in her hand. But what was she going to do with it? Austin had no idea, and he suspected Claire didn't, either.

Directly behind Austin was Graa^lok's youngest cousin, Nan^hal, just Austin's age. They'd had a long talk alone—well, almost alone—in a corner of the cave, because she'd wanted to know everything about him. He hoped that Nan^hal noticed how Tony was relying on Austin now.

"Tony Schrupp. This is Lieutenant Lamont, US Army. Can you hear me?"

This time Tony answered. Austin, who hadn't known there was radio to the outside, either, watched the television window. Lamont wasn't on it. Then he was, standing beside a low gray metal structure. An air shaft, not yet sealed against the spore cloud.

"I hear you," Tony said. "Don't touch that air shaft. Go away."

"I don't want to kill you."

"You won't," Tony said. He jerked on a lever.

Then, all at once, the cave exploded into sound and the TV window into dirt and flying rocks. Austin went numb for a moment until he realized no one inside was hurt because the explosive had gone off outside.

Tony said to Beyon-mak, "Did you get him?"

"I don't know yet. He was standing pretty close to the shaft and the bomb had to be farther away so as not to—"

A gunshot. A few seconds later, something dropped through the air and then the loudest noise and brightest light Austin had never imagined and he couldn't hear, couldn't see, was dying . . .

He wasn't dead. Smoke choked him and sparkly light blinded him but he wasn't dead. "Mom!" he cried, groping around the cave floor for Kayla. He didn't find her until a fan switched on and the smoke blew away and he could see everyone: not dead, not even injured, just some terrified and some furious, and Beyon-mak, weirdly, smiling at his equipment. Smiling!

"That was a flashbang," Lamont said. "Next down is a smoke bomb. I could smoke you out and pick you off one by one, but that's not what I want."

Tony's face was so nearly purple that he looked like a leelee. Austin had seen that look before. Tony was not going to back down, not ever. Tony said, "You can't have Dr. Patel. She's with us now."

"I'm not!" Claire shouted.

"I don't want Dr. Patel," Lamont said. "I want the call-back device. Send someone out the cave entrance with it and my squad and I will go away."

"The what?"

"Don't play dumb with me, Schrupp. You know what I mean. Pyramid-shaped device to call back the infected colony ship. Send one person out with it, alone, and I won't drop explosive charges down this airshaft or bomb both your entrances till rockfall seals you in."

Beyon-mak whispered, "*Both* entrances. He doesn't know about the third, or the—"

"Shut up," Tony said, which shocked Austin almost more than anything else that had happened. Tony telling Beyon-mak to shut up!

Austin suddenly felt as if it were his head that contained explosives. Other entrances, flashbangs, Tony's bombs and Lamont's bombs, a *call-back device* . . .

Tony said, "Lamont, I don't know what the fuck you're talking about!"

Austin said, "I do."

Leo strained to hear the radio conversation, or whatever it was. He couldn't see the transmitter-receiver and he was just far away from Owen that only words or parts of sentences were clear. "Dr. Patel. . . . both entrances . . . call-back device . . ."

Nothing he hadn't already guessed, except that he doubted Owen would just take the call-back device and go meekly away. He'd have to kill all the hostages in the cave and call it collateral damage. Did Schrupp know that? Probably, but as far as Leo could see, Schrupp didn't have a lot of choices. Unless there was more to the cave than Owen figured.

Certainly there was more to Owen than Schrupp figured.

Leo's guts roiled. He didn't let it interfere.

More words he couldn't hear. Then Owen said, "Okay. Now." Owen started moving in a wide circle away from the airshaft, away from Leo, down the mountain. His head moved constantly, scanning the ground for more explosives and the rest of the terrain for, presumably, Zoe. As he drew closer, Leo saw that Owen's left arm hung limply at his side; the blast had torn his shoulder to ribbons. His rifle was back in its sling and he carried his Beretta in his right hand. "Berman!" he shouted.

No answer.

I could do it now. But there was always the chance that Leo was wrong. He could be wrong about Owen, he'd never wanted anything so much in his life as he wanted to be wrong. He had to know, for sure. This was *Owen.*

Owen vanished behind the rise of rock. They descended the mountain in parallel, Leo south of Owen. Leo stopped just above and to the right of the cave entrance and took a position behind a boulder. Owen kept going, onto the flatter land below, then far enough away to be within shouting distance but out of weapons range, unless the entire fucking plain was booby-trapped.

Leo waited. Who would it be? He was pretty sure he knew, but maybe he was wrong.

He hoped he was wrong.

———

"You knew about this, too, Graylock, and didn't say a *thing*?" Tony said. "Not a fucking thing?"

"I didn't know what it was!" Graa^lok said. Tears filled his big dark eyes, squeezed out onto plump cheeks. "I didn't!"

Austin had retrieved the pyramidal call-back device—was that really what it was?—from the sand in the small cave beyond the fallen rocks. The rocks had fallen more, and for a sickening second he'd been afraid that either Beyon-mak's bomb or Lamont's flashbang had destabilized the whole cave and the roof would fall on him. Or that the rockfall had buried the device deeper. Or something. But the pyramid was there, and he shook the sand off it and clambered back over the rocks, their sharp edges cutting his hands and covering him with silt.

The call-back sat on the floor of the central cave while they all stared at it. Then, as fast as a diving bird on fish, Beyon-mak swooped down to run his hands over it, put his face close, lift it as delicately as if it hadn't been shaken by earthquakes and rattled by rockfalls and scraped along by Austin.

"There are round bumps on all four faces," Beyon-mak said. "That's all. I'm guessing a long and complex sequence of presses—but who knows what they are? Austin?"

"I don't know!"

"Of course he doesn't know," Tony said. "Probably nobody knows, or maybe the Mother of Mothers does—it doesn't matter. We don't want the ship. But that goddamn Ranger does, and he can have it. We're taking this thing out to him."

We. But there would be no we. *One person,* Lamont had said.

Tony said to Austin, "If you and Graylock found this thing and didn't know what it was, how does Lamont know it even exists? Who did you tell about Haven?"

"I . . . Noah followed me here! But he said he already knew, Tony! He knew you were here!"

"Of course he did," Beyon-mak said, straightening. He had sand on the knees of his pants. "But he didn't know about this device. Who did you tell about it?"

"Nobody!" But he had a sickening memory of talking to Leo. What had he said to Leo, he couldn't remember . . .

"It was you," Tony said. "It had to be you. Nate, Graylock, take everybody into the backup cave."

Claire said, "Backup cave?"

Tony actually grinned. "Separate airshaft, separate third entrance, tight closing door. Don't underestimate our planning, Doctor."

She said, "I'm taking the device out to Lamont."

"You are not. We need you."

"Oh for God's sake, Schrupp, *think*. He's not going to shoot the messenger or bomb the airshaft. What he wants is to go back to Terra and take his Rangers and protectees with him. I'm a protectee. If he has me, Branch Carter will computer-generate all possible sequences for that device and press those bumps in every single sequence until he gets that ship here. Or maybe the Council of Mothers knows the sequence. Either way, we'll lift off and leave you to your postapocalyptic world-building on Kindred. But if it's not me who takes that thing out there, Lamont will keep at you until he gets all his protectees. I've watched the man for months and you have not. He's obsessive-compulsive with paranoid tendencies and the stress of this environment has pushed him over the edge."

"I don't care if he's hallucinating green elephants and talking to his dead grandfather. You're a Terran doctor and we need you more than Terra does. Sorry, Dr. Patel. We'll treat you with every respect and courtesy, but you're not leaving World. Austin, you created this mess—you take the device out to Lamont."

Kayla, who'd been standing at the edge of the circle, screamed, darted forward and clutched Austin. Tony peeled her off him and handed her to Graa^lok, who could barely hold her. Exasperated, Beyon-mak helped him. Kayla went on screaming. "No, no, not Austin, no—"

"Get them to the backup cave!" Tony said. "All of them!"

Graa^lok looked at Austin. Graa^lok's face twisted in anguish and indecision. Austin hated him; Graa^lok always got the best choice, the safe deal. But then Austin nodded and said, "Take care of my mother," and Graa^lok nodded back. For a moment Austin felt good; he was doing the right thing. The feeling didn't last.

When they had all gone through a locked door that Austin had always assumed was another supply area, Austin faced Tony. "Will you let me back in? After I give the device to the lieutenant?"

Tony hesitated. "That bastard shot out all the cameras. And there aren't any monitors in the backup cave . . . Tell you what. You stay outside until the Rangers lift off in that second ship. Then come ring the bell and I'll let you back in, through the airlock in the backup cave."

Austin looked at him. It might be a long time before Branch figured out the code that Beyon-mak spoke about. It might not be figured out before the spore cloud hit. With the cameras shot out, Tony couldn't see anything outside to tell him if the cloud had hit or not, which was only an approximate date. Even if there was an airlock, and there probably was, Tony would not risk spore contamination of Haven. He needed Graa^lok's sisters and cousins to stay healthy and have babies who would inherit Terran immunity. He needed to keep his "protectees" safe from the riots and food shortages and roving bands of the collapse of civilization.

Austin would not be allowed back into Haven.

He could scream like Kayla. He could hang on to a table and refuse to go. He could act like a little kid, but Tony would get him out by sheer force if he had to, or if Tony didn't, then Lamont would bomb Haven if he didn't get the device. If that happened, Austin's mother and Claire and everybody would die, anyway. Including Austin.

He wasn't a little kid anymore. He was a man. His mother was his lahk, and maybe even Claire was, too. Bu^ka^tel.

He straightened his back and looked Tony in the eyes. "Do you think Lamont will shoot me?"

"I don't see why he would. He's getting what he wants, isn't he? You heard Dr. Patel. He wants to go back to Terra."

"Okay." And then—without a quaver, sounding strong, and he was proud of that—he said, "Give me the device."

"Well, there it is."

Of course it was. But Austin refused to feel stupid about what he'd said. He picked up the call-back and headed for the tunnel to outside.

Owen waited for someone to emerge from the mountain, and Leo waited for Owen.

He could wait in the same position, barely breathing, for as long as he had to. The rising sun was behind him; the wind was too light to interfere with anything; the brush and rocks on the upland meadow below him were only waist-high. Leo sweated inside his armor and helmet; he ignored it. The orange light, though nothing like a sunny day on Terra, was enough to see by. Only his own memories hampered him.

Delirious and cursing, his body a mass of sores, his head about to explode from fever. Owen carrying him down the mountain on his back, murmuring over his shoulder: "Easy, buddy, we'll get you to the medics, not your fault it's just fucking poison ivy. . . ." Owen visiting him in the infirmary, trying to convince him to recycle through Ranger training. Owen and Leo in a bar somewhere with two girls, Owen laughing but even then, even with a rhinestone blonde on his lap, Owen had been reserved somehow, holding back, in control . . . Owen getting Leo here to Kindred, counting on him to stick no matter what, using him . . .

The last thought wouldn't stay. It was still Owen carrying him down the mountain, saving Leo's life. Always Owen carrying him down the mountain.

In the meadow, Owen shifted position.

A figure crawled from the bushes at the base of the mountain, stooped, picked up something pyramidal and started across the meadow. Austin.

Leo was too far away to hear any conversation. But he already knew what Owen would say: *Leave it there.* "There" would be half-way between Owen and the mountain, where Owen could retrieve it without letting an enemy, even a thirteen-year-old enemy, get too close. Almost Leo could hear the words in his mind.

Except there was another sound, behind him. "Throw away the rifle, Leo. Without turning around."

Zoe.

Time slowed down. He had days, years, eons to assess the situation. Even if her feet were free, her hands were still cuffed behind her back. She had her sidearm, but did she have a way to use it or was she bluffing? Or had she worked her body through the cuffs to get her hands in front? It was possible but only if you were very thin, unusually flexible, and willing to dislocate your shoulder. Zoe was thin; he had no idea if she was unusually flexible; she would dislocate anything on herself if she thought it was her duty.

Would she shoot him? In a pulse beat.

Leo didn't turn around. He had one chance: to convince her.

Austin started trudging across the plain.

"Zoe, listen. Austin is bringing Lamont the call-back device. But he doesn't want it to call back the ship. Dr. Jenner thinks there's something on the ship, another damn microbe"—he couldn't remember the fucking term—"that saved the leelees on the ship and might save

Kindred, too, if they can get it here. But Lamont doesn't want to save Kindred, he wants it destroyed. Everybody on it, all the Kindred. You've seen how he despises them, he fucking hates them, maybe because of the spore cloud hitting Terra, and he won't call back the ship. Not right away, anyway, he'll hide the device until the spore cloud devastates Kindred and nearly everyone here is dead, and *then* he'll go home. But all the Terrans and Kindred in the cave—they know he's got it now, so he's going to have to kill them all. Even Claire Patel. He'll kill them, Zoe. He'll have to."

She hadn't shot Leo yet. She'd heard him out. Hope flashed through Leo like a jolt of electricity.

Then she said, "Bullshit. Lamont don't like Kinnies, but he isn't going to destroy them! Where do you get this fucking garbage?"

"It's not garbage." Austin was a third of the way to Owen, his arms wrapped awkwardly around the device. "Owen stole those vaccines. Not the kid—Owen. I *saw* them, in his lockbox, early this morning. He didn't want Kindred vaccinated with the good stuff from Terra."

"You're fucking crazy, Leo."

"*No.* He's going to shoot that kid. He can't have witnesses."

Austin plodded closer, shoulders slumped over his burden. Owen raised his weapon.

Zoe said, "He's just being cautious, warning the kid not to come too close, he could be a suicide bomber . . ."

"*Austin?*"

No more time. Owen's gun was coming up. His mouth worked. Austin, obedient, put the device on the ground, and there was no more time at all.

Owen carrying Leo down the mountain . . .

Leo fired. The distance was no more than eight hundred yards; his best kill ever was nearly 2,200 yards. Simultaneously, two more shots shattered the meadow. Owen's rifle and Zoe's Beretta.

Leo was rolling to the ground the second his bullet left the barrel.

He knew he was fast—in Brazil he'd changed weapons faster than the rest of his company could reload. But Zoe was close. Her bullet took him in the right side. He drew his sidearm and aimed, but there was no need. She stood completely still, her gun awkwardly in her cuffed right hand, the left dangling from her side, her mouth open.

"He . . . he killed that kid."

Leo got to his feet, holding his left hand over his side, feeling the blood trickle between his fingers. "Drop the gun, Zoe."

She did, unblinking, her face blank until it crumpled into pain that had nothing to do with a dislocated shoulder. "He killed that kid. You were right."

Leo holstered his Beretta. The motion made him dizzy.

Zoe said, "Is Lamont dead?"

"Yes." Leo didn't have to look.

Then he slumped to the ground, and everything went black.

He didn't think he was out that long, but when he came to, the sun beat down directly overhead and Zoe was gone. His armor had been removed and his shirt torn into bandages. Hers, too, he guessed— the pad of blood-soaked bandages on his wound was thick and the cloth tied around him to hold them so tight he almost couldn't breathe.

He tried to raise himself on one elbow to see if Owen's and Austin's bodies were still there, but the movement caused something to rip, pain to shoot through him, and the conviction that he had better lie still until help came or he died.

One or the other.

But he would have liked to see Isabelle again. Just once more, with the orange sun shining on her pretty hair.

CHAPTER 18

Salah stood before Noah Jenner and said, "Count backward from one hundred."

"One hundred, ninety-nine, ninety-seven . . . uh. . . . no, wait. . . . ."

"Can you name your siblings, Noah?"

A blank stare and a wince of pain, presumably from the headache that Noah had denied having.

Salah closed the door quietly. He found Claire's useful medical suitcase and raided it. In the deserted kitchen he filled with water three of the sturdy, lightweight metal canteens the Kindred used. No plastic bottles here to clog land or oceans, both of which would soon be free of most, if not all, human life.

The early morning sun slanted long shadows across the refugee camp, now almost deserted. Abandoned tents sagged beside blackened cook fires and the rutted tracks of supply carts. It looked not like the well-run refugee camp it had resembled before, but more like a Terran homeless jungle. The Kindred remaining were mostly families with vaccinated children, those that had somehow alienated their lahks too much to return to them, and maybe a few who figured their survival chances were better near the Terrans, either for medical help or looting. Experiments, outcasts, opportunists.

Six steps away from the compound and Kandiss, on the roof, spotted him.

"Go back inside, Doctor."

Kandiss was silhouetted against the lowering sun; Salah had to shade his eyes to see him clearly. Of all the Rangers, he had the least sense of Kandiss. The huge man had said nothing when Salah treated his injuries, mostly cuts from flying debris after the bomb attack. He'd refused any further questions about his concussion. Kandiss had never come to Salah with a minor illness caused by the alien environment. Even less than Lamont, Kandiss did not interact with the scientists. Although Salah had seen Kandiss's entire medical history and psych profile back on Terra, both were so sparse and unremarkable as to define "normal." He had a mother and two sisters in Florida. His service record was impeccable. Salah had never detected coming from him any whiff of Lamont's racism, Berman's fierce passions, Brodie's unthinking optimism. He no idea who Kandiss really was, or what Kandiss felt about the four horsemen of the apocalypse set to come trampling over the gardens and lahks of Kindred.

"Private Kandiss, please listen to me. Lieutenant Lamont and Specialist Berman have been gone since yesterday, much longer than two ten-mile hikes and a negotiation with Schrupp should take them. That suggests there was some kind of incident. They both may be injured and need medical attention. I'm a doctor. We can't"—he told the lie as convincingly as he could—"afford to lose any more Rangers. We need all of you. Let me go see if Lamont or Berman need medical help."

Kandiss said nothing, which Salah interpreted as a good sign.

Salah hoisted his makeshift backpack. "I'm confident Lieutenant Lamont will bring back Dr. Patel," he said, although he was confident of no such thing, "but if Lamont or Berman are injured, Dr. Patel might need these medicines and this equipment. She didn't take anything with her when she was kidnapped. I'm going to bring the items that might mean the difference between life and death for your two Rangers."

That sounded both simplistic and melodramatic, even though it was true. Salah didn't know what tone might move this silent soldier with whom he had nothing in common. Not that he had anything in common with the other three Rangers, either. He waited.

Finally Kandiss said, "Can you track?"

"Yes," Salah said—another lie.

Kandiss snorted. "Walk ten degrees east of north."

Something landed at Salah's feet. A compass. Yes, of course— Kindred had a magnetic field similar to Earth's. He had never thought about it before. Kandiss's directions—an order, actually—would include any necessary recalculation to make the compass useful.

He started walking. Ten miles would tax him, but he could do it. He hoped. He'd never been much of an athlete, and weeks of indoor activity at the compound hadn't helped. He could have exercised like the Rangers did, but he hadn't.

The backpack grew heavy. He felt exposed in these mostly tree-less fields, empty except for grazing animals. One kind pulled carts, he knew that much. The other kind were splashed with blotches of different colored paint in different parts of their anatomy, maybe a more humane version of cattle branding. Their coarse hair was long and uneven—was this an animal that was sheared regularly for cloth but hadn't been during this crisis? Salah had no idea. There was so much he didn't know about this planet. And, he realized for the first time, so much he didn't like. The light, the slow pace of lahk life, the deliberate and stubborn avoidance of tech . . . Kindred was admira-ble, far more admirable than Terra socially, environmentally, eco-nomically. The culture was everything that Salah had always said he believed in. But—

He wanted to go home, to Earth. He wanted it as much as Lamont did, although for completely different reasons. He did not belong here, and never would. From temperament or age or background, he did not have the adaptability of, say, Claire. Or of Brodie.

"You're off course," a voice said behind him, "and you're a terri-ble traveler."

Isabelle. Salah had not even heard her approach.

She said, "I could have been anyone sneaking up on you."

"But you're not," he said, irritated because she was right. "Go back, Isabelle."

"You're going to Tony's hideout and you're off course."

"I'm following the course Kandiss gave me."

"Has Kandiss ever been there? Neither have I, but I've hiked in those mountains before. You need to go farther that way." She pointed.

"Thank you. Now go back."

"Why?"

"This could be really dangerous, Isabelle. Lamont is paranoid, impaired by too much popbite use, and too trigger-happy. Please go back."

She said flatly, "You're protecting me."

"I'm trying to."

"Does it occur to you, Salah, that maybe I don't need protecting? That I don't want to be protected? I'm a *mother*."

"You're not a soldier."

"Neither are you. But I know this world better than you do, and I know soldiers better than you do, too."

"That's all true. But—"

"But I'm a woman. And you're a Terran male, who thinks women are to be shielded from danger even when they're like Zoe Berman. Or me. At least Leo Brodie forbade me to go with him because a civilian might interfere with his mission, not because I need protecting from reality."

Brodie had gone to the mountains, too? Salah hadn't known that. He didn't like it.

"Isabelle—"

She walked ahead of him, veering to the east. She said nothing more but Salah heard the loud sound anyway: another door closing between them.

After another mile of tense silence, during which the mountains seemed no closer and Salah felt himself flagging, Isabelle said, "Look. Straight ahead."

Salah strained his gaze. The sun was low now, dusk gathering on the dark-purple landscape. A figure staggered toward them, fell, got up and went on. It carried something bulky and heavy. Salah couldn't judge size from this perspective . . . Austin?

"Zoe," Isabelle said and sprinted forward.

By the time he caught up, Isabelle crouched beside Zoe Berman, who lay on the ground, scowling up at both of them. Salah bent and said, "Where are you injured?"

Isabelle said, "Austin? Leo?"

"Both shot," Zoe said. "Both alive when I left but bad off. Last night. Did what I could."

"Shot? By Tony Schrupp?"

"No," Zoe said, and passed out.

Salah examined her shoulder, gently palpated her belly. Spleen, bleeding into the abdominal cavity. It was amazing that she'd made it this far. These Rangers were almost another species.

Wryly, he realized what he'd just thought.

Beside Zoe stood a pyramidal object of gray, untarnished metal. The call-back device. This alien object might both aid Kindred in the spore plague and—which Salah suddenly hungered for as if he'd been starving—take Salah home.

Isabelle took Zoe's goggles off her helmet, put them on, and fiddled with them, looking like some caricature of an alien insect. She stared into the distance. "Someone's coming. A group of people." And then, "Oh my God!"

She took off running.

They were carrying him carefully, on a simple litter made of cloth strung between two poles. Every time the litter jarred, it hurt. Leo bit down on his tongue and said nothing.

Lu^kaj^ho murmured something incomprehensible in Kindred. Isabelle's language lessons had deserted Leo; he said back the only thing he could remember: "I greet you, Lu^kaj^ho." Lu^kaj^ho smiled.

Once they reached the flatter meadow, it was better. Less jolting. The three Kindred cops—that was how Leo still thought of them—made their slow way south. The sun was lowering behind the mountains. A moon, almost but not quite full, shone above him. The procession passed something that smelled warm and spicy. Leo closed his eyes. If he lived, he would like some of that spicy smell around him. Hell, if he died he'd like it around him, too.

"Leo."

His eyes flew open and she was there, bending over the litter. Leo scowled. "I told you not to come."

Isabelle ignored this. "I greet you, Leo." She touched his hand gently, as if the injury were there.

"Well, I goddamn greet you too, Isabelle, but I told you to stay put. Kandiss? Did you shoot him?"

"Of course I didn't shoot him." She gave a strangled little laugh, almost a sob. "I can come and go."

But Bourgiba couldn't, not without Kandiss's permission, and now the litter was lowered to the ground and the doctor was removing the bandages Zoe had wound around Leo. Leo pressed his teeth together so hard they could have broken rocks. He wasn't going to wince in front of Salah Bourgiba.

Bourgiba said, "The bullet's still in there."

News to Leo. He kept his eyes on Isabelle.

"I'm going to give you something for pain," Bourgiba said. "At the clinic, I can operate. Can you swallow?"

"Yeah." Of course he could swallow—Zoe hadn't shot his throat. Was this doctor competent?

Of course he is, idiot. Keep your eyes on Isabelle.

She gave him the pill with water from her canteen, raising his head so he could drink. He groped for her hand and kept it. *Take that, Doctor.*

The pain pill must have been more than that. The only words he managed to say before he slid into blackness were, "Austin? Zoe?"

But nobody heard him. Isabelle jabbered in Kindred to Lu^kaj^ho and the other two cops. Then her hand slid out of his, or his from hers, and the world went away.

Marianne sat beside Branch and silently counted losses and gains. Branch, cross-legged on a pallet with her laptop and the call-back pyramid on the floor beside him, wouldn't have heard if she'd spoken aloud. Probably he wouldn't have heard Gabriel's trumpet. His thin face scrunched with concentration.

Loss #1: Leo Brodie had been shot, his liver nicked by a bullet that had apparently done other damage as well, and Zoe Berman had a ruptured spleen. Salah, despite a single quiet comment that he was not a surgeon, had operated on both, with Isabelle and Marianne as untrained nurses. Both Rangers would recover but would need care. From whom?

Loss #2: Austin Rhinehart was luckier. Owen Lamont's bullet— and what kind of fanatic would shoot a thirteen-year-old?—had only grazed his head, due to Leo. Isabelle had found Austin lurching toward home, crying, blood streaming into his eyes. Head wounds, Salah said, bled a lot even if superficial. Austin had a monster headache but would be all right. Except—what did it do to a child to be shot by an adult he had trusted?

Loss #3: Claire, Kayla, and, according to Austin, a bunch of Kindred girls and their mother, were still hostage in Tony Schrupp's survivalist bunker.

Loss #4: Mason Kandiss no longer guarded the compound. He had gone to bring back, or to bury—Marianne wasn't clear on this— his lieutenant's body. "A Ranger never leaves a brother behind,"

Isabelle had said. Marianne, who neither understood nor sympathized with a creed that placed unit loyalty over, say, intent to destroy an entire civilization, had bitten back her retort. Anyway, there wasn't much to be guarded against; the camp was quiet.

Loss #5 was anticipated: In six days, the spore cloud would strike Kindred.

Well, then, gains. Gain #1—

She couldn't think of anything gained in the last several days.

Isabelle entered the leelee lab with Salah, Ka^graa, and an old woman who had to be a mother. Who? From where? Everyone sat down, exchanging *I-greet-you*'s in low voices, and Marianne suddenly flashed on faculty meetings at the college where she used to teach. A life ago. Several lives ago.

"Okay," Branch said, finally aware that the room held other people and he was on stage. The tips of his ears grew red, but he had obviously thought through what he wanted to say. "We have the call-back device. Now we have to figure out how to use it, and we do that by thinking like an alien."

All at once redness seeped from ear tips to his whole face. "I didn't mean . . . not that Kindred are aliens, I mean the other ones, the aliens who designed this and . . . not 'other aliens' I didn't mean to say that either—"

"Branch," Marianne said firmly because there was no time for this polite fumbling, "we know what you meant. Get on with it."

"Okay. Yes." He drew a large breath, while Isabelle translated. "Worlders press a button, or something like that anyway, on their colony ship and it goes to . . . wherever it went. They press a button on their other ship and it goes to Earth. We press a button on the *Friendship* and it goes to Kindred. So there were preset variations in the original plans the master aliens left, or else the ships are programmable, which makes more sense. And since so far no humans know how to program them, they're programming themselves on a simple return-to-where-you-started loop. Press the button and you reverse the flight plan.

"But what if no people are left to press that button, which is the situation on the colony ship now? You don't just want to abandon an expensive thing like a starship. So you build and leave behind an unbreakable call-back device. This."

He put his hand on it, and Marianne suppressed her impatience. Everyone here already knew this. Branch had a careful, linear mind, touching all bases, a good thing in a researcher, but—

"With your call-back device," Branch finally continued, "you build in a code to use it, because even if the device can't be damaged by anything short of a nuclear bomb, it can be stolen. Remember, you don't know how the stone-age people you're leaving all this with— you don't know how they're going to develop, what kind of society they'll create. The device could be stolen, misused by terrorists, lost for millennia—which it was. Applying the code has to be intuitively obvious—just press the right bumps in the right sequence. The code itself can't be too simple or it might accidentally be set off by, say, rocks falling on it. But the code might be lost or misremembered. So although complex, it has to be something that could be figured out by a society advanced enough to build the ships in the first place. A sequence of numbers that is basic to the universe.

"So what do you use?

"Not every single possible combination of pressing all sixteen bumps. That would be 20,922,789,888,000 possible sequences, and then only if the device is activated by a sequence using all sixteen bumps. At two seconds per trial, running them all would take over five million years. And the correct sequence might not even require all sixteen bumps. Is everybody with me so far?"

Marianne nodded. Branch waited until the low murmur of translation caught up.

"You can't use constants from physics, either, like the speed of light or Hudspeth's constant because they depend on units—meters, kilograms, joules, seconds—and there is no telling what units your stone-age society will develop if it ever builds starships.

"So you make sure that any ship still capable of being recalled sends its own code. That's what I think is coming from the ship . . . listen."

They had all heard this, but Branch played it again anyway from his receiver: one tone, pause, six tones, pause, eleven tones, pause, sixteen tones, pause, nine tones, pause, fourteen tones, pause, three tones, pause, eight tones, very long pause, one tone. Long silence before repeating.

"So the problem is to translate that bunch of numbers into some sequence of pressing bumps on the call-back device. You can't just press the numbers from the ship onto the pyramid because how do you know where to start? And there are still millions of possible combinations. No good. I think the transmitted numbers are supposed to be the *key* to the actual code to press. But the sequence doesn't match any mathematical sequence—not primes or Fibonacci or anything else I can come up with. It might be based on some common, indisputable number like the days in a Kindred year, but I can't make anything like that work, either. Yet the sequence has to be something known to the Kindred who will build these ships. I just don't know what!"

Salah said, "Branch, it seems to me you've made a lot of assumptions here. Three of those tones are in two digits—eleven, fourteen, sixteen—and you don't know that the numbers are even in base ten. The 'master aliens' might count in base six or base twelve—why assume they use base ten?"

"Because humans do," Branch said, wiggling his fingers, "and they gave the code to humans."

"Why assume the tones implies another number to press?"

"I told you. There has to be a way to narrow the possibilities and this is the most logical."

"Why assume the transmission from the ship is a call-back code at all? It could be a Mayday call for help or—"

"Because I fucking have to assume something!" Branch flared.

They were all so tired, Marianne thought: tired of tension, tired of violence, tired of not succeeding at anything. Tired of this planet.

Branch got himself under control. "Look, the universe runs on mathematics. It's the only shared language across all advanced cultures, all sciences. The transmitted numbers have to mean something."

"You did a good job," Isabelle said. "Look, let's sleep on it. Maybe someone will come up with something."

Branch looked at her, his eyes pleading. He was so young. Approval still mattered to him as much, or more, than survival.

Isabelle repeated, "You did a good job."

Leo woke and, without thinking, groped for the sidearm he had insisted on keeping on his pallet. It wasn't there. He bellowed, "Hey! Somebody!" and Kandiss came into the room. The big Ranger, in full kit, loomed over the pallet, his face blank.

The two men stared at each other. If Kandiss was going to kill him, there was nothing Leo could do about it. He said, "Give me back my weapons."

Kandiss ignored that. "I buried him."

Owen. Of course Kandiss had retrieved and buried the body. Leo said, "Zoe told you what happened."

"I want to hear it from you."

Leo told him. He couldn't tell if Kandiss believed him, or even heard him. Kandiss never blinked; his face never twitched. When Leo finished, he repeated, "Give me my weapons."

Then Kandiss did react. "I don't have them."

It took Leo a moment to absorb this. He let out a string of curses worthy of Zoe. "Find my weapons and bring them here."

"Yes, sir," Kandiss said.

Sir. Leo was now the ranking soldier on Kindred, the CO. Christ on a cracker. Leadership was exactly what he didn't want, what he'd dropped out of Ranger School to avoid. Although somehow he seemed to have been exercising more of it despite himself: making decisions, recruiting locals, shooting his CO.

A sharp pain in his heart, which Leo ignored because he had no choice.

Before Kandiss could return, Salah Bourgiba came in. "How are you feeling, Brodie?"

"Just dandy. Never better. Austin and Zoe?"

"Both will recover."

"Did Isabelle take my weapons?"

Bourgiba's brows rose; evidently this was news to him, too. "Isabelle?"

"Send her in here. Jenner, too!" Then, remembering who he was talking to, he added a grudging, "Please."

Bourgiba left without a word, but Leo didn't need words. Looks were enough. Bourgiba disliked him as much as he disliked Bourgiba.

Leo tried to stand up, couldn't, and sank back onto his pallet. He was as useless as a toddler. Kandiss returned and said, "Your weapons aren't in the compound."

"Where are Lamont's?"

"I have them."

"Bring them here, Kandiss. And— What is it? Why do you look like that?"

Kandiss looked away, looked back, bit his tongue. For Kandiss, this amounted to major drama. He said, "Sir, Lieutenant Lamont had a nonregulation weapon on his person."

"He did? What?"

"I'll bring it."

He returned with Lamont's rifle, sidearm, helmet, all of it. And something else. Leo picked it up: a metal canister about six inches long and three in diameter, marked only with the code A45D6. Plus a device about a foot long. Leo said, "What is it?"

"Don't know."

"Is it . . . this looks like a mounter that might fit onto a rifle. Is this canister some sort of explosive? Can Zoe come in here?"

"Doc says no."

"Then I'll go to her. Help me up."

Torture getting to his feet, torture walking even with Kandiss's support. Leo ignored the pain and hoped that motion wasn't tearing apart anything important inside him. Zoe lay on a platform bed in the next room. She stared at him stonily.

He thrust the canister at her, along with the mounter. "What's this?"

Zoe's stoniness vanished, either in relief that Leo wasn't going to rehash what happened on the mountain or in simple astonishment. She said, "Where'd that come from?"

"What is it, Zo?"

"Experimental. Not approved yet, nobody has them, too dangerous. I'm not even supposed to know about them, but there was this looie on Terra who—"

"I don't care how you know. Lamont has this. *Had* this. What is it? An explosive?"

"Yeah. Has almost the impact of a shoulder-launched missile but is fired right from standard rifle. Only thing is, nearly half of the field trials blew up the rifle, the tripod, and a crater big as a refrigerator."

"Huh," Leo said. "My weapons are missing. You know who took them?"

"You lost your weapons? Again?"

"I was being operated on!"

"So was I, but I have mine."

Leo didn't ask how she'd done that. Maybe Kandiss had held them for her, maybe somebody else. "Take me back to my room," he said to Kandiss. "Bring me Noah Jenner."

Jenner looked better than when Leo had seen him last—sharper, more focused—although he still had a lump on his forehead the size of a walnut. Noah glared. *Another one that doesn't like me. Well, tough shit.*

"I have your weapons," Jenner said, "and you're not getting them back. We do things differently here, Brodie. We're grateful for your help in getting the call-back device, but there will be no more killing. I'll take these things, too."

"Try," Leo said.

Kandiss took a step forward.

Jenner looked at the huge Ranger, pressed his lips together, and left without another word. Leo said to Kandiss, "Did Jenner leave the compound with any duffel or box that could have held my kit?"

"Supply carts have been coming and going all day, sir. They're moving the vaccinated kids and their mothers into the compound before the cloud comes. I'm frisking everybody."

Leo considered. His side hurt but his head felt clear. "Okay. Let them come in but check any supplies for contraband. You guard the door and periodically scan from the roof. Also, tell Isabelle Rhinehart I want her to bring me Lu^kaj^ho and his cop squad."

Kandiss stiffened. Leo didn't have to be told that Kandiss didn't want armed Kindred males inside the compound. Leo said, "They're on our side, Kandiss."

"Yes, sir."

"Really." Immediately he knew he shouldn't have said that; in Kandiss's world, a superior officer might give information, but he never justified his orders. In some ways, the Kindred cops were actually easier to deal with than Kandiss.

What the fuck? What did he just think? How could he relate more to these alien cops than to Army?

When Lu^kaj^ho entered with his men, Leo told them all, in a halting combination of his Kindred, their English, and some pathetic pantomime, that they were now part of compound security. He wanted Lu^kaj^ho on the roof and cops on the east, south, and north doors, all of them to take orders from Kandiss. He made sure Kandiss understood this as well. The whole thing would have been easier with Isabelle or Bourgiba to translate, but Isabelle wasn't around and Leo would not ask Bourgiba. He needed to learn to make himself understood to Lu^kaj^ho's squad; he was now their commander.

He'd never wanted this.

After they'd all left, he closed his eyes for a few minutes. But he couldn't sleep. Asleep, he dreamed about Owen. Awake, he also saw Owen's face constantly, but it was easier to explain to himself yet again why he'd done what he had to.

Besides, he had to check, clean, and load all of Owen's weapons. They were his now, and nobody was going to get them from him again.

CHAPTER 19

Austin lay on his pallet in the clinic and thought about the ways he'd fucked up.

He'd trusted Tony. He'd trusted Lieutenant Lamont. He'd taken his mother—his mother!—to a place where she was now a hostage. He'd taken Claire Patel there, too—another hostage. He'd let Lamont shoot him so that now he had a gash on his head and a shattered shoulder and might not be able to ever use his left arm again. He'd cried in front of Isabelle. He'd found and brought the call-back device, yes, but now there was another piece he hadn't found or brought back: the instructions on how to use it. He was a total fuck-up and probably Leo hated him now. Along with everybody else.

Dr. Bourgiba came in to check his head, and Austin lay mute and stiff—he was stone! rock!—and didn't answer any questions. He didn't cry out when it hurt, either, which was something. But not much.

Then Isabelle came in and Austin turned his face to the wall. Why didn't they just leave him alone? He made loud noises in his head so that he couldn't understand what Isabelle was asking him, and when she laid a hand on his head he screamed, even though it didn't hurt at all. "Go away! Go away!"

She did. Austin let the tears come. He wanted his mother, and that was the biggest fuck-up of all because he was too old to cry for his mother, he was *thirteen*.

The door opened again. Austin turned his head back toward the wall but jerked around again when he heard the next voice.

"Hey, buddy," Leo said.

Leo leaned heavily on Isabelle's arm. She lowered him to sit at the end of Austin's pallet, back to the wall. Leo breathed heavily for a few minutes and then said, "Thanks, Isabelle. Leave us guys to talk now, okay?"

She did, closing the door behind her. Leo looked strange out of soldier clothes and without helmet or weapons. He wore a loose Kindred wrap and he was barefoot. A tube came from his side into a bowl he'd put on the floor. "Damn drainage pipe. I might as well be a sewer. Bourgiba says that on Terra this would be a sterile tube with a bag or some shit like that, but they don't have one in the clinic. Listen, Austin, we need your help again. You did a great job, incidentally, getting that call-back device out of that survivalist shit hole. Nobody else could have done it, certainly not your buddy Graa^lok."

Leo had pronounced it right, Austin thought dazedly, with the rising sound in the middle. Tony never did that. And Leo had said . . . that Austin did a good job?

"Here's the thing," Leo said, and his voice, too, dazed Austin—it sounded like an adult talking to another adult. "There have been developments while you were in sick bay, so I'm going to brief you. Dr. Jenner and Branch Carter are working on a way to call back the colony ship with that device you rescued. They haven't figured it out yet but maybe they will, they're smart people. They might call the ship back so they can let loose that germ on it that's supposed to stop the spore germ."

Austin already knew that much; he'd known it before his disastrous trip to Haven. He could tell that Leo was skeptical about some of it, or maybe all of it, but that he was waiting to see what happened.

"But now," Leo said, "we have another problem. Most people left the refugee camp once it was clear to them there weren't any more vaccines in there or any way to make more, thanks to that terrorist attack."

The attack where Leo shot the attackers. How many? What did it feel like to kill somebody? Did Leo feel bad about shooting Lieutenant Lamont? He didn't look like he felt bad.

But Austin was learning that people weren't always what they looked like. Tony, for instance.

Leo continued, "But now people are coming back to the camp, because there are rumors out there that we Terrans are going to set off a second plague." Leo considered. "Which, I guess, we are, if the scientists can figure out how. But nobody out there really understands about these virophages—hell, I don't understand them either—and so everybody's scared. For their kids, mostly. The vaccinated kids and their mothers have all been brought into the compound for their own safety. Probably you heard some of the babies crying?"

Austin nodded.

"Yeah, it's a nuisance. But the crowd out there in the camp is getting bigger and more dangerous looking because they're mad as hell at us. Even though we're only trying to help. But that always happens when you go into a foreign country."

"It does?" Leo blurted out.

"Yeah. It did in Brazil, in Iraq—hell, it happened on Earth when Kindred came to warn us about the spore cloud. That's why the Russians got so pissed. Half the population just wants to blame somebody and there you are. Shoot-the-messenger stuff."

Austin didn't know what that meant, but he nodded anyway.

"So what I need to know is where these rumors are coming from. I got my squad out asking questions but—"

"What squad?" Wasn't Lieutenant Lamont dead and Ranger Berman shot and . . . could just Ranger Kandiss be a squad all by himself?

"Oh, nobody told you? I swore in some of the Kindred cops, and six other recruits. Ten all together. They're the Kindred-Terran Peace-keeping Force now."

Austin felt his mouth fall open. The Kindred-Terran Peace Keeping Force! He said, "Do they have weapons?"

"Some, yeah. They need more, but we can't deal with that now, we need to focus on intel. The people in the camp don't trust my squad, they think they're turncoats. It's not a really rough crowd out there, Austin, not compared to . . . well, maybe they're rough enough. We don't want another assault on the compound. So I need to know just what the mob out there has been told about this 'second plague' and how they learned about it in the first place. Either we have a leak here or else they learned some other way. You have any ideas?"

All at once, Austin's chest felt like one big bruise. This was horrible, this was the worst yet. Leo's eyes gazed at him levelly, not trusting like his mother's but something better than trusting, some bond of equals. Austin had to tell him the truth.

"It was me," he managed to get out. "I told Graa^lok's cousin why Dr. Jenner wanted the call-back device. We were just talking and she was curious and . . . I made her promise to not tell anybody. Tony has radio transmitters and now he has a lot of people that speak Kindred and maybe . . ."

"I see," Leo said. "Pretty girl?"

"Yes."

"Listen, Austin, don't blame yourself. This is a good thing, in the long run."

"It is?"

"Yeah. If the ship gets called back, and if it releases virophages, and if they cure people of spore plague, then the people will know it just didn't happen by itself, we caused it. You see? Otherwise it might just look like the whole spore-cloud thing was wrong. It's good that people have more information, even if it came from that asshole Tony Schrupp."

There was something wrong with this reasoning, something more than just the long string of ifs, but Austin couldn't quite see what it was. Relief overwhelmed everything else. Leo wasn't blaming him. Another assault on the compound, if it came, would not be Austin's fault. Still—

But—

Leo didn't let him think. "Here's the other thing," he said. "This is a lot to ask of a wounded warrior, but I'm going to. There's a lot of little kids in here now and mostly their mothers are looking after them, but there are some older ones who were vaccinated too. Nobody who speaks their language, which is only Isabelle and Jenner, has time to tell them what's going on. So I'm going to send some of them in here and let you brief them, as my representative. Tell them whatever you think is appropriate for them to know. You're on my staff now, okay?"

Austin nodded, torn between that wonderful sentence (*You're on my staff now*) and a deep reluctance to lecture a bunch of kids. But Leo didn't give him time to say no. He bellowed, "Isabelle!" and the door opened like she'd been waiting just outside all along.

Four kids came in with her: two boys about ten and a tiny girl of six, holding the hand of an older girl. Austin blinked. The older one was his age, the prettiest girl he'd ever seen, prettier even than Graa^lok's cousin. She smiled shyly and said in Kindred, "I greet you, Austin-mak."

Austin-mak. The title for an honored person of higher rank and not of one's own lahk.

Isabelle said in Kindred, "This is Jen^la^hon and three children of her lahk."

Austin said to the girl, "I greet you, Jen^la^hon."

He didn't even notice when Isabelle helped Leo out of the room.

"You were too easy on him," Isabelle said to Leo.

He grunted, easing himself back onto his pallet, sticking the end of the tube into his pants instead of the bowl it was supposed to drip into. Let the damn thing drip blood and fluid down his belly, that was better than going around looking like unfinished plumbing. He said, "You're too hard on him."

"He kidnapped Claire!"

"We'll get her back. We'll get all of them back. Tony Schrupp is a dirtbag but not a killer, not really. He only tried to take out Lamont in some sort of self-defense."

"Lamont—"

Leo held up a hand. "Don't, Isabelle." He wasn't ready yet to talk with her about Owen. Maybe he never would be.

"All right. What do you need me to do now?"

Several answers rose to mind, but this wasn't the time. Also, Leo doubted he'd be able to follow through, not for a while yet, although Bourgiba said his liver seemed to be healing well. Why was a liver so fucking important?

He said, "Check on the squad for me, ask if Lu^kaj^ho and his guys need anything, and what they're hearing. Make sure Kandiss isn't shooting anybody. Go up on the roof, I told him to let you, and eyeball the camp for me. Tell me everything you can, but do not go into the camp. I mean it, Isabelle. Don't set foot out of the compound."

"All right."

She didn't argue, and Isabelle not arguing was a welcome thing. Still, it was probably temporary.

"Leo," she said, "what if Marianne and Branch can't get the ship back here?"

"You know what. We go to the original plan, plan A."

"Everybody either gets sick or dies."

"And then we go on from there. Rebuilding with whoever gets well."

She bent over and kissed him on the lips. Leo's eyes flew open. The kiss was sweet, sudden, and brief. His chest swelled like he'd been shot all over again. She said quietly, "I love your optimism, even in the face of everything you must have seen and done."

Then she was gone, opening his door to the sound of babies howling, then closing it again without looking back.

Marianne stirred a big pot of vegetable stew in the clinic kitchen. At least, she hoped it was going to turn out to be vegetable stew, given that she was unfamiliar with all the ingredients and had never been much of a cook anyway. She should have left this to someone else, but Isabelle was busy with Leo Brodie, Salah with doctoring, Noah with recovering and tending his wife and daughter, and the Kindred mothers with their kids—no, that wasn't true. Marianne was making stew because she could no longer sit beside Branch, "helping" to search for a way to turn a series of random numbers into a meaningful sequence. Branch was tireless at what Marianne was coming to see as a hopeless task, but Branch was young. Marianne was not.

One tone, pause, six tones, pause, eleven tones, pause, sixteen tones, pause, nine tones, pause, fourteen tones, pause, three tones, pause, eight tones, very long pause, one tone. Silence.

The stew turned out edible, more or less. (How much longer would they have electricity for cooking veggies? How much longer would they have veggies?) She helped serve it to everyone jammed into the compound. Full of people, empty, full again—both compound and stew bowls. There was something profound in there, or at least notable, but Marianne was too tired to find it. Her back ached. Her head ached with thinking, except when it ached from trying not to think the same thoughts over and over.

One tone, pause, six tones, pause, eleven tones, pause . . .

"Mom," Noah said, "go to bed. You look exhausted."

"You do, too."

"I'm recovering from a concussion. What's your excuse?"

"I would laugh but I'm too tired," Marianne said. "Did Isabelle take stew out to the soldiers?"

"I did. I need to do something."

Marianne looked at her tall, alien son, with his artificially copper skin and surgically altered eyes and the same sweet smile he'd had as a little boy. There was nothing she could do to help him save the life he loved except what Branch was already doing, Claire had already done, and Leo Brodie was trying to do from his sickbed. The only thing Marianne could do for Noah was spare him more anxiety.

"I'm going," she said. "Tell Lily good night for me."

"I will," Noah said, although they both knew that Lily had been asleep for hours. But when the world was ending, Marianne had discovered, tiny normal things mattered. A lot.

To her surprise, she fell asleep almost immediately. It was a deep, restful sleep, without dreams, until, abruptly, she woke.

Silence. Darkness. Both total and complete, as if she lay in a cave, or in the womb. But an image danced before her, clear as one of the countless drawings she'd made in college biology class, nearly fifty years ago.

Marianne pressed a button on her Terran watch, which was useless for telling the time here but good for illumination. In the tiny light of its dial, she made her way from her room to the leelee lab. Branch lay heavily asleep on a pallet beside the call-back device.

One tone, pause, six tones, pause, eleven tones, pause, sixteen tones, pause, nine tones, pause, fourteen tones, pause, three tones, pause, eight tones, very long pause, one tone. Silence.

Marianne switched on a light; Branch did not stir. Gingerly she lowered herself to the floor and pulled the call-back device to her.

A four-sided pyramid, with four bumps marching down each side. Did it matter which of the bumps near the apex she called "one"? Maybe not, for what she had in mind. The universe runs on mathematics, Branch had cried, with all the passion of the young scientist. He was right, of course. The physical universe ran on mathematics. But the human universe ran on something else, something that had to be known to any race who could follow master plans to build a starship.

One tone, pause, six tones, pause, eleven tones, pause, sixteen tones, pause, nine tones, pause, fourteen tones, pause, three tones, pause, eight tones, very long pause, one tone. Silence.

She pressed hard on one of the bumps near the apex. Her finger counted off the other three bumps on that face: two, three, four. Then the bump at the top of the adjoining face would be five and the one under it six. She pressed it hard.

Probably nothing would happen. Talk about your long shots. . . .

The third button down on the next triangular face would be eleven, and the bottom button on the fourth face would be sixteen. She had spiraled down the pyramid, pressing. Her fingers returned to its pointed top, pressing the button on the face opposite where she had begun. That was bump nine. Then fourteen, three, eight, spiraling down the face of the pyramid, tracing a distinct pattern.

A double helix.

But what about that last single tone, following a much longer pause, that completed the code from the colony ship? What was that?

A ship's number. It was the first one built, the first one launched, forty Kindred years ago. But where . . .

The whole thing was probably futile anyway, so did it really matter? Marianne returned her finger to the first bump she'd pressed and pressed it again, as hard as she could.

Blattt!

Marianne cried out, the noise was so loud. She slammed her hands over her ears. Branch woke and groped for a knife from under his pallet. The door flew open and Noah, in the room across the hall, rushed in.

Blattt!!!!

Then Leo Brodie stood in the doorway, leaning against the jamb but upright, a rifle in his hands. He yelled something but no one could hear him, or anything else, until the device stopped blatting and a silence, shocking after all that noise, fell. More people crowded into the corridor, kept back by Leo's slumping body.

Branch said in an incongruous whisper, "What did you do?"

Marianne said, "I think I just called back the ship with the virophage."

CHAPTER 20

In the two days since Marianne had called back the ship—if that was indeed what she had done—Salah had watched the refugee camp fill up again. People came by bicycle, by truck, by animal cart, on foot. They left their lahks just days before the spore cloud hit. Nearly all of them were furious.

"Why?" Branch had asked, puzzled. "If they think they're going to die anyway from *R. sporii*, then why not stay at home and die there?"

Branch genuinely did not understand—from youth, from temperament, from the mostly sheltered life of well-off parents followed by academic research. Sometimes Salah felt very old.

"There are rumors on the radio that there is a second plague on the ship that's coming here. A plague we Terrans are going to set loose on Kindred."

"It's a *cure*," Branch said. "We hope. And if they know they're going to die of the first plague anyway—"

"Branch," Salah said, "which would you rather face: a bout of cholera alone or a bout of cholera followed by malaria when you've already been weakened by the cholera? They hope that some of them will survive *R. sporii*, and they're probably right. They don't want to then be hit with another unknown plague."

An irreverent verse flashed into Salah's head: *When the wit began to wheeze / And wine had warmed the politician, / Cured yesterday of my disease / I died last night of my physician.* Mathew Prior, in the irreverent eighteenth century.

No one on Kindred would appreciate it. No one.

"Then," Branch said, "why doesn't the Council of Mothers tell them different?"

"Tell them what? Nobody, including us, knows how the virophage will affect humans. The camp is full of scared and angry people both wanting to stop a second plague and looking for someone to blame. That happened on Earth, too, you know."

"I know," Branch said, so somberly that Salah wondered if he had overestimated the young man's innocence, after all. "I wish we knew exactly when the ship will arrive. From the astronomical data I know the location of the colony planet, but distance doesn't seem to correlate with how the drive works."

"No," Salah said.

Branch looked at the clinic ceiling, as if it were the sky. "I wish I knew when it will arrive."

"When is this fucking ship getting here?" Zoe demanded.

"No idea," Leo said.

They had met in the clinic kitchen, both hungry, though neither of them were supposed to move yet. Bourgiba had explained that he was not a surgeon, that the best he could do with what he had here was what he'd done: remove Zoe's spleen and patch up Leo's liver. Leo was grateful for the medical help but hated the inactivity. It gave him too much time to think. He was grateful when Kandiss or Lu^kaj^ho came in with reports, even though the reports were all the same: Nothing happening. People are angry. No ship yet.

It left Leo with too much time to think about Owen. He tried, instead, to think about OPORDS, about assessing defenses and effectively deploying personnel. Thinking like a leader, and wasn't that a kick in the head? *Him.*

Which led his thoughts back to Owen.

So he was almost glad to meet up with Zoe in the kitchen. They eyed each other warily. He had injured her; she had shot him.

He waited to see what she would say.

"Just before I got deployed here," she said, "my platoon did a night parachute drop. We dropped from eight hundred feet with zero illumination and seized a landing strip for follow-on forces. Three of us including me had injuries from a hard landing but we went on the assault anyway. Mission successful."

"Where was this?" Leo said, because it was clear he had to say something.

"Not sure. Mideast someplace." She reached for the soup ladle.

Evidently this story settled something in Zoe's mind, although Leo had no idea what. He said, "Uh-huh."

She said quietly, "You did right, Leo. I'll say so at the court-martial."

"Thanks." Court-martial? For that, they had to first get back to Terra. Unless Kandiss decided to somehow arrest Leo and take control of the squad, which Leo doubted. It would require too many words.

Not that Leo himself was doing all that great at military protocol. Zoe didn't treat him with much deference, and the whole idea of military chain of command was foreign to Lu^kaj^ho.

The Kindred, now an Army private second class, appeared in the doorway to the kitchen. His report was just more of the same: more people in the camp, no attacks, no visible weapons, a lot of refugees accompanied by children, and no ship.

"How many be children?" Leo asked.

"Now it is about half."

"*Half?* Are kids?"

"Yes."

After Lu^kaj^ho left, Zoe said, "You speak the lingo pretty good."

"No. I don't."

"You think we got kid suicide bombers?"

"I don't think so. They didn't do that before, and Kindred aren't really vicious or ruthless." *Not like in Brazil.*

"Then why all the kids? In a strike zone?"

"I don't think that they think it's a strike zone, not this time."

"Then what is it?"

"I don't know," Leo said. "Maybe a hospital zone, for vaccines? Hand me that ladle or are you going to eat all the soup yourself?"

She handed him the ladle. "Leo . . . I mean, sir . . ."

"Leo is fine."

"What I said about a court-martial when we get home . . . It's going to be twenty-eight years after we left."

"Yes."

"Twenty-eight fucking years. That's too long. I won't know anything, all the ordinances'll be different."

"They'll send you back for more specialist training."

"Maybe. But I don't know if—"

"It's here!" Austin screamed, bursting into the room. "The ship! It's in the sky! It's coming down!"

"Let's go," Leo said, and reached in his pocket for the dose of Owen's popbite.

It was much larger than the *Friendship*. That was the first thing Marianne noticed: the ship's size. Well, it was a colony ship, not a diplomatic flagship. The huge, bullet-shaped vessel of gray metal hovered over the compound, blocking the orange sun. She had been afraid it might return to the ruined city where it had been built, and then what would they have done? But the ship was here.

"Homed in on my transmitter," Branch said with enormous satisfaction.

They stood in the cleared zone outside the compound, what the Rangers called the perimeter. Their necks bent far backward, along with nearly everyone else from the compound and the camp. Ranger

Kandiss and some of Leo's cops stood between the Terrans and the camp, weapons in their hands, but only Kandiss watched the Kindred instead of the ship.

"It's beautiful," Branch said. "I wonder who they were?"

He meant the ship's designers, not the colonists. His remark jolted Marianne, who'd also been admiring the ship's beauty, back to reality. This lovely vessel was full of dead human bodies, of chittering leelees, of a microorganism that had won its evolutionary battle against *R. sporii*. That, however, was no indication that the virophage could enable humans to do the same.

The ship stopped hovering and moved north, to the large empty grazing lands between the compound and the mountain.

What was Leo doing? Austin had watched him swallow a pill and give one to Ranger Berman. They'd both gone back to their rooms and come outside dressed in armor, carrying weapons, walking much steadier than before and without help. Leo gave the ship only a quick glance. He climbed a ladder to the compound roof. Why?

How come nobody told Austin anything?

Dr. Bourgiba said, "Brodie. Climbing to the roof could tear your stitches. I told you so. And you've taken popbite, haven't you? It's counterindicated if—"

Leo wasn't even listening. Slowly he climbed the ladder. One of the new Kindred soldiers, Heemur^ka, climbed behind with Leo's gear. Ranger Berman took her place beside Ranger Kandiss on the ground. Austin put one foot on the ladder.

"Are you crazy?" Isabelle hissed, grabbing him. "You are not going up there!"

Dr. Jenner said to Isabelle, "I don't understand! What are they going to do?"

So nobody had told her, either, and Dr. Jenner was a *mother*. Well, no, she had refused to be a mother, but she was an old woman anyway and still she didn't know what Leo was going to do. Austin felt a little better.

Five hundred yards away, the ship began to land.

It was big, and it settled down easy as a soap bubble. No noise, no fire, no nothing. Leo had been a teenager when the Kindred ship came to Terra and he'd had other things on his mind, like avoiding jail, but he remembered the TV broadcasts that showed the *Embassy* landing just like this in New York Harbor. No drama, just a perfect piece of machinery.

Leo, the popbite singing in his blood and brain, settled into position on the roof. Heemur^ka handed him his weapons.

"Shit," Heemur^ka said; he was learning as much Terran as Leo was learning Kindred. But then Heemur^ka added, "I greet you, ship."

Why didn't they give their ships names? Weird.

The moment the ship touched ground, the Kindred in the camp ran toward it. Men, women, little kids. Okay, they had probably rehearsed mentally just as much as Leo's squad had. They formed a line between the compound and the ship, several people deep, facing the compound. They were not going to let anyone, Terran or Kindred, near the ship. Dr. Jenner had already told Leo that the door could not be opened by signals from the outside, and she should know—a decade ago on Terra, she had been sealed inside the *Friendship* with an entire battalion of NASA technical experts outside. Leo didn't know if these doors could be forced open manually from the outside, but it didn't matter. The Kindred who massed in front of them in grim-faced protest weren't taking any chances.

Leo knew what they were counting on: That neither his Kindred recruits nor Leo himself would shoot several hundred Kindred, half of them kids carefully placed in front. They were right. He wasn't Owen. But that wasn't the problem he faced now.

"Lu^kaj^ho," he called down, "tell them to move away from the ship. Now.

"And tell them why."

Salah grabbed Isabelle's arm. "What's going on? What's Brodie going to do?"

"I don't know but—" She started to climb the ladder.

Another of Leo's pseudo-soldiers said, "No, Isabelle-mak." There followed a furious exchange in Kindred that Salah could not follow. He glanced around for the Rangers; Kandiss was out of sight around the corner of the building. Zoe stood at the east door to the compound, her face disturbed about something.

Isabelle stopped yelling and again put her sandaled foot on the bottom rung of the ladder.

The Kindred soldier brushed her off and grabbed the ladder away from the roof.

"Give it to me!" Isabelle said.

The man didn't even answer; he handed the ladder to another Kindred, who carried it quickly away.

Before Isabelle could even react, Zoe had put her rifle into its sling and made a cup of her hands. "I'll lift you up," she said urgently. "Talk Brodie out of it. The missile is experimental. One in two chances it explodes and kills him. And us."

Missile? Brodie had a missile up there? Salah was no military expert but he hadn't seen anything as big as a shoulder-mounted launcher.

Zoe's eyes glowed with the feverish shine of popbite; probably she thought she could lift a mountain, but she wasn't that long out of surgery. Salah said, "Isabelle," and made a cup of his own hands. Isabelle stepped into it and Salah threw her as high as he could, wrenching his shoulder. Isabelle grabbed the edge of the roof and pulled herself up.

"You can't, Leo," Isabelle said.

"Get the hell off here, Isabelle!"

Heemur^ka moved between her and Leo, making sure she didn't get close enough to interfere with the shot. The mount was affixed to his rifle, the canister loaded into it. Leo kept his gaze trained on the ship and the crowd gathering in front of it. More kids, and now a few old ladies, one carried on a litter. Mothers.

Isabelle said, "You're going to blow a hole in the ship, aren't you. To release the virophage. But it's not a bullet because a bullet wouldn't even dent that hull. It's a powerful explosive from Terra and it's not reliable. One in two odds of blowing us all up."

"Zoe tell you that?" Damn her to hell, Leo had trusted her.

Isabelle didn't answer his question. In the field, people crowded closer to the ship. In his scope, a tiny girl, pale blue dress on her little copper body, crooned to a doll in her arms.

Isabelle said, her voice steady but not completely hiding desperation, "Okay, assume you're willing to risk killing yourself, me, your squad, and half the people in the compound if the explosive blows up in your face. Are you willing to risk killing all the people hit by the blast or flying debris near the ship? All those kids? That's not you, Leo."

Leo said, "Drop her off the roof, Heemur^ka."

"No! Stop!" And then a blast of Kindese, which Leo ignored.

Four of the Kindred-Terran Peacekeeping Force approached the crowd surrounding the ship. The Kindred soldiers were armed but held their weapons loosely, unthreateningly, as they began to talk to people. Talk, persuade, cajole, threaten—*Just get them away from there by telling them why.*

Isabelle shouted at Leo, "You don't even know that setting the virophage loose will work! It's only a desperate gamble!"

Then Leo did answer her. Without turning, without taking his gaze from the scope, he said, "Isn't a desperate gamble better than everybody dying for sure?"

He didn't hear her answer; Heemur^ka dropped her over the edge of the roof. Presumably somebody caught her because a few moments later she was with the group that Zoe and Kandiss were herding away from both the compound and the camp, up the hill to the south. They would take everybody to Isabelle's lahk house, to safety, with or without its lahk mother.

Heemur^ka said in Kindred, "I greet you, Leo-mak."

What the hell? They hadn't just met. They were here on the roof preparing to die or kill or both, preparing to set loose a plague on the planet—a *second* plague—and Heemur^ka was saying, "I greet you"? Some crazy fucking Kindred custom that Leo didn't know about? A death ritual, like those songs that kamikaze pilots sang before they took off?

Leo said in Kindred, "I greet you, Private Heemur^ka," and kept his finger on the trigger.

Halfway up the hill to the lahk, forced along by Kandiss and Zoe, Salah had had enough. Enough of being herded, enough of esoteric master-alien codes, enough of not being able to make his own decisions. Enough of death. Enough of this planet, just as he had once had enough of Terra. Nothing to choose between them for human idiocy.

He stopped walking and said to Zoe Berman, "I'm going back."

"No," she said. "You're not."

"I won't go anywhere near the compound, anywhere near Brodie. I won't interfere with whatever he's going to do. But I can help move people away from the ship. They don't trust Leo's Kindred soldiers because they think they're turncoats. They might trust me, a doctor. At any rate, I can speak the language. Let me try. Please."

He tried to say more with his eyes: to remind Zoe that she had been forced to trust him once and he had not betrayed her. How much was he getting through to her? He couldn't tell; she was half popbite now.

Finally she said, "Kandiss won't let you go."

"Then he'll have to shoot me."

Salah started back down the hill. Each step, he half expected a bullet in the back. But instead he heard Zoe's voice, indistinct but passionate, presumably addressed through her wrister to Kandiss.

No bullet hit him.

And then Isabelle was walking beside him. "I speak Kindred, too, Salah."

"Go back. It's too dangerous," he said, fear and determination removing from his mind that they'd already had this conversation once before. Too late, he remembered.

"Shut up," Isabelle said, and said no more.

What the fuck? Bourgiba and Isabelle moved into Leo's field of vision, crossing the open space between the compound and the protesters by the ship. That's what they were—protesters, not enemies, just trying to protect their kids. Owen had never understood that. Owen had never understood a lot of things.

There was nothing Leo could do about Isabelle and Bourgiba.

"Heemur^ka," Leo said in Kindese, "go now. I be okay. You go. Safety."

Heemur^ka answered in a burst of Kindred that Leo couldn't follow, and then stayed put. Nothing Leo could do about that, either. If Heemur^ka was willing to risk his life for his CO and their shared mission, that only meant Leo had done his job. "You'd have made a good Ranger," Leo said in English.

Another burst of incomprehensible Kindred. But Heemur^ka grinned.

Things began to look better. The peacekeeping force was moving unchallenged through the crowd, talking and explaining, and now Isabelle and Bourgiba joined them. Much hand waving, mouth moving, pointing at the ship and then at Leo, clearly visible on the compound roof.

People began to move away from the ship. At first, just a few, then more. The persuaders were getting it done.

Heemur^ka jabbered something in Kindred and pointed.

Without moving, Leo shifted his gaze to the right. A group of Kindred—seven, eight—ran from the deserted camp toward the dispersing crowd. Two were women, one gray-haired but still fast.

Heemur^ka said in English, "Shoot. Now."

Shoot? Why? The group wasn't even armed; in their pale unisex dresses there was no room for weapons. All they were doing was joining the protest.

Heemur^ka said, "I shoot!" and raised his pipe gun.

What the fuck? "Hold your fire!" Leo said, but either Heemur^ka didn't understand the English or pretended he didn't. He fired his pipe gun.

The shot hit nothing—he hadn't intended it to. It didn't even make the advancing group slow down. And then they had reached the crowd and mingled with them, joined the talking and waving and pointing.

Heemur^ka said, "Bad people! Say not true! Make people to go to ship!"

Leo got it. These were the agitators, the haters, the "bad people." They didn't believe the Terrans could be trying to accomplish anything good. They weren't just trying to protect their own; they were the type who wanted to eliminate anything not their own, and they would tell any lies they had to in order to accomplish that. To "make people go to ship," even if it got those people killed. Leo had known them in the United States, in Brazil, in the Army itself.

Owen, it had turned out, had been one of them.

Five hundred yards away, people were hesitating, reversing direction to head back to the ship. Only a few, at first.

Then more.

Salah laid a hand on the arm of the first person he recognized, a gentle woman named Fallaabon. He had treated her rambunctious little son for a broken finger when the child had fallen from a tree near the refugee camp, one of the few occasions when the Kindred had not used their own doctors. Perhaps none had been handy. Salah spoke to Fallaabon as quickly and decisively as his Kindred would allow, explaining about the virophages, the leelees alive on the ship, the need to blast open the hull, the danger of taking her child too close to it. Others gathered to listen. Salah framed everything in terms of the children and of bu^ka^tel, at least to the extent he understood that enormously complicated concept. Obligation to her lahk, to the greater good, to the future, to the planet itself.

More people gathered to listen. Some nodded and began to move away from the ship.

Salah had lost track of Isabelle and of Leo's cops; it was a big crowd. But less big than it had been. After half an hour, it seemed that they were making headway—people were leaving.

Then, somehow, the momentum reversed. Others were making speeches, too, Kindred with a different agenda. People still listened to Salah, but not as many, and some slid their eyes away from him and made a gesture that he had only seen associated with dung.

He saw Fallaabon lead her little boy back toward the ship.

The longer Leo hesitated, the more people had time to move themselves and their children close to the hull.

Leo had shot civilians before. Women, too, and even a kid. But they had all been credible threats to either his own platoon or to the Marines he'd been protecting. This was different. Nothing in his training or history or temperament prepared him for this.

If he fired the missile, it would—if it didn't blow up—breach the side of the ship, letting loose Dr. Jenner's virophage but also killing innocent men, women, kids.

If he didn't shoot, the Kindred would take up their wrongheaded, determined position right up against the ship, convinced they were protecting themselves from plague, until four days passed, the spore cloud hit, and they all died of spore disease anyway. Or didn't.

What if the virophage didn't even work?

What if it did?

Kill maybe two dozen to save a planet?

He was not supposed to have to make this sort of decision. He was a sniper, and this sort of decision was supposed to be made farther up the chain of command so that Leo could obey orders. But there was no farther up this particular chain of command, and time was running out.

Leo sighted, adjusted for the freshening wind, squeezed the trigger, and fired.

The canister left the launcher without exploding. A moment later, the longest moment in history, it hit the hull of the ship broadside and tore a hole the size of a pickup. The blast shattered the air. Flying shrapnel, screaming, bodies falling to the ground.

Leo lowered his weapon and scanned the carnage, looking for Isabelle.

Salah felt it before it actually happened. How? No time to think, and the sensation was beyond thought, anyway. Brodie was going to fire. Salah *knew* it.

Fallaabon's little boy turned and, still holding his mother's hand, smiled and said something to Salah in Kindred. There was no time to answer. There was only time to act.

And to think, as he threw his body on the mother and child, *This is my decision. Mine, by myself, for myself.*

The ship exploded.

CHAPTER 21

Marianne woke to the sound of wind outside the compound. Not a religious person, nonetheless her first thought was a fervent *Thank God!* Which god? It didn't matter. They needed wind.

There had been no wind the day the ship landed. No wind as they counted the dead and buried them. No wind as Isabelle, dry-eyed but clearly only by an effort of will, stumbled through a poem over Salah Bourgiba's grave. Marianne didn't know the poem and was surprised that Isabelle did, but Isabelle was endlessly surprising.

> *Already my gaze is upon the hill, the sunny one*
> *At the end of the path which I've only just begun.*
> *So we are grasped, by that which we could not grasp*
> *At such great distance, so fully manifest—*
> *And it changes us, even when we do not reach it,*
> *Into something that, hardly sensing it, we already are.*

It sounded like something Salah might have taught her. Had Isabelle loved Salah? Marianne didn't think so, even though they had been sleeping together.

The Rangers had not attended Bourgiba's burial. Mason Kandiss had watched it from his post on the roof. Leo Brodie had had the good sense, or decency, or something—categories were so confused here—to stay inside the compound. What Brodie had done made possible Kindred's only hope of planetary survival. It had also killed twenty-four people, ten of them children.

Marianne wondered if, circumstances permitting, Brodie would ever visit that other grave in the mountains, the one that Zoe Berman had told her about. Kandiss had dug the grave and scratched the name on the boulder acting as headstone: LT. OWEN RYAN LAMONT.

However, Marianne didn't give much thought to Lieutenant Lamont. Her mind was full of the virophage.

How much wind? She rose from her pallet and made her way to Big Lab. In the predawn, Lu^kaj^ho stood guard at the east door. She saw with a little shock that he carried not a clumsy Kindred gun but an Army rifle. Leo Brodie's? Owen Lamont's?

"I greet you, Dr. Jenner," he said in lilting English.

"I greet you, Lu^kaj^ho."

A lot of wind, fresh and cool, in a starlit sky. In this continent slightly south of Kindred's equator, winds blew east to west. This couldn't possibly be better. The virophage would be carried across much of the landmass. If, of course, it was actually an airborne pathogen. If there was enough of it. If it could protect humans as well as leelees. If—

Enough.

Somewhere in Big Lab a baby cried, but no one else seemed awake. Marianne knew better—Branch would already be seated at what remained of their equipment, now all crowded into the leelee lab. The young man apparently never slept, no more than the Rangers did.

In the lab, Branch peered through a Kindred microscope.

"They're too small to see," Marianne said, although of course Branch knew that. Even the virophage's host, *R. sporii*, was too small to see. They needed an electromicrograph, which of course they did not have.

"Look at this," Branch said, without preamble. He got up to let Marianne at the microscope.

"Branch, there's wind."

He smiled. "I heard it. But look at this, Marianne. It's tissue from the lung of an infected leelee."

Marianne sat on the stool. As soon as the smoke cleared around the colony ship, Branch had gone inside, heavily masked. He had come out with sacks of leelees, chittering and smelling just as bad as their planet-bound cousins, even as other leelees found their own way out of the ship. Branch had described an interior full of flourishing plants, teeming fungi, and bodies that were nothing but skeletons, all soft tissue having been microscopically consumed by forty years of hothouse microbes. The whole thing, Branch said, had looked like a terrarium from a horror movie, and Marianne had decided that she didn't need to experience it. They had the leelees.

Branch had set up fans inside the ship to blow infected air out, but that hadn't been enough. They had needed wind, and now they had it. The incubation period of *R. sporii* in humans—Terran humans, anyway—was three days, which was how long the spore cloud had been on Kindred. Not that nonscientists could tell that: the cloud was silent, diffuse, invisible. But those infected would fall sick today.

Unless the virophages protected them—completely, partially, or not at all.

This made Branch's research pointless, even if he'd had the most sophisticated equipment at the CDC. But research was what drove Branch, just as it drove Marianne, and so he was researching. Cultures with cells grown from sacrificed leelees dotted the room.

The image in the microscope showed three intact lung cells and parts of two others. Somewhere in each cell, too tiny to be seen, was *R. sporii*, and somewhere inside that was the virophage. The cells looked normal.

"You showed me this before," Marianne said. "It just shows that the leelees aren't infected."

"It shows their lungs aren't infected with Avenger. Now—"

"Wait—what did you just call the virophage?"

"Avenger. Well, I have to refer to it as something. The first viro-phage ever discovered was called Sputnik!"

"I know," Marianne said. Sputnik was Russian for "fellow trav-eler," and the researchers who discovered it had an unfortunate penchant for whimsy.

"*Anyway,* now look at this. They're neurons from an infected leelee's brain, from the area that seems to correspond roughly to Ter-ran mammals' cerebellum." He removed the slide from the micro-scope and replaced it with another. "I stained them to emphasize receptors."

Marianne peered into the 'scope. Four neurons—Branch had always prepared outstanding slides—and none of them looked like the cerebellum neurons of leelees sacrificed from Kindred. There were more axons and more receptors, bristly outgrowths that made the cells look like particularly dense hedgehogs.

She said, "I'm a geneticist, not a neurologist, but that looks like a lot more going on in the leelee brain than in the leelees we're famil-iar with." She glanced at a cage of live leelees, chittering and stink-ing. "Have you observed any behavioral differences in the ones you captured from the ship?"

"Nothing. And of course there's no reason to think the virophage is responsible, but still . . . That's an awful lot of evolution to have occurred in forty years without some unusual trigger."

Marianne stood. "If it *is* evolution. If it is due to the virophage. But it doesn't matter right now. The only thing that matters right now is the effect the virophage has on *R. Sporii* in the human body."

"I know," Branch said. "But . . . still . . . if only I had a gene se-quencer and electromicrograph!"

———

Three days later, in midafternoon, the first Kindred died of *R. sporii*.

It was an adolescent boy in the camp. Marianne never knew his name. The compound had no doctor now, and when a young girl came running across the perimeter for help, Marianne had none to give. Noah went back with the girl, returning to the compound a half hour later. He looked dazed.

"It happens so fast," he said.

"I know," Marianne said. She had seen it on Terra: adult respiratory distress syndrome, a catchall diagnosis. Gasps for air as lung tissue became heavier and heavier with fluid seeping into the lungs. Each breath required more and more effort. An X-ray of lung tissue—if they had that equipment here—would show "whiteout"—so much fluid in the lungs increasing the radiological density that the image looked like a snowstorm.

Noah clutched at Marianne's arm as if he were a child again and she, his mother, could fix anything wrong. But she couldn't, and in a moment he dropped her arm.

Marianne scanned the horizon. Trees waved gracefully in a west–east wind. Would this poor boy's death be an isolated case? An outlier or a harbinger?

Science always proceeded by trial and error, by living with doubt, by refusing to grab prematurely onto certainty. But this was a huge trial, a massive amount of doubt, and devoid of any certainty at all.

Wailing rose from the camp.

Zoe Berman, in full gear, approached Marianne and Noah. "Go inside now," she said, eyes on the camp, "just in case. Lieutenant Brodie's orders."

And just who had given Brodie that field promotion? Marianne didn't ask. The military unit, grown ever larger with Kindred recruits, was something she didn't understand, nor want to. With a final glance at the camp, the blowing trees, the clear sky, she went inside.

It was going to be a long day, an even longer night, and no one would sleep.

———

Isabelle stood in the doorway of the ready room, a child in her arms. At least the kid wasn't crying, Leo thought. And it was alive, unlike the children who had died when he fired on the ship. That had been necessary, but he knew it would haunt him for the rest of his life. Awake, asleep, in dreams. Maybe someday he could talk about it with somebody—Isabelle?—but not now. He said, "Any more deaths?"

"No. And according to the radio, the spore cloud hit days ago ago."

Leo nodded. He hated not being out there with his peacekeeping force, but Dr. Jenner had told him that if he did any more climbing around, he would tear open his stitches and die. Leo didn't know if this was true and he suspected she didn't know, either, but it worked okay for him to direct the mission from the ready room. He got reports about the camp from Lu^kaj^ho's infiltrators, about any external threats from Kandiss and Zoe, about the vaccinated kids inside the compound from Isabelle, about radio reports from Isabelle and Noah Jenner, the only two left who were fluent in both Kindred and English now that Salah Bourgiba was dead.

Did Isabelle mourn him? She looked heavy-eyed and limp, but everybody looked that way. Waiting, not war, was the real hell.

He said, "Well, that's good, right? Maybe the virophage worked. At least in the camp."

"Maybe." The child whimpered and she shifted it in her arms. Isabelle looked good with the dark-haired, copper-skinned baby. If she married a Kindred, her child would look more like Lily, a mix. But Isabelle hadn't married any of the Kindred men.

She said, in an attempt at lightheartedness, " 'Lieutenant'?"

"Lu^kaj^ho started that shit," Leo said, with disgust. "I think because Owen was called that, he assumes it's a title for whoever is CO. Then Zoe did it, one of her twisted jokes. Only Kandiss has the sense to ignore it."

"It's not a joke, Leo. Your unit wants you to be lieutenant."

"Yeah, but the US Army back home has other ideas."

"Are you going back home, Leo? If it becomes possible?"

So they'd arrived here. Already. It took Leo by surprise—the timing did, anyway. But it wasn't like he hadn't, in the long stretches of sitting here on his pallet, thought about it.

He looked her straight in the eyes. "I don't know, Isabelle—am I? Going back to Terra?"

But whatever he'd hoped to see—some sign, some plea—wasn't there. However, it wasn't not there, either, a maddening state of push-pull. If Isabelle had been a different woman, he'd have thought she was jerking him around. But he knew she wasn't.

All right, then—let's do this. He said, "Did you love him?"

She didn't play any games about pretending not to understand. "No."

He digested this: the speed and firmness with which she answered. He said slowly, "A lot depends on what happens with the cloud. If the virophage doesn't work and everybody dies, and if it's possible to reprogram the ship, will *you* go back to Terra?"

"I don't know. If the virophage does work, or partially works, and there is still a civilization here to rebuild—will you stay on Kindred and help build it?"

"I don't know," Leo said. "I'm in the Army, you know."

She grimaced. They both knew that too many Army regulations had already been jettisoned. And what did he face if he went back to Terra? Court-martial?

He said, stalling, "You know these people a lot better than I do—is there going to be what Tony Schrupp says, rioting and looting and a general breakdown?"

"I don't know," Isabelle said, "but I don't think so. You know what, Leo—I think we all see the world mostly like we are inside. Tony was always a suspicious grabber, and so he's suspicious about grabbing. That's why he built Haven. Marianne has always put her faith in science, and she still does. And you were always a leader underneath, making your own judgments, and so now you can lead the unit."

"You don't know me, Isabelle. I was no leader."

"Maybe you were and didn't know it. We might need an army, Leo. We never did before, but before there was enough to go around easily, with very old laws and customs and such. If all that goes, things might be more disrupted. Humans aren't naturally peaceful. We're biologically hierarchical and territorial. Only abundance, a monoculture, and intense indoctrination kept us so peaceful for so long."

The stilted words sounded like Salah Bourgiba, the intellectual. Maybe it was all true—actually, it was what Leo himself believed, just not in such fancy words—but he still felt a flash of jealousy that she was using Bourgiba's phrases.

Heemur^ka appeared in the doorway and spoke in rapid Kindred. Leo felt his adrenaline jump-start. But then Isabelle translated.

"He says no more deaths in the camp, no planned violence. People are waiting to see what happens with the spore cloud."

"Which means that if more people die, there could be trouble. Here's what I want you to tell him." Leo laid out the operation orders in case of attack, and everything else went on the back burner.

For now.

Austin woke with a start. He had struggled to stay awake all night, to hear everything, but sleep had grabbed him without his even feeling it, and now it was morning.! *Shit!*

The radio in Big Lab still received broadcasts. Noah sat on a cushion near it, a cup of nakl in his hands, leaning toward the radio to shut out the noise of fussing little kids and a wailing baby.

"Noah-kal—what news?"

"One more death in the camp, and other places are reporting

only a few so far. That means that either the virophage mostly worked or—"

"I know what it means," Austin snapped. When were they going to stop treating him like a little kid? He stalked to the piss closet, then the showers. When he was clean, he listened to the radio for an hour before going outside. The sun was well over the horizon, and the wind blew.

Ranger Berman was on roof duty, with two of Leo's peacekeepers on the ground. "I greet you, Private Heemur^ka."

"I greet you, Austin."

"I greet— What's that?" He was the first to spot it, a figure trudging over the horizon toward the compound, carrying something big. A second later he heard Ranger Berman on her wrister, although he couldn't distinguish the words.

The figure plodded closer. Another few minutes, and Austin was sure. "It's Claire!" He took off running before anyone could stop him.

She was dirty, tired, and angry. "Austin. You. The least you can do is help me—here, carry this!" She thrust at him a big piece of equipment. He recognized it. It was heavy.

"How did you escape? And how did you get this through the crawl tunnel?"

"I didn't and I didn't." Then she softened a little. "Graa^lok let me go, with this."

"*Graa^lok?*"

"Tony has a radio, you know. He—"

"I know he has a radio! I'm the one who brought it there!"

"Good for you. They've all heard that the virophage has kept deaths from *R. sporii* to a very few, relatively. Graa^lok understands the science, at least after I explained it to him. He believed me, unlike that moron Tony, and Graa^lok felt bad about my abduction. As you should, too! In the middle of the night, he smuggled me out the third entrance to Haven and let me take this. That entrance is a lot bigger."

Bigger! That meant that all Austin's dismantling of supplies, crawling with them through the tunnel, getting scraped and bruised—all had been unnecessary. There was another, bigger entrance that Tony never showed him.

"But Graa^lok contaminated Haven with—"

"There's an airlock. A real one. Beyon is a good physicist, I'll give him that, and Graa^lok a good engineer."

"But Tony will kill Graa^lok for letting you go!"

"Austin," Claire said, "I'm not going to stand here arguing what Graa^lok did or what Tony will do or anything else. Now carry that thing, and start to make up for all the trouble you caused."

She walked forward and Austin had to follow. She didn't seem to understand that he was really a hero.

More deaths from the spore cloud were being reported on the radio. Isabelle and Noah plotted them on a map that Noah drew of the continent. Marianne and Claire studied the map. The pattern was clear.

No one else had died in the camp. The farther east you went, the more deaths. Most clustered on the east coast, beyond a mountain range that blocked wind, and to the far north, where the land was rockier and less fertile. Mostly herders lived there, with some fishermen and scientific outposts. Those fared the worst. The map was almost a perfect epidemiologic match to the wind direction and strength.

The virophage had saved millions of lives, without causing sickness in humans. It was a miracle. It was scientific triumph. It was evolution in practice, and sometimes, Marianne thought, evolution was on your side. Sometimes.

"About one-twenty-fifth of the population is gone," Isabelle said, "four out of every hundred. That's still enough, along with the Russian attacks, to cause major disruption in how everything functions."

"But maybe not enough to cause collapse," Noah said. He held Lily in his arms, and Marianne saw all over again how much her son loved this planet and his life here. He added, more somberly, "Apparently there are groups that still blame Terrans for everything, including the spore cloud."

As there were on Earth. Marianne didn't want to think too much about the past. She turned away from the discussion and to her work.

Claire Patel had brought a gene-sequencer from Haven. Zoe Berman and Mason Kandiss had taken some convincing that the sequencer wasn't a bomb in disguise, but Leo Brodie was in charge and he explained to the unit what it was. Marianne would like to have heard that explanation; what Leo knew about science would fit on a thumbnail, in a large font. But he wasn't stupid, Marianne had to give him that.

The gene sequencer was Terran, brought to Kindred ten years ago. Old, cranky, outdated, but running. Marianne and Branch obtained a virophage sample from dead spores—not an easy task, in itself—and sequenced its genome.

The genome was tiny, only twelve-thousand base pairs making up eighteen genes. Eight of them were completely unknown to the database on Marianne's laptop. Five of them corresponded to known genes for RNA viruses. The other five were also known: they were exact duplicates of genes in *R. sporii*.

So this was not the first time the two viruses had encountered each other. Somewhere in the unimaginably distant past, spore cloud and virophage had met. The virophage had raided its host's genome, as microbes did all the time. The virophage could even be a genetic "mule," carrying genes between many viruses on planets, on asteroids and comets, in the drifting cold of space. Virophages stole from viruses, modified viruses, destroyed viruses, and viruses did the same to each other. Marianne realized yet again she was looking at the very oldest form of evolution—a jump through time that made the time dilation between Terra and Kindred completely irrelevant.

This was the real, fundamental battle, and it would outlast every other form of life.

As well as affecting every other life-form. On the colony ship, the virophage had changed parts of the leelees' brains. It wasn't obvious what effect this had on the animals, if any. But it had happened.

Marianne touched her forehead, wondering.

Leo had recovered from his gunshot wound, and Zoe from her surgery. "I feel fine," he said irritably to Dr. Patel, who had insisted on a thorough exam. "You don't need to do that."

"Yes, I do," she said. "You're a very bad patient, Lieutenant Brodie. And Ranger Berman is worse."

Leo had given up on trying to get anybody to address his unit by their right ranks, including the unit. He said, "I have better things to do than to lie here and—"

"Lieutenant," Lu^kaj^ho said over his wrist radio, in Kindred, "two groups come at the compound, one by north and one by south."

"I will come now," Leo said in Kindred.

Dr. Patel said in English, "You're picking up the language really fast."

"Have to. Thanks, Doc." He was already scrambling into his armor.

By the time he'd climbed up to the roof, it was obvious who the group from the north was. Young women, led by Graa^lok. Austin raced out of the compound, past the now deserted refugee camp, to meet them.

Leo said to Lu^kaj^ho, "The prodigal son comes home."

"What is this?"

No way Leo could explain. Actually, Leo wasn't sure, either, what the story was about—it was a phrase people used. From the Bible, maybe? Or Shakespeare? Most everything seemed to come from Shakespeare.

Salah Bourgiba would have known. Hell, he would have recited the whole damn poem. If it was a poem.

Leo said to Lu^kaj^ho, "It is not a thing," and turned his scope south.

A group of men on bicycles, heavily laden with gear. This was more serious. Leo snapped out orders. Before the bicycles got into firing or bomb-throwing range—assuming they had no weapons more advanced than Leo had seen here before—Zoe had the peace-keepers in defensive position. Kandiss had hustled the group on the plain into the compound, along with Dr. Jenner, who'd been pick-ing vegetables in the kitchen garden. Leo had his full kit brought up to the roof. Then they all waited.

The group on bicycles got closer. They were all old men.

Leo set his lips together. One thing that had made defense eas-ier on Kindred than in Brazil, in Afghanistan, in so many other military missions, was that the Kindred did not use suicide bomb-ers. Owen had never believed that, and Kandiss still didn't, but it had proved true. The Kindred weren't fanatical enough, or cruel enough, or maybe just plain insane enough to throw away their lives. But things change, and there was nothing like a major plague to change them. These old men could have decided to take out the Terrans who, they might believe, had taken out so many of their own, and to do so by ending lives near their end anyway.

Except that for old men, these looked like a pretty healthy group. Only one rode in a sort of cart behind a bicycle. The rest pedaled away. One reached under a tarp over his gear and Leo trained his rifle on him.

"Hold your fire," he said to his wrist radio.

The group drew closer.

Then Isabelle, who must have just heard that her sister had returned from Haven, was running down the hill from her lahk to the compound—no, to the men. Damn the woman! She was always where she shouldn't be . . . Leo would kill every last one of those gee-zers if they so much as touched her.

She threw her arms around one and hugged him hard.

Christ on a cracker— Who was that? Who were any of them?

Lu^kaj^ho said over Owen's radio, now his, "Lieutenant, these be no danger. They be jukno^hal."

Leo didn't know the word. "What? Who?"

"They build the ship."

What ship? Was there a ship being built somewhere? A starship, a sailing ship, what? He needed Isabelle to translate, but Isabelle was down there making a fool of herself. Hugging and laughing. Laughing?

"Berman, send Noah Jenner up here," he said to Zoe.

"Roger that."

A few minutes later Jenner ran out of the compound toward the old men. Leo cursed. "Berman, I said to get him up here to trans-late!"

"I told him. He ran off. Unless I shoot him . . ."

"Forget it." *Civilians.*

The group made its way to the compound. Zoe and Kandiss inspected their bundles. Clothing, food, water, a pet cat.

"Well, sort of a cat, sir," Kandiss said. "In a cage. Purple."

Leo lowered his rifle. He didn't know whether to feel relieved, furious, or foolish. Isabelle left him no room for any of the feelings. She said to him as soon as he'd climbed down from the roof, "I greet you, Leo. Let me introduce you. These are the builders." She began a long series of names, clicks and inflections, none of which he could remember. Each man said, "I greet you, Leo-mak."

Even less idea of the chain of command than his unit.

Leo said, "I greet you," to each of them and then to Isabelle in En-glish, "Who are they? Why are they here?"

"They built the colony ship, almost forty years ago. They know as much about it as can be known. Ful^kaa here"—she pointed to the old man in the cart—"he was the chief engineer and brilliant, I'm told—absolutely brilliant. He heard on the radio that the ship had been recalled, that we had the device to do that, and everything that's happened since. These men have all left their lahks to help you repair the ship." She paused and looked levelly at Leo.

"Repair it," she said, a challenge if he ever heard one, "and use Branch's reprogramming to send it back to Terra. With anyone who wants to go."

CHAPTER 22

Three months later, the camp was full again.

This time, they were not protesters or attackers or desperate people seeking vaccinations. This time, they were pilgrims. At least, that was the best word Marianne could find for them, since not even Isabelle seemed able to explain exactly why they came.

"They want to touch the ground where it happened," was the best Isabelle could do. "It's not a religious thing, exactly—but isn't *not* a religious thing, either. This is where the ship brought the virophage and the ship came from their ancestors—you've noticed that most of the pilgrims are young—with the bodies of the colonists on it, and also this is where the virophage came from that saved Kindred. Both those that lost lahk members to *R. sporii* and those that didn't come to touch the ship. We touch, you know—the ground, the trees, the rivers. Real, feeling interaction with the ecology is so important."

But the ship wasn't part of the ecology. Kindred hadn't designed it or even built the star drive that made it possible, which was the work of the unknown "master aliens." And it was the *Terran* scientists who had saved the planet. Marianne did not point all these things out. If this was Lourdes or Mecca or Stonehenge, then let the pilgrims come. They did no harm, although the "security risk" of their constantly changing presence drove Ranger Kandiss crazy.

Kandiss, not Brodie. Over the three months of people coming

and going, of creating and applying materials to repair the ship's hull, of fluctuating food supplies as harvests suffered from the diminished number of farmers and the loss of the three major cities, Leo Brodie had surprised Marianne with his acceptance of everything, with his calm, with his—there was no other word for it—ability to command.

And now the ship was ready. It had been repaired, cleaned of forty years' of untended and, in some cases, unintended life-forms. It was stocked with supplies. The last groups of pilgrims were arriving. The ship had finally, according to Terran custom rather than Kindred, been named: the *Return*. And now decisions had to be made about who was going to Earth and who was staying here.

Marianne played with Lily every chance she could. She talked with Noah, got to know Llaa^mohį. Her long-lost son, wonderful daughter-in-law, precious grandchild. Every time Marianne thought of leaving them, her heart flamed with pain.

But she had two other children and two other grandchildren, and this was not her world. She had never really thought it was. Marianne was going home.

"Is he ever coming out?" Austin asked Graa^lok. He meant Tony, of course. The boys talked endlessly about Tony, about Haven, about all that had happened. That's how they referred to it: "the all." Probably nothing so exciting would ever happen on World again.

Well, that might be okay.

"He'll come out," Graa^lok said. "Someday. Probably he's waiting until the Rangers are gone so they won't punish him for . . . the all. Austin—"

"I'm not going to Terra!" Austin said fiercely, as he had said a hundred times before. "They can't make me! I'll run away! I'll go back to Haven! I'll make Leo throw bombs down the airshaft to get me out, like Lieutenant Lamont did!"

"Leo-mak wouldn't do it," Graa^lok said. He had lost weight, eaten by guilt over his part in "the all."

This was true. Leo wouldn't do it. But Graa^lok was missing the point. "I'm not going," Austin repeated.

"Your mother wants to go."

This, unfortunately, was also true. The chance to return to Terra had made Kayla happier than anything else had in years. Maybe ever. "I know she's going," Austin said miserably. "But I can't go, Graa^lok. I just can't. I live here. I wouldn't have any friends there, or a lahk except for Mom, or anything."

The boys fell silent, unable to picture life without a lahk.

"They can't make me go," Austin said.

Graa^lok said nothing, staring down at his sandals to hide his expression.

The night before launch, the camp was again deserted. Apparently the Kindred felt the need to let the Terrans be alone with the ship. Leo didn't understand that and didn't try, but he was glad about it. He wanted to be alone.

He walked out from the compound across the field to the north, passing two groups of skalethi. One lay asleep in a clump, as they always did, looking like a football pile-on trying to recover the ball. The other group stood cropping grass, also in unison. On Kindred, "herd animals" applied to more than humans.

"I greet you, skalethi," Leo said, in Kindese. The animals ignored him.

The ship loomed dark against a field of stars. Leo put his hand on the hull, which felt cool and smooth. Inside were supplies, pallets, room enough for a whole colony of people instead of the few that were going.

Five Kindred, two of them scientists, including boss scientist Ka^graa. Only five. Leo knew now what it cost Kindred to leave their lahks, but these had chosen to go. Some people, Terran or Kindred, were always what Dr. Jenner called "outliers": different enough from their own culture to go off seeking another one. Ka^graa, whose wife was dead, was taking with him his oldest daughter. The mother of her lahk had agreed.

Kandiss was going. He had wanted to leave Kindred since the minute he first set foot on it. The Seventy-Fifth Regiment was his life, and he was going back to it.

Dr. Jenner and Branch Carter were going. So was Dr. Patel, who'd said she'd be needed to oversee the microbe adjustment necessary for the Kindred to live on Terra and the Terrans to get their original microbes back. Leo, remembering what that involved, winced. But it was necessary if you wanted to go home.

Kayla Rhinehart was going. She hated Kindred worse than even Kandiss did. Although it was Leo's unspoken opinion that Kayla would be a pain in the ass wherever she went. Kayla raised the question, though, of Austin. The kid kept yelling that he wasn't leaving Kindred, and then the next minute watching his mother like he had to take care of her no matter what. Terrible to make a kid responsible for a parent like that—it should be the other way around. Not that Leo had ever personally known either arrangement.

He didn't know what would happen with Austin. And that raised the question of Isabelle, who had also always taken care of Kayla. Leo and Isabelle had avoided each other these past weeks. A lot of the time she was gone, working on the Council of Mothers to rebuild Kindred's government. Leo supposed she was also grieving for Salah Bourgiba, as well as for her planet. He'd gotten his language instruction from Austin, which gave the kid something to do since he refused to return to school and nobody had actually made him do so.

Noah Jenner, his wife, and their little girl would stay on Kindred, of course.

And Zoe? She had looked Leo straight in the eyes and said, "You tell me first, Leo." He could have pushed her for an answer, but he didn't. He already knew it. She had had at least five conversations with him, spread over their weeks on Kindred, about how tough it would be to skip twenty-eight years on Earth. Maybe more than five, if you counted sideways hints. But Zoe was a soldier—if her CO told her to return to Terra, she would. If not—

The wind picked up, that wind that had saved so many lives, bringing to Leo the same spicy scent of fruit and leaves as when he arrived. Weird to have no seasons. No seasons, no other continents, no other languages, so many restrictions on having kids and not having normal tech and not making too much money. Weird to give away a big chunk of what you did have, every illathil. And still pay taxes. Weird to live by bu^ka^tel, which Leo still didn't really understand. Weird and unnatural and—

Isabelle came across the starlit field toward him.

He knew it was her long before he could make out her face. He knew by her gait, by the way she held her head, by her Isabelleness. His heart began a slow, steady thud like a dance beat, or a dirge.

"I greet you, Leo," she said in Kindese.

"I greet you, Isabelle," he said in the same language.

Then, for what seemed a very long time, neither spoke. Finally Leo could stand it no longer. His lips felt dry, but he got out one word. "Austin?"

"He's staying here."

"Poor kid." Leo meant it.

"You understand, don't you, his dilemma. Either choice, he loses something."

"Well, that's always how it goes, isn't it?"

For answer, she moved into his arms. Her lips were soft and full and sweeter than anything had ever been before in his life. But after one long kiss, he held her slightly away from him and braced himself for another loss. If that had been a good-bye kiss. . . .

He said, "Your sister?"

"To Terra. You knew that."

"And if Austin isn't going to take care of her, are you?"

"No. I belong here, Leo. And . . . and you?"

"I'm staying. I sort of think I'm needed here. Even though that sounds so full of ego shit."

"It's not. World does need you. And so do I."

So not a good-bye kiss. Leo seized her again and held her close. They would stay here, and he would learn this planet and organize some sort of army that could protect it if the Russians ever returned. Or if the Kindred "no war" tradition changed. This planet needed an army; it just didn't know that yet. He'd have Lu^kaj^ho to help him recruit, and Zoe to help train new units. If he stayed, Zoe would, and it would be a good thing to have your best friend as second in command.

Owen . . .

No. This was different. Owen was over. This was a new day, and he and Isabelle had places in this new world and work to do. Separately, and together.

The ship lifted. Marianne watched a planet fall away below, as she had twice before. On the *Endeavor*, on the *Friendship*, and now on the *Return*.

She had no idea what she, what any of them, might find on Terra. Twenty-eight years would have passed there by the time their ship landed. She had left a planet facing political, economic, and environmental struggles so violent that they mirrored the Darwinian arms race of *R. sporii* verses its virophage. Not an unapt comparison, not at all.

Branch said, "I wonder how long before we jump."

Neither Marianne nor Claire answered him, because there was no answer. All they could do was wait and see.

She had a headache, right behind her eyes. Well, no wonder—little sleep, too much stress, and anyway she was too old for this. From now on, she would stay put.

"I have a headache," Branch said.

Claire frowned and touched her own forehead. Had they all caught a last bug, the Kindred equivalent of a cold? Well, it didn't matter, not compared to the bigger adventure. Some of their band— she'd almost thought "lahk"—had stayed on Kindred to rebuild, because humans always do.

She wished them well.

The stars blinked out, and the ship jumped.

ACKNOWLEDGMENTS

I would like to thank my beta readers, all three of whom were a tremendous help with this novel: Douglas Pressley II, US Army, for his help with military matters; Dr. Maura Glynn-Thami for sharing her medical expertise and providing me with "doctor words"; and my husband, Jack Skillingstead, for his always valuable literary insights.

I would also like to thank my agent, Eleanor Wood, for her indefatigable efforts on my behalf.